NEAR SOMEWHERE

A NOVEL

EDWARD COZZA

Winner-IPPY Gold & 3 Beverly Hills Book Awards
for
Nowhere Yet

Foreword by Chef Dean Fearing

Pinot
Dog™

Encintas, California

Copyright © 2015 Edward Cozza
All rights reserved.

Except as permitted under the U.S. Copyright Act of 1976, no part of this book may be reproduced, scanned, or distributed in any printed or electronic form without written permission from the publisher. Please do not participate in or encourage piracy of copyrighted materials in violation of the authors' rights.

This is a work of fiction. Names, characters, places, and incidents either are the products of the author's imagination or are used fictitiously. Any resemblance to actual events or locales or persons, living or dead, is merely coincidental.

Published in the United States by Pinot Dog, Encintas, California.

www.edwardcozza.com

Cover design by Patricia Bacall
Cover photo by Remy Haynes
Author photo by Starla Fortunato

ISBN: 978-0-9881906-3-4

PRINTED IN THE UNITED STATES OF AMERICA

For Mary Elizabeth,
I could not have written one, now two books, without you.

NEAR SOMEWHERE

A NOVEL

FOREWORD

A lot of famous writers give endorsements to writers they have never met. I sort of have a problem with that, but that's just me. I met Ed Cozza when he came to my Dallas restaurant when he was in town for a book signing and bourbon tasting event at Stanley Korshak for his first novel. I have friends who work there and they asked me if I would like to come to the event, and being originally from Kentucky, I am somewhat familiar with bourbon. I wondered what bourbon had to do with a book signing, but it sounded like a good idea to me.

Ed stopped by for lunch the day before and the day of the event and we had a chance to talk. He told me had been a fan of mine for a very long time, and I was sort of leery when he said that, because what else is he going to say? He elaborated further and told me he had long been following the Southwest cuisine movement and had cookbooks of mine, as well as the cookbooks of some of the other chefs who were contemporaries of mine (Del Grande, Miller, McGrath). He told me he used to watch the PBS series, *Great Chefs of The West* and also had the companion book to the series. I had not heard anyone reference that series in a great long while, so I figured he was genuine in his praise.

I went to his "Bourbon and Book" event and made my Grandmother's Bourbon Cheese Ball (served with Triscuits, of course, 'cause that's how she did it!) for the occasion. We tasted several of the bourbon selections and decided we might actually be kindred spirits, no pun intended. There was a fine turnout for the event and the folks at Korshak invited him back for the release of his next novel, which, if you are reading this, you now have in front of you.

That night after the book event, he brought his friends for a big dinner in the Wine Cellar at my restaurant and we all had a great time. He signed his book for me and I figured that would be it, but it was not. I read the book, *Nowhere Yet*, and noticed his characters liked to eat and drink with a certain enthusiasm, so it occurred to me that some research had been done somewhere along the line. I didn't figure Ed would merely ask someone what it was like to enjoy great food and libation.

Ed doesn't live in the Dallas/Ft. Worth area, but he always comes to my restaurant whenever he comes to town. He has a couple of close friends here, so it sounds like there is always a potential storyline being worked up by that crew when he is here. The last time he was here, he asked me if I would write the foreword for this book. I said yes, but what else could I say? I got to thinking that maybe I didn't know him well enough to do that. This got me to rereading his first novel and then got the chance to look at his newest offering. Ed stays true to having his characters experience things that I think all people want to experience. Being in the hospitality business, I like to believe that people want to enjoy a wonderful meal and feel at home, even when they are a long way from home. Ed told me that in all the years that he has been traveling and a long way from home, the things that kept him together during all that travel was writing, and good food. He said he didn't realize at the time that the dining experiences would have such a great impact on him and that they would make him feel so at home. People made me feel at home when I came to Texas, so I could relate to that.

I have had the pleasure of having done several cookbooks, but not a novel. I only say that because Ed's novels always seem to have real life, and real food alongside of each other. Some people might find that odd, but as Ed described above, there is strong connection. So when you ask why is a fellow like me, who loves to give folks a culinary experience they can't get anywhere else (but loves more to make folks feel at home) write this foreword? Maybe it's because I like to think that along the line I can give comfort to people, like the characters in Ed's books, like Ed, and take away their troubles for a while. It all sort of connects, and that is why I ultimately agreed to write this foreword.

Ed will be back in the restaurant in a few days, and we will talk about great bourbon (bourbons that we used to have no problem getting, before everybody decided they just had to have a spirit they never tasted before, that somebody told them to buy), and we'll talk about our promise to get together to play guitar, to talk about our favorite boot makers, and enjoy food we both love.

I hope you enjoy this book and that you take the time to get together with people you care about, take the time to share a great meal, and do both as often as you can. You need some inspiration to get together? Read this book. You don't cook? Come here to Dallas and I'll do it for you. Give me enough notice, and Ed might just be here, too.

Chef Dean Fearing
Fearing's, At the Ritz Carlton, Dallas
Dallas, Texas

CHAPTER 1

Beverly Hills
Present Day

Townes sat looking over the glistening swath of turquoise of the massive swimming pool, thinking it the largest he had ever seen, the landmark pink building of the Beverly Hills Hotel a backdrop to the near-blinding reflection of the Southern California sun off the water. It might not have appeared to have such a shimmer to the other inhabitants, they being perhaps more accustomed to the absolute shine of prosperity, but for Townes, the luminous expanse was overpowering. Even the fragrance of the water was impossible to ignore. All the travel, all the nights alone, all the people from around the country with whom he had connected had brought him here. He had always wanted to come to this place, but never by himself like all the other places he had been. He wanted to come here with someone that he cared about, someone who cared about him. He wanted the ache to stop. He wanted the voices in his head to check into a different hotel. Maybe his friend Crosetti was right. Maybe now he was finally near *somewhere*. So much had happened. It was going to take some time to determine his next move.

The most troubling thing was his best friend being missing. Townes was still not sure what to make of that. He was going to try to put that out of his mind, hoping nothing terrible had happened and that his friend would make his whereabouts known when he thought the time was right. He reached for a newspaper but the paper felt odd, scratchy to his touch and decided he was in no mood to read. He brushed his now-long blond hair back with his hands, pausing momentarily over his eyes, wishing his headache had also checked into a different hotel. He looked at the woman in the chair next to him. Seeing her there, reading, brought a flood of memories, some he wanted to forget. She was tanned, and her ponytail poked out the back of her baseball cap, which was the same color blue as her bikini. Her slight scent of coconut oil blended nicely with the entire scene. He wanted to say something but it was difficult for him. Talking to her might not go well and he did not want to take that chance. Maybe they could talk later, that might be easier. If he waited, maybe he would not have to talk about how everything had happened, and why he felt stupid about some of what happened, or what didn't happen, in the first place. She could be understanding or she could be annoyed that he brought any of it up. Maybe she did not want to talk at all. She had been quiet the entire time she was there, so she probably didn't want to talk.

But so much had happened. Seeing Annie that first day. Spending time with Kat. Meeting Ashley. Wondering why Zeeder was gone—missing. There had been so much and now all of this. The thoughts just made Townes's head hurt more. He didn't know if he had done the right things, made the right choices, or not. He thought the choices were the right ones, but he couldn't help but wonder. All the hotels, all the restaurants, all the bars all over the country that he had seen by himself had now brought him to this one place. People would ask him about it and that is what he would tell them. More importantly, that is what he told himself. He took a sip of his Old Tom Gin Collins and closed his eyes.

CHAPTER 2

Dallas
Prior to Present Day

Playing human bumper pool at the Dallas airport terminal did not help ease Townes's mind. His emotions seemed unhinged. An earlier mirror assessment had given a reading of fatigue, with burnout as a more than probable contributor. He wished he were home. Though Dallas had not been too difficult, the long roll call of all the other trips had really started to take its toll. It had been building for a while, but this was the first time it was noticeable. Had he not met up with his winemaker friend Crosetti while he was there, Townes might have just thrown his briefcase in Turtle Creek. The end of his rope was spelled out in the big letters on the top of the eye chart and he was having no trouble reading them. He was not currently prepared to deal with what he needed to do to make such a large adjustment. With so little rope left on the spool, he needed to figure something out, and figure it out soon. The agenda for the trip had been short, including dinner with Crosetti, with no business to get in the way and no hard conclusions cast.

Crosetti helped him keep his mind off of it. Crosetti, and an exceptional amount of Pinot Noir and bourbon. Someone had wisely vetoed the tequila suggestion, which was now listed with the all-time good decisions of his life. The use of restraint was to be applauded, especially since it was restraint by both him and Crosetti, which was rare. Still, they had put a serious dent in the wine cellar of Fearing's Restaurant at the Ritz, and the previously ample stock of bourbon at the Rattlesnake Bar would now need reevaluation of its actual numbers.

Crosetti said, "We must have needed to do it, or it would not have happened, and thank goodness we didn't drink the tequila, or we might have gotten drunk." Townes now doubted the last part of Crosetti's statement. Air travel after that night was postponed until now, as Townes chose instead to see if there weren't some regenerative properties by the swimming pool, under the shade, asleep.

Townes had never enjoyed flying, he always just tolerated it. Now, with this Dallas trip, it had become more than just an annoyance. He was anxious even before boarding the plane. He broke out in a sweat and felt nothing but nerves as he waited to board. Having some drinks beforehand would've helped, but would certainly make him feel like hell when he landed. Drinking or taking meds just to be able to fly was something that would bring only bad results.

The fall weather was a pleasant change, and he enjoyed seeing leaves turning, feeling the air, more crisp than the perpetual spring where he lived, but the anxiety made him uneasy, and he was thinking about getting back home to La Jolla more than he normally would. With no one to go home to, he didn't get homesick on the road. He thought about the great meal at Fearing's, though it was now a bit fuzzy. *What was it they had?* Tortilla soup, maple peppercorn-soaked buffalo tenderloin, jalapeño grits. He could taste the cumin, the maple, even today, and wished he were sitting back at that restaurant, instead of being here, trying to dodge idiots talking on their phones. The meal was spectacular. Crosetti kept raving all night about it. "It reminds me of eating back home at the vineyard … only inside," he'd said.

Townes and Crosetti had started the evening at the Rattlesnake Bar, and he would undoubtedly be in better condition if not for that first stop. There would always be lots of wine with a man that owned his own winery, so it wasn't like they needed a jump-start. They would of course find the bar again after dinner, only to finish the evening with a couple of Ashton VSG Torpedos and maybe one too many Elijah Craig Bourbons. The total consumption being a respectable showing for four, maybe six men, yet there were only two. Crosetti was in town for a wine event, so there was never a chance of a shortage there. Townes might say too much wine, but Crosetti would say "There's no such fucking thing as too fucking much wine." They had laughed so much, his sides were still hurting. Crosetti commented on the number of women, how they were all so impeccably attired, as if they worked at a clothing store, maybe the nearby Stanley Korshak, perhaps. Not like Southern California.

"I live out in the sticks, they don't dress that way there, but I'm just observing, not bitching. I want to buy wine for all of them!" Certainly when the girl who was seated by the picture of the ocelot had her date's hand inside the front of her shirt, that merited further comment. They did not ask the girl by the picture of the ocelot if she were giving turns to the patrons to put their hand inside her shirt, like her date was doing, but after several drinks, Crosetti came very close. Now that Townes tried to remember, Crosetti may have asked her after all. Crosetti said he recalled a somewhat racy bar from earlier in his life that was called the Ocelot Club. Rough place, outskirts of town, sultry women. Some sort of power, this ocelot thing, and perhaps she was unaware of it.

"I never went in there, I was too young, too scared. Now I'm just too scared," Crosetti laughed, shaking his head, his shoulder length black curly hair moving around as he did. His large, strong frame honed by a lot of difficult outdoor physical labor shook with energetic and infectious laughter. His Hawaiian shirt stood out in contrast from the button downs around the room, from the white shirt and black sport coat that Townes wore.

Townes had enjoyed the night with Crosetti. It was good to get together and laugh until they were near sick. With all the traveling, Townes could really use some laughter. They were just glad to get together, to speak of things more and less meaningful than a stupid business trip. It had been too long since they had aired things out. It was a night to savor, one to take home to help postpone the loneliness waiting for him.

Crosetti was right about the food. Thinking about the food always seemed to help the miles go faster. He could find comfort in the grits, because they didn't serve grits where he lived. They tasted as if they were milled in the kitchen, even though he knew that they weren't. The jalapeños were fresh, with just the right amount of heat. Buffalo was not something that could readily be found in Southern California. Oddly enough, it actually made him think about the now farfetched concept that these animals used to number in the millions. Maple? No, somebody always had some sort of health statement about anything sweet being bad for you, so that was a rarity also, save for some cheap imitation syrup served with a breakfast that clearly stated that there was not even a trace of maple in there, and that some sort of cactus syrup was better for you. Tribal chatter would ramble that gluten was a co-conspirator for all human ills, and that you should, by god, not think of eating any, even though he had only met two people in his entire life who had an actual legitimate allergy to it. He wanted his house to smell as good as this restaurant. Maple, so simple.

Sitting down to a wonderful flavor bounty like this always gave him a vision of some things he was missing. That food kept him connected. That, and it smelled and tasted great, and taste was often something that took a separate and different trip than the one he was on. When trying to recall the sensory highlights of a trip, oftentimes there were none. He always tried to change that whenever he could. The cumin in that tortilla soup would have a much greater impact on him than on the other diners in that restaurant, as he would recall it for weeks after.

Townes's day job, a consulting business, took him around the country. It was rather a double edged blade, this constant going. It kept things from getting stale around home. It was a solitary life, but it fed his novelist alter ego, and his experiences gave him more than enough to write about. Townes wanted to be his alter ego more than he wanted to be a consultant, and he wrote while on the road. "Never a lack of crazy shit to see on the road." When he wasn't traveling, his second alter ego played music in local venues around San Diego with his friend Zeeder.

Townes and Zeeder both lived in the California beach enclave of La Jolla. They didn't think their music was going to take them anywhere significant, they just enjoyed playing. The money wasn't great, but it was "better'n no money, but not much," as Zeeder would say, so they did it and it didn't hurt to have the diversion.

"It'll do 'til we figger out what we're going to do when we're wildly successful," Zeeder also liked to say. He was a somewhat mysterious fellow, an artist and musician, from somewhere in the South, most likely Kentucky, as most of his references were about that part of the world. No real visible means of support, and when pressed would say only that he had once won the lottery, but that was running out. He would also say about their music that their slow, inevitable rise to fame would give them "ample time to train ourselves to deal with the enormous weight of monumental success. That, and the groupies."

"There are no groupies," Townes would counter.

"'Zactly! We is honing our abstinence, as well," Zeeder would reply.

He was as fine a person as anyone he had ever met, and even though Townes knew very little about Zeeder's past, he knew that if he called him right now and asked him to come to Dallas, he wouldn't even ask why, he would just get on a plane and be there.

Living alone and being on the road by himself so much of the time was getting to him, and Townes was no longer sure how long he wanted to stay on this particular path. He enjoyed pieces of it all, but felt his life had a large void that needed tending. Tending by a woman who would share his life. He enjoyed his work, but it seemed a burden now. He was starting to think his dreams of becoming a successful writer someday were maybe just that. The small chance of success was clouded by having no one to share it with, should it even come. Traveling actually kept things fresh, but not having someone to go home to weighed heavily. If he didn't have the dog, Angelina, things might be quite pitiful. That he had started talking to the characters in his book was starting to worry him.

"All things in time … providing I live to be one hundred …"

For now, he just wanted to try to relax, to think about how great it had been to see his friend Crosetti. They got a chance to talk about the manuscript Townes had finished and they had decided—well, Crosetti had decided—a glorious celebration was necessary, whether the book ever got published or not. He blocked out the streams of people, the strange smells found only in airports, sort of like a cinnamon roll pizza, topped with dirt, body odor, and disinfectant, as best he could, choosing instead to recall the smell of the fresh cooked beignets of last night's dinner. The constant blaring of the announcements overhead, sounding like people were deliberately talking over the loudspeaker, as if not to be understood. Cramming into the plane was another story, awful at best. It never got better, or easier. Ever. It ate at him constantly. It was only on this recent trip that the anxiety had taken him so hard. He knew he'd be able to forget if had a bunch of drinks, but he wasn't going to do that. He reluctantly boarded, found his way to his seat, donned earplugs, sunglasses, and closed his eyes.

"Just one more," and he drifted to an uneasy sleep.

CHAPTER 3

La Jolla

Townes put the key in the lock and opened the door. The house was dark, quiet, but smelled like home, no trace of airport scent. He entered, dropped his bags to the floor, and pushed the door closed behind him, taking time to lean against it to ensure it latched, keeping all that lay on the other side at bay, at least for now. He paused, turned, the palms of his hands pressed against the door, his head moving slowly forward until his forehead rested against it. He closed his eyes, took several deep breaths, in and out, and stood there for several seconds before he turned back to survey the interior. There was a stack of mail on the dark coffee table, and a handwritten note on top of the stack.

> *Dog eating me out of house and home.*
> *You owe me thousands of dollars, in dog treats alone.*
> *Dog also preventing my giving proper attention to tour buses of beautiful women that keep stopping in front of the house.*
> *PS-Got a gig tomorrow night. Vacation is over ... come get dog!*
> *Z*

"Music ... with no airplanes," Townes sighed.

He didn't even bother to turn any lights on, reading Zeeder's note by the porch light shining in from the outside. He didn't need the light to tell him he was home, the dark was just fine with him. He made his way through the house to the kitchen and turned on the faucet. He let the water run for a few seconds and then leaned over to drink from the stream. It reminded him of hot summer days and garden hoses when he was young; the water tasted better like this. The plane ride dried him to the bone. He drank until he could drink no more, shutting off the water and wiping his wet face and chin on a shirt sleeve.

"Make some gal a great husband someday," he thought.

He dragged his dried body around the house, reacquainting himself with everything, delighting in the fact that he was here, in this place, not in someone else's place. He looked out the window for a few minutes. He had just come from out there, and for the past several days could think of nothing but being back here. Just the two of them lived here, he and the dog, Angelina, but the joy in that was considerable. With a faint light coming in from outside, he could barely discern dog toys lying around the house on the floor. It would be good to see her. She would be mad at him that he had been away so long, but that anger would last only a few seconds. Even if she were upset at his being gone, that was good. At least someone knew he had been away and had some feelings about that.

"Might be the only chance I get for someone to give a shit."

He kicked off his shoes and tried to stretch his tight legs and body as best he could. He felt compacted and dehydrated like one of Angelina's rawhide bones, which he hoped he didn't step on in his bare feet in the dark, those hurt like hell. He unbuttoned his shirt and stood there yawning and stretching in the living room, head side to side, rolling it back and forth. He ran his fingers through his hair and let out a groan. It would take him a couple of days to recover from the trip. Maybe tomorrow he could get some sort of a workout in to help purge the toxins of the road. Crosetti was to blame for putting a few toxins there, though he would disagree with calling them toxins. The music would help cleanse him. It would be good getting back to playing with Zeeder. It was always therapeutic and made him feel as if life really had more than one dimension to it. It was the music, not the performing in front of people that gave him peace of mind. Zeeder was the talent and Townes felt fortunate to have him as his friend, fortunate to get to play with him.

He moved to where his guitar stood, picking it up and playing it in the dark. He closed his eyes and drifted around the house as he played. The music scraped the dust from his soul, sending the runoff to the nearby Pacific shore and out to sea. He was tired, the session didn't last long. He put the guitar back in the stand and shuffled to the bedroom where he sat on the bed and laid back with his feet still on the floor. He barely heard the hum of the airplane now, the short guitar session having cleared most of it from his exhausted brain. There was still some residual rumble and turbulence.

He got back up and made his way to the kitchen, opened the cabinet door, taking down a bottle of Maker's 46. He opened the door to the freezer, took out four ice cubes, and slid the ice gently into the glass, trying to avoid unnecessary noise. He poured just the slightest bit of bourbon in the glass, listening for the comforting crackling sound. He let the glass sit there for a few minutes, feeling the outside of the glass with the knuckles on his right hand. When the glass felt right he took a sip, breathing slightly through his mouth. Letting out the breath, he set the glass on the counter, shuffled back to the bedroom, sat back on the bed, and swung his legs up, laying diagonally across it. He looked at the ceiling once, closed his eyes, and hummed the words to one of the songs he'd just played. Sleep came quickly.

CHAPTER 4

It was a chamber of commerce morning in La Jolla. Townes was happy to participate. He showered lazily, dressed in jeans, a linen shirt and sandals and took off walking to meet up with Zeeder who would give him grief about the shirt, yet oddly enough he would recognize the fabric. Angelina would be some kind of upset if she knew he were back and had not come to get her, but he guessed she probably knew already that he was back. Zeeder did not live far, no air travel, only feet required. Townes was hungry, but wanted to see Angelina more than he wanted to eat. Besides, she was always happy to eat with him, wherever that might be.

He headed towards Zeeder's apartment on Prospect Street. La Jolla was always quiet in the mornings, and today was no exception. The sky appeared to have been freshly papered with the most winsome shade of blue, a bit of wispy white overlay, always a formidable tonic in the compound against jet lag. Townes was still dragging from the travel, but the fresh air was good. Now all he needed was Angelina and a coffee shop, home to the only activity in town at this hour. The hour wasn't early by other cities, but time ran differently here. He drew in a deep breath and absently rubbed his temple. He remembered hearing someone describe jet lag as feeling similar to having a head injury. It was a dullness that overtook him and never seemed to leave the entire time he was traveling. He never grew used to it, and it took longer and longer to get over it once he was home.

The walk to Zeeder's in clean, ocean air would go a long way to assisting in revival, and Townes was all for that. He had not been gone all that long, but, if Dallas were any indicator, the trips were taking more out of him than they used to. It was good to get away and gain perspective, but the drudgery that came with that somehow overwhelmed the other. He longed for a day when, just maybe, he would travel because he wanted to, not because he had to.

"All you have to do is get this book published," one of his characters said to him, "and get a couple million people to buy it ... which should only be ... just about impossible." Townes put his finger in his ear.

He covered the few blocks between his and Zeeder's place quicker than he thought he would, considering his legs were not moving like he wanted them to. He walked up the steps and opened the gate. He could hear Zeeder playing guitar on the deck. Townes stepped through the gate and the music stopped. All he could hear then was the thumping sound of the dog's tail hitting the wooden deck. As soon as she saw him, she hopped up and ran, jumping on him, almost knocking him down. She was a small black American Labrador, but she was adept at rendering him helpless when she wanted to. She was maybe fifty pounds, but when something needed her attention, her frame seemed more powerful that the size.

"Angelina running away from your music now?" Townes said, rubbing the dog's head.

"I hope not. That might bode ill for tonight." Zeeder said. "Of course, it might only be bad iffin we was a playin' to a pack of dogs, 'stead of people ... the venue did not specify." Zeeder continued to play. He was in his usual attire of T-shirt, cargo shorts, and sandals. His brown hair long, his beard short. "You spectin' company wearing that shirt?" Zeeder said, sipping from a green bottle.

"What's this pooch doing here?" Townes was now down on his knees scratching the dog, getting reacquainted. "No company, just comfortable."

"She ate me out of house and home and—"

"I know, she kept the busloads of beautiful women from finding their way up here."

"Well, somethin' like that."

Townes stood up and looked at the panoramic view of the ocean. "When the hell are you going to get a place with a decent view?"

"I'm hoping to make it big someday and get just that very thing."

"You have made it big, look at this," Townes said, motioning with his arms.

"Well, it is certainly a matter of perspective."

"Isn't everything?"

"That depends upon the perspective itself."

"Thank you for validating my statements. You truly are a genius."

"Well, that's not a matter of perspective, that is simply fact, an understated fact at that, though you make your point quite well. Thank you, and you could continue iffin you wishes, but only for several hours."

"Thank you for looking after the only woman in my life … it's a big help always. What are you drinking?"

"Well, it is a tremendous imposition, but I have adapted and keepin' a ledger of what you owes me. And I'm drinking an Ale-8. Want one?"

"Has what I owe you reached into the millions yet? What's an Ale-8?"

"'Proachin' that. I am near retirement with what you owes me," Zeeder said, pressing his chest out, shaking his long brown hair, rubbing his beard. "You ain't never heard of Ale-8, then I guess you can't have one."

"Retirement? Geniuses don't retire. Have you not read the manual?"

"No I have not. Would you give me one, as I certainly want to go by the book."

"Love to. Playing at Jack's tonight … did you say?"

"Yes, they lowered their usual standards and are allowing us to alienate their clientele with our confusing and irreverent selections."

"You didn't tell them where we live, did you?"

"Nosir. Why?"

"Well, we are within walking distance, should they become an unruly mob and bust out the pitchforks, torches and such. Would hate to get tarred and feathered at my own home … just seems wrong."

"Perhaps we should wear disguises and play under 'sumed names, whatcha think?" Zeeder asked, looking off in the distance.

"Might be good to ease into the neighborhood rather than attack it," Townes said, now smiling as the dog stared up at him adoringly while her tongue lolled happily, dripping slobber on Zeeder's deck.

"If memory serves me correctly, we played there recently, and we used our quasi-real names … cleverly leaving a disguise kit in the alley out back … but I could be wrong."

"Rarely. Your memory is pretty good, Bill."

"Zeeder."

"Precisely."

"Is you up to the performance?"

"Yes," Townes said, soaking in the adoration and the view.

"I was only asking because you just returned from travel and might not be your usual jovial and perplexing self to reap the enormous personal rewards that come with giving the patrons the utmost in background music, or music to get inebriated by ... whichever the case might be," Zeeder said, tilting his head. "They's kinda the same thing though, not sure why I broke them into two categories. I generally don't get this existential this early in the morning."

Townes looked at Zeeder, starting to say something, but stopped. He started again. "Don't I always answer the call?"

"Yes, and quite wonderfully."

"How have you been?"

"Purdy good. Dallas, was it any count?"

"You know the saying: everything is big in Texas, bar bills, anyway." He yawned. "Saw my buddy... had a pretty riotous time at a great spot, Fearing's, it's called, if you ever get to Dallas. Ate like kings, drank at least a barrel of wine ... followed by ... at least a barrel of bourbon. No arrests."

"Sounds purdy fair. How's your buddy?"

"He's a crazy sonofabitch, but he's doing real well and it's always a treat to see him, though my head seems to hurt like a bastard the next day for some reason. We laughed until I thought I was actually going to be sick. That's the story I'm going with, anyway."

"Perhaps the food was suspect, 'cause I knows there was nothin' wrong with the bourbon." Zeeder smiled.

"Food was incredible, so that wasn't it. We came to the usual conclusion."

"Bad ice?"

"Yep."

"Figgers. That'll always get ya."

"It's always easy to come home to this," Townes said, looking at the ocean.

Zeeder nodded. "The dog says you mights want to think about gettin' a place with an ocean view, else-wise she may be considerin' tradin' up and a leavin' ya for a better opportunity. A man with just such a view."

"Tough to compete with that. Boyish charm only gets a person so far these days. Location is still important."

"You ought be a writer-type feller," Zeeder said, mimicking a writing motion.

"Aspiring."

"Same thing."

"Hardly." Townes shook his head.

"Back to the perspective thing again."

"My perspective is that I write, but not very well. You play the guitar, but you do it very well."

"Betcha you's tired of being right all of the time."

"I am never right, except about this. Well, part right. You are an artist, as well."

"How is that different from you a bein', or not a bein', a writer in your mind?"

"Your pictures, they are great and you have sold some of them ... profession realized."

"What I realize is that we all have our talents, we all have our failures, and your failure is at realizin' your talents," Zeeder said, hitting a quick, loud chord on his guitar.

"Wow."

"Exactly. Now you play something," Zeeder said, handing the guitar to Townes.

"What, me play this? I don't know how to play anything."

"That's a damn shame 'cause you got a gig tonight to play with me up the street at a local establishment, so I find that to be problematic to a successful session, which could result in withholding of payment by said establishment, and potentially damaging reviews by others wishing to possibly pay for our services at some later date. One o' them there domino things, 'sentially."

"Could you say that again slower, and I'll write it down and use it in my book," Townes said, as he played a song, looking first at the dog, then out to the ocean.

"Surely not! But I might ... for a fee."

"Where did you learn to speak like that?" Townes fingers picked out the tune.

"Are you a askin' me or askin' the dog?"

Townes said nothing and kept playing, smiling at the dog, at Zeeder, at the ocean. The dog walked over and bumped Zeeder with her nose, then walked back to Townes and lay down on top of his feet. Townes smiled an even bigger smile and looked up into the sun and the blue sky, closing his eyes and letting it all wash over him.

"Welcome home," Zeeder said.

CHAPTER 5

Townes took Angelina and started walking back to his house. Having forgotten to eat, a detour to an outdoor café was plugged in to the itinerary. Several choice presented themselves, with the one that had a water bowl on the sidewalk receiving the most votes. Angelina stopped and looked at the bowl and looked at Townes.

"This one to your liking, is it?"

She wagged her tail twice then moved closer to the bowl and started to drink. Townes sat at one of the tables situated on the sidewalk, and soon a waitress appeared.

"Hello, I'm Savannah," she said, smiling at the dog. "Separate checks, or both on the same one? I can do it either way," the waitress smiled.

"Oh, I hope she's paying, I don't know how much money I have, if any."

The dog looked up at the waitress, water dripping from both sides of her mouth, and wagged her tail.

"Does that mean she has the money?"

"Not sure. It could be a trick, I've had to wash dishes before."

"We'll take our chances."

"Thank you. Bring some green tea and a blueberry muffin, she'll have a plain bagel."

"She want anything with that ... cream cheese, lox?"

"No thanks, she's watching her weight ... me too, actually."

"Okay. Donuts probably out of the question, then. Would you like some more water?"

"Maybe, but you have to ask her."

"More water, Miss?"

Angelina moved her tail.

"Coming up," Savannah left, whistling a tune.

One of the pearls of living in this part of the world was always being able to sit outside. He watched a vehicle pull up and park in front of the coffee shop, a man and a woman inside. He looked back to the dog, who was sniffing around the other tables looking for food. Townes snapped his fingers and the dog stopped, looked up and returned to Townes's side. She looked at him, sat down and put her head on his leg

"You're all right. You have breakfast coming." She moved her tail, her head still resting on his leg, all the while holding Townes in her gaze.

"You don't need cream cheese." Her tail moved again.

Townes could hear the couple getting out of the vehicle, but paid little attention. The man walked past him into the coffee shop and began to harass the waitresses to get them an outside table "muy pronto." Townes thought he might have breached protocol by sitting down at the first table he came to, but after being unable not to hear the commotion the man was making, determined he just wanted everyone else to know he was there. The woman stood alone and Townes now looked at her. She was partially bent over, adjusting the blue warmup jacket she was wearing, looking like she had just come from a tennis court. She straightened up and Townes could not look away. She had golden shimmering hair that had obviously seen a lot of sunshine. Her skin was tan, her face natural looking, no visible makeup, Townes could see none was needed. He could not see the eyes behind the sunglasses she wore, but he somehow knew he would like what was hidden behind the dark shades, should the chance be given. She looked athletic, with a determined movement about her when she walked, flaxen hair tied back, and it bounced with her purposeful stride. She looked up and down the sidewalk while her companion was impressing the wait staff and inside patrons with his overall importance and need for immediate attention. The woman could also hear him from outside, turning away from the entrance, looking around again, as if now not wanting to be here, maybe not wanting to be with him. She looked towards the dog and then she looked up at Townes. Angelina's head was still resting on his leg and, as if on cue, the dog turned her head and looked straight at the woman. In return, the woman gave both Angelina and

Townes a brilliant smile, one that delivered warm breezes and sandy beaches and cool nights under the stars. It was the kind of smile that could take him to places he had always been wanting to go.

The smile was cut short, though, as her companion made a clamorous exit from inside the shop.

"Just get us a table … out here … unless that would be too much trouble," he said, adjusting his untucked bistro shirt that was covered in paisley designs almost as loud as his voice. Townes was fairly certain he'd seen pictures of that exact same design in a newspaper article with photos from a microscope about a terrible contagious disease. There may have been someone who was on the other side of town that didn't hear what the man said, but probably not.

The smile immediately dimmed, and the woman looked down at the ground, then went over to where her companion was standing. She looked shorter with every step she took towards him, the waitress shaking her head and seating them, the woman now looking somewhat sad as she sat down. Townes pursed his lips, letting out a breath, holding the woman firmly in his gaze, the dog now looking up at him. He was embarrassed for the woman, though he was certain she did not need his contribution, as she was obviously humiliated enough on her own. Townes looked down at Angelina.

"Yes, I did see her. She must be a jet lag mirage." The dog looked back towards the woman, then back at Townes. Townes looked at the woman, then back at the dog.

"Nope, real, and unbelievably so."

He was awestruck, and now embarrassed for himself. The woman was beautiful. There was something about her that fascinated him, even though he'd never seen her before. He couldn't remember being fascinated like that in a very long time, if ever.

"Late breakfast for two," the waitress, Savannah, interrupted Townes's pondering.

"What?" Townes said slowly, his concentration now broken.

"What are you looking at, sport?" The woman's loud companion asked.

Townes looked away.

"Your order … for you and your associate," Savannah said, standing there, the plates in her hand.

"What … oh … yes, the food. Thank you."

The waitress looked at Townes, then looked at the woman and her companion. "Asshole."

"Excuse me?"

"Not you ... him. What a tool. I've seen her somewhere before, I just don't remember where. Glad I'm not her. You want me to pour coffee in his lap?"

"You would do that?'

The waitress just smiled.

"It somehow has a nice ring to it. I've got a decent bit of jet lag going here this morning, and normally wouldn't think of ... no, you're right, he is a tool, I would think of doing that."

"I can, it's really easy," she said.

"He doesn't seem like the kind of guy who would take it in the proper spirit."

"You mean in the spirit of here's a steaming hot cup of shut the fuck up?"

"Something like that, I guess, yes."

"I won't go overboard. I offer to pay for his breakfast after I do it, I'll bet he tries to get me fired. He does, I can always do something else."

Townes looked at the waitress, looked at the man, looked longer at the woman. "Thank you, you made my day."

CHAPTER 6

The woman from the coffee shop. He wished he knew her name so he could stop calling her that. Not that he talked about her to anyone but Angelina, but still. A name would be nice since she had taken up residence in his Townes's head. Normally it was only characters from his book who lived in there, but this new inhabitant was far more impressive and he was sure she wouldn't argue with him like they did. It wasn't just how she looked. There was something more to his fascination than that. Living in La Jolla and traveling like he did, Townes saw beautiful women with considerable frequency. What was undeniable, was this woman seemed to have an even greater beauty coming from within. It was impossible for him to forget someone with that much radiance. He just knew there was more than just a good looking person here and he was stunned at how strongly he felt it.

"Leave the nice woman alone," he said to himself. Don't bother her with your troubles, feelings, dreams, history, favorite drinks, favorite color ... blah, blah, blah. Maybe you don't scare 'em off, the right things, and the right person will come your way. Or, you could be single all your life ... lose your dog to guy with an ocean view." Those were the arguments his book characters would offer up to him. He wanted to quit thinking about the woman from the coffee shop and how his life was going, or not going, but it was difficult to do, as her companion sat there and continued to extol the virtues of himself all the while she said nothing and looked like she wanted to be anywhere but there.

Let me take you away from here. You don't look happy, and I know I'm not happy, so maybe we could help each other. I might not be the best guy in the world, but I sure as hell am not as bad as that loudmouth sonofabitch. That's what he wanted to say. But he didn't.

Angelina and Townes returned home, Townes sagging into a chair to look through his mail and make some notes on his trip. He was having trouble focusing. A workout would probably do him good, but so would just sitting on his front porch. The dog had had her workout for now, and she was resting on the floor. Townes looked at her, then at the couch, and determined there was a pretty good message in all of this. A little nap wouldn't hurt.

He kicked his shoes off and laid down. He lay there looking around until his eyes began to flutter closed. He thought of the music he would play later that night, making sure he not move too deep into that, or he would never drift off to sleep, and would soon hop up to start working on the songs. He let that thought escape and moved to thinking about the view of the Pacific from Zeeder's deck, and how tranquil it was. He drifted with the water and it let him move easily back and forth and into a calming rhythm, a rhythm that gave him a feeling of warmth and let all the anxieties he had from the recent trip blow away with the ocean breeze. He moved ashore and began to walk along the beach. There was a light breeze and he could feel it in his hair, as it seemed to move him toward something in the distance. He moved with the wind and it took him closer to what stood out on the beach. That same blue sky he saw earlier, though he wasn't really seeing it the same as before. It was framing something down the beach. He walked towards it until he got close enough to see it was a person. He stopped and looked back towards the path he had made. It was blurred and the sea was washing away his footprints. He shook his head and looked again toward the person, who was now further away than before and certainly less clear. He looked back towards the tracks and they were now gone. He looked again in the direction of the person and the distance between the two of them had again increased. He looked down at his feet and the sand and sea water were turning into dirt and dust and beginning to blow around him. He looked back to the tracks, now gone, the beach now gone, as well, replaced by a dirt road, grape vines on either side. He began to laugh at the increasing futility, more a nervous laugh than one of amusement. He looked towards the person. A loud ringing made him look up. He started falling forward so quickly that he saw nothing but black. He opened his eyes, the beach, the person, were gone, leaving only a ringing telephone, Angelina looking at him. His heart was pounding. He sat up from the couch, gave his head a move from side to side, blinked his eyes and got up to answer the telephone.

"Yes."

"I wasn't sure if you would be back yet." Zeeder.

"I am, sort of."

"Is you all right?"

"No. What's up?

"I forgot to ask what time you wants to git together, you know, before yer much anticipated performance."

"Are we performing? I thought we were …" Townes stopped, having trouble remembering.

"Providin' the very finest of background noise for people to drink to."

"Something like that."

"Won't these folks be awer-stricken by yer acerbic charm? The real question is …"

"Pitchforks and torches, I know."

"I can only hope there is a semi-deserted castle, complete with moat we can flee to."

"I'm sorry … still tired from the trip … and I had a weird dream."

"Did you call that woman from my art class yet?" Zeeder asked.

"What does that have to do with anything?"

"Well, she is purdy nice, and she might be someone you could spend some time with … besides yerself, and them voices in yer head, o'course."

"Why don't you call the woman in your art class?" Townes yawned.

"I did. She don't like me."

"What's not to like?"

"I thought the same thing. I don't mean she don't like me, don't like me, I just ain't her type. We's friends."

"And you, for some reason, think she would like me?"

"What's not to like?" Zeeder repeated. "Yer table manners seem to be sufficient."

"Always an underrated attribute. So we have two likable fellows … that somehow seem to be resistible."

"Perplexin', ain't it?"

"Very. I don't know if I'll call her if she can resist a great guy like you. Besides, I think I fell in love today," Townes said quickly.

"That is a bit of a scary concept, you fallin' in love. Not sure what to make of that. I might be able to get unskeered ... iffins you was to turn on a flash-o-light, er somethin'."

"It's not dark out."

"I know, but I spook easily. Plus, I was a speakin' figuratively. Wantin' further information and such. Can't believe you missed the flashlight metaphor."

"It could have been a dream, or hallucination, brought on by fatigue, sleep deprivation ... and something else, I forget."

"Amnesia?"

"I don't remember. She was a striking woman, I do know that much about her ... dream or no."

"Did you's speak with her? Speak to her? Knock her over? Go through her handbag? Did you ... do I needs to go on?" Zeeder asked, letting out a big breath.

"No. She was with someone. Sort of a loud guy, pretty edgy. A prick, really."

"So she is unaware that she is wastin' her time with him, when she could be givin' thanks to every waking moment with you."

"Not sure I would go that far. I would probably be giving the thanks for every waking moment with her."

"Did you tell her that she could greatly improve her life, and in witnessing one musical session, she could more than likely fall in love with one of two well-meaning, quasi-talented musicians?"

"Nope. Told her nothing. I was sort of awestruck. Besides, she was with someone like I said."

"Never heard you talk like this, not since I made your acquaintance," Zeeder said.

"Is it wacky to get this worked up about someone I don't know, and who appears to be with someone else? It is wacky, isn't it?"

"Wacky. Is that a technical-cal term?"

"Not that I am aware of."

"You would really like to have some company, I think, and thus the attraction to this woman. You know nothing about her, however, so perhaps you should make some sort of effort to ... you know, gain some sorts of understandin' 'bout her celestial make-up of bein'."

"What the hell are you saying?"

"You best be findin' outs more 'bout her."

"How am I supposed to do that? I don't even know if she is lives around here."

"Well, you kin go 'bouts this in a couple a different ways. You kin go back to the coffee shop ... asks them iffin they knows her."

"Good thought."

"Or, you kin wait 'til the screamin' ladies throws theyselves atcha during tonight's performance, and let that wash this person from yer recall ... and get on with the show."

"You, are brilliant, as always," Townes said.

"I finds it extremely difficult to disagree with you when you are correct like that. In my case, I mights say I is a social savant."

"Tomorrow I'll go back to the coffee shop and ask, Mr. Savant."

"Very good idee-er, I wish I had thought of it. I might have thought to modify that plan to take place today, iffin it was me a gonna done it, while it was, you know ... fresh in their minds as to who it was yous a askin' them about."

"We have a show tonight."

"Yes, I heered that sommers, but not fer several hours yet, sos git to it. I don't want you attempting to play your best tonight and coming up with reasons your heart possibly is elsewhere. You will be singing ... save that sentiment for your writin'. It might pen out more meaningfully. I damn sure hate a sloppy sad singer."

"You're right. I'll go back before the gig. I hope they're still open."

"Good thinking," Zeeder said.

"I only get these good ideas every once in a while, so I had better act on them."

"Yep."

"See you later."

"I should hope so."

Townes looked around and grabbed the dog's leash off the arm of the chair. She swung her tail repeatedly and headed towards the door. Townes attached the leash and they were off again, walking the direction they had come from on their way home from the coffee shop. It was difficult to tell who was more excited. Both walked quickly and each held themselves in a manner that indicated purpose and anticipation. Perhaps the dog believed there would be a repeat food order, or maybe it was just the joy of two walks in a single day. Townes was hopeful that a piece of a puzzle could be provided and he could proceed on with assembling the rest of it into a really nice picture. He was comforted by the day and by the thought of discovery, as he and Angelina kept up their brisk pace until he stood before the door to the shop.

"Closed. Please Come Back Again," the sign read.

CHAPTER 7

Townes and Zeeder met at Jack's Painting and Cocktail Lounge and prepared for their evening, checking their instruments and what minimal equipment they had. They tuned their guitars with quiet but anxious focus and it was not long before all was ready.

"What was her name?" Zeeder asked.

"They were closed. I couldn't find out anything," Townes said, still disappointed.

"What a shame. She didn't leave you a note or anything?"

"No note, no acknowledgement of my existence. No treasure map."

"Well, don't give up. You still have Angelina ... 'til she leaves you for a man with an ocean view."

"You are a beacon of hope."

"Without even a tryin' and anything for you, my com-pad-ray."

"If you saw her, you would understand my plight."

"I haven't seen her, and yet I sense the potential of your plight and fear it may impact your musical performance type abillilaties this evening."

"Abillilaties? Is that a southern word? What about the pain and struggle of trying to find out about this woman giving a soulful touch to the music?"

"I'm not for certain where that word came from, and I think you read that pain and struggle and soulful statement on the back of a box of some sort of musicians', or maybe book writers' cereal. It was a joke, and not to be taken literal ... unless you are doing that writing stuff, of course, which you well may be, I never knows. I tells ya stuff, just for conversation, but now I have to worry about you puttin' it in that book o' yorn, so I might just start keepin' my comments to my own self," Zeeder said, smiling.

Townes stopped what he was doing and looked at Zeeder. "I don't have any idea what you just said." He turned back to his business. "I'm going to stop thinking about her and with a little luck, we are going to do very well this evening, and if that luck holds, we escape with our instruments and bodies intact," Townes replied.

"I certainly hope so. It is so distractin' to have all those women throwin' theyselves at us like they do, and is so tiring having to run from them all the time. I swear, sometimes I just get so tired of runnin' away from them that I just gives up and gives in to their improper advances. After that, I'm plumb wored out."

"Your imagination is better than mine, and I'm supposed to be a writer."

"It keeps me from bein' an all too easy target for prospective wives and record company representatives. I need a defense of some sort," Zeeder said.

"And a fine defense it is, as you are managing to keep both away, and quite effortlessly I mights add, and for this I commends ya. God damn, I'm starting to talk like you."

"That is probably a might scary to you, but I am right proud of ya."

They had a very short drink of bourbon at the bar, a tradition for them, then took their places and did a few more checks before they began to play.

"Welcome to Jack's Painting and Cocktail Lounge, and we hope you enjoy your evening here," Townes said softly, then the two began playing.

The time passed quickly and the bar was nearly full by the time they were halfway through their first set. It was a relatively young crowd with a near equal mixture of men and women. The atmosphere of the place lent itself nicely to the smooth flow of tunes from of Townes and Zeeder's playlist. The crowd was appreciative of their selections and both were pleased with the applause. Townes was tired, but that was posing no immediate threat, with the music and the polite crowd actually diminishing the weariness and adding to his enthusiasm. It was good to be back playing music, and playing music in a place as nice as this. Townes watched the crowd, and acknowledged them with a smile and a nod as they did the same. He noticed the makeup of the group. He never failed to be fascinated by the contents of every bar he had ever been in. One fellow, by himself at the bar, speaking with the bartender occasionally, and engaging him in conversation when the barman had a minute.

"That would be me," he thought.

An older man and woman, both nicely dressed, he wearing a necktie, both of them drinking martinis and looking at each other with true purpose when they spoke. These people had been in love for a long time, and were clearly in love still. They were very distinguished looking and touched each other gently and often. It was not normal to see someone here with a necktie.

"I should hope to be so in love, so long, and look half that good," Townes thought. "I would wear a tie everyday."

The comfort with which they interacted revealed the depth of their feelings, and their love could be sensed from across the room. Townes admired it and was happy just for the fact that he could witness it. There were several younger couples, too. They were more lively, more animated, their various drinks in a myriad of colors. They were dressed nicely, as well, though no neckties. Townes felt somewhat stupid for just now noticing that everyone had dressed quite well and that it had taken him so long to notice. Most of the places they played, people wore shorts, sandals, and T-shirts. The younger couples laughed loudly and clinked their glasses frequently and with exuberance. The women held onto the arms of their companions, and smiled at each other a great deal. Townes was not convinced that the women were that fond of each other, though their smiles never waned.

The wait staff moved briskly. The bartenders had little time to stop and take in the scene, but managed to do so occasionally. To take their measure was probably to determine the pace they would need perform their duties, more than to actually view the crowd. Focusing on the composition of the music as well as the composition of the patrons made him feel more like he was part of that river than just watching it roll past. It was necessary for him. He was never sure why.

Two women walked in and one caught Zeeder's eye and waved. Zeeder bumped Townes with his foot and cocked his head toward the door. As they made their way to one of the few unoccupied tables, one of the women smiled at Townes, and he couldn't help but smile back. He glanced at Zeeder and saw that he was watching the exchange with interest. They finished the song and announced they were going to take a short break, then return to play another set. There was polite applause and both looked at each other, then back to the crowd, smiled and thanked them for their applause.

"What was that about?" Townes asked.

"I reckons they was all drunk when they got here and know nothing about music, and are probably making some sort of signal by putting their hands together, in hopes of summoning other members of their tribe to come with clubs and help them bludgeon us into leavin'," Zeeder replied.

"Where do you come up with this? I think you should be the writer."

"But I'm the painter and musician with the tortured soul, tryin' my best not to breakdown cryin' in front of everyone. Speakin' of art, that is the girl from my art group. 'Tractive, ain't she?"

"Yes, she is. I am still not believing you aren't asking her out."

"She is not interested in me--I done told you that. Personally, I think she is looking for a writer."

"Did she tell you that?"

"No, I just have a feeling. Let's go introduce you to your future bride. I should unquestionably be best man, if it's any count, plus receive a finder's fee."

Townes looked at Zeeder and gave no reply. They left their chairs and made their way over to the table where the two women, one blonde, one with black hair were sitting. The blond woman wore a blue peasant blouse, the other woman wearing a turquoise colored shirt with sequins. Townes hesitated as Zeeder moved more quickly getting to the table, Townes lagging behind. The blonde woman stood up and greeted Zeeder with a hug.

"Hi Zeeder, you sound great! A true artist all the way around. I am so impressed," she smiled.

"Thank you. It was recorded earlier … by someone else," Zeeder laughed.

"Who is your sidekick, there?" she asked.

"Katrina Ballas, this is Townes Mantle. Townes Mantle, Katrina Ballas"

"It is very nice to meet you, Katrina, thanks for coming out," Townes said smiling.

"Are you kidding? I've been anxious to meet you and listen to you guys play ever since Zeeder mentioned it with the art class … and call me Kat."

"He is really good," Townes said, nodding at her.

"You both are really good. Oh, I'm sorry, this is my friend, Gina Berlotta," Kat said, introducing them.

"Hello, Gina. Nice to meet you. Thank you for coming out," Townes said, still smiling.

"Pleased to make your acquaintance," Zeeder said.

"I like your music," Gina said, fixing her gaze on Zeeder.

"It's all Zeeder. It is just a ventriloquist thing that he does. It's kinda a mystery how he pulls it all together," Townes said, making a sweeping motion.

"Townes is very modest," Zeeder said quietly.

"You are both great!" Kat said, her palms extended.

"Well, thank you," Townes said slowly.

"Zeeder tells me you are a writer?" Kat asked, looking at Townes more intently.

"I do some writing ... mostly I do other things, some consulting, to support my writing habit."

"You write about consulting?" Gina asked, turning her head.

"He is multifaceted," Zeeder grinned.

"No, I am a business consultant, and I write a little."

"He writes a lot. I've seen him, pen and paper and everything," Zeeder added. "He's writing a book."

"Oh that's great! What kind of book is it? A business book?" Gina asked, not really understanding.

"God no, I'm not smart enough to write about anything factual. It's a novel ... I just finished it."

"What?" Zeeder asked, turning to look at Townes. "When did you do that?"

"Not that long ago, really. My editor has been showing it to some literary agents. I didn't want to say anything to jinx it, that sort of thing," Townes said, rolling his eyes.

"That's great news. Woulda been better what you woulda told me, however, I wouldn't let your oversight stand in the way of us celebratin', as am always lookin' for a reason," Zeeder added.

"That's really great news," Kat said, smiling at Townes.

"Extremely," Gina added, looking at Zeeder.

Townes looked around and seemed at a loss for words. The congratulatory part made him uneasy.

"Well ... it's just writing, it doesn't mean anything," he said, finally.

"Doesn't mean anything? *Are you kidding me*? I don't know anyone that has had a novel published," Kat said, her eyes opening wider.

"It's not published," Townes added.

"Still, it is a real accomplishment and something very exciting. Have you been working on it—a long time, I would guess?" Kat asked.

"It took me my whole life, up to now, to write this ... but I really only started it a year ago, so not sure when the meter started running on the project, technically speaking," Townes nodded.

"Well, from that standpoint, it is tough to say, though I don't think you should count your entire life in the equation. The main thing is that you did it, no matter how long it took. A year is not that long," Kat said, tilting her head.

"When was you a gonna tell me?" Zeeder frowned.

"I don't know, sometime, I guess. I just got back in town last night."

"Have you told the dog yet?" Zeeder asked.

"Not yet, she's been at your house, remember?"

"Yes, I reckon I do remember, as there was considerable effort required to keep her happy, not to mention the cost involved."

"I know, busloads ..."

"Precisely," Zeeder said.

"What are you talking about?" Gina asked.

"Nothing, er ... not nothing, but just the dog. It's a long story," Townes said.

"The dog ghost-wrote the book, or the other way around?" Kat asked, smiled, narrowing her eyes.

"Good question and one that I have not thought of. That would 'splain a great deal," Zeeder said.

"I don't believe I have to disclose, in either case, do I?" Townes smiled.

"That is for the book police to decide, and of course, the book court," Kat said, smiling back at Townes.

"Until that time, no comment," Townes said, motioning his hand from side to side.

"He's funny about his writin' that a way," Zeeder nodded.

"How about we talk about you artists for a while?" Townes asked.

"I'm not an artist, not in the class. I'm just here for the music," Gina smiled, looking at Zeeder.

"What would you like to know?" Kat responded.

"How do you decide what art classes to take?" Townes asked, leaning closer to her.

"How do you decide what writing classes to take?" Kat asked, leaning closer to Townes.

"I'm not taking any writing classes, and we are not supposed to be talking about me anymore, we are supposed to be talking about you artists. How do you decide which classes?"

"Well, you just try some and see if you like them, or you just pick-up ideas, techniques, or concepts from different teachers, different genres. Something like that," Kat shrugged. And it's art, so it's fun."

"I was just gonna say the same thing she said," Zeeder said.

"If you have passion, it is all part of the process," Kat added.

"I can appreciate that," Townes said, looking at Kat.

"Do you have passion?" Kat asked, leaning forward.

"He's very passionate about everything," Zeeder said, casting his arms wide.

"I'm asking him," Kat said, not looking away from Townes.

Townes held her gaze level with his own before he answered. The pause was slight, but noticeable. "Very much so," he finally said, looking straight at her. "Life is difficult and sometimes I think passion is all that keeps me going."

"That is a wonderful thing," Kat said, as she reached across the table and touched his arm.

"I'm not smart enough to—"

"You said that," Kat said, cutting him off.

"So I must be correct in my assessment of my lack of intelligence, compensated by lots of passion … or something like that," Townes laughed.

"I would take passion over intelligence any day, but I suspect that you are a great deal more intelligent than you give yourself credit for," Kat replied.

"He's purdy smart, all right," Zeeder added.

"Zeeder is the smart one," Townes said, matter-of-factly.

"Well, I wasn't a gonna say nothin', but since you brought it up …" Zeeder grinned, puffing his chest out slightly.

"We're not going to take I.Q. tests or anything, are we?" Gina laughed, still looking at Zeeder.

The others chuckled.

"I'm not," Townes said.

"No."

"Nope."

"Good. I'm glad we got that settled," Gina said. "Plus, I'm just hanging out, I'm not in the art class, so don't ask me. I just wanted to clear that up. I might have some art questions of my own," she said, looking at Zeeder.

"Not sure I can answer them, but I'd give it a shot, you wanna ask 'em," Zeeder smiled.

"Do you always talk like that?"

"Likes what?"

"See, I just love that."

"Got no eye-deer what yer talkin' about."

"Yeah, you do." She smiled.

As Townes looked around the room, Kat glanced down at his hands, noticing him rubbing his left thumb back and forth across the tips of the fingers of his left hand.

"What do you prefer, writing or playing music?" Kat asked.

"I like them both. They clear things out … make things better."

"Do you have a great deal of clutter?"

"Clutter?"

"Yes, you said they clear things out. Is that like clutter, do you have clutter?"

Townes smiled. "More than some, less than most … or the other way around, I'm not sure about the clutter of others. What clears things out for you? Painting maybe?"

"I suppose so. I haven't been at it very long, but I do enjoy it. It is relaxing, so I suppose you could say, yes, it clears things out."

"Good, we all need that. What do you do when you are not painting?"

"I'm a doctor."

"Wow!" Townes said, slapping the table.

"Wow, what?"

"I just think that is really something."

"Why is that?"

"So … so much knowledge, so much skill, such … it's just, I don't know … admirable."

"Because?"

"I'm not that smart and am in awe of people that are that smart. That and what you do makes a difference."

"How do you know? I didn't tell you what kind of a doctor I was. Maybe I perform gruesome experiments on lab rats."

"Do you?" Townes asked, leaning back in his seat.

"No."

"Then you make a difference." He tapped the table. "And we need more people that make a difference."

"Well, see, I'm not sure I have made that much of a difference, not yet at least. I am wanting to go out of the country, do some work there. Maybe that will make a difference."

"I think you probably have already made a difference, you just don't see it."

"Maybe you have made a difference," Kat leaned in.

"I'm pretty sure I haven't."

"Your music makes a difference."

"Giving people the finest in background music to drink to hardly qualifies as a difference," Townes said, looking around the bar.

"Your book will make a difference. It is hard for me to explain, but ..." Kat paused, touching Townes on the arm, closing her eyes for a moment.

"It's not published yet. How can you know that?"

Kat opened her eyes and blinked several times before looking into Townes's eyes. "I can't really explain how I know that, but I do. Your book is going to be quite successful ... a movie, or series, or something."

"And you know that how?"

"It is really difficult to explain."

"I didn't even tell you what I write about. What if I write gothic, slasher, romantic graphic novels?"

"You don't."

"Maybe I do."

"You don't." She touched his arm and looked at him for a moment. "You write about ... regular people kind of things ... good things."

Townes did not know what to say. He returned the gaze. "Given the importance of the issue at hand, maybe you can explain it to me sometime ... sometime when we have more time and less people around. Sometime ... maybe we could, should have that conversation soon."

"Maybe we could."

CHAPTER 8

Townes woke up, repeating a ritual that was becoming all too familiar with him and tried to get a grip on where he was. He was clinging to the side of the bed, as if to keep from falling out of it. He was not sure how this happened and was trying to generate the electricity necessary to get his brain jump-started enough to have some hope of getting his memory to return to tell him his location and why he was in a position to be clinging to the bed. His eyes were beginning to gain focus and it appeared that there was a very good possibility that he was in the own bedroom and was in his own bed.

He leaned back in the bed to avoid rolling out of it. Something soft, yet tipped with sharp points was pressing into his back and keeping him from enjoying the center of the bed. He reached his arm back, as best as he could, to feel what was pushing him out and poking him. He heard a groan and with it felt movement, freeing him from the pressure forcing him from his bed.

It was the dog. She had stretched to what seemed to be the length of two dogs and was now collapsing back to normal size, allowing Townes to roll back towards the middle of the bed. He looked at Angelina sleeping on the bed and held his hands up to his head, rubbed his eyes and laughed out loud. He reached over and gently patted her on the belly. She stirred further and lazily looked up to see what was interrupting her sleep.

"Nails in my back ... and they turn out to be yours."

The dog groaned and went back to her sleeping pose. Townes rolled out of bed lazily and looked back at her, shaking his head. He thought about the evening before, how it had turned out, meeting Gina and Kat. Gina was rather quiet but still pleasant. He ended up talking with Kat for quite some time between sets. She was fascinating and seemed excited to talk about writing and music and kept trying to get him to tell her about the book. Having just met her, he was a little reluctant, but found it easier the more they talked. She was very sharp with a quick wit. She had little trouble laughing, and smiling, her personality such that a person felt comfortable being around her and if one wanted to know what was on her mind, one need only ask and Kat would oblige. She was not overly talkative, but she didn't back away from an opinion either. She had a refreshing way about her. Townes was intrigued by her interest in the things he was doing. The sixth sense she had was really amazing, sometimes able to answer the questions she asked of him herself. Her comments about the book being successful, the movie angle. That part really got him going.

I told her what I did, but strangely enough, she seemed to already know, he thought. Physically, she could have been the sister to the woman he saw at the restaurant. She was also very tan, fit, her hair golden, just like the other one.

He gave up on the thought of trying to reclaim his territory in the bed and decided not to get back in it. Still groggy, he moved slowly around the house, still thinking about last night while he worked on trying to wake up. He remembered Kat asking him if he could do anything he wanted, what it would be. He told her he would be what he is now, only better. He asked her the same question and she replied that she would be an artist. Townes thought that puzzling. He remembered the conversation returning to the passion portion and back and forth from there. He was fascinated at her being a doctor and he asked her about it. He couldn't decide if she was shy about it, or if it was just something she didn't reveal about herself. She was plenty open about herself when they spoke, just not about that. Townes did not generally reveal that much about himself, so it was not really fair to hold her to a different standard, especially since her profession was of such great substance. If she had reasons for discussing or not discussing what she did, it was her choice. He didn't press her. If she wanted to discuss it, she would. Townes felt calmed talking with her. He wondered if they would get to talk together again. He hoped they would.

Angelina was now stretched back out to take full advantage of the now vacant bed. She was enjoying the newfound extra room, yet still kept an eye on Townes for sudden movement towards the doors, or in case a steak should fall out of his pocket. Townes thought more about Kat, thinking maybe he should call Zeeder and get her phone number. He looked out the window, his mind returning to the woman from the coffee shop. She had stayed in his mind, yet he still knew nothing about her. Nothing except that he felt warm when she took off her sunglasses for that brief moment and looked at him with eyes blue like the nearby ocean, so maybe that was something. Angelina raised her head off the pillow as Townes looked out the window. She looked directly at him, a challenge of sorts.

"What?"

She slapped twice on the bed with her tail.

"There's no way she's there two days in a row. After jackass yesterday, she may be too embarrassed to come back, but I do need to go back and ask if they know her."

Angelina continued to look at him, then glanced towards the door, then put her head back on the pillow.

"You don't know that."

She let out a long sigh.

"All right, we'll go."

Angelina snapped up and began to stretch, first her neck then her hind quarters, shook twice and leapt down off the bed. Townes let her into the backyard. He returned to the bedroom and dressed, putting on sandals, jeans, a baseball cap, and a T-shirt Zeeder have given him that said "Garden & Gun" on the front of it. He grabbed the leash and attached it to her collar when she returned from the back yard.

"You just want the smoked salmon with the bagels, you know she won't be there."

Angelina moved her tail from side to side.

"I thought so."

They left the house and headed back to the coffee shop. One woman, one day, and he knew nothing about her, save for the fact she had an obnoxious boyfriend, husband, or whatever he was. And she was beautiful. And she had looked at him. Right at him. And those blue eyes made his legs weak.

You know fucking zero about this woman, one of his characters said to him.

Angelina looked back at him and swished her tail.

"Right, I do know one thing about her," he said, as if the dog had posed some point of order.

Angelina turned back towards the sidewalk and the view of the journey ahead. They were both anxious to get back to the cafe, though for different reasons. Townes wondered if the staff knew and could divulge the identity of the beautiful blonde.

What if the waitress doesn't know? What if she knows but won't tell me because I could be a stalker? What if they have changed their policy about serving dogs outside ... and she thinks I'm a stalker? What if ... she thinks I'm a dipshit for talking to characters in my head ... and thinking about all the reasons she won't tell me?

"Table for two, or does your partner prefer to stand?" The hostess smiled.

"I think she'll sit, though the chair is probably not the kind she is used to, no offense," Townes laughed.

"What kind of chair is she used to?" The hostess chuckled.

"Leather, something a little larger that she can curl up and go to sleep in ... in case of an emergency, but nothing is scheduled for a while."

"She that particular?" the hostess asked, as she looked down at the dog, who was now panting, excited.

"Well, she has certain standards, as I'm sure you have a certain standard, and well ..." Townes said, his voice trailing off, realizing he was jabbering.

"The leather chairs for outside won't arrive from Italy for another couple of days, so how about if I bring a bowl of water? Would she consider just hanging out with you and tolerate the sidewalk as is until we get it carpeted?"

Townes looked at Angelina, who was looking at the woman, waiting for her to magically produce a plateful of food. "Well?"

The dog looked at Townes and sat down. "I think she will be fine with things as you have them."

"Splendid. I'll send your server right out," the hostess said as she turned to go back inside.

"Wait," Townes said.

"Yes?" The woman said.

"Were you working yesterday, by chance?"

"No, I wasn't."

"Is there anyone waiting tables today that might have been here yesterday? I can't remember the person's name that waited on me yesterday, I'm bad with names."

"Not sure, why?"

"I am looking for someone ..."

"I think we all are," the hostess said, smiling, cocking her head to one side.

Townes laughed, realizing what he had just said. "What I mean is, there was someone here yesterday, and I am trying to find out her name, so I was wondering if, well, there was someone here who might know her. Does that sound too, well, weird?"

The hostess looked at Townes and then at the dog, then back at Townes. "You look OK to me. I'll see who was here yesterday," she said as she started again for the inside.

"Great, thanks ... I mean, I really appreciate it," Townes mumbled after her.

He noticed Angelina had modified her activity to something between panting and drooling. "Hey, this might work," Townes said, smiling back.

Angelina was now looking towards the inside of the restaurant, the smell of bacon almost more than she could stand. Other people were sitting at the outside tables now, and she was giving all of them a complete visual inspection, sniffing the closer ones.

"That's a pretty dog," one of the women diners near them said.

"Thank you. She's not bothering you, is she?"

"Not at all."

"She probably will at some point."

"Not possible, is it sweetie?" the diner said happily, looking at the dog.

A waitress came to Townes's table. "Hello, how are we doing today?" she said, patting Angelina on the head. "Hey, I remember you!"

"Doing just great, thanks. Sorry, I'm bad with names."

"Savannah, and yes, I'm here most every day, except for the days when I work up in Encinitas at The Craftsman," she replied, still patting the dog. "You should come up there sometime too."

"I'll do that. I'm Townes, this is Angelina. Listen, there was a woman here yesterday, and I was just wondering if you knew her."

She looked at Townes and then back at the dog. "This your dog, or you just dog sitting?"

"I think I belong to her more than the other way around. Does it matter if we belong together, or if I'm dog sitting?"

"Both are acceptable, one just shows more commitment. What kind of work do you do? We didn't get into that yesterday. First dates are always tricky."

"Business consultant. First dates?"

"Yuck!"

"Writer and musician?"

"Sounds much better, don't you agree? That's what you should say when people ask you. I am a writer ... and a musician. You could even choose either one of those, depending on the day."

"When you put it like that, definitely. The yuck one pays the bills."

"Pays the bills ... until ..."

"Pays the bills ... until ...?"

"Pays the bill until you become an overnight sensation. What kind of writer?"

"Novel. First one."

"Cool! Can I buy it? Warwick's Book Store is not far from here, I'll go buy it when I get off work, but you have to tell me the name of it."

"Not published yet."

"Shit! I mean ... shoot! I wanted to buy it. But written though. Finished?"

"Written and finished," Townes said, tilting his head back after hearing the words.

"Good going. So you could use a break. I write music, and one of these days ... maybe I could use a break too. You want to look at some of my songs?" Savannah smiled.

"OK, but I'm not ... I'm only a local musician. Yes, a break would be nice."

"I heard that. Who you looking for?"

"Yesterday, when I was here, around one: blonde, tan, workout clothes."

"Most, if not all the women in La Jolla."

"Shoulder length, tied back."

"Most if not all ... I used to be blonde, but today, as you can see, my hair is red, *red*!"

"Your hair looks great. This woman, she looked, I don't know, she looked ... resolute, wonderful smile, amazing blue eyes ... perhaps carrying a burden. Quiet herself, but had a loud, overbearing fellow with her," Townes's voice faded as he described the woman's companion.

"Hmm ... sounds like you are a writer."

Townes did not seem to hear that part. "Very fit, very ... attractive. No makeup."

"You going to order something?" Savannah smiled.

"It would probably help, wouldn't it?"

"Many things, most certainly."

"Green tea, carrot juice, smoked salmon, capers, no onions, extra bagel."

"Nothing for Angelina here?"

"She'll have the extra bagel."

"Coming right up."

"Do you know who I'm talking about? I think we had a discussion about pouring coffee in his lap …"

"Yep, I do remember that. Sorry I don't really remember her all that well, but that a-hole with her … man, he was a piece of work. I felt sorry for her. You should ask her out. I've seen her somewhere, but I don't remember where. I've worked in a bunch of restaurants, so no telling. I used to live out in Palm Springs, so maybe that was it. For some reason I'm seeing her with a taller guy, dark hair. I think he was really good looking too, if that's who I think, but I can't be sure. I think … I think I'm rambling, sorry. Yep, I remember jerkasaurus. Normally I would never think of passing a plate around the kitchen for all of us to spit on, but I had to make an exception in his case.

"I'll see what I can do … and I'll be right back with your order."

CHAPTER 9

Townes and Angelina returned to Zeeder's apartment after breakfast. Zeeder was on the patio painting. It was normal for Zeeder to be outside either painting or playing music.

"Well, looky here. Aren't you that singer man what was a playin' at the bar last night?" Zeeder asked, not really looking up from the canvas.

"No, you are thinking of my partner," Townes said, obviously in a good mood.

"I didn't sing much, as I recollect."

"Look at you. Creativity just oozing out of you. It would never even occur to me to try to paint and play the guitar ... at the same time."

"Well, I ain't a gonna argue with you, especially on such a purdy day. Speaking o' purdy, how did you get along with Kat? 'Peared to me, you was a gittin long quite nicely, iffin I'm recollectin' correctly."

"She is fascinating. She is sort of, I don't know, sort of mystical. She knew a lot about me, things I didn't tell her."

"Are you sure you is a-feeling all right, or do you need to sit a spell? You want I should get you some medicine, I think I got some bourbon around here sommers."

"I feel great. Back home, beautiful day, good gig last night, met a really interesting woman, I have a fine dog, and a fine ... albeit eccentric friend. I think I'm covered. What the hell you painting, anyway?"

"I am not at liberty to discuss that, but I am glad to hear the word 'fine' appear with such frequency in your speakin'. With regards to me, o' course."

"How's 'bouts that?"

"Indeedee. Can I get you somethin'?"

"Just ate, thank you, but I did have a question earlier regarding Kat's phone number, unless that is forbidden."

"I should think she might be amenable to that, based on last night's chemistry." Zeeder said, focusing on his painting. "I asked you to call her before, guess it woulda help what I have given you the number."

"Something like that. Are you sure it's OK? I wouldn't want to break any ... artists' gaggle trust, or anything."

"I actually think we are a pride, but I don't think that would be problematic, given that the apparent results of your last rendezvous with her seemed to indicate possible favorable tendencies," Zeeder continued to apply the paint to the canvas without looking up.

"I don't know," Townes said, taking a deep breath, and holding it in for an extra count before releasing it loudly.

"You don't know what, 'zactly?"

"She's a doctor, that's pretty big time."

"Big time what?"

"Big time."

"You said that. I'm trying to discern what that means."

"She is way out of my league."

"I could paint a mustache on you, iffin you think that might help elevate your status," Zeeder gestured over towards Townes with his paint brush.

"You know what I mean," Townes leaned away.

"I do not."

"Doctors are, you know ... smart and such."

"Oh, that is so, you know ... stupid and such," Zeeder continued to extend the brush in Townes's direction.

"They have it all—the brains, the discipline, the grooming. I groom my dog."

"Did you like her?"

"Yes."

"Did she like you?"

"I think so I hope so ... probably, maybe ..."

"Let's say that you call her and if she doesn't wish to see you, she will respond towards that end."

"She's a doctor. She's used to doctor parties, and finer things, and artists and such. You're the artist—you should call her."

"She ain't interested in me.

"How do you know?"

"Talk amongst the pride. Ain't like we ain't friends, or don't like on another. I just ain't her type."

"Seriously? Maybe it's because you don't use the word 'ain't' enough." Townes smiled.

"I think Gina and I mights be more compatible-bull," Zeeder said, making a gesture as if he were directing a symphony.

"How about that."

"Tryin' to get her to come over fer a visit sometime."

"What does she do when she is not painting?"

"Not sure."

"Well, her interests are arts and artists, you are stacking this nicely in your favor."

"I seed her first," Zeeder pointed at Townes.

"Not to worry. I need to focus on writing, not on a woman, or women."

"Which is it, one or more than one?"

"Writing. I said writing needed to be the focus."

"I heard more," Zeeder held the paint brush up to his ear.

"You are painting, and this ocean view is making you light-headed."

"If you say so. By the way, the fellers in the band wants us to join them for something they have coming up."

"Yeah, what's the gig?" Townes looked out at the ocean.

"Highfalutin gig."

"I thought the band only played dives ... and drunken private parties."

"This would be half of that."

"Since you said it was highfalutin, that leaves only the drunken private party half. Where?"

"La Jolla Country Club."

"La Jolla fucking Country Club!?"

"I only know it bys the name I gived ya. I don't know it by the one you just said. Yer language has gotten goddamn downright shitful, case you was a wonderin'," Zeeder said, raising his eyebrows.

"Our band ... at La Jolla fuc ... at La Jolla Country Club?"

"Our band. Some sort of wine tasting, fund-raiser."

"Was it a mistake?" Townes asked, stroking his chin.

"No."

"Somebody cancel?" Townes said, now scratching his head.

"I'm not the booking agent or band leader. Fudgie is in charge of that, and he said it was on the up and up."

"On the hoi-polloi is what you mean, and Fudgie has been known to have lapses of judgment."

"Hoity-toity might be what I meant, I gets 'em mixed up," Zeeder said, scratching his head.

"Do they know about that band, the band members?"

"I'm not the ..."

"I know, I know. When is it?"

"Oh, we got several weeks."

"Still, I guess we'd better practice."

"Fudgie said the same thing. Don't wanna suck," Zeeder said, shaking his head.

"Don't wanna suck, so Fudgie's in, obviously. Everybody else in—Stretch, Saxman?"

"Sounds like it."

"That would be something. We've never been kicked out of a country club. This could be a first. Well, we haven't played with those guys in a while, so be good to let off a little steam. If it's a wine thing, I'll get my winery buddy Crosetti to come down."

"A first for us, or for the country club? They have probably kicked people out before, just not of our low caliber," Zeeder said, moving his paintbrush in a downward motion.

"Well, I always say, I'd rather be kicked out than kicked."

"Really, you say that?"

"To get kicked out, you had to be let in in the first place. You can get kicked anywhere."

"Never thinked of it that-a-ways. Did you think that on your own, or was somebody a kickin' you while you was a thinkin' about it?"

"Artists."

"I would love to see one today, truly would."

"Go look in the mirror."

"Surely not! Why break the streak now? Two hunnerd fifty days on the job without incident."

"Country club ... hmm." Townes shook his head.

"Let's get back to the women."

Townes still held his gaze on the ocean in the distance and said nothing.

"This is the point in the conversation where you respond to my recent query," Zeeder used the paintbrush to gesture towards Townes.

"What?"

"Quite the intellectual response. How many years of higher edumication?"

"What do you want to know?"

"See, was that so difficult for you to say? You said woman, or women, remember, you said it."

"Just someone I saw. She was ... I don't know, just ... she was just really something," Townes said smiling, gazing out towards the ocean.

"She was a looker, that what yer sayin'?"

"More than a looker."

"More than that? Not sure I ever saw that."

"Change your life more than that."

"And you knows that from just a lookin'?" Zeeder said, holding the brush up to his eye like a telescope.

"Never saw one like this before, not even close."

"You should not gawk, you know."

"I wasn't gawking. She just had this ... something. I don't know. I'm trying to forget about it," Townes said, blowing out a loud breath.

"Certainly someone making that kind of impact should be forgotten. Perhaps you could poke an eye out, that would make about as much sense."

"What!?"

"How about Woman Two? Would that be Kat?"

"She was very intriguing. I swear she is clairvoyant. I'm surprised you didn't go out with her. I think I said that, didn't I?" Townes seemed a little confused.

"She's not interested in me, and I know I said that. Your confusion may be a symptom of a greater ailment. Perhaps these two women have you a might perplexed. Maybe I should fetch the medicine."

"Like I don't think it is that difficult to perplex me? Like I know anything about women. Would you like me to go on?"

"Always, and most certainly I would."

"Artists."

"Where!?" Zeeder said, looking around quickly, then back to his painting.

"Kat is very special, and I would like to see her again."

"How 'bout the mystery woman, would you like to see her again? Or, now that you have had time to think, do you opt for the poke an eye out thing?"

Townes looked up from his ocean stare towards the sky, then down to follow the shoreline. "Of course I would like to see her again."

"What do you know of her?"

"Just a hair past nothing."

"That's better than nothing or less."

"Nothing or less is probably more accurate. I will, hopefully, snap out of it. Maybe if you gave me Kat's phone number that would help ... if you would."

"I will, and gladly."

"Thank you. How did the country club thing come together exactly?"

"Not sure. Fate, perhaps. Fudgie didn't say," Zeeder mumbled, holding the brush in his teeth as he looked at the developing picture.

"Do you think we will have to move out of La Jolla proper after they throw us out of the country club?"

"More than likely. Identity change most certainly, cosmetic surgery possibly."

"Altering our appearance. You think that serious?" Townes held his hands over his face, leaving only his eyes showing.

"Only if we want to avoid the inevitable tribunal."

"Man, I hate that tribunal shit," Townes said.

"As do I."

"Are we making any preemptive adjustments, you think?"

"I might pack and forward my things immediately prior to expedite my departure from the lower forty-eight," Zeeder said, making a sweeping motion with his hand.

"I mean to the music."

"Oh, probably just the usual."

"Turn it up."

"'Zactly."

"Well, this will be a growth experience for the boys," Townes said, looking down and shaking his head.

"You mean you and me will grow in a different way, from having to live on the run."

"Look, if you and I can ... wait, if I can play at Jack's with you, then growth is possible."

Zeeder took the brush out of his teeth, a puzzled look on his face.

"You are equipped for that, I'm not. We did it together, it worked out. Your maturity and talent compensated for my long list of shortcomings, too long to paraphrase," Townes said, looking at the ground.

Zeeder's chin went down to his chest. "I think ..." he paused, scratched his head with the hand holding the paint brush, careful as to not paint himself in the process.

"You think what?"

Zeeder said nothing, and walked from the patio into the house before responding. "I think writers are nonsensical."

"It is a requirement," Townes said back.

Angelina had been resting on the patio the entire time and now looked up when Zeeder went in the house. She looked towards the door to the house, then up at Townes.

"I don't understand him half the time either," Townes said, looking down at her.

Angelina looked back towards the door, then let out a sigh and went back to resting. Zeeder returned with a piece of paper, handed it to Townes, then resumed his position in front of the canvas. The paper he gave to Townes had something painted on it.

"What is this?" Townes asked, handling it gently.

"It's Kat's phone number."

"You painted it on here?"

"Yes I did. You are very observant," Zeeder grinned.

"What if it ... it's still wet."

"Paint can be like that. Wet sometimes, dry others."

"This is a test, isn't it?" Townes laughed.

"Perhaps."

"And I have to be careful."

"Only with the paint. You will then be just beginning your journey," Zeeder gestured, following the horizon.

"I'm taking my dog and leaving."

"Why?"

"I have to go call this number, or ..."

"Or what?"

"Or hang it up to dry."

CHAPTER 10

Townes and Angelina returned home, taking a roundabout route, enjoying the welcome gift of an unbooked day. He thought about the conversation with Kat, only to quickly drift to the mystery woman he had seen at the cafe. Both women were perplexing him. He didn't want to put them out of his mind, but rather in a different part of his mind. Kat was perplexing because of her clairvoyance, the other because just seeing her hit him like Angelina would after he had been gone. He knew he needed to focus on his novel. He went back and forth within himself, and with the help of the voices of the characters in his head, one day thinking it was going to happen, and the next that he was as crazy as he could possibly be, and why in the hell did he think that there was even the slightest goddamn chance in the world that he would get even a second look from an agent, when so far he hadn't even gotten a first look. There was no basis, at least none that he knew of, for Kat's comments about the assured success of the book. That follow-up conversation with her about her knowing things he had not yet told her was going to happen. All this uncertainty troubled him and he wanted to get back to feeling grounded. Angelina pulled hard on the leash.

"What?"

She had found some dogs and the smelling ritual had begun. The other dogs were Australian Shepherds, each black, white, with slight brown mixed in, one glassy eye.

"I'm sorry," the woman on the other end said. "They are very friendly. Oh,

Townes, hello. Gina, we met the other night … no, last night, was that right? I have trouble keeping track."

"Yes, yes, hello. Nice to see you again," Townes said, trying to keep the canine klatch from becoming entangled.

"Your dog, she is very pretty."

"Yours are, as well."

"Thanks. Hey, where do I know you from, I mean besides the other night?" Gina asked.

"I'm sure I don't know. Isn't that what I'm supposed to say to you?"

"Why, do I look familiar?"

"No, just a phrase a guy would use, but I do wish that I knew you from somewhere."

Gina blushed. "Hey, I really enjoyed listening to you and Zeeder, at Jack's last … whatever night," she laughed.

"We didn't disrupt your evening by playing badly, did we?"

"No, you were good. I enjoyed it."

"Thank you. We had fun as well."

"Kat was excited to go. I'm glad we did. You play there a lot—maybe that is where I have seen you before. Is it always just the two of you?"

"Yes, just the two of us and we do sort of play there a lot. We have a few more nights there this week. We have an alter-ego band that we play with sometimes, but we never get invited back when we play somewhere, noise ordinances and such. I'm pretty sure you weren't in any of those places," Townes said, his voice fading.

The dog leashes were now tangled, forcing Townes and Gina to take action to avoid further macramé. The dogs seemed to be laughing. First one, then the other, would attempt to move away from the fray, only to move back in, thus making the knot a bit more difficult to untie.

"I hate when they do this," Gina said.

Townes just smiled and worked to solve the puzzle of lines.

"Would you and Zeeder play for a party I'm having?"

Townes was now down on one knee to get the dogs leashes undone. "I don't see why not would have to check the schedule," Townes said, grunting a bit from trying to hold all the dogs.

"What would you charge for something like that?"

"That would depend on what you had in mind."

"An informal cocktail party, casual, nothing stuffy. Tiki torches, Hawaiian shirts, skirts, that sort of thing. We're not, er ... I'm not stuffy," Gina smiled.

"I like the sound of all of that. Where would it be?"

"At my house."

"Where do you live?"

"Here."

"California here, San Diego here, La Jolla here?"

"Above La Jolla Shores here."

"I only ask because we get a lot of folks vacationing here and you never know where they might live. Well, sounds like travel to the venue would not be an issue" The leashes now made free again.

"Thanks for untangling them ... so travel not an issue?"

"Not an issue. We charge more if we have to travel. If you lived in Alaska, we would really have to ding you," Townes grinned.

"You are funny. And I really like your friend. He's very witty. Does he always talk that way, you know, that southern thing?"

"Pretty much, he does. Don't encourage him to talk that way, I'm trying to get him housebroke. So here in La Jolla, what do you do?"

"Does it matter?" Gina said, raising an eyebrow.

"No, just curious."

"Price difference?"

"No, just curious." Townes repeated, scratching his head, looking at the leashes.

"How much?"

"Very reasonable."

"I can do reasonable."

"When do you need us?"

"In a couple of weeks."

"I think it's all right, but I have to speak with my partner about our schedule," Townes said, rubbing his chin.

"He do all that, does he? He didn't mention that last night. Maybe because I was asking him all kinds of other questions so I could listen to that drawl of his."

"Yes. He is the brains ... and the talent. He forgets things, too. He might forget your name even. He won't ever forget a face, but he does have trouble with names. "

"If he is the brains that forgets names, what does that make you?"

"Extremely fortunate, I guess. I forget names too, I must confess. But I am

55

lucky to play with him, and have him as a friend."

"I should say, but I think you are a bit modest. Modest, and reasonable, if nothing else," Gina smiled.

"If nothing else."

"Can I contact you to give you the details?"

"Yes."

"If you are placing it in your calendar, it's Gina Berlotta."

"I will do my utmost best, without having my calendar right now."

"I have recently gotten reacquainted with some old friends, and I wanted to have a party to continue the reconnection. We hadn't seen each other in a long time, and it sort of made me realize some things have been missing in my life. Maybe I can convince them to have the next party after this to sort of keep the momentum. If not, that's OK too, but I am going to follow up on our recent get-together," Gina reached down and stroked her dog, and looked as if she were miles away.

"That sounds nice."

"It is. We've known each other a long time. It had just been so long since we'd gotten together that no one really knew where anyone else was in their lives. It was a pretty moving experience. Wasn't designed to be that way, just turned out that way. Some outsiders, now new friends, got involved and well … let's just say there were some fireworks," Gina continued to pet her dog and look off towards the ocean.

"Fireworks?"

"It's a long story. The best part of the story was that my friends got me thinking about the path I was on, and I decided to change it. Kat was very … probably the most instrumental in this, and my friend Annie."

"Sounds …" Townes paused, "Serious. Did you say Annie?"

"Yes, Annie. Well, it is serious, but the best part about changing paths, is that you can choose to also make it more fun—choose the fun path."

"I am all for that," Townes looked up into the sky.

"Nothing wild."

"Hmm, too bad."

"Why?"

"Just kidding."

"Some of us, like I said, are getting reacquainted, so wild really isn't in the playbook, at least not yet anyway. We had some wild at our recent get together. I hope that should last us a while."

"So you are capable of wild?"

"Well, I didn't really have a hand in the wild part, I was just there," Gina said, her hand outstretched.

"I've said that before."

"No, really."

"No, really. Where was the get together … I mean where the wild showed up?"

"Palm Springs. Rancho Mirage."

"Not usually associated with wild."

"Right? I have, er, had a place out there, and this was the first time I've had wild come to visit. It wasn't that wild, but it was out of the ordinary."

"Wild like …"

"Wild like a friend of mine punched this asshole in the face wild."

"Guys do that sometimes, but still uncomfortable," Townes said, again scratching his head.

"My friend that punched the guy was Kat."

Townes let out a whistle. "Well, can't say as I've seen that, and I've seen some stuff. Was thinking about calling her after last night, but maybe I should wait. Well, I would assume your party will have a different guest list, so how many?"

"Ahh, twenty-five, thirty, tops, probably less, but yes, different guest list. Go ahead and call her, she likes you."

"That's good. Sounds like it would be not as good to be on her bad side," Townes said, again scratching his head with his free hand. "Food at this party?"

"Of course, why? Did you pick up a flea?"

"No, nervous habit I guess, sorry. We like to eat, which means you get a discount if we can have some. You sure she was talking about me?" Townes asked, starting to scratch his head, but catching himself.

"Yes, she was talking about you. Back to the food thing. Starving musicians, just come to La Jolla to walk your dogs?" Gina grinned.

"Well, I think it's not quite that simple."

"Where do you live?"

"Here."

"Here California, here San Diego—"

"Ha, here La Jolla," Townes cut her off, feeling stupid he had asked her those same questions.

"What do you like to do for fun? I mean when you are not playing music, walking Labradors, doing the business stuff, and writing, which I think is very cool, by the way. You were kind of cryptic last ... or whatever night it was." Gina asked.

"Does it matter?" Townes said, smiling.

"Yes."

"Why?"

"You are coming to my house, and it sounds like you will also be dining there, but if you have a hobby of being an elephant trainer, well, if you brought your students, they might trample my lawn."

Townes laughed and looked again to make sure the dogs were not braiding the leads. "No elephants. A little business, a little writing, a little music. Probably not enough fun in the equation, but I am working on that. The animal you see is the only one, and she trains me."

"She hasn't done so bad, it looks like."

"She doesn't have much to work with."

"You said you were not yet published, right?"

"Not yet, but hopeful," Townes said, patting his leg.

"Maybe I can help you."

"What do you do? Wait, sorry, I think I asked that before."

"Right now, nothing."

"Nothing?"

"Yes."

"I have experience in nothing, though it hasn't worked out," Townes paused. "Yet."

"Maybe you're not doing it right," Gina said slowly.

"I would say that based on my results, I am definitely not doing it right. It's working better for you?"

"So far."

"It's not too much responsibility, the hours and such?" Townes grinned.

"Yes it is a lot of responsibility, the scheduling and such."

"I'll have to remember that next time I give it a go. Maybe it will work better if I had the instructions."

"Not just anybody can pull it off."

"I should think not."

"Let's just say I am in between, in transition. I'm really not so sure I'm supposed to be doing nothing. So, you will do the party, and it will be reasonable, like you said?" Gina asked, leaning forward. "And you will bring your partner?"

"Yes, pending partner agreement, and reassurance that we don't have to draft a 'wild occurrences' rider into the contract."

"Of course, and of course not. You will let me know?"

"Certainly."

"Would you like to know how to get in touch with me?"

"I very much would, yes."

Gina laughed silently and reached into her pocket, pulling out a clip with some money and some cards with it. She took one of the cards from the stack and handed it to Townes.

"This is me. Call me when you speak with your partner. It should be fun. You will meet some great folks, and maybe they will have you play at their place sometime. You never know what will happen."

"I have found that to be implicitly true," Townes said, cocking his head to one side.

"Good."

"Good."

"This will be no exception. You can bring your dog, if you would like, she seems very well-behaved," Gina said, looking at the dogs who were both now sitting, panting, and watching the street activity.

"She is well-behaved, I am the unruly one. I wouldn't want to complicate things at your get together."

"Well, whatever you want to do, the offer is there."

"Thank you, that's very kind."

"Why don't you give me your number as well and that way I can call to remind you, in case you turn out to be, you know, a flaky musician."

"I suppose that is always a possibility, but I hope that affliction doesn't show itself," Townes smiled, pulling his wallet out of his front pocket, and took out a business card, and handed it to Gina.

"Well, you went somewhere and got cards printed, so that would show some initiative."

"How do you know that's me?"

"It has your name on it?"

"Good point. It must be me then."

"Well, let's hope so."

"I'll call you when I find out the schedule. I'm looking forward to this."

"It'll be fun."

"Fun always works for me."

CHAPTER 11

Townes and Zeeder were booked again at Jack's Painting and Cocktail Lounge. They talked about the upcoming country club gig with the band, and Townes's recent conversation about playing the party at Gina's house while they set up.

"This life on the road could prove difficult. Think that's why I never really toured," Zeeder said, looking away, as if seeing something far off.

"We're not going on the road. Two gigs, both in La Jolla," Townes countered.

"Still."

"You have a one block, or two block radius restriction, do you?"

"Well, I guess not. I just don't want this thing to get out of hand and start riding around in a bus ... though I would go to Europe ... or Australia," Zeeder said, nodding.

"As long as it's not on a bus?"

"Well, it would have to be a nice bus."

"I'll make note of that. No school busses."

They were prepping for their evening event as they talked and set-up their four guitars, a mandolin, a couple of amplifiers, microphones, cables, music stands, CD's business cards and tip jar. Townes was always getting on Zeeder about forgetting the last three.

"How is it you keep meeting these women?" Zeeder asked, pausing from his set up.

"What do you mean? Townes responded.

"The lady with the dog today, the mystery woman the other day, Kat. Those certainly would qualify as women." Zeeder went back to his equipment preparation.

"Yes they would qualify. Let's see, you introduced me to Kat, and Gina came with Kat the other night, so you already know Gina. All in all, I wouldn't call that unusual, but your standards are quite different."

"Yes, they is."

"I don't think there is really a discussion here." Townes did not look up from his attention to the gear. "You meet people don't you? You met Gina, you met Kat. I should be asking you. I think you said you might be trying to get together with Gina. She specifically said she wanted to see you, so, so you met them too, or first, or what the hell ever."

"Reckon I did, at that. I don't have a good memory. But it does seem to happen to you fairly often."

"This is a first," Townes smiled.

"A first?"

"First time I ever met two women in one week ... I mean outside of business, which doesn't really count."

"I think you mean three," Zeeder added.

"Haven't met her yet, just saw her, so that one doesn't count. I would like to meet her, but ..." Townes took a breath. "Besides, what's the big deal? I had a nice conversation with Kat and ran into the lady with the dog, er, Gina."

"And she wants you to come to her house."

"Come to her house, with you, and play music for her party. I wouldn't say that is anything beyond that description."

"What about the mystery woman?"

Townes accidentally turned the amplifier up and it made a shrill, high-pitched sound, very unpleasant to hear, prompting Zeeder to jam his fingers in his ears "Sorry," Townes shrugged. "I don't know. Don't even know much about her."

"Much? What the hell kind of thing is much?" Zeeder was now tuning his guitar. "How much?"

"A name, her name, she's got a ..." Townes's voice trailed off, looking more at the guitar than at Zeeder.

"She has a name. That's wonderful," Zeeder said, very deadpan. "That is really good that she is not one of the no-name women roamin' the countryside in packs, searchin' for a moniker. Now you don't have to get caught up in any time-consumin' name-the-woman-contest, or go get a book of names and read them to her until she smiles at one she likes. Does she have the gift of speech, as well?"

"I don't know. I know her name, though we have never spoken. And I might take this opportunity to mention that for a Southern gentleman, you are kind of a sarcastic prick sometimes," Townes smiled.

"Well, is that how you are going to talk to this woman, what's-her-name?"

Townes smiled, looked around at the music equipment, and around the bar, the door, the kitchen, surveying the scene. "Annie. Her name is Annie."

"At the risk of sounding like a sarcastic prick, that's a start. How do you know this?"

"I just do."

"Yous went back and asked the folks what work at where you see'd her, like I told ya to, didn't ya?" Zeeder said, slowly nodding his head.

"Yes."

"How much did it costs ya?"

"Two of the largest meals I have ever in my life seen, with a tremendous gratuity." Townes said, rubbing his fingers together.

"Big eater, big tipper."

"Something like that. I had help with the food."

"Was extra bacon involved?"

"Yes."

"Great plan. Are you not pleased that you thought to return to the scene of the incident and question the suspects?"

"Quite pleased."

"Are you going to tell me anymore about this mystery ... 'scuse me, this Annie?"

"No. I think I'm going to play at a nice bar and hope the patrons are not susceptible to outbursts of violent behavior," Townes said.

"Or that they brought any piss peaches with them to throw, but that goes without sayin'. Would ya tell me at the break, or do I have to stage a walkout?"

"Piss peaches?" Townes laughed. "Maybe if you play really well, I might tell you."

"Well then, that sinks it. I was a plannin' to play really shitty, so that means I won't hear no more about the woman. Fuck!" Zeeder said quietly, kicking the floor. "Piss peaches is the ones that is beyond rotten."

"I guess I won't be telling you, then."

"What iffin I promise to try not to play shitty, even though sometimes I can't help it?"

"That's what I usually say."

"Well then, that's where I heered it. I knew it sounded familiar."

"Well, I am sure you will play fine; it's always me we have to worry about, but we'll both try to not play shitty. And … I'll tell you at the break."

"Good 'nuf."

They started to play. The crowd was light when they arrived to set up, but the bar began to fill up quite quickly, the atmosphere changing with each new person who walked through. Townes always took notice. The bottles on the shelf behind the bar more resplendent with the music, the light shifting as people entered, almost as if the vessels moved ever so slightly to the music. Patrons soon began to rush in, then seemed to move in a less deliberate, slightly unhinged, smoother fashion. This was where the people were going, the hurry was over. Townes always enjoyed the early movements of their nights in the bar.

For all present, there was promise, there was hope, the entire evening lay ahead. There existed a delicate balance at the beginning of the evening that did not always carry through to the end of the night, with the most modest of movements somehow, sometimes managing to push the thin atmosphere away from there, and replace it with a different, heavier type of thing altogether. Townes still preferred the beginning of the evening. It was more peaceful. The people had not had the chance to judge the inhabitants or the music. The early scene was pristine and could be filled in accordingly, depending on how the evening proceeded. The clink of glasses, the flash of a silver cocktail shaker, the conversations blending together make a potent tonic that could take you away with them, sweep you away, or knock you flat on the floor, with someone to brush over you, or throw you out later. Townes didn't know if it was always that way when playing in this type of setting, or if it was that way wherever he played. He always preferred the gentle, well-meaning unfolding, always wanting to keep it simple, keep it slow. The overfilling of the coupe later would make it more difficult to savor and the taste would not be as sweet, would not be as promising as the early pouring. Hope, Townes thought, came in many flavors, in many vintages. The music could slow things down, could slow him down, if sometimes only for a fleeting moment.

He saw a woman sitting in a booth, all by herself. He wasn't sure but he thought it looked like Kat. He squinted his eyes to see that it was in fact Kat at the table by herself, she raising her hand ever so slightly to acknowledge Townes's inquisitive gaze. She had returned for more, or it was just a coincidence. Townes nodded his recognition, and Kat smiled back at him. This was in keeping with the previous thought of the early pouring. He wondered why she was alone. Surely she was meeting someone and he would be here any minute, and she was just killing time by herself. Yes, killing time, in a bar, by herself. That's what attractive doctors do, go to a bar and hang out. Hang out, pick up guys, pick up musicians. The voices of his characters were really letting him have it. Townes looked away and smiled to himself, stilling the conversation that nothing could be thought wrong, the distance not that far.

She smiled back at Townes, as if she knew what was driving his music. This was the type of moment that made up for all the crappy places he had played, and all the less desirable things he had seen, all the ugliness that sometimes came later in the night. A soft smile and a gentle wave. He felt he could play all night now, and would not be fazed by anything. Anything, except the woman in the pink blouse that came through the door and found her way over to the table where Kat was sitting. The two hugged briefly. The woman sat down at the table with Kat, her back to Townes so he could only see the back of her head and no longer see her face, but he had seen her face when she walked in.

Townes looked down at his feet, around the room, then back to the table where the two were sitting. They were obviously good friends. They laughed delicately, but often. Townes looked at Zeeder, Zeeder flashing a comical look his direction. It was all they could do to keep from just stopping in the middle of the song and laughing out loud. Townes's fingers suddenly felt as if they were glued together, his stomach felt uneasy. Zeeder's expression became all the more comical. Townes was starting to crack, but held his ground, looking everywhere except back to the table where the two women were seated.

Zeeder moved his leg over towards Townes and began to tap Townes's leg with his foot. Townes's face was starting to wrinkle, and he was beginning to sweat. Zeeder only maintained the beat against his leg, doing everything he could to keep the torture in motion. As Townes looked over to the table, where Kat was talking, smiling, she lightly raised her hand to point in Townes's direction. Her friend turned to look. It appeared she moved so slowly that Townes thought he might be asleep somewhere and was now only waking. She turned at last, and he thought he had swallowed a couple of small birds and they were now raising hell in his stomach.

He kicked Zeeder back. The woman now fully twisted in her seat to see what her friend had pointed to. The song ended and the woman smiled at Townes. She paused a moment, as if she had seen him somewhere before. Townes had certainly seen her before.

CHAPTER 12

Townes could hardly wait for their set to end. Zeeder kept shaking his head and laughing to himself. Townes tried not to look over at their table, but his attempts repeatedly failed. Both women were now watching the musicians more intently, or were being very polite. Kat had known they were playing here tonight, so her interest seemed genuine, and that made Townes feel good. Her friend may have happened there by accident, or perhaps Kat had invited her there to listen to them. Maybe Kat just invited her there because it was a nice place and it had nothing to do with them wanting to hear the music. Townes always hoped that someone came to hear them on purpose.

Townes's mouth was dry, his anxiety unsettling. Maybe they were just meeting here and then going someplace else. *Goddammit*, he thought, *keep your mind on what you're doing*. Zeeder was barely able to keep from laughing out loud at Townes's anxiety, kicking him whenever Townes would look over at the table. Townes looked down at his feet again. His characters were laughing, too.

He had played for lots of people, and wondered why he should be nervous now. He barely knew Kat, and he did not know the other woman at all. That was certainly nothing to be nervous about. They did not know if he was good, or bad, or anything of the sort. But if he played shitty, that they would know. Would they get up and walk out, the two of them, shaking their heads in disgust as they left the bar, all the while saying, "We thought you were going to be good, and you ended up being shitty"? Is that what they would do? Maybe they would. Maybe they would just refrain from further eye contact, then they would just leave quietly, so they would not have to speak to them about how shitty they were. No small talk. No having to lie and tell them they played well and really enjoyed it, when in fact they did not.

Goddammit I hate this, Townes thought. Hate what? *Oh, having a fucking conversation with people in your head while you are supposed to be playing music. An almost certain formula for playing shitty, so knock it the hell off!*

Zeeder was looking at him again, which this time made Townes think he was playing shitty. Zeeder shook his head, as if he knew Townes was having the conversation with himself, with others, and was showing his disapproval. Zeeder was right. The conversation in his head should end right now. Well, at least the argumentative part. One sided opinion might be fine, but it was probably wise to curtail the mental joust as quickly as possible, as no good could come of it. The song finished and Zeeder made no effort to begin another number. Townes looked at him. Zeeder said nothing and offered no explanation.

"Music?" Townes asked.

"Nope," Zeeder replied.

"Music?" Townes again asked.

"Too much thinkin' gettin' in the way. Perhaps a break would be in order. Maybe I could ask the audience if any of them would be interested in taking your place whilst you went over and talked to a couple of the ladies at the table over there. I'll wait. Take your time. Maybe the management won't notice that the music that they paid for is suspiciously silent. What woulds ya bet?"

Townes could say nothing. He looked over at the table again, then back at Zeeder.

"Take your time, I'll just be a sittin' here a waitin'. You have been so focused on the music tonight, that I cannot believe you have noticed there was anyone in this establishment at all."

Townes burst out laughing in to the microphone, then announced that they were going to take a short break, and would be right back.

"You handled that well," Zeeder said, bowing his head.

"You want to ... oh, thank you. You want to go over there with me?"

"Not just yet. I'm going to pretend to be messing with the rig here, all the while keeping a watchful eye on you, should the need arise to have someone call the paramedics to come resusimitate you. You'll be a thankin' me later ... should you live through the ordeal."

"I'm not really sure what the hell you said, but I appreciate the vote of the confidence. It is a great comfort."

"It, at the very minimum, is the least I can do," Zeeder said, leaning up out of his bow, lifting his chin high.

Townes looked back with an expression of partial understanding, yet still puzzled, managing only a short "Right."

He started to move a few steps towards the table then stopped. It occurred to him that he had not been invited to come to the table. He could not just burst upon those two women, it was not polite. He was working, they were guests and maybe they did not want to speak with him. It was merely coincidence that they were here, maybe, maybe not. Only they knew and it would be improper of him to just barge in on them. He turned back to Zeeder and looked at him, even more puzzled than before.

"Boy howdy, that was quicker 'n quick. Did they hold up a sign that said 'you suck', or did they throw somethin' at you?" Zeeder said, his arms folded across his chest.

"I can't just go over there. It would be rude."

"And the last time that stopped you was ...?"

"Well, it's never too late to practice good manners," Townes replied.

"And you are startin' now for reasons I am obviously unaware of."

"She is a doctor. She didn't come here to be ... you know."

"I don't know. What I do know is I am a goin' to go over and extend a greetin', like any non-socially-challenged person would do," Zeeder said, bobbing his head up and down.

"Well, I don't know." Townes still had the puzzled look on his face.

"Maybe you should go home and think about it some more ... but I keeps all the money fer tonight, 'cause you was too mentally constricted to play," Zeeder said, moving his hands as if he were counting money.

"What!?" Townes said quickly.

"Hello. I hope I'm not interrupting creative artist discussion here," Kat said quietly, having walked over to them during their exchange.

"No, no, just helping the stripling here with a little courage work. Seems he's a bit skittish about comin' over to yer table."

"Thanks, asshole," Townes said under his breath.

"Is that so?" Kat asked, leaning in towards Townes.

"I didn't want to interrupt ... you and your friend," Townes said, pawing the floor lightly with his foot.

"It is all right if you come over. I came here to see you two. I invited my dearest friend in the world, Annie, to come hear you guys play. Come over. I want you to meet her."

"You have to tell him he won't be intrudin', and that he didn't suck, else wise we'll be here for a long time chasin' this dog," Zeeder said, doing his best to say it without moving his lips.

Kat chuckled, and looked at Townes, reaching over and putting her hand gently on his shoulder. "I would like you to come over, as I came here to listen to you. It would be great if you stopped by the table. And, you didn't suck."

Townes smiled. "Well, that sounds like a good idea then."

Zeeder watched the exchange and turned to Townes. "Kat, I'ma gonna call you ... every time I can't get him to do somethin'."

"That would be fine. I would be glad to help. That wasn't so difficult," Kat said, now looking at Townes also.

"I should warn you that I'll be a callin' you quite a bit. He's quite obstinate, you know," Zeeder said, raising his eyebrows.

"He really seems quite harmless, at least from what little I know about him," Kat was looking Townes up and down.

"Well, mostly harmless, but certainly he can be quite exasperatin'. At least I thinks so," Zeeder scratched his ear.

Zeeder placed a firm hand on Townes's shoulder and smiled, not showing his teeth.

Townes started to say something, and seemed to become agitated, but Kat again placed her hand on his shoulder, motioning him towards the table she had come from, her friend still seated there alone.

"OK," Townes nodded.

"Excellent! I love progress," Kat nodded in return.

They walked to the table with Kat leading them, Townes behind her, Zeeder last, prodding Townes as they walked with words not quite loud enough to hear, and Townes holding his hands behind his back, middle fingers extended for only Zeeder to see. Townes wished the walk was just a little longer to give him time to clear his head and focus completely on the front of the procession and the destination. He was no longer hearing Zeeder. His only concern was ahead of him, but that concern was considerable. He was actually trying to clear his mind while trying to think of what to say, which meant he would probably say nothing, or at least nothing that would make any sense. Her first impression would be that Townes had only recently mastered the art of speech. That conversational speaking lie in a future tutorial, with a date to be determined. There was too much clutter in Townes's mind, and the short saunter from where they had been playing seemed longer than the actual distance, which just added to the clutter. It was a walk across a cocktail lounge, not the entirety of La Jolla.

"These are my music and art friends, Zeeder and Townes," Kat gestured towards the two as they arrived at the table where the other woman sat. "And this is my friend, Annie."

"It is nice to meet you," Townes said, extending his hand, but managing to stumble on his last step.

"Most certainly," Zeeder said, chuckling at Townes's miscue.

"It is nice to meet you, too. Gosh, you guys sound great. Kat told me about you. I wanted to come hear for myself," Annie said smiling, looking longer at Townes.

"Well, thank you for coming out," Townes said, checking to make sure his feet were not still moving.

"Well, just hope we didn't cause any hearing damage, or least not much," Zeeder said, noticing Townes checking out his feet, giving him a slight nudge.

"Gosh, no. It was very good."

"You don't have to say that. We like to hear it, but you don't have to say it," Townes said.

"We won't try to stop you from sayin' it, however," Zeeder added.

"I told you they were good, and funny too," Kat said, touching Townes on the shoulder.

"You were right on both," Annie smiled, looking at Townes. "I really want to hear more. Unfortunately, I ... uh, have to leave now, but I hope I get to hear you play again sometime." She seemed uneasy, still looking at Townes, then looking away.

"Oh, that's a shame. I hope it isn't something serious. And I hope you can come back sometime, though we might be worse ... well I might be, he never is," Townes said, nodding once, slowly facing Annie.

"You have to go?" Kat asked, tilting her head.

"Sorry, but I have a patient I need to tend to. I hate to leave, but I have to." She looked uneasy.

"That is too bad. Sometimes we get better as the night progresses," Zeeder offered.

"Golly, you were just great, so I don't believe that," Annie said.

"Well, sometimes," Townes said, looking down.

"They are lying, they always play great, and they never get bad," Kat said, smiling at the two. "At least not that I've heard."

"I don't think they could play bad," Annie said, grinning at Townes.

"Yes, we could," Townes and Zeeder said in unison, stopping, then looking at each other.

"I bet not," Annie said, noticing that both men had said this at the same time.

"Never on purpose," Zeeder added.

"True," Townes seconded.

"It's too bad you have to go. We will just have to get together another time," Kat said, looking disappointed.

"That would be great. It was nice meeting you … and listening to you play, even if it wasn't for very long. I'm just … busy, but maybe next time," Annie said, getting up from her seat.

"Well, thank you for coming out, even if it was just for a little while. I hope we will see you again," Townes replied.

"I'm sure you will. Kat will see to it. She is always determined," Annie said, looking at Kat.

"Of course, I will see to it. I want to support these artists," Kat said, holding her arms out toward Townes and Zeeder, "and one of my life missions is to get her to have fun. Just once I want to hear her say she is having fun, and not say she is busy."

"I have fun," Annie said softly

"Of course you do, you think," Kat said quietly

"Artists? Zeeder is the artist," Townes said, looking at Annie.

"Townes is the writer," Zeeder said, also looking at Annie.

"You guys have all kinds of talent," Annie said, her eyes wide, but giving a non-approving look to Kat.

"Yes, if we could only find what mine is," Townes said.

Annie looked at him and started to say something, but just smiled and moved towards the door, with Kat accompanying her.

"Well?" Zeeder looked at Townes.

"Well what?" Townes glanced at Zeeder out of the corner of his eye, still keeping watch on the women walking away.

"Well, what are you a gonna do?"

CHAPTER 13

New York

Townes stared out the window of the jet and tried not to be terrified. He watched the shapes and colors change, the greens to browns to reds. Another trip, but it might do him some good, providing he did not have a complete panic attack. The business didn't clear his head, but at least the change of scenery placed some different colors on his palette. He had been out just the week before, so he only had the chance to change suitcases when he was home, or that is how it felt. Going from playing music to talking with someone for hours on end about business was about as far apart as two things could be. He didn't think he knew very much about either. He wasn't sure how he managed to do them both, not remembering a time when he was not doing either one. Formal training for either was something that escaped his memory, as well. Did he just wake-up one day and tell someone he knew something about business? He wasn't sure. Music? How that happened, he wasn't sure. Writing? How that happened was no more clear than the others.

He thought that for someone who used to be pretty sure of himself, he was now not very sure of quite a few things. At the moment, what he was sure of, was that he was having serious difficulty relaxing on an airplane. Maybe the perpetual cycle was what was giving him fits. He closed his eyes and took a couple of deep breaths, thought about Annie, thought about Kat, and drifted off to sleep.

New York sprawled below as the approach to the airport shortened. It was a massive change of pace and culture from southern California. Townes always looked forward to a return visit. Real seasons, complete with real changing colors, followed by real cold. The more he visited, the more he loved New York. When people asked him about the city, he generally told them to "just go there."

The downside was that the cross-country flight always made him feel like crap by the time he got there, and his new traveling partner, anxiety, just made it that much worse. He would slog off the plane and into the airport, the entire daylight allowance nearly gone. And because it was fall, the allowance was short anyway, but what you got in the fall during the daylight in New York was spectacular.

The airport terminal seemed to have a much different hue than the one he had departed from. This one was gray and dark. Not unfriendly--it just spoke of a different way of life that sometimes left an unfamiliar residue. The luggage could not get there quickly enough. The walk from the gate to the carousel was a good means of getting his legs going again after not using them for five hours. Just enough time to remind him of the airport aroma that he could always do without. If it was a good day: disinfectant, old shoes, pizza, coffee, the occasional Cinnabon. He tried not to think of what the restrooms always smelled like.

He went down the gray stairs to the baggage claim. Five yards beyond was where the limo drivers were standing, holding up their small printed signs with the names of the lucky ones, the ones who could relax while getting the last bit of geography between the airport and their destination covered. Today he was one of the lucky ones.

He moved towards the man holding the sign with his name on it. Townes pointed at him, while still moving towards where the baggage would be regurgitated.

"Hello," Townes said.

"Hello," the man replied.

"How is the weather today?"

"Nice earlier, then a storm blew through and rained and got cool. Pretty nice now," the man said.

"Excuse my poor manners, my name is Townes."

"Nice to meet you Townes, I'm Anthony."

"Nice to meet you, Anthony. I hope the weather is nice the rest of the week."

"I think it is. Maybe a little rain by the end of the week."

They made their way to the baggage claim carousel and stood awkwardly as the others from the flight found their way to the same location. They waited for the buzzer to sound and the luggage sidewalk to begin its movement. It was always uncomfortable, everyone looking at each other for a sign that somebody knew this was the correct place the luggage would be. Those who had some friend or loved ones waiting for them usually did not bother to look around. They were happy and busy speaking with someone who was happy to see them, someone who cared about them and that they cared about. The rest were tired, uneasy, and cast glances around to see if anyone in the group had some sort of luggage premonition they could pick up on. Everyone sizing each other up, wondering what they were doing, what additional journey was still to come and would that journey be with, or without luggage. This segment of travel was not as bad as the preflight anxiety, but still was uncomfortable, and Townes always felt this part to be a purgatory of sorts.

"How many bags?" Anthony asked.

"One."

"I can carry that briefcase for you now," Anthony offered.

"That's all right. I don't mind," Townes answered.

They stood for what seemed like an hour waiting for the bags to begin their parade route around that end of the large room. Townes watched the families, the business types, the friends, the military people, all sharing in the same anticipation of getting the hell out of there, and the annoying detail of waiting for whatever things you brought with you. He always thought about going somewhere and not taking anything with him. Clothes on his back, paper and pen to write, book to read, no bag, nothing else. He imagined the conversation:

How many bags will you be checking?

None.

You are limited to one carry-on bag, and it must be ...

No bags, nothing.

Nothing at all?

"No, nothing. *You charge me for taking luggage, which is total bullshit, then you ask me why I don't have any. I'm going to sit over there until you make your goddamn mind up.*"

He would just exist with what he had on when he left and see how that would work out. He probably could not travel anywhere that he would have to be around people, since a change of clothing would be out of the question.

He could also just buy anything he needed. That was such a revelation. Go with nothing, get what you need. *How much would he need? What would it take to just get by?* This was not particularly fascinating, but it was where his mind would go when he was once again in a mindless situation like waiting for luggage. His characters helped him pass the time. Besides, this was not a place where he would deal with more complex problems. He always wondered if the really smart people used this time to figure out difficult problems, or if they were thinking about how to design a better baggage system, or how to feed the world, or give them unlimited energy at a low cost. Were they thinking about these things, or were they thinking about what drink they were going to order when they got to the bar, or what they were going to have to eat that night, and how bad that guy next to them smelled, and how ugly that other guy's shirt was, or how pretty that girl over by the door was. He wondered if they had voices in their heads too. A buzzer sounded and Townes flinched.

"You OK?" Anthony asked.

"Yes, er, fine," Townes answered.

"One bag you said."

"Yes, one bag."

The buzzer went off, signaling the actual arrival of the long awaited luggage, and at least five people jumped, so startled by the loud noise in the midst of their pacing. There was nearly a stampede, but the herd settled as soon as the first bag came out from behind the doors. Where could it have been all this time?

"About time," Anthony remarked. "I was gettin' ready to go back there and smack somebody."

Townes just shook his head, a half-smile all he could manage. The bags began to emerge from behind the closed door and onto the moving path that snaked its way around the room and back out of sight, emerging again out of the same door they had originally appeared. He had actually seen someone run up and start pounding on the wall when the bags made their momentary disappearance, thinking they only had one shot at claiming them and then the bags would be given away, or perhaps sold. As more bags began to materialize on the moving path, the entire thing began to slow to almost a stop, only to lurch forward momentarily and then almost stop, only to repeat the same movement, over, and over, the noise dreadful. Townes imagined what a steam locomotive might look like. Perhaps they had installed a steam-powered system since he was last there, and it was now producing this *chug-chug* effect, and in a matter of minutes bags would be whirring around the track at amazing speeds and he might perhaps have to throw his entire body at the precise moment to retrieve his streaking luggage. The more likely possibility was that the machine was broken and not running worth a damn and everyone was just going to have to wait that much longer, as the thing never really got moving. At this point, he was willing to go with either theory. He wished this had been the trip where he had brought nothing.

The *chugging* motion of the luggage machine only served to make the entire group more anxious than they already were. Many would look around at one another, as if to ask: "can you believe this," or "this isn't right, is it?" Looking for some affirmation from the others that something was in fact wrong, and that, yes, it was going to take longer than normal, and short of mob violence, there was nothing they could do to relieve the tension and anticipation of pondering about the arrival time of their familiar vessel.

"Shit," the fellow next to Townes muttered. He was not the only one. There were collective sighs, groans and words in languages he was not familiar with, but that would probably translate to being the same word. The unpleasantness of the entire situation was further enhanced by how loud the stopping and starting was. Not only was it slow, but clamorous as well. Each start, each stop, a drum beat, a length of large chain being dropped on a metal surface.

"Great," Townes said.

He imagined he was walking on the beach in La Jolla and hearing only waves. Angelina was with him. She was trotting along the edge of the water, a tennis ball in her mouth. There were just the two of them. He tried to clear the loud noise out and turn it into the sound of the waves breaking just offshore. He thought about Annie and Kat, and how nice it would be to be walking with one of them on that beach right now. It would be good to be anywhere but here listening to this constant pounding. He went back to the beach in his head. *What did he really know about either one of them?* He had seen Annie first, that day at the cafe, and he felt sort of silly that he was so smitten with her. Some things are hard to explain. To think that they would actually meet was beyond possible, and yet they did and she was friends with Kat. How could that be? Kat, he had at least spent some time with. She was so different, not like anyone he knew, and she knew things about him he had not told her. She was very sure of herself, and he could definitely spend more time with her. He wanted to ask her more about how she knew the things she did. He wanted to walk on the beach with her and the dog. He could ask her if she wanted to walk on a beach, or if she wanted to go with him and carry an extra sledgehammer into the back room of this airport and pound the living shit out of whatever contraption was making all the racket.

He had lost the beach mirage amid all the clamor. He looked around. The faces of the other passengers had not softened any. If anything, they had hardened and they were more restless. The herd was acting like a storm was coming. All they needed was a clap of thunder, or someone yelling out, and they would stampede. Whether or not they just start running around, bumping into each other, or actually organize into formation and collectively ram their way through the doors that purportedly were the source of the noisy stop-and-go carousel was still uncertain. At the least, they could attack whatever dragon was making the dreadful noise, putting an end to the madness. Whether they would be satisfied with that limited destruction was not apparent. They were brooding. People were beginning to groan more loudly, more frequently. He could not swear that he heard them pawing the ground with their feet, but Townes thought that it was possible. Where would they go after they had broken the door down, only to find no luggage? The newsstands would surely be next, then the food places. There was going to be coffee spilled everywhere.

CHAPTER 14

The limo ride from the airport was a change of situation that Townes never minded after spending the majority of the day with so many other people, pressurized in a large, cramped, and constantly humming container hurtling through the sky. The sound of the car wheels on the road and the reduction of occupants to just two, along with the absence of pressurization was a welcome alternative, and his anxiety dissipated quickly. He had taken the earliest flight out, so it was still light out. Getting into New York and having the sun participating in the day always helped with post-airplane rejuvenation. Looking up at the buildings always gave him pause. The city was magnificent, and he decided that those who continually expressed their dislike for it usually had no idea how it really was. How it was at this moment, just light enough to see and just cool enough to feel the fall weather. It was energizing.

He was baffled at how much he had grown to love it here considering he'd been raised in a small town. It had just grown on him over the years and he was fine with that. Even through traveling was increasingly distasteful, he would always make time for a trip to New York.

"Just to the hotel, sir?" Anthony asked.

"Yes, thanks."

"You got it."

The drive through Queens, after leaving the airport, made Townes feel real again. He never felt *real* while he was flying. Moving at such a high speed, at such altitude, always felt imagined. Driving down the street, seeing children playing in front of their houses, people talking on street corners. This was real. Seeing the buildings was real. Bumps in the road were real. These were a nice recalibration from the plane.

He was anxious to get to the Ritz. He knew Milton would be holding court at the bar he always called him before he made his travel arrangements, just to make sure. A Barman Extraordinaire, as far as Townes was concerned, and it would be great to see him. Townes was always amazed at how Milton remembered everything. Obviously, not living in the city, Townes couldn't be categorized as a regular, yet Milton remembered everything, every time. He never asked Townes what he wanted to drink. He knew what Townes wanted to drink. He was a magnificent barman, but his real gift was connecting people. He knew when you were feeling bad. He knew when you were feeling good. He always made a point of introducing you to the other people around you. They had known him for twenty years, thirty years, and when they left, they now knew you, and you them. You felt like you were going to a family gathering, only no one was going to argue with you. If a person could not enjoy themselves here and be comfortable, then they should be asked to leave the city.

The ride across the bridge was the last wake-up call before the skyscrapers would become home for the next several days. The change of pitch in the road was telling you that you were about to get into the big current and that you had better remember to be a part of that current, or that slipstream would sink you, but not before it bounced you, eventually slamming you into a great number of rocks before it took you under. If you became one with the current, it could take you places and show you fascinating sights in a way that only being part of the flow could do. It had taken Townes several visits here to realize it, but now it made him feel good because he knew some people who never discovered this. The current gave you an incredible energy that left you tired, yet completely satisfied, at the close of each day. It could carry you or it could drown you.

The car was on Central Park South before he knew it. Car doors opened, bellmen moved to greet guests, assistants waited to be of service, the front desk there to touch, all staff sincere in their acknowledgements. It was as if his feet swung out of the car and never touched the gray pavement or interior parquet. The quick ride in the small elevator took no time. He was being shown his room by the most pleasant of souls and it all felt so good. Yet he was so wrung out by his travel anxiety, he little remembered the conversations with any of them. His new traveling partner was not helping him in the least. It was not that he did not care, it was the subtle mental beating that a cross country flight, complete with this new found anxiety, would administer. He would try to circle back with all of them to show respect and gratitude.

He looked out the windows on Central Park to catch the last slivers of the day peeking between and over the buildings. He hung clothes on the wooden hangers in the closet, and placed the other items in the dresser drawers. He learned a while ago that taking everything out of the suitcase made the temporary stay seem more palatable, giving more order to his life. He changed out of his wrinkled travel clothes, went into the bathroom and drew some warm water onto a washcloth to knock off some of the gritty travel film that had hitched a ride on him somewhere along the way, repeating the procedure with cold water, leaning over the sink, taking a deep, quick breath. He continued to stand over the sink, water dripping from his face. He looked up to the mirror, blowing out a breath before he straightened up and brushed the water from his face up onto his hair. He stood looking at the mirror for a few moments before toweling off, trying unsuccessfully to ignore the lines he saw in his face. He ran his fingers through his blonde hair, applying a light splash of Tom Ford cologne before placing the towel around the back of his neck. A fresh shirt, pants and sport coat made him feel somewhat whole again. He took the elevator to the lobby, the doors opened, and he was back in the current, somewhat renewed.

The bar was full, as usual. It wasn't large, by any means--sixteen, twenty chairs at the most, configured in an L-shape with a couple of immense wood pillars placed just where they should not have been. The pillars were big enough that they should have been in the front of a building somewhere, certainly not in the middle of a bar where the barman would almost have to climb up on the bar to look around them. It was really the only flaw of the building and the hotel itself all else seemed as it should be. The patrons all dressed nicely. It was right before dinner and people were attired accordingly for New York. It was a stark contrast to the over-casual look of Southern California, where everyone looked like it was really a bother to get dressed at all for dinner. It was as if were they wearing anything besides merely a swimsuit, then they had gone to great effort to put on shorts, sandals and a T-shirt.

I was out getting the newspaper this morning in my shorts and T-shirt and someone grabbed me and took me out to dinner. I didn't have time to change into something more crappy looking. Townes shook his head.

Townes didn't mind the casual nature of California for the most part, but it was a welcome change to dress for proper cocktails and dinner. It made the rituals seem as if they were supposed to happen. Drinks and dinner, something pre-arranged, not accidental.

He made his way past giant pillar number one to get a view of who was behind the bar. There was usually someone famous in the bar, but Townes was more concerned with whether the resident celebrity was behind the bar, and Milton indeed was there, and was extremely busy. Along with adding different ingredients to his drinks, he added immeasurable warmth, probably the single most important ingredient that he never failed to add to include in his cocktails. This ingredient kept everyone feeling at ease, whether they had a drink or not. Sometimes the secret ingredient was lost on a patron, someone who just could not muster up manners, or a pleasant tone, all received that component, a few did not understand it. Milton was someone you wanted to go see and wanted to spend a portion of your time with. He sang a verse of a song as he walked between visitors, pulling the bottom of his black vest, straightening his tie, which was never left loosened, and brushing the sleeves of his white shirt. Townes was standing behind a couple seated at the bar when Milton looked beyond them and at him. He smiled at Townes, stopped his movement, and held up his outstretched hands.

"Where have you been?!"

"All over," Townes replied.

"All over what?" Milton shot back.

"All over … the country, I guess."

"You guess? Did you guess that you would be in serious trouble for waiting so long to come and see me?" He came out from behind the bar, the two shook hands and embraced. "Welcome back, my friend, how have you been?"

"I have been fine Milton, how have you been?"

"Eh, I have the greatest job in the world and would not trade it for anything. Been a little under the weather, but I think I'm better now," Milton replied, in a thick Brooklyn accent.

"I hope so. I would quit coming to New York if you weren't here."

"If I wasn't here, you wouldn't know where to go in New York, because I always tell you where to go and what to do. I'm not here, God help you, you're lost." Milton patted Townes on the back, returning to his post behind the bar.

"Right as always, Milton."

"Of course I'm right. Let me get you something, my friend who has been all over, except for here. I think you need a Manhattan. You remember that drink, don't you? Been making them since before you were born. I'm going to make it with some really good rye and some orange bitters, and you are going to love it! Come down here and sit down."

"I am sure it will be to your normal outstanding standard," Townes said, moving to the one remaining open chair at the bar.

"Man, it is good to see you. You are still out there, that crazy California?"

"Yes, crazy California. Not quiet and subdued ... like New York," Townes replied, almost whispering the last part.

"Where are you, Los Angeles ... no, San Diego, am I right?"

"Yes, San Diego."

"Crazy people out there in California," Milton said, gesturing westward with his hand.

"And you would know that how?"

"I read the paper. I watch the news."

"That's true, crazy people in California, and I have never seen anyone in New York ever do anything crazy, nor have I ever read about anyone doing anything crazy in New York. The city is so nondescript, I am not sure why I come here at all. So dull, no variety, nothing to see, nothing to do," Townes said, smiling.

"So when you are not picking on helpless bartenders, what do you do?" Milton asked, his hands on his hips.

"I don't think I've ever seen a helpless bartender. Do they exist?"

"How should I know? I'm always here."

"Well, they don't exist here, now do they?" Townes said, leaning towards Milton.

"Such a tough customer. Comes in a couple times a year, picks on me. Are you married yet?"

"Not yet."

"What are you waiting for?"

"Small detail," Townes said, pinching his thumb and forefinger together.

"Which is?"

"The right woman. Minor thing, but I'm funny that way."

"Well, you are not getting much younger. Not that you look old. In fact, you really look good. I should look as good as you do. Standing back here, looking like you, I would have lots of offers for marriage. Maybe you should be a bartender."

"You are already married."

"You back here, with my talent, you'd be married in a week."

"A week? If I had your talent, I would be married in a couple of days," Townes laughed.

"A couple?"

"Well, I would need one day ... for the paperwork."

"Paperwork?"

"Well ..."

Milton shook his head and laughed. He took a mixing glass, added ice, Michter's Rye, some Carpano Antica sweet vermouth, some orange bitters. He stopped and held his nose to the bottle of rye, smelling deeply.

"Damn that's good." He then moved down to tend to some people at the other end of the bar, the mixture still in front of Townes. Townes looked around, feeling comfortable back here with his old friend. Milton had a marvelous way of making you feel like you were part of the New York aristocracy. Townes thought that if you were a friend of Milton's, you were definitely part of an elite group. He knew a great many important people. Townes thought himself unimportant, except for the friendship which he held very dear. Milton returned, stirred the drink. He held his knuckles next to the glass.

"You're not going to shake it?"

"Why, it's not a malted. You want to make this?"

"No sir, your domain, you reign."

"It is not my domain. It is the domain of my customers, my friends, though I am betting you can't make one of these as good as I can."

"Probably not."

"Kids," he said shaking his head, drifting back to the other end of the bar, the contents still sitting in front of Townes in the mixing glass.

Townes shook his head also, smiling and taking a deep breath, letting it out slowly. It was great to be back in New York. Milton returned, checking each patron along his route back, making sure everyone had everything they needed. The ladies at the bar held their hands out, a sign of affection, Milton touching them as they did.

"You have everything you need, my darling?" he would ask.

"As long as you are here, Milton, we have everything we need," a woman replied.

Townes marveled at his fluid movement, his genuine concern, his care.

Milton was now back in front of him, repeating the process. He placed a strainer on top of the mixing glass. He reached down and pulled up a cocktail glass that had been conditioned with ice. He dumped the ice out, placing the glass first on a bar napkin, then moving it closer on the bar in front of Townes. He then reached for a jar of Luxardo cherries, taking out one cherry with a long handled silver bar spoon and placing it in the chilled vessel along with an orange rind. He then poured the strained mixture into it, filling it from a high level above to its absolute top, with not a single drop left in the mixing glass, not single drop spilled on the bar.

"How do you do that?"

Milton smiled, then started to sing a song.

"Welcome back. Enjoy this, my friend." He took another sniff of the bottle of rye, smiled, replaced the cork, then was off, back down the bar again.

Townes had to lean over the drink to sip directly from the top of the glass without picking it up, so he wouldn't spill it. It was just as he had remembered Milton's Manhattans to be. He instantly felt warm and at home at the same time. He may have been away awhile, but this welcome always rang true. He closed his eyes after that sip, and the room itself became more fluid. Things were moving now, and moving favorably. He would be in New York for a few days--three, maybe four--and this was a fine start, which he always tried to make of point of getting. This was not southern California. You needed to get your mind right from the outset, or the city would take you, run you over, and leave you piled by the curb with the rest of the discards. Townes knew he might be a bit slow tomorrow, but he would not be without commitment. He was here and this first stop comforted him. The city was in him now, at least one large sip's worth.

CHAPTER 16

The long trip, the piano playing in the hotel lobby, the cocktails, and the comfort that Milton had graciously shared made Townes ready to go to bed. There would be no walking the city tonight. He was too tired, and now too at ease to get out on the pavement. He had a lunch meeting tomorrow which might afford a walk maybe a run in Central Park in the morning. He was groggy now and the fine libations Milton had served up were letting Townes drift more than usual. He thought about Angelina, wondered what she and Zeeder were doing. It was nice sitting here, and would be improved only if the dog were there with him. The bar was thinning out, the pace slowing. He thought about Kat, how she was calming, reassuring, and he liked her, even though he did not know her very well. If she were here right now, they would know each other a lot better in no time at all, though with her telepathic way, she seemed to already know quite a bit more about him than he knew about her.

It would certainly relieve some of the pressure from Milton that Townes had at least talked with the same woman on successive nights. Milton would be pleased, and would kiss her hand and tell her to "be patient, but not too patient" with Townes, and that he was delighted to see Townes taking a few minutes away from work to spend with her. Milton would take his digs at Townes, but always in a way that let him know he cared about him. Generally after that, he would treat him like he was going to get the keys to the city soon thereafter. If you did not love Milton, then it was guaranteed that you had a serious character flaw, and you should take your sorry ass somewhere else.

Getting to know the doctor better might be a good thing, and slowing the business things down a bit might not hurt either. He had been on the road a good number of years and this had precluded any meaningful relationships. It was not that Townes didn't want to spend time with someone. It always seemed like he had been too busy, too removed, not spending enough time with anyone to get to know them very well. It may be time now, but he did not have the manual on the subject, so he was not sure. If Kat were here, he would introduce her to Milton and just let it roll from there. He might take her up to Bemelmans Bar at the Carlyle and introduce her to Bobby the bartender there, so she could see that Townes was friends with some of the best bartenders in New York. *And that is important, especially since you live in San Diego*, one of his characters said.

That was the tale right there. He was friends with the best bartenders in New York, but he did not have a wife, or steady girlfriend. He was friends with people on the other side of the country, but in the rare time that he was home, he came home only to his dog. He was tired and thought it time to at least think about going to bed. Fly across the country, drink with Milton, and forget to eat dinner. That might have something to do with how he felt right now. He had forgotten one of the most important rules when sitting with Milton. You had to eat, or you might require members of the Ritz staff to carry you back to your room. He supposed they could load him onto one of those brass luggage carts, that would be easier. He could sleep in the bar, though it had been a long time since he had done anything like that. He was sure it was not at a Ritz. Upstairs lodging probably was not an option at the last place this had occurred. Was it in a booth?

"Surely not!" Zeeder would say.

He needed to call it a day. Luxardo cherries were not enough of a meal. "Milton, maybe I should eat something."

"You got that right. What did you have on the plane, a pistachio, or a cracker?"

"Neither."

"Then yes, you should eat. I'll bring you something," Milton said, and he was off in a blur.

Townes knew the meal would help. That first Milton cocktail put some starch back, but if left unattended, the ritual could be problematic. Food would be good. He was always content here, always happy here, but his previous thoughts about companionship were hanging with him. What if he had someone to bring here? Wouldn't that make an already fine experience better? Someone to share it with, that would settle a great deal of things. It might start a great deal of things as well, but for now, the idea sounded good.

One of the bar staff was back with a place setting in front of Townes, with Milton following closely behind with a couple of plates in his hands.

"That was awfully fast, did somebody send something back?" Townes asked.

"Very funny, Mr. Southern California. I had already put in an order for you. Sheesh, who do you think you're dealing with here!?" Milton said, placing the items in front of Townes. "We have some lobster corn dogs here, and here we have a bowl of steamed mussels, with some toasted bread for that good broth down there. Bone-appetite-ay, the French people say. I never been to France, but I hear that's what they say. Brooklyn, we never said that. Eat up, you're wobbling in the chair there, and we haven't had anybody fall off a chair here in years. Your picture goes on the wall here if you do. Eat up, eat up." Milton and Enrique turned and were away again.

Townes did not know what to say. He always underestimated Milton, probably because he did not see him more often. Every time he came here he was amazed at what would occur. He would not underestimate him again. Townes dug into the food like he had not eaten in a week. Lobster corn dogs and steamed mussels. "What I usually have at home ..."

"I almost forgot the Chablis," Milton returned, placing a glass in front of Townes, filling it with wine. "Gotta have this for the mussels," Milton smiled.

"I was just telling myself that I won't underestimate you again."

"Always talkin' to yourself. You are starting to sound like me, and you ain't that old."

"Starting to feel old."

"You know you can call me tomorrow at home during the day if you need anything."

"That is very kind of you, but you know I wouldn't bother you during the day. My job is to bother you at night, in-person."

"Atta boy. So you will be here, tomorrow night to bother me in-person?"

"Yes."

"What are your plans for tomorrow night?"

"Not sure yet, but they will begin here with you."

"Do you have a date for tomorrow night?" Milton said, turning his head.

"That would require knowing a woman in New York."

"It happens. Some people know women, and go out with them. I read about it in a magazine."

"Not me."

"What about in San Diego?"

"What about it?"

"Do you go out with anyone there?"

"No, not really."

"I think you are working too much."

"I actually am starting to understand that. I did meet someone, but we haven't really been out together. We just met," Townes said, looking down.

"Progress! That is progress. How long have I known you?"

"About ten, maybe twelve years."

"And in that time you have told me about how many women?"

"None … maybe one."

"Progress! We will discuss this more tomorrow. You finish your dinner." Again Milton was off.

Townes shook his head as he watched the man, singing, joking with the other people at the bar as he moved along. Townes raised his glass of white wine to the man walking away from him. Unlike the Manhattan, he was able to pick this glass up without spilling it. The food and the wine tasted grand, and Townes now could focus a little better, feeling slightly more back on his game. He would finish his dinner, finish his wine, and head upstairs to bed, not wanting to get too far behind on his first night here, though it was never easy getting away early. It was always so peaceful, and Milton so accommodating, that it was just easier to stay, to talk, to meet people. It was different in California. Everybody was driving somewhere, so no one stayed anyplace for very long. They had to get back in the car and drive. Here, they were walking, or could get someone to drive them. That lent itself to settling in, if ever so slightly, more than back home. He would enjoy himself and head upstairs. Getting out without a nightcap from Milton would be next to impossible, so Townes was happy to oblige. One Blanton's before bed would not make the elevator numbers illegible.

Townes moved slowly back through the lobby to head upstairs. He saw a woman with two dogs come in the front entrance, moving the same direction. The dogs saw him and ran towards him. Townes crouched down to better reciprocate their greeting.

"Look at you two, such fine pals," Townes said, petting them both. "What kind of fellows are you?"

Their owner moved quickly to gather the dogs back into her control. "This one is a Wheaton Terrier, this one is a Shi Tzu. I am sorry for the bother," the woman said. "They get crazy sometimes after they have been in the park."

Townes looked up at the woman, a floppy hat mostly covering her light brown hair. She wore a baggy but expensive-looking sweater, warm up pants, and not-quite-dark glasses. Her skin was pristine, her voice soothing.

"Nope, no bother. They are a welcome sight at this late hour. I left the love of my life just this morning, and this is just fine," Townes said, wondering what he had just said.

"Wife, girlfriend, or ..."

"Dog. Even better. No offense."

"But of course, and none taken," the woman responded.

"They are handsome boys, but I don't think Milton is going to be at the bar much longer, so you had better get them in there for last call," Townes said, slowly standing, finding it a bit more difficult than he wished it to be.

She grabbed up the smaller of the two canines, produced a leash out of her purse and was struggling to put it on the larger one.

"Let me do that for you," Townes said, the dog still by his side and not appearing to be in any hurry to get away from him.

"You are very good with them. They really like you."

"Ah, if only people did."

"I am sure that anyone that my dogs like this much cannot be that bad with people."

"Well, most people run when I do this," he said as he clicked the leash in place. "There, now you can take them in to Milton."

The woman laughed. "No more drinks for them tonight. We just went to the park, and we are not wanting a return trip out there until morning, right, guys?"

"So they have already seen Milton tonight then? I know how they feel. What might everyone's names be?"

"Pete, Scruff...and Ashley."

Townes looked around the lobby. "Are you missing one?"

"I'm Scruff," the woman smiled.

"Oh, I'm sorry. I didn't ..."

"That's OK."

"I hope I ... you don't look like a Scruff, more like ..."

"This big guy is Pete."

"Well, I am Townes," he said, patting both dogs on the head, and holding out his hand with the leash in it, forgetting it was there.

"Nice to ... oh, thank you," she said, taking the leash from Townes.

"It's nice to meet all of you. If you need someone to walk them for you, I will be here at the hotel a couple more days."

"Well, they do seem to like you, and it is hard sometimes to coordinate everyone's schedule, but I don't want to bother you."

"Hey, I understand. Don't want a stranger looking after your family."

"No, it's not that, really it's not."

"Well, OK, but if you change your mind, just leave word and I will take them around the park. I do have references here at the hotel, though they are unfamiliar with my dog experience. You could start with that fellow behind the bar in there. He would verify that dogs probably understand me better than people, and vice versa."

She laughed, "I might just do that."

"Well, I hope so," Townes replied.

"It was nice to meet you, Townes. Say good night boys," Ashley smiled.

"It was nice to meet you ... Scruff," Townes said looking at the woman. "Oh, and Pete, and Ashley."

The dogs and Ashley gave Townes one last glance, and off they went to the elevator. Townes scratched his head and looked around the now mostly empty lobby. He waited for them to go up, then pushed the call button on the elevator, getting inside when it arrived. He inserted his key to get his floor number. Back in the room he looked at the turned-down bed, the chocolates on the pillow. He took one, unwrapped it and leaned his head against the window, looking out at the dark Central Park below.

"Scruff."

CHAPTER 17

Townes awoke the next morning, struggling to figure out what city he was in, thinking he might have been over-served last night, quickly dismissing that theory and moving to the concept that the ice had been tainted, --it had happened before. He remembered something about dogs but was having difficulty piecing everything together. The usual thickness from flying never failed to show up and throw its very worn but still dark tarp over him, but not before filling his nostrils with sawdust and placing a small bit of bubblegum in his ears. *There, now try to function normally.* That is how Townes felt. He moved to the window, looking out, hoping there would not be a search light shining back at him or that he would not be staring at some dreadful brick wall in some city that he couldn't recall the name of, having gone there by mistake. None of those. The scene outside was either an exact replica of Central Park, complete with surrounding buildings, or he was in New York.

"That's the one," Townes said, the tarp perhaps tearing a bit so he could discern his location. He thought that if more details from the previous evening were to slip through, he could clear up a few things, getting on with what he was actually supposed to be doing.

"The dogs had a woman with them," he murmured. "They must have been taking her out for a walk. She was probably restless," he yawned, stretched, tapped on the window, and made a pointing gesture at the landscape beyond the glass.

He completed the air travel grime removal more quickly than anticipated, shaving and dressing with newfound momentum. He checked that it would be a sunny day, so the traverse to his client's office should not be difficult. Breakfast beforehand would help cut a larger hole in the tarp. He started to exit the room, noticing an envelope had made its way under the door. He opened the door, removing the bag containing the morning newspaper, and the sign warning outsiders to refrain from dealing with the room inhabitant, at least at this time. He moved back into the room, opening the paper to scan the headlines. He was hoping to see a headline and story declaring:

CALIFORNIA MAN WINS WORLD'S LARGEST LOTTERY JACKPOT
A La Jolla, California man won the world's largest lottery jackpot yesterday. The man, had also just been notified that the most prestigious publishing house in the world had decided to publish his debut novel. The publisher anticipated bestseller status, with a Pulitzer Prize certain to follow. The unnamed man was thought to have been seen last night, drinking in the bar of the Ritz Carlton Central Park, and was unavailable for comment.

That was Townes's hope, but that was not on the front page. Maybe the story was inside. He would check later. He picked up the envelope, with his name on it, that had found its way under his door. "Maybe from the lottery people ... or my new, unknown publisher," he said, exiting the room, and heading for the elevator to the third floor club lounge, in search of breakfast. He still had the unopened envelope in his hand as he entered the club lounge.

"Good morning, sir," a woman at the entry desk greeted him, her tone proper, respectful.

"Why, yes it is," Townes replied, using her same low decibel level.

"May I assist you with anything this morning?"

"I don't think so. I would like to get some breakfast, so I think I am in the right place," Townes said, glancing to his right, where ten feet away there lay a cornucopia of breakfast fare.

"Very good, sir. Your name?"

"Oh, my apologies, Townes, Townes Mantle," he said, extending his hand.

"Welcome, Mr. Mantle. My name is Lauren. Please let me know if I might be of service. Would you like me to mail that letter for you?"

"What, er ... this? Oh no, but thank you. This was under my door this morning, so I probably should open it. Could be an eviction notice, could be the lottery people," Townes smiled.

"Well, let's hope it's the latter," she smiled back at him.

"I will let you know, either way. I'll try and not yell too loud if it is the lottery people."

"Yes sir, I will hope for that."

Townes made his way to one of the small tables by the window. He looked out across the street to Central Park, the hansom cabs in an orderly line. He looked again at the horses attached to them, thinking maybe he might have an idea how those horses felt. *Something heavy strapped to you, following the same trail every day*, one of the voices said. Townes put his finger in his ear.

"Good morning, sir. Would you care for some coffee?" the man asked.

"Yes, decaf with cream, thank you," Townes replied.

He looked around the finely appointed room. It was like someone had invited you into their extremely nice home and had decided to place a great amount of wonderful-looking and delicious food in their study, leaving you alone with the other guests to separately enjoy it. There were a few others scattered about. He could hear no conversation loud enough to understand. They were all quiet, or the bubble gum was still firmly lodged in his ears. The man quickly returned with the coffee and cream.

"Thank you," Townes responded.

"You're welcome," the man answered, quickly leaving.

Townes added the cream to the hot, aromatic liquid, his gaze still on the horses across the street. He reached for the coffee, realizing he still had not opened the envelope.

"Hmmm."

He got up and moved to the table of food, scanning the selections, fascinated not only by their fine fragrance, but also by their artful appearance. Smoked salmon, capers, a croissant, with a bowl of blueberries, raspberries, blackberries and cream he thought would make for fine fare this morning. He returned to his seat, opened the envelope, the stationery from the hotel feeling crisp in his hand, crackling as he opened it. This fine linen paper always felt most proper. He did not think the lottery people knew he was here, but maybe Zeeder had told them. He removed and unfolded the note inside the envelope, glancing back at the horses out the window.

Townes,

It was very nice meeting you last night. I was wondering if I could take you up on your offer to walk the boys in the Park. I have to go down to the theater this morning, and won't have time to take them. I understand if you don't have time, especially given such short notice. Give me a call.
Ashley
Room 1300

Townes looked up from the letter and back out the window again at the horses. She had wonderful handwriting, and there was just maybe a hint of a smell of jasmine on the note.

He enjoyed the food, the berries now seeming fresher than they were just moments earlier. He looked back at the letter, holding it in one hand, while he tasted bites of the salmon, washed down with the freshly brewed coffee. It would be far too easy to sit here all day. He finished his food and coffee, got up from the table, reached into his pocket and pulled out a couple of dollars, leaving them on the table. He walked over to one of the house phones at the other end of the lounge. He picked up the phone, dialed the house operator.

"Ritz Carlton Central Park South, how may I assist you?"

"Room 1300 please."

"Certainly, one moment. May I say who is calling?"

"Yes, this is Townes ... uh, Townes, the dog walker."

"One moment. Have a nice day."

He was placed on hold. He thought if someone called his room, no one would ask who was calling, they would just put them through.

"Hi, Townes."

"Hello, Ashley. I understand the boys are in need of some outdoor activity."

"Oh, you are so sweet. Are you sure you don't mind doing this ... I mean if it is a bother, then I can get someone ..."

"It is no bother at all, and I would love to."

"Oh, thank you so much."

"What do I need to know?"

"Oh, nothing special, just normal dog stuff. They are good boys and should not give you any trouble."

"You want me to keep them on the leash?"

"You can, but that is up to you. If you let them off to run, they will come back as soon as you say 'boys.'"

"Great. My appointment is not until later, so we have plenty of time. What do you want me to do with them when we get back?"

"If I am not here, just talk to Felix out front. He'll bring them up."

"All right. When would you like me to meet you in the lobby?"

"In ten minutes, but you can come up if you like."

"I don't want to get in the way. Besides, you don't know me, so I understand."

"Oh, I got very good references on you," Ashley laughed.

"They must have thought you were talking about someone else."

"You are funny, and so nice ... just like the references said. I'll be down in ten minutes."

"Great."

"Bye."

Townes hung up the phone, walked over and grabbed a small pastry, and went back to where he had been seated earlier. He sat again for a moment, enjoying the cruller, looking at the turning leaves out the window.

Waiting for Ashley down in the lobby, he could again tell he might have stayed a bit long at the bar last night. He was OK when he was moving, but when he sat, he wanted to go back to bed.

"Bad ice," he muttered. A walk in Central Park with the dogs would go a long way towards getting that tarp off for the remainder of the day. He should give Ashley some money, or a gift of some sort for letting him walk her dogs. That was going to make him feel much better, and that was worth something.

"Hi!"

Townes turned and Ashley was there with the dogs.

"Hello there, all."

"I cannot thank you enough."

"I'm the one that should thank you. The theater? Do you work there, or are you getting tickets or something?" Townes asked, reaching down to pet the dogs.

Ashley looked at him with a puzzled look on his face. "Well, I sort of work there. You are too sweet. Milton said it might be like this."

"What?" Townes now had the puzzled look on his face.

"Nothing, you are just sweet. Now you boys behave and do what Townes tells you," she said, bending down and kissing both dogs on the head, handing the leashes to Townes.

"We will be good, we promise," Townes said. He wondered why she had given him that look. She was probably used to dealing with people that could hold a thought better than he could at the moment. He was curious what job she had at the theater, maybe set designer or something.

Townes exited the hotel, glad for the doorman, two dogs pulling him that direction in a hurry.

"An actress, maybe," the cool air hit his face as he went through the doors of the hotel out into the day towards the park, the hansom cabs still lined along Central Park South. Fall had started, only a few green leaves remaining, many had turned to orange, to yellow. It was cooler today than when he had arrived, the air feeling good on his face. That is what fall in New York could do for a person. If he did nothing else today, getting out and walking some nice woman's dogs in Central Park would seem a good achievement. Maybe if he did this every time he was in New York he would be more relaxed. He wondered where he could advertise himself as a substitute dog walker. Surely there must be someplace he could do that. He imagined the notice:

In the city from time to time.
Willing to pay for the privilege.

Well, it might work, one of the voices said.

The dogs were having a great time. He had bonded with them quickly. He let them off the leashes at Sheep Meadow, but they stayed close to him. He didn't worry about them taking off. Ashley was correct, they were no trouble. All three leisurely crossed Sheep Meadow, then circled the area they had crossed. Townes would have been content to do this for the rest of the morning, and he was sure the dogs would be, too. But his day job duty called and he had to prepare for his client meeting later, so they turned back and headed to the hotel. Calling to reschedule because of dogs would probably not be well-received:

Yes, something has come up and I need to walk this really nice lady's dogs today, and I won't be in until tomorrow. Thank you for your understanding.

That would be the preferred course of action. Rest up, walk the dogs, maybe see the lady again later that day, spend some time with her. That would fit nicely, taking him to about the time Milton would be starting.

Spending the time in Central Park with the dogs proved quite the restorative. He never got a chance to spend much time in Central Park. He would go once in a while, have a cigar, but not really explore much of it. To be able to wander around, letting the dogs sort of guide him wherever they wanted to go may not have been a carriage ride, but it was relaxing. This form of travel made him think more about what it might be like to be able to do this more often. They headed up to the Lake, over to the Boathouse, then along East Drive, pausing often to delight in the fall kaleidoscope the trees were displaying. He needed to get back for his meeting, but was thoroughly enjoying his time in the Park with his two new friends. He thought about nothing in particular, which was a change of pace for him. He usually gave so much thought to everything going on, and not enough of this, this sort of pleasant nothingness. When he got back to La Jolla, he might have to do more of this, less of the other.

Got an ocean and a dog.

He reluctantly arrived back at Central Park South and the hotel. For as long as they walked, Townes felt invigorated.

"Welcome back, Mr. Mantle," the doorman said. "Did you enjoy your walk?"

"Yes, thank you, it was quite nice. I actually would have gone a lot longer, but the dogs said they had an appointment to get to, so we came back. Maybe when they get finished they would take me out again. What do you think?"

"I don't see why not."

"Could you have someone take these fellows up to my friend's room?"

"These are Miss Meacham's dogs."

"Yes they are. She said that you could take care of that, is that right?" Townes smiled, now knowing Ashley's last name.

"Yes, I will have someone see to that," The doorman said, moving to the inside of the building, speaking with another man. The other man moved towards Townes.

"Hello, sir, how is everything today?"

"Fine, thank you," Townes said, recognizing the second man. "Hello Dima."

"Hello, Mr. Mantle, it is good to see you again. I can take the dogs up to Miss Meacham's room. She mentioned that you would be walking them. How was your walk?"

"It was great, wasn't it, guys?" Townes said, looking down at the dogs, who were enjoying watching and sniffing the people coming and going from the hotel.

"I am glad to hear that," Dima said, taking the leashes. "Is there anything else that you will be needing?"

"Not that I can think of, but I will let you know," Townes said, reaching into his pocket to get some money to give to Dima.

"That is not necessary, Sir. Miss Meacham has already taken care of things," Dima said, refusing the money.

"Are you sure?"

"Quite sure, Mr. Mantle. Thank you."

"All right then. Thank you."

Dima moved away from Townes, taking the dogs with him.

"So long boys. Maybe see you tomorrow," Townes said.

The dogs stopped suddenly and paused, looking back at Townes. The suggestion seemed to be all right with them. Dima was startled, still moving forward, his arm jerking back when they stopped at the sound of Townes's voice.

"Sorry Dima, just saying good bye to the dogs. I didn't mean to foul up your program there."

"Not a problem, Sir. The dogs seem quite fond of you."

"They are good boys, very smart, well behaved ... much more than me, on both counts," Townes said, smiling.

Dima seemed perplexed by this, but said nothing, leading the dogs away. Townes paused, shaking his head.

"I guess I have to go that way myself, so I hope I can tag along for part of the trip."

"Certainly, Sir," Dima said as they now all moved towards the elevators, the dogs glad to have Townes back among the pack.

CHAPTER 18

It was not a long walk to his appointment, only a short distance from Central Park South. He was preoccupied from thinking about Ashley, thinking about Kat, thinking about walking the dogs. He was lucky he had remembered to change his clothes. Long as he and the dogs had been on their Park tour, it still was good to walk to his appointment.

The walking made him think about how much he used to walk, thinking about the remorse he felt a few years back when he took a load of things, including his old backpack, to the Salvation Army. It used to be that it was nothing to strap on the pack and spend days walking. Every time he came to New York he thought about the life he used to have. That life seemed, like the backpack, to now belong to someone else. Not enough walking, entirely too much talking, but this trip was going much better than the norm. After all, he'd met a really nice woman and got to walk her dogs.

The work now felt mundane. He liked dealing with the people. He thought he was good at what he did, though he did not consider himself to be all that smart. He was pragmatic and not emotional in his approach to his consulting business. He did his best to quickly assess the situation and give a recommendation. He actually was quite baffled that people were willing to pay somewhat large amounts of money for the service he provided, which he believed to be nothing more than applying common sense. Things were not always obvious to him, but apparently they were less obvious to those willing to pay for his services. He had been doing this for a while, and it held little magic or mystique any more. He always did his best to do a thorough job. He would not let his growing indifference keep him from delivering the best work he possibly could. It was easy to him. Maybe it was driving him to do other things—the writing, the music--to find better balance and allow for more of a reach, or stretch of his imagination. He wasn't sure he was any good at music or writing, but they were enjoyable. He had been writing for years, articles for magazines and newspapers, but nothing big. He considered that kind of writing as a line of work to be even less like real work than the consulting business, but it was a lot more interesting.

He thought of his novel. His editor was circulating it to literary agents, thus far with no success. The thought of actually getting it published might not be in the complete outer reaches of his imagination, but it was in an adjoining zip code. He wanted it, but doubted it, wrestling with the thoughts of success daily. On this trip, aside from his consulting work, he was to meet with his editor. He hoped to get some news about getting the book on its way. He would meet with his editor tomorrow, after he finished his day job.

He thought about when he started writing more seriously, as opposed to just musings and journal-type crap. Once he did that, he started looking at things differently, which actually helped him sleep better, quelling certain anxieties, incubating others. The change of approach was not a total epiphany, but it was as close to having one as he had ever had. He thought it a strong message that he needed change. He generally avoided such introspection but this wave came in pretty strong. He was going to see where it took him. That seemed contemplative enough.

As for the music, he and Zeeder played pretty much whenever they could, and getting paid for it seemed almost as funny as getting paid for his consulting work. Somebody thought it was good. They played in another band with some other friends, when they all wanted to let off steam and push things further than the music he and Zeeder played. When the band got together, sometimes it took a couple of days to recover. Sometimes that was a good thing, sometimes not. Either way, it wasn't consulting

The rest of the day moved along quickly. Had he not spent time last night with Milton, the day might have been a little shorter, but it always seemed to put years back on his life, so being a little slow today was a small price to pay. Being with Milton was like being with family, only he never argued with you, was never disappointed in you, was never upset with you. With family, someone was always pissed off or upset about something they were not telling you. With Milton, these situations simply did not present themselves. It was not a subservient thing either. He could be quite direct to combative customers, but to those he cared about, he made you want to spend time with him every chance you got.

The day finally wound down, and Townes and his client agreed to meet again the following day even though he didn't want to take up much of their time with another long meeting. *Especially when he could be walking dogs and getting paid nothing*, one of his voices said. He scheduled a late morning session and thought about taking the dogs over to the park.

It was rush hour in New York, the sidewalks full, everyone in a hurry to get home. Townes was in no hurry on his walk back to the Ritz. He still was uncertain of Ashley's position with the theater. He could not ask for much more out of a day, so the fact that he was now packed in with the mass of humanity did not enter his mind. He was not stuck in traffic, behind the wheel of a vehicle, or stuck in an airplane, so this was not so bad. He felt so much better now, he might even buy something from a street vendor. He would go back to the hotel, check in with Milton and see what developed from there. Some of the finest restaurants in the world were here, but the prospect of a table for one never really appealed to him. He usually dined at the bar, even if cocktails were not involved. At least at the bar, especially in New York, the barman was always good company, always knew what was going on around town. If they were good, and they usually were, you had someone to talk with. Townes was never good at being a loner. He hated being alone, and did not want to get better at it.

The morning and evening rushes in New York had a distinctly different feel than in Southern California. People probably felt the same in both places, groggy and maybe not in the best of spirits in the morning, tired, but glad to be heading home in the evening. At the Ritz, two doormen greeted him warmly.

"How was the day, Sir?"

"No arrests, no injuries," Townes replied.

"Sounds like a success."

"Yes, I thought so. How about your day? Everything all right?"

"Absolutely. No winter yet."

"Yes, a great fall day, I'm not ready for winter yet."

"Based on your tan, I'm guessing winter is not much of a concern for you."

"Well, as usual, you guys are right," Townes said, smiling, as he entered the hotel door, held by his conversation friends. The second set of doors was opened from the inside by a familiar face.

"Hello, Mr. Mantle, it is nice to see you again."

"Hello, Dima. How are you?"

"I am very well, thank you."

"Glad to hear it."

"I have a message for you. It is from Miss Meacham."

"No problems with the dogs, I hope? I did just like she said, and ... we didn't go to the Sabrett's stand, even though I tried to talk them into going."

"No, no, the dogs are fine," Dima laughed.

"That is a relief," Townes let out a breath. "I thought maybe I did something wrong. Hate to get fired on my first day."

"No, no. She asked that I give you a message if I saw you. Let me go over to the front desk and retrieve it for you. I will be right back," Dima said, moving quickly.

Townes walked over to one of the ornate lobby chairs, relieved that everything was all right, the lobby quite full of people this time of day, the conversations blending with the music from the grand piano by the back wall. He pulled off his overcoat and scarf, looking around the comfortable setting. It was not the usual din of the standard business hotel. The ambience of the place, along with the music, gave it a more refined feeling. No one was yelling across the room for their friend to "get me another beer while I go to the bathroom." No one in this lobby wore tank tops, board shorts or flip flops. For this he was grateful. That kind of behavior suggested the pending extinction of good manners, giving Townes a tremendous headache whenever he encountered it, which was more often than not. This hotel was one of the outposts of decorum. It made a great many things all the better. He studied the fine dark wood walls and columns and the large paintings. They would quickly leach out the noise, creating an entirely different world from the one he left two days ago. One could relax in an instant here.

He found a vacant chair and draped his coat and scarf over the back of it, placing his briefcase on the floor next to it. He sat, the chair giving his legs and lower back immediate respite. He thought he had not walked far, then remembered he had started the day with the dogs in Central Park, and shook his head. Dima returned from the front desk, looking around the lobby, envelope in hand, Townes waving to get his attention.

"Here you are," he said, extending the envelope.

"Thank you. I was just going to sit for a minute. I ended up walking more than I thought today."

"Sit as long as you like. Would you like me to get you something?"

"No, no, that's all right. I would be in trouble if Milton saw me sitting out here."

"I can help you move your things into the bar, or I can have them taken up to your room, if you would like."

"Thank you, Dima, that's not necessary," Townes said, starting to open the envelope.

"Very well. I will be right over by the door should you need anything."

"Thank you very much."

"My pleasure. Have a good evening."

"You too."

Dima moved away from Townes, and back over by the entrance. Townes opened the message from Ashley.

Townes,

Thank you for walking the boys today. That was really sweet of you. I have left two tickets for tonight and tomorrow night's shows at the Nederlander Theater (208 W. 41st Street) for you and a friend, if you would like to come. They will be at Will Call under your name. I really hope you can make it. If you want to get together after the show, that would be great too. Please come!

Ashley

He looked up from the letter and grinned.

CHAPTER 19

Townes walked around the corner of the lobby lounge to the bar. The bar was crowded, as usual, and Milton was the epicenter. There were no seats available so Townes had to stand. He would wait for just a few minutes. He was going to the theater, still wondering what Ashley's job was.

"Yes sir, what will it be this evening?" Milton asked, Townes's back towards him. Townes turned his direction. "Hey, there you are!" Milton's tone was noticeably more upbeat.

"Good evening, my friend."

"I was just talking to someone about you," Milton said.

"That is what I hear."

"She's a sweet girl, Ashley."

"Yes, she seems to be. She left me tickets for the show tonight. What exactly does she do at the theater?"

Milton got a perplexed look on his face. "You don't know?"

"I'm not from here."

"I'm not going to tell you."

"Come on."

"Are you going?"

"Yes."

"Good, she can tell you when you get there, I would rather it come from her."

"You are pretty tough."

"All my life, babe … grew up in Brooklyn," Milton said, flexing his arms. "You're really not going to tell me?"

Milton paused, looked back down the bar and back at Townes. "No."

"She must be an actress, or maybe the director."

"Maybe." Milton paused. "I think you need a Martini tonight."

"A Martini."

"Yeah, I never heard of it 'til today, so I am going to have to look it up," Milton eyed a chair that just opened up. "I got some Brooklyn gin that you are going to love. Got to help out my friends from the old neighborhood. Let me go get that chair," he was moving that direction before Townes could further object to his nondisclosure.

Townes moved down the bar to the vacant seat. Milton had already cleared and cleaned the hard-to-come-by real estate.

"What was that drink called again?" Milton asked, assembling the ingredients as Townes took his seat. He was already humming a tune, the gin and the Boston Shaker in front of him. He smelled the top of the bottle after he opened it. "Man, that smells good! From my hometown too, how can it be bad?"

"Martini, I think you said."

"Oh, yeah, one of those new mixologist's drinks, with stewed figs, and cilantro … or some shit," Milton laughed, moving like he could do this blindfolded and undoubtedly could.

"I hate cilantro. You remember how to make a Martini?"

"Well … you know, my memory is not what it used to be. I don't think I put any sauerkraut juice or used coffee grounds in this, but you taste it and see what you think." The clear, cold liquid, now pouring from the shaker glass into the cocktail glass, pouring completely to the top, the blue cheese stuffed olives on a napkin to the side of the glass, as there was no room in the glass for anything else. Townes would again have to lean forward to drink it without spilling it. "But I think it is supposed to taste just like that," Milton said.

Townes drank it becoming cold and warm at the same time. It was perfect.

"How many of these do you figure you have made in your lifetime?"

"I can't count that high, I didn't go to college."

"Well, this one is perfect."

"It's the Brooklyn Gin, I'm tellin' ya. Local boys do good."

"You still are not going to tell me what Ashley does?"

Milton looked at the cocktail, looked at Townes, then again smelled the top of the bottle of gin, smiling before he replaced the large cork top.

"No. I'll be right back. Do you want something to eat?"

"Maybe something quick, I need to get to the theater ... find out what your friend does there."

"She's your friend now, too."

"You know her better. You at least know what she does."

"You will too. I'll see what we have to eat around here," Milton said, scurrying off. "What would you like?"

"Whatever you bring me."

"Done."

Townes shook his head, watching Milton quickly move away. He leaned over to take another sip of the Brooklyn Gin Martini. Two more leaning sips and he might be able to pick up the glass. He was going to have to go and find out Ashley's occupation himself. There were worse things. Her note and show tickets were not an indication of his termination as dog walker after only one outing, at least. Townes laughed out loud, enjoying the ice cold libation and the prospect of seeing Ashley again. He looked around the bar. It had quieted, but not much, and was probably because Milton had gone in the back room. Milton now reappeared from the back, the pulse of the bar quickening as soon as he returned. He paid attention to everyone and made sure they were all taken care of. He had some plates in his hands, making his way towards Townes, promising those he passed on the way that he would be right back. He had smoked salmon, prepared as decorative small flowers, set on cucumber slices, some Creme Fraiche, topped with caviar. There were shrimp on the other plate.

"They were going to throw this out," Milton said, placing the food in front of Townes. "I hope it's all right."

"It looks great, and is just the right size," Townes responded.

"How's the drink?"

"Just the right size, also."

"Would you like another one?"

"I do need to make it to the theater. Another might put me off course."

"I'll make it a short one."

"And that has happened before when?"

"I don't want you to lose your nerve and chicken out on seeing Ashley."

"I won't chicken out."

"That's right, especially not with me looking after you," Milton said, already in the process of making the second martini.

"Maybe you should come out to San Diego and do this. I don't have anybody there to look after me like you do here. I would do a lot better if you were around more."

"I'm always here."

"Yes, but I need you out there, too."

"I couldn't be there. I don't have a car, or a driver's license. Besides, palm trees make me nervous. I wouldn't last five minutes out there. You don't have a bartender out there to keep you in line?"

"No."

"Well, there's your problem."

"I just told you that. I need someone like you, but I don't think that is possible."

"Probably not," Milton said, placing the fresh cocktail in front of Townes.

Townes sighed, taking a bite of the salmon. "You make it pretty hard to get up from here."

"Don't eat so fast, you'll get sick," Milton said, moving back to the other patrons.

Townes finished the last of the first drink and moved it out of harm's way. It was easy to forget whatever he was thinking about before he walked in here. With the addition of the second martini, he was becoming less perplexed about Ashley and more relaxed. It didn't matter what she was at the theater she was a very nice person.

He wondered what Kat was up to and thought he might call her before he left for the theater. Nothing serious, just keeping in touch. Maybe they could get together when he got back. He thought about asking her to come out and meet him in New York, but that might be a little premature. He had not known her that long. Maybe she could ask her friend Annie to come with her, then it wouldn't sound so crazy. *No, that would sound more crazy,* he thought. The two of them could come out and meet him. *He could introduce Kat and Annie, who he didn't know at all, to his new theater friend, whom he had no idea what it was she did, and they could have all have a great time,* a voice said. He sighed again. The salmon, the shrimp, and the two ice cold martinis made it difficult to pry himself out of the chair. He could stay here all night, but he knew Milton would not let him. He needed to settle up before he stayed too long and missed the girl. He would not be calling anyone tonight, maybe tomorrow. He got Milton's attention and told him he needed to go.

"You just got here."

"Ashley … theater … remember?"

"Oh, yeah, yeah, yeah. You gotta get out of here," Milton said, placing the bill on the bar.

"Since you won't tell me what she does, I am off to find out just what it is this woman does do," Townes said, pausing before signing the check.

"Sounds like a good plan, but I'm not sure what you just said."

"That's your fault."

"You get back early, I'll be here 'til close. Otherwise, I want a full report tomorrow night."

"You can count on it. Thank you for looking after me."

"Someone has to. No one doing it back home."

Townes headed out of the bar, back through the hotel lobby lounge area towards the front door. Dima was still stationed up front.

"Everything all right, Mr. Mantle?"

"Yes, Dima, perfect."

"Very good, sir. Would you like me to take your briefcase up to your room?"

"Oh, yes, I guess I left it by the chair out here."

"No problem, sir. I will place it in your room."

"Thank you for looking after me. I seem to be getting forgetful. Listen, is the car here now?"

"I believe so. Where would you like to go?"

"Nederlander Theater, West Forty-First Street. If it isn't available, could you get me a cab?"

"No cab, no. Let me check. Please come with me."

"That would be great, thank you."

"My pleasure."

They went out through both sets of doors. It was a great deal cooler now than earlier. Fall was definitely here. Dima made his way to a sleek, black, shining Bentley, double parked out front. Townes thought it to be a Bentley, but he wasn't really focused. Dima spoke with the man tending the vehicle, then motioned for Townes to come to them.

"Not a problem. Mathew will be happy to take you there."

"Thank you," Townes said, reaching in his pocket for money to give to him.

"That is not necessary, sir. Enjoy yourself and tell Miss Meacham hello for me."

"How did you know I am going to see Ashley?"

"It is my job to know my guests."

Townes smiled, touching him on the shoulder as he got in the car. The car moved away from the curb, into the night. Townes was tired now, but excited to be riding in a very nice car instead of a cab and heading to meet the mystery lady, Scruff.

CHAPTER 20

The ride to the theater took no time at all. Townes was glad he had decided to forgo the walk. Sometimes when he was in New York, he forgot how much he had walked during the day. If this last walk turned out to be twenty-plus blocks, that could wear him out. Hoofing it after a couple of Milton's martinis had a tendency to make Townes's motor run a little hotter than normal, so riding in the house car was a good idea. He had done that walk down Sixth Avenue after drinks with Milton before, peeling his clothes off as he walked, to no avail, to keep from overheating.

"Hello Ashley. Sorry about the sweat, but I just had two martinis and walked twenty blocks," would not make the best impression, regardless of her job. He thanked the driver, giving him a tip, and walked to the Will Call window. He thought it funny that no matter how tall or how short you were when you went to one of these, you still had to bend down to speak to the person on the other side of the glass and intercom. Yes, there were in fact tickets there in his name. So far, so good.

The woman smiled at him and slid the envelope with the tickets in the slot, asking him for ID and a signature. He entered the theater and looked around at the internal trappings, the old Playbill covers mounted on the walls, the chandeliers hanging purposefully, the smallness of the coat room. It was all as it probably always had been, save for the carpet which had probably been replaced countless times. He wondered how many pairs of shoes that floor had seen.

He passed the bar area, thinking he was still topped off from his last stop, and would not be needing any further libation prior to the show. He found an usher and asked the location of his seat. The usher pointed him to the last entrance on the right side of the theater, telling him someone there could show him to his seat. Townes thanked them and proceeded in the prescribed direction. The theater background noise, more like a hum, was almost trance-like, a combination of the guests' anticipation and the remnants of the noisy street. He produced his ticket for the usher. The usher handed him the Playbill, then asked if he would like some assistance finding his seat and Townes accepted. The usher led Townes all the way down to the first row of seats, his seat on the aisle. He removed his coat and scarf, sitting down, placing them on his lap. He observed the ornateness of the theater hall, obviously built in a time when people still cared about such things, a time when it was important to make people feel they had come to a fine place to see an equally fine live performance. A very luxurious hall that spoke of a time when not everyone wore flip-flops everywhere they went. He thought it a shame few things were built that way now.

The theater felt small, which made it even better. You didn't need binoculars to see the performance, even if you were in the very last row. This certainly was not a concern for Townes, as from his seat he would be able to catch one of the cast members, should they accidentally fall off the stage. He was worried that if he sneezed, it might disrupt the production.

"The production!" Townes said, louder than he meant to, thinking Ashley might be listed in the handout.

He opened the booklet, flipping through the first few pages of ads and articles about other shows and actors you should not miss. It was on page sixteen that the participants of this performance were listed. There was a large list of people, obvious that it was no simple task to put one of these shows on. There had to be over fifty names listed, varying from sound to stage, to costume, to actor, to ... Ashley was listed at the top, with two other actors, in the boldest of type.

Townes looked up from the page to see if the entire audience was looking at him, the last one in the building who did not know she was starring in the play, giving rise to a feeling that he needed to get out more, pay better attention to things going on in the world. She was an actor and he didn't even know who she was. Maybe if he went to the movies once in a while, went to a Broadway show once in a while. He always thought about going when he came to New York, but going by himself was not something he found inspiration in. He felt stupid. No wonder she thought it funny when he asked her what she did at the theater. Milton was probably laughing at him right now, and would be sure to remind him of his ignorance for many more visits, which Townes felt was more than justified.

Now that he was thinking about it, he did recognize her name, and he may have even seen her in a movie once, though it had been quite a while since he had been to a movie. With the business, the travel, the music, the writing, there did not seem to be time. Milton would remind him that there was always time, saying something like, "There are so many great cocktails out there, but once in a while you need to stop and drink one." Now that he knew someone in the movies, he just might have to start going, at least to her movies.

The house lights flickered, letting everyone know the play was about to start. He was still thinking everyone was looking at him due to his stupidity. Bringing down the lights could not come soon enough. They made some announcements about not taking pictures, turning off cell phones, and not unwrapping and eating hard candy.

Do people still do that? Townes thought.

The lights dimmed and the show was off and running, moving faster than he thought possible. Even though there was a complete order, or symmetry to the thing, he could not believe how quickly it advanced, never seeming to drag, no need for explanation or adjustment. It was all carefully laid out and in-motion in such a fashion that he almost thought he was in the thing himself. He did not know if that was because how it was timed, or if it was that he knew someone in it, having walked her dogs that very morning, which now seemed like days ago. There was applause for the actors, purposely laughable parts, and parts that gave pause. He was enjoying every minute. With his proximity he was waiting for the people on stage to ask him what he thought, or maybe to direct him to go and get something for them, something pertinent to this story, to this moment. He was ready.

The first act was over before he could completely resolve his understanding. House lights back up, curtain down, he was almost out of breath. He was not sure that was the effect they were striving for, but he thought it might be at least in the desirable top three. People got up to stretch their legs, to make a trip to the lobby, maybe unwrap that hard candy they had been holding on to. He was comforted that no one commented on his internal confusion, even as he reminded himself that it was impossible for anyone to know what he was thinking.

He read the Playbill during the intermission, a good third of a page devoted to Ashley. There were a couple of movies listed that Townes had at least heard of which made him feel a little better. He reread the section a couple of times, flipping back to where her picture was placed with a half a dozen of the participants. The two inch square, black and white photo of her did not jump off the page at him. She looked vastly different than when he had met her, she not wearing a stocking cap and dark glasses in the picture, so this also made him feel better.

He was certainly enjoying the performance, at least the first act. He had never seen a Broadway show where he had walked the dogs of any of the participants. She was good at her craft, and aside from his initial observation, and during the intermission of the surroundings, during the production, he would keep his focus solely on her. The crowd began filing back in, and Townes was excited to see the remaining action, eager to see Ashley continue her performance, which thus far had been great. He was tired now, but he would enjoy the rest of the play. The second act was every bit as good as the first. It flew past with even greater speed. He was there thanks to his new acquaintance, who was bathed in light, looking considerably more regal without the stocking cap, standing just a short distance in front of him. The end of the play came sooner than he wanted it to.

He wondered what it felt like, doing what she did. It was different than he and Zeeder playing music at a bar. People sometimes paid attention to them. Sometimes they paid no attention at all. When his friends came, that was when he enjoyed it most. That made him think about Kat. Here he was, clapping for his new friend, thinking about Kat. Technically, he had spent more time with Ashley's dogs than he had spent with Ashley, or Kat. He would certainly like to spend more time with Kat, wanted to know more about Annie, Scruff, Kat ... Townes rubbed his eyes.

Martini's wearing off....

CHAPTER 21

The applause continued, and the curtain came down. Townes was very glad for the ticket. He would be sure to leave Ashley a note back at the hotel.

"A note," he said, remembering a note that was in the envelope with the ticket, wondering why he didn't read it before. Milton's martinis could sometimes have that effect on him.

He took the envelope out to view the contents. There was a note with a backstage pass to meet Ashley after the show. He made his way to the front of the theater and asked an usher about the meeting.

"Excuse me, could you help me with this?" Townes asked, revealing the note and the pass.

"Let me see," the usher said, surveying the papers. "Come this way."

Townes followed, thanking the usher for her help, explaining he had not been backstage before.

"Well, you won't be able to say that after tonight," the usher said.

The usher led Townes through a maze of props, curtains, ropes, and people, all the things he would expect to be back there, uncertain of the order, or disorder. The small, maze-like hallways smelling somewhat stale, and like four hundred coats of paint. They came to the dressing rooms, the usher handing the papers Townes had given her to a man by the doors to the dressing rooms, speaking to him softly, Townes not able to hear the conversation.

"There you go. He'll take you from here," she said.

"Thank you."

This was the baton hand-off, the man by the many doors, motioning Townes towards a particular door where he could see a couple of people, one of them Ashley. She was sitting with someone and looked up and smiled when she saw Townes.

"You made it!" Ashley smiled, with Townes stepping forward tentatively. "It's all right. You can come in."

He entered her dressing room. The room small, but larger than he thought it would be. "Yes, thank you for inviting me. The show was … it was, well, fantastic."

"Oh, thank you so much for coming."

"The show … you … were great, the show was great. I really had, er, enjoyed seeing the … you, the show."

Ashley chuckled. "Thank you. It's OK. You need only be nervous if you are onstage. There are no critics back here … I hope."

Townes laughed, seeing Ashley could tell he was nervous. "Good. Would hate to get a bad review. You were great … I said that, didn't I?"

"Thank you, and yes, you did say that, but it's OK to hear it again, just in case no one else thought so."

"I'm sure they all felt almost as strongly as I did about you."

"I hope so. Thank you for coming … I said that, didn't I?"

"It was my pleasure, and you did say that … I'd better go before my repeating myself rubs off on you any further. *Knucklehead*, a voice in his head said.

Ashley laughed, touching him on the arm. "I can't imagine."

"Well, it happens," Townes said, sharing in her laughter.

"I know it's late, but I'm starving, so would you like to get some dinner?" Ashley asked.

"Oh, that would be good, yes, I'd like that."

"It's not too late for you?

"No, not at all. When I'm traveling, I don't really know what time it is, or sometimes even where I am."

"Really?"

"Except for when I'm in New York. Pretty hard to confuse that with anyplace else, I guess."

"I love it here."

"Strangely enough, I do too," Townes said, looking around.

There was a pause and they looked at each other smiling, both content to feel something good had happened, both somewhat weary, but still feeling good about the moment.

"I need to let you get changed," Townes said.

"I won't be long. You can wait … There's an area out there with some comfortable chairs, something to drink," Ashley replied, her eyes still acknowledging the moment.

"All right. Are you sure *you're* not too tired?"

"I am tired, but I am famished. I don't care if they have to stitch me in tomorrow, I'm hungry. Are you sure you're not too tired? You've had a longer day than I have."

"Well, I don't know about that," Townes said, again looking around.

"We need to spend some time together, because the boys have spent more time with you than I have. I want to be able to compare notes with them," Ashley smiled.

"I gave them a couple of treats, so their votes are already bought and paid for."

"I think they have a good opinion of you, even without the treats, and I trust them."

"I guess we'll see at dinner."

"Yes, we will. I won't be long. Thank you again for coming," Ashley said, leaning over and kissing Townes on the cheek.

"Are you kidding? It was my pleasure and thank you for inviting me. I'll be waiting out here somewhere, unless they throw me out."

"They won't. I promise."

They went to an Italian restaurant, Felidia, not far from the hotel. Ashley looked splendid in a silk, ruffled cuff white blouse, black pants and a cobalt blue jacket. The proprietors were friends of hers and were ecstatic to see her. The entire staff welcomed her with hugs and kisses. She introduced them to Townes. They all showed him nearly the same affection. He was with Ashley, so he must be their friend as well. It was a dark interior, but a very homey place with a heavenly smell of what Townes imagined Italy would be like. They were taken to a more private area, a table with a "Reserved" sign on it. Perhaps they knew she was coming, or maybe it was always her table, based on the greetings. It was a whirlwind of introductions and embraces, and before he knew it, they were sitting down. Elegant flutes of something bubbly were on the table along with some small plates of introductory offerings to welcome them.

"I guess ..."

"I come here sometimes," Ashley said, squinting.

"So it would appear."

"They are so sweet, and the food is always perfect. Too perfect, actually. I really have to watch myself when I'm here, or the costume people have to let out my clothes," Ashley laughed, raising her champagne flute to Townes. "Here's to a pretty good day, and to learning more about the man my dogs are so fond of. Always celebrate the victories."

Townes touched his glass with hers. "And here is to a great performance, and to learning more about you ... if that's not too bold ... and what was that last part?" Townes said, more quietly.

They again touched glasses and smiled.

"Just something I say ... always celebrate the victories. I really like Prosecco," Ashley said.

"Yes, it is very nice."

"Not too formal, not too casual."

"I never thought of it that way, but yes," Townes said, looking at his glass.

"That's a good concept, isn't it?"

"Yes, I would say it is."

"I mean, for something to be both, that's good, right?"

"Yes ... yes, it really is. Is that from one of your performances?"

"No, it's from me," Ashley said, giggling.

"Even better."

"So let's hear about Townes, the man my dogs seem to love. Tell me the things they seem to already know," Ashley said, lowering her head, so she would have to look up.

"I didn't tell them everything. I wanted to be somewhat mysterious, so they would want to see me again."

"Well, they do, but I need to know more about you first. You seem a little mysterious ... in a good way. I don't see a deep, dark past in your face. I see more of someone doing a great many things, good things."

"Not yet, but I'm trying."

"My sense is you do better than try."

Townes laughed at that. "I'll give you the short version."

"Now, but you must promise you will give me the longer version at some point."

"Maybe the short version won't inspire you towards hearing a longer version," Townes said, rolling his eyes.

"Not possible."

"Well, I'll do my best."

"Stop stalling, talk ... about you."

"I'm not good at that."

"Nobody is give it a shot."

"Hmm, OK. I have a little consulting business, and I'm almost a writer, and almost a musician, living in La Jolla, California. Never married, one labrador."

"Are those in order?"

"No, the dog comes first, always."

"Agree. Writer, musician?"

"Well, I try."

"What kind of writing, what kind of musician? This is good." Ashley grinned, leaning closer.

"Half-assed, both categories."

"Not possible. What kind, tell me?"

"I play some clubs around town and ..."

"And what?"

"And I am trying to get a novel published."

"This is too good!"

"Not yet it's not," Townes said, again rolling his eyes.

"But it will be."

"I am full of hope ... among other things, my friend Zeeder would say."

"I think you are onto something. Look at your face," Ashley smiled.

"I try not to."

"No, you have a great deal of sincerity. Not too casual, not too formal," Ashley grinned, as she sipped her Prosecco. "You're struggling with the confidence, even though you shouldn't."

"You're thinking of the wine, or something."

"No, you! How close are you?"

"Book is finished. Trying to get someone to pick me up. Editor is supposed to be circulating it around."

"You are just all kinds of good, aren't you?"

"I'm not the lead in a Broadway show."

"Stop it! This book stuff is exciting! When do you hear?"

"I don't know. It would be nice to hear something while I am in town, but that is a stretch."

"Oh, you must believe in yourself."

"I saw that on a box of tea once," Townes said, scratching his head.

"I'm serious! You have to. This is exciting."

"I haven't done anything yet.

"You wrote a book."

"I don't have a publisher. Anyone can write a book."

"Someone will pick it up, and not everyone writes a book. I haven't," Ashley said, touching his arm with her finger.

"I don't know about that, and it seems these days everyone does write a book, which doesn't seem to help with the odds. Besides, you don't know what kind of writhing I do. It could be mentally deranged crap."

"Don't focus on the odds, and you are not capable of mentally deranged crap, at least not from what I can see. Let's drink to your getting published."

"You just met me, you don't know that."

"I can sense that your work is not mentally deranged … and that it will be successful."

"How can you tell that?"

"We can talk about that. Is there a female character in this book?" Ashley asked, turning her head to the side.

"Isn't there always?"

"Have you written a screenplay?"

"Sort of putting the cart before the horse, don't you think?" Townes said, cocking his head.

"Just want to put a positive spin on things. I suppose you can do that later."

"I suppose you are right, and I appreciate your being positive."

"It is what keeps me going."

"That, and dogs," Townes said, gesturing with his champagne flute.

"Hell yes, dogs!" Ashley said, reciprocating the gesture.

"To dogs"

"To dogs."

"May we never be without them."

"Never ever."

"Never ever."

They touched glasses again and sat, taking in the warmth of their surroundings. The precursor to the edible celebration was a bottle of Gaja,

Barolo, which they both found to be luscious. After that the food began to arrive in waves. There really had been no mention of what they wanted to eat, it just came in several small plates. There was a trio of spreadable garbanzos with some bread that seemed to have been baked seconds earlier. The lightness of the fresh pasta, combined with the smell of both cooked and freshly grated truffles was intoxicating. Tuna crudo, asparagus and prosciutto, veal tenderloin with fava bean puree and truffle sauce, and those were just the dishes he could remember. The plates were many, but they were all small, giving them just a taste of everything. Townes did not need to order, the seemingly instantaneous feast was more delightful than anything he could have decided on.

When he asked Ashley about it, she just smiled, saying: "I come here sometimes." After a certain point, he really did not think he was hungry, yet managed to take such pleasure in every offering that all plates were taken away empty. Dining like this made conversation easy, as everyone was comfortable, and just a little bit tired, which maybe made for a slight easing of any inhibitions either might have. Ashley could be quite guarded, she had to be in her profession. Townes could see it being almost a reflex for her. The longer they sat, the more they talked, the less guarded she was, yet she still did not reveal everything, and he understood and respected that. She had gotten the referral on Townes from Milton, and that seemed to be all she needed. She did not like to talk about herself, but that spoke to her character, not to wanting to withhold anything.

The food kept coming, and neither was in a hurry to leave. Though it was apparent that Ashley had this treatment here all the time, Townes could not remember ever having such a meal with a woman. He had dined at some great places, but generally at the bar, by himself. Her willingness to share her company was welcomed even more than the non-stop wonderful food offerings. Townes purposely did not look at his watch, for fear of what it would tell him. She asked more about Townes's life, to the point that he was embarrassed to talk so much about himself. Every time he attempted to find out about her, she diverted the conversation, saying there was nothing to tell. That certainly was not the case, in his opinion. She was an actress. There undoubtedly was a great deal to tell. Her life had to be a lot different than the average person, but she did not want to talk about herself. She said only that she was very fortunate, worked hard, and had gotten a couple of breaks, to get where she was. She said she enjoyed the work she did, and hoped it would continue, but that if it did not, she would still be happy.

Townes was amazed at her total absence of self-importance. He did not know any famous people, except for Milton and Crosetti. Townes thought an actress would be different than this and he was glad she was how she was. She made him feel comfortable, she did not seem affected in any way. She did her job because she enjoyed it. If her job changed, she would probably enjoy that too.

They both became weary at the same time. It was getting to be quite late, yet they only noticed due to the emptiness of the restaurant. Just them and the staff. Ashley breathed a huge sigh of contentment, and Townes reluctantly suggested they get back to the hotel, lest the production company have him shot. Ashley suggested that after such a display of consumption, the six blocks walk would do them good.

The walk was just as delightful as the dinner. Townes kept thinking once Ashley got outside and back into the invigorating fall air she would come to her senses and realize he kept her out too late, but this was not the case. She put her arm in his and strolled gently, occasionally humming, in between asking him what he liked to do, what would he like to do that he had never done, and what would he do, if he could do anything he wanted. Townes laughed and asked the same questions of her, and she saying only that she would be walking down the streets of New York with him.

They made it back to the hotel and though late as it was, thought it a good idea to stop by the bar and say good night to Milton. It was something Townes always did, so tonight would be no exception, except that he would be stopping by to see him with a beautiful woman. It was late, but he would probably be wrapping things up at the bar, and sure enough he was, there at the opposite end of the bar from them, putting bottles away when he noticed them come in, too far for him to see who it was.

"Sorry folks, we're closed, but come back tomorrow and the first round is on me."

"That's a shame. I wanted a really fancy drink before I went to bed, something very difficult to make," Ashley said.

"Yes, me too, and you shouldn't be offering to buy strange people drinks," Townes added.

"Ooh look at this! Hello my darling, is this man bothering you?" Milton stopped what he was doing and walked towards them, and out around to the front of the bar. He hugged both of them, kissing each one on the cheek.

"He's not bothering me, much. How are you dear?" Ashley asked, returning the hug and kiss.

"Not bad for an old man," Milton said, wiping his brow.

"You're not old! I think you're perfect."

"I have to agree with her, Milton. Though I not might be thinking about that exactly the same way she is," Townes smiled.

"Not braggin' if you can do it," Milton smiled, holding up his arm to flex his muscles.

"Not at all," Ashley said, hugging him harder.

"Come sit and talk to me while I finish up," Milton said, moving back behind the bar.

"We don't want to keep you, we just wanted to say good night," Townes said, enjoying this time at the bar more than usual.

"Who's keeping me? You sit, watch me fill out paperwork, what could be more exciting for either of us?"

"Are you sure?" Ashley asked.

"I can do this in my sleep sometimes I do. I might be asleep now. You wouldn't know."

"We would see your pajamas, that is always a tip off," Townes said.

Milton laughed, shook his head and disappeared behind the door to the back.

"He always moves so smoothly," Townes said.

"I never thought of it that way."

"I was here with a friend one time, and he was mesmerized, just watching Milton, how he moved around the bar."

"It comes from the soul," Ashley said, squeezing Townes's arm.

The large dinner and the long day had caught up with them. Both were content with the silent setting of the closing bar, their good friend somewhere nearby. Townes smiled, nodding his head.

"What?" Ashley asked softly.

"This is my favorite time here."

"How do you mean?"

"When everyone is gone, when it's quiet, but Milton is still here. I can't tell you how many times I have sat right here, after a chaotic day, a long flight from California, whatever. Just sat here and enjoyed this."

Ashley looked around the silent room, then back to Townes.

"It is like nothing bad is going to happen to you, no matter what. You are in a sanctuary, a protected place, with the master of protection ... or something like that," Townes said, rubbing his hand gently on the bar.

Ashley said nothing, mirroring his eye movement, as if they both knew exactly the same thing, looking at exactly the same areas of the bar at the same time.

"This is why I come here, Townes smiled"

CHAPTER 22

Milton reappeared with two wine glasses, both filled with a generous offering of something gold in hue.

"Good thing I caught them before they threw this out," he said, placing the stemware in front of Townes and Ashley. "Some pretty good Sauternes, I don't know."

"Thank you, Milton," Ashley said.

"Yes, thank you, Sir."

"Eh, hate to see waste when I can pour it for two of my favorite people. How was the show tonight?"

"It was tremendous," Townes said.

"He's exaggerating," Ashley said quietly.

"I'm sure he's not. This boy always tell the truth, that's why I like him. No BS," Milton smiled.

"Being a writer, being in the business world, that statement is virtually impossible."

"Yeah, I guess you're right at that. Well, he doesn't BS me, and if he BS'd you, I would hear about it and then he would hear about it."

"Yes, you would," Ashley said, looking at Townes.

"I thought about adopting him, but I don't know," Milton said, patting Townes on his hand then turning to resume putting the bar to bed for the night.

"I have a couple of paying jobs, and my own health insurance," Townes said.

"Done!" Milton said, not looking up from his detail.

"Isn't he sweet?" Ashely said.

"I love him."

"So do I. He's also never wrong about people"

"Well, everyone he's ever introduced me to was all right."

"I would say that's accurate, especially in your case."

"He might have stretched the truth a bit, in my case."

"He most certainly did not. I wouldn't be spending time with you, were that the case."

"He probably put something in your drink, has you off balance."

"Not hardly."

"Well, here's to Milton," Townes said, raising his glass.

"Yes, here's to Milton. We're drinking to you, Milton."

"Thank you, my darling," Milton said, blowing a kiss without looking up.

"It's not the first or last time either," Townes added.

"Bless you both."

Townes and Ashley smiled at him, then at each other. They were at peace before, but the inclusion of their friend in their serenity made it all the better. As Townes had said, nothing bad was going to happen to you here. Their light breathing, Milton's occasional clinking of bottles and talking to himself were the only sounds in the bar.

"It's late and I don't want to be in trouble with the production company for keeping their star out too late."

"I'm in the production, I'm not a star, and you need only be concerned with not being in trouble with that wonderful man there with the reading glasses," Ashley said, motioning to Milton putting away bottles and marking them on a paper on a clipboard.

Townes laughed. "Never will get on his bad side, I promise."

"Good."

"And you are the star," Townes said, taking a drink.

"I don't like that term, so please don't use it."

"All right," Townes said, feeling terrible he had done so. "I'm sorry, I …"

"Shh, it's OK. Listen, how would you like to come up and see the boys? They would like that."

"They've probably forgotten me already."

"I really don't think anyone ever forgets you."

"Everyone forgets me, or tries to. Isn't that right Milton? Everyone forgets me."

"I don't remember," Milton said, again not looking up.

"See?"

Ashley laughed and touched Townes on the shoulder. "You two should be on the stage."

"Not me, they'd bust out the rotten produce," Milton laughed.

"Not me. Being the writer is enough. Only have to deal with scathing reviews, but no risk of getting whacked with a piss peach."

"A what?"

"Nothing … just no on stage for me."

Ashley frowned at Townes. "Milton, we are going to leave you to finish. I will try to get by tomorrow to see you."

"All right my dear," Milton said, taking his reading glasses off and returning to where Townes and Ashley were seated.

Townes and Ashley got up to bid him good night. Milton hugged and kissed them like before.

"Thank you for coming in to see an old man."

"We didn't see one, but if one comes in, tell him we didn't get a bill for the drinks," Townes said.

"It was a vision problem."

"Vision problem?"

"Yeah, I couldn't see charging you for something they were going to throw out. Good night. I'll see you tomorrow," Milton said, hugging and kissing them again, then returning to tend to his work.

"Hard to argue with him, isn't it?" Ashley said.

Townes held up a finger, watching and waiting for Milton to walk away before he reached in his pocket, pulling out his money clip. He took some bills out and put them on the bar. "Now we can go," as he started walking. "I tried arguing with him once, but that ended pretty quickly, so now I just do as he says."

"Well, he said he would adopt you."

"There could be a lot worse things, so that would be all right."

Ashley smiled, locking arms with Townes. "Let's go see the boys."

"OK."

They got in the small elevator and took it to Ashley's suite. The hallway as silent as anywhere a person would ever go. The dogs greeted them at the door, excited to see them both.

"See, I told you."

"They're excited to see you."

"To see us."

"Sure. Do we need to take them out?"

"No, one of the hotel people took them out already, so they should be good. You boys need to go out?" Ashley asked.

The dogs moved towards the couch, in no hurry to leave. Townes got down on the floor and rubbed his head on both dogs, scratching and petting them.

"I told you."

"I love dogs."

"You think they don't know that?"

"I feel sorry for someone who doesn't love dogs. I think they are missing a lot," Townes said.

"Come sit a minute."

"I need to let you get your rest."

"Shush. Come look out the window," Ashley said, leading Townes and the dogs over to a couch by the window. Central Park bathed in darkness, save for the street lamps, the buildings a frame for the dark canvas, dotted with lights.

"Your view from the top here is quite a bit better than mine," Townes said as he sat down, the dogs settling at his feet, Ashley sitting next to him, putting her head on his shoulder.

"Thank you for coming to the show, going to dinner with me, and ... walking the dogs. I'm tired all of a sudden," Ashley said, her eyes closing.

"Thank you for ..."

Ashley put her finger over Townes's mouth. "No talking, just quiet ... with dogs ... stay for a while ..."

Townes let out a short breath, Ashley's finger still on his lips.

CHAPTER 23

Morning came, the daylight view of Central Park now spectacular with the addition of colors. Townes walked quietly around the large suite, not wanting to wake Ashley. There were some photos around the suite, of Ashley at the theater with people, a photo of Ashley with Milton, photos of Ashley and the dogs in Central Park. There were no photos that indicated a boyfriend or husband. He had not asked her and he thought she certainly would have said something. It was hard to keep secrets in the world she lived, so the best way to do that was probably not to have any. There was much he did not know about her but he knew she would tell him whatever he asked her. The dogs came out of the back of the suite to greet him.

"You guys be quiet," Townes whispered. "Don't want to wake the boss."

He walked softly back from where the dogs came, peeking through the slightly opened door to see Ashley in the bed smiling back at him.

"It's OK, I'm awake ... sort of," she said, closing her eyes and stretching.

"I didn't mean to wake you."

"You didn't, these guys did. They do that more often than not."

"I took them out this morning. How are you this morning?"

"Oooh, I'm tired, but I feel good. Staying with a wine nightcap probably saved me. Thank you for taking them out."

"Happy to do it. Yes, finishing the evening with a plus-sized cocktail from the big man downstairs can sometimes make for a cloudy morning."

"Uh huh. Are you leaving?"

"I was just wandering around your house … your room here."

"Did you find anything interesting?"

"Great view, nice dogs, you. Those all fall into that category, I think," Townes smiled.

"Well, I was with you up until that last one, I really don't think I am that interesting."

"I know someone who says that same thing, I disagree with them on that point, just like I disagree with you."

"Well, I don't know them, but I do know I am right on this one."

"You can say that, but I'm not buying it. You were so great in the show last night. I don't think someone can do that sort of thing and not be interesting."

"Sure they can, it's just acting," Ashley yawned.

"Which is interesting, just by its very nature."

"I don't know."

"It's connecting, or making a connection, that sort of thing. I read in the *New York Times*, I think, I forget when, that going to plays and going to sporting events are sort of the same. There is a personal connection made that stays with the person … the attendee, sort of forever."

"Really? So seeing me in a Broadway show makes me like the Yankees?"

"No!"

"Well, that's what you said," Ashley said, sitting up in the bed.

"There is a connection made. It's live, it's real, it stays with you. TV, movies and such make everything seem easy when it really is not. It is hard for you to get up there and do that, no retake, no do over. Baseball game, same way. There is tomorrow to do it better, or different, but the same person might not be there watching you, watching the Yankees, so they will remember … they will connect with what happened that day they were there."

"So I am like the Yankees," Ashley said, rubbing her eyes.

"No, nothing like the Yankees."

"Are you a baseball fan?"

"Huge baseball fan and you are not anything like them."

"Well, we should go to a game together sometime and see," Ashley said, pulling Townes into the bed.

Back in his own room, Townes was giving thought to going back to sleep when the phone rang.

"Yes," he said, answering the phone.

"Hi … it's Kat. How are you?"

"Kat. I'm … I'm good, how are you? Kind of early out there, isn't it?"

"Yes, I have a bunch of things to do and was up, so thought I might call. That's all right, I hope?"

"Of course it is! I was going to call you today anyway to see how you were doing."

"You're just saying that."

"No, I'm not. Why would I just say that? I wanted to hear your voice."

"Really?"

"Yes, really."

"Well, I like the sound of that."

"Me too. How is paradise?" Townes asked, scratching his head.

"Great, as always. How is New York?"

"Great, as always."

"As much as Zeeder says you are in New York, I'm sort of surprised you don't live there."

"One day, maybe. A place here, a place there. Got to hit a pretty good lick first."

"That sounds good. I don't know if I could live there, but maybe."

"Here and there, just about the best of many things."

"I suppose. When are you coming back?"

"A couple of days, I think. I have a couple more meetings."

"Good meetings, or the other kind?"

"Well, I always hope to avoid the other kind. I have a book meeting,"

"That's good, right?"

"Let's hope. How's the doctor business?"

"The same. It is exactly the same. Always booming, I am somewhat fatigued to say. I would feel better if everyone's mental health suddenly was perfect and I had to become a potter, or something, I don't know," Kat said, matter-of-factly.

"Would you like to get together when I get back? This sounds sort of like a career crisis."

"Yes, I would like that very much. I might need a change of scenery."

"I would like that. It would be great to see you. It shouldn't be more than a couple of days. You have to tell me about this clairvoyant, or whatever thing it is you have."

"Umm. I don't know."

"You start telling me things about me, after knowing me for a few minutes, I think that merits a bit of explaining."

"We'll see."

"Maybe you already can see."

"Hah, funny."

"I am curious about this."

"We'll see."

"I certainly hope so."

"Well, enjoy New York, and good luck with the book stuff."

"Thank you. I'm meeting with my editor. Hopefully that will go well."

"I'll keep my fingers crossed."

"Thank you."

"Maybe we will celebrate when you get home."

"Well, I'm not sure about that," Townes said, shaking his head.

"We can celebrate your return. How does that sound?"

"All right."

"Oh, my friend Annie, she said to tell you hello."

Townes paused, and said nothing.

"Are you still there?"

"Yes, yes I'm still here. Annie, how is she ... how is she doing?"

"She is fine. She said she really enjoyed listening to you the other night and she wants to see you again ... or, hear you again, whatever."

"Well, yes ... well, that ... tell her thank you, and we'll be playing somewhere ... at a bar near her soon," Townes stammered, rubbing his forehead.

"Ok. Do you have a schedule?"

"Zeeder does. Ask him, if you see him."

"I will. Annie said she would like to hear more of you next time, more than last time ... longer, I mean."

"Did she have to go meet her husband, or boyfriend, I don't remember."

"No, a patient. She's not married, no boyfriend."

"Good ..."

"What?"

"Good, that I now remember why she had to leave. I couldn't remember why. She seemed very nice."

"She is completely nice ... too nice, really."

"How's that?"

"Just that she is a really fine person, that's all. People take advantage of her sometimes."

"You're a nice person."

"Thank you, but it's completely different with her. She has had people in her life that she would be better off telling thanks but no thanks. You know what I mean?" Kat said the last part more loudly.

"Not sure."

"We can talk about it when you get back. It's like ex-boyfriend kind of stuff. Better off giving them the shove off," Kat said forcefully.

"Oh. Not sure I see, but OK."

"Good luck with the book. Don't forget me when you are a successful writer."

"You are a successful doctor, don't forget about me when you hang up."

Kat laughed. "I might. Not likely, though."

"Well ..."

"Well what?"

"I won't if you won't."

"Deal."

"Good."

"Look forward to both of us getting together ... and not forgetting."

"Me too. See you when I get back."

"Bye."

Townes hung up the phone and fell backwards onto the bed. He looked up at the ceiling, rubbing his eyes with his thumb and forefinger. He paused, then looked out the window.

CHAPTER 24

Townes showered and dressed, putting on dark slacks, blue dress shirt, and dark sport coat. He had meetings with his client from yesterday, then with his editor. He had a great deal of anticipation for the day. Maybe it would continue as well as it had begun. He was a little tired but moved to get out of the room as quickly as he could. He got to the door of the room, again finding an envelope had been pushed under the door. He opened and read the letter inside.

Townes,
Thank you for everything yesterday. I had a really great time. The boys like you a lot, and they are pretty good judges of character, so I'm thinking you might just be all right. I would really like to see you again, so let's get together before you leave the city, your schedule permitting. I can see why Milton wants to adopt you.
Love,
Ash

Townes smiled, and thought this was going to be a pretty good day. He stopped by the club lounge, greeted Lauren at the desk, and proceeded to get something quick, yet still civilized, for breakfast. He pulled Ashley's note out of his sport coat pocket, reading it again, hoping he would feel the same after his meetings. He glanced at the paper, checking for nothing in particular.

He had some fresh berries and cream, coffee and a croissant. A nap would be nice.

He again walked to his client's office. He had not walked the dogs today, so the distance seemed shorter than yesterday. He had it on good authority that the dogs liked him, so maybe he could walk them again before he left.

He had been thinking about Kat, even before she called. Zeeder had been trying to get him to call her, and maybe he should have done that before. He thought that her being a doctor put her out of his league, but that did not seem to be an issue for her. Ashley was an actress, which certainly put her way out of his league, but that did not seem to be an issue for her, either. Zeeder had said "it don't matter none what nobody does, iffin they get along together." He needed to look at it that way, as the other way was pretty ridiculous when he sat and thought about it. He knew nothing about Annie, though he knew more now than he knew an hour ago. She seemed as out of his league as the others but at this point he was beginning to hear Zeeder's philosophy, complete with his Kentucky drawl.

After his business meeting, he left to meet with his editor. Normally Townes only spoke with his editor over the phone. This time he wanted to meet in person. It had been a while since they had gotten together and his editor had been, or he hoped had been, circulating the novel with his contacts in the business. He had been in the business forever, and knew a great number of people in it. Yet the idea of getting published seemed, to Townes, like his new female friends, out of his league. It was a constant battle to not listen to the voices about that. He thought it was like an aspiring baseball player, and that Ashley was right, that if he ever thought about the odds of actually making it professionally, he would never even pick up a ball.

He had a little longer walk to meet his editor for their lunch at the Four Seasons Restaurant. He would stay on Park Avenue to Fifty Second Street to get there. It was a fine, fall day, and he enjoyed the walk. The installation art on Park was always something to see. The gorilla statue reminded him of one of the guys in the band. He laughed when he thought what Zeeder might say if he were here. He was not sure that Zeeder had ever been here, but thought it would be quite an experience for him. Zeeder only really talked about Kentucky, sometimes Tennessee, with no real references to anywhere else.

The Four Seasons was buzzing like always. Not loud, but more of an "important-things-are-going-on-here" type of vibe. Townes always tried to have lunch here when he came to New York. It was better to dine with someone here, but if no one was available, Townes came here anyway and ate at the bar. Patrick, Townes's editor, had been working with him for quite some time on the book. Maybe Patrick was tired of working with him. Maybe it was too draining to work with a first time writer. Patrick had a stable of writers, good ones, real ones, accomplished ones. Townes had once remarked that his client list was like a big bowl of fruit, and Townes was the potato in the bowl. Maybe Patrick was going to thin the bowl.

Townes checked in at the captain's station. He was early, but he didn't mind waiting. He chose to sit at the bar, both for a drink and for the view of the bustle of this storied establishment. He watched the chain mail curtains undulate with a hypnotic movement, always a calming detail of the place. Townes always imagined being here discussing a big business deal, maybe a book deal. The barman welcomed him and asked him what he could bring him. Townes ordered a club soda and bitters. He didn't need a cocktail before lunch. He hoped he could say the same after the meeting.

Watching the patrons, watching the billow of the metal curtains, was all a pleasant interlude. He knew he had to stay in motion while he was in New York. He could hang out on the beach back at home. New York offered a contrasting type of therapy that he was glad to receive. The ambience was a different flavor to savor, just as the dishes they served would be.

Townes saw Patrick enter the restaurant, He put some money on the bar, thanked the barman and made his way over to meet Patrick, where they embraced.

"Hello sir," Townes said.

"Hello Townes. You must be the most tanned person in here. California still seems to be to your liking."

"No, I got this walking around the city."

"Yes, and I surf on the East River," Patrick laughed. "How are you?"

"I think pretty well, but you tell me. How are you?

"Well. How has the city been treating you?

"Better than I have a right."

The maître d' led them to their table.

"I'm sorry, I forgot to ask you if the Grill Room was all right. Did you want to sit in the Pool Room?"

"No, this is fine. I like both of them equally."

"Me, too."

They were seated and both men looked around the restaurant.

"It is always comforting to know a place like this still exists," Patrick said, taking a full breath.

"I agree."

"I've been coming here for more years than I can count, and I never get tired of it. Of course, I don't come here that often."

"I try to get here whenever I'm in New York, but it doesn't always work out," Townes said.

"So we agree that it is all right that we are here?"

"I think so."

"You think so?"

"Well, it is always good to see you in person, and it is always good to come here ... unless you have bad news."

"Ever the optimist."

"Hey, I don't know how all this works."

"Why do you think I have bad news?"

"I don't know ... maybe that thinning the fruit bowl thing."

Patrick laughed, shaking his head. "I'm not a farmer."

"I have the utmost respect for the trade, but depending upon the weather it is really a harsh way to make a living, almost as bad as consulting and trying to get a book published."

"Indeed it is."

A waiter returned to their table, mentioning the specials, asking them what they would like to drink.

"I think a drink would be good. How about a Beefeater Martini, up?" Patrick said.

"Very good, and for you, sir?"

"Old school, huh? OK, well, hmm, all right, I'll have the same. Olives too, please."

"Yes, olives," Patrick said.

"As you wish, gentlemen. I shall be right back."

"We don't get together that often ... well, never, actually ... so you know, a drink isn't a bad thing, right?" Patrick asked.

"Well, I've never thought of a drink as a bad thing," Townes smiled.

"Good, I didn't think you would object."

"Not now, not ever."

"Not ever?"

"You know what I mean."

"I do not always know what you mean, only how I interpret what I think you mean, as an editor …"

"Right, but currently you are not editing, you are sitting here with me, at the Four Seasons, ordering Martinis."

"I have a lot of great memories of this place."

"Living in New York, all you have to do is get in a cab, or walk to some of the finest places anywhere."

"Well, living here, one tends to take it for granted that this is possible, that this is available."

"How can you take it for granted?" Townes asked, looking around the room.

"Poor choice of words. My meaning was that you live here, you do this. You do not know that it is not the same elsewhere, say in warmer, western cities, as an example. You go to grade school where the playground is asphalt, you assume it is the same elsewhere."

"Grade school? Wow! That one takes me back."

"Yes, well, the similarity of the comparisons should give you ample visualization," Patrick said, starting to fidget.

"Always the editor. Are you—"

"Here you are, gentlemen: two Beefeater martinis," the waiter said, placing the drinks in front of the two.

"Ah, excellent," Patrick said.

"I will let you enjoy your cocktail. I will be back to take your order. Do you have any questions about the menu?"

"Not yet, but I may after the drink," Townes smiled.

"Excellent, sir. Enjoy."

Patrick lifted his cocktail, the frost showing on the glass. "Here's to you Townes and to the best of luck in your literary journey."

"Thank you," Townes said, raising his glass.

They drank, each taking a breath after. Townes set his drink back on the table, Patrick held onto his, taking another drink.

"Yes, excellent memories, excellent memories," Patrick said, taking another drink.

Townes took another small sip to see if Patrick would follow, the action. He did. The waiter had just set the drinks there and Patrick was nearly ready for a refill.

"Is everything all right?" Townes asked.

"What? Oh, of course. Where is that waiter?" Patrick said, looking around, finishing his cocktail. Locating the waiter, Patrick made eye contact and gently moved the glass from side to side, the waiter nodding.

Townes took a sip and started looking at the menu, shaking his head at the items listed. "These all sound really good."

"Hmm? Oh ... I guess I should take a look."

"You don't normally see roasted squab, black trumpet risotto, foie gras, truffle sauce where I live. Hell, the dumb bastards where I live outlawed foie gras. Can you believe the stupidity of that?" Townes said. "The complete outlawing of any and all meat can't be far behind out there."

"What? Oh, really ... hmm," Patrick looked to focus on the menu.

Townes shook his head and took a sip of his drink as Patrick finished his. "It is just a different class of culinary excellence. Maybe if I go up to Beverly Hills, I could probably eat like this ... Beverly Hills Hotel. Up to Napa, The French Laundry. One day. Need a reason to celebrate to go do that. I always wanted to stay at the Beverly Hills Hotel."

"Where?"

"Where what?"

"Where did you say?"

"I said I wanted to go up to Beverly Hills, eat and stay at the Beverly Hills Hotel. Go up to Napa, eat at the French Laundry. Are you OK?"

"I ... um ... I just ..."

The waiter returned with another martini for Patrick. "Here you are, Sir. Would you like another martini, as well?"

"No, I am fine, thank you. Maybe a glass of the Lucia Pinot Noir."

"Very good. Are you ready to order?"

"I think so. Patrick?"

"Hmm? You go ahead."

"Duck consommé, the bison carpaccio, and the squab."

"Very good. And for you sir?"

"Duck consommé, and the dover sole."

"Excellent," the waiter said, clearing the spent martini, setting the new one.

The waiter walked away. Townes just continued to look around the room, fascinated by the chain metal curtains, the elaborate chandelier above the bar. The high ceilings, the windows, the light made him feel like he was floating.

He could sense something was wrong but was not going to press Patrick on the issue. He was quite certain the rapid-fire first, and the quick-to- follow-second martinis would assist Patrick in saying whatever was on his mind. Townes was content to float.

"I came here once, with some big shot writer. I forget when it was. He told me I was wrong to try to alter his work, and that I was just some stupid fucking editor, and he said he could hire another one … in the bathroom passing out fucking towels," Patrick said, taking a drink. "You know what I told him?"

"Not yet."

"I told him he couldn't hire the men's room attendant to edit his work. He asked why not and I said because I was already working with the attendant on his novel because I wanted to finally work with a writer that didn't have his head shoved up his own ass."

"What did he say?"

"He laughed, told me to shut up and finish my lunch."

"Did you?"

"Of course, I finished my lunch. We were at the Four Seasons. Fuck that sonofabitch. I need another drink."

"OK."

"There were some good times here."

"Like that one?"

"That wasn't one of the good ones. I just thought it interesting."

"At least," Townes chuckled.

"I gave your manuscript to Arielle to see if her agency would pick you up."

"And what did she say?"

Patrick took another sip of his martini then paused. "She said no."

"No. That's it, she just said no? No comments? I don't expect somebody to just pick it up, but I would like some comment to know what or how to improve."

"She said it wasn't compelling."

"That is of such great help. I'll just go back and make it compelling. What the fuck is that supposed to even mean?" Townes probably would not have phrased it quite like that, had martinis not been involved.

"It's a hard business."

"That's what everyone says, and I am well aware of that. Don't get me wrong, I certainly appreciate you giving it to her … there was no guarantee anyway, but when it is someone you are close to, I would think they would offer up something like ... tell your boy he needs more ... more, whatever. Not just "it's not compelling." So, now what? Any other agents you can recommend? Hell you must know a hundred."

"I do, but ..."

"But what?"

"You know, this book is good ... for what it is," Patrick said, looking around the room.

"Good for what it is?"

"Yes, for what it is."

"I have no idea what that means. Before, you told me you liked it."

"Yes, well, the business is changing, the agents, the world, everything is changing. I'm not sure. I'm just rambling. The book world is different now."

"I was only going by what you said when we were working on it, and you said you liked it. If you didn't like it, maybe when we were working on it would have been a good time to tell me you didn't like it, or whatever, but not now that we are done. I guess I ... should have ... ordered that second martini."

CHAPTER 25

Townes didn't remember much about the walk back to the Ritz. He found himself walking through Central Park. There was no need to hurry. This was just another in a long line of rejections, and his editor seemed to be having some sort of personal meltdown, unrelated to their relationship. He would no longer be helping Townes with the book. Having Patrick tell him he was like a son to him was of little consolation. It wasn't personal, but it still was not pleasant.

He walked around the reservoir, past the back side of the Metropolitan Museum of Art, along East Drive, over to Bethesda Fountain, to the band shell, down the Mall and Literary Walk. He paused there, steeped in the irony, sitting down on a bench. Fall sounds were different than spring sounds. They were muted, like the colors. The sun was getting lower. That point of the park was always breathtaking. The orange hues, the dusty sunlight coming through the graying buildings were not going to lift him today, but he still felt them.

He wanted to call Ashley, but he didn't want to bother her. He had just spoken to Kat that morning. He laughed when he thought about wanting to talk to Annie.

I know we just met, but I have this huge crush on you, because I saw you and your ass clown boyfriend one day at the cafe. I was with my dog, and I came back to the cafe the next day to find out your name, and then you showed up with Kat at the bar we were playing. Well, I just wanted you to know that I got turned down again with my book. My editor is joining the French Foreign Legion, or some fucking thing, and ... well, you were the person I most wanted to call. He stuck his finger in his ear. The sounds of the Park, of the fall, were better than the sounds in his head.

It was getting dark now and he thought sleeping on the bench in Central Park was probably not the best idea. He continued south, past Driprock and Dipway Arches, over to Columbus Circle, having overshot his exit by several blocks. He stopped, leaning on the wall that separated the Park from the city. He leaned over the wall, looking back into the Park. He then put his chin on the pitch of the wall, looking down it, eyeing first the Park, then the sidewalk, the people walking towards and away from him. He then repositioned his head on the pitch looking at the buildings across Central Park South, then turning to look back again, into the Park.

"I'd better get back to the hotel," he said, as more than one passerby looked at him. Milton would be at work by now. He thought he might really need his services. Townes got to his room and saw that he had a message from Ashley.

Call Me.

"Hey, somebody that wants to talk to me," he said, dialing the phone.

"Ritz Carlton Central Park. Yes, Mr. Mantle."

"Yes, Miss Meacham please."

"Very good, Sir I'll connect you."

The phone rang.

"Hi, Townes, how is everything?"

"Uh, I would not know where to start. How is everything with you?"

"Everything is fine. I just wanted to know if I could see you tonight after the show."

"Um, yes, that would be great. Are you sure you won't be too tired?"

"I will be tired, but I want to hear about your day. Maybe you could find where to start by then."

"Maybe."

"I know you were meeting with your editor. I just want to hear about everything."

"It would be great to see you, but I'm afraid there won't be much to tell you on that front."

"Oh, no ... oh. I just wanted to get to talk with you, you know, before you become too famous. You might not have time for me later."

"I could not imagine ever not having time for you. The too famous part doesn't appear to be in the cards today."

"You can't say that."

"I think I can always say the first part. The other part seems destined. I haven't done anything yet."

"You can't forget me, and the dogs, they will be so excited to see you again, before you are famous."

"I ... I haven't ..."

"Save it for later, we can talk all about it."

"All right. Any place in particular you would like to go?"

"Maybe Marea. It's just down the street from the hotel. I can meet you there, before eleven? That's not too late, is it?"

"No, it's not too late."

"Great, I'm looking forward to it."

"Well, break a leg ... is that what they say?"

"Yes, it is. I'll see you later to hear the story."

"It was nice of you to ..."

"Shh! See you later. Bye."

Townes hung up the phone and scratched his head. He walked over to the window and looked at the people walking below. This actress had just asked him if he wanted to see her after she finished her performance, and said she was excited to talk to him about his day. He moved to the bed, kicked off his shoes and laid down. The day had been a sour apple. He wanted that taste out of his mouth. He would do his best to avoid telling Milton what had transpired. Right now he needed to rest.

He slept soundly, dreaming of walking where he had just been. He was walking, holding Annie's hand. They were only walking, no conversation. She was seeing the Park for the first time, he serving as her silent tour guide. They sat on a high point, some large rock formation, saying nothing, taking it all in. Then, he saw Annie alone, a long ways away from him where she sat on the rock. It began to rain on her. She was looking down, tears in her eyes, her clothes becoming wet, but she just sat there. When he looked again, his view was of a vineyard. Townes awoke suddenly, expecting to be on the beach back in La Jolla. He looked around, trying to get his bearings.

He lay there, thinking about what his next move with the book should be. No agent, editor gone south, no prospects. He thought about Annie, Ashley, about Kat. He was pretty sure they were not thinking about him, but at least one of them wanted to have dinner with him later.

He sat-up, deciding he would get changed to go downstairs to see Milton.

He had slept longer than he thought he would, and he didn't want to stay at the bar too long before he went to meet Ashley, as conversation could be challenging after a prolonged stay with Milton. Milton didn't overdo his craft. He was never going to crank out as many drinks as he could possibly serve. He just had a wonderful way of making a person feel at home, which sometimes created a serious losing track of time.

He dressed and went downstairs. The bar was quite busy, as usual. It was not a large bar, so it only needed a few people there to make it full. It was not like it was an entire room, more like a large hallway with a coatroom, as Milton had described it. In spite of possible architectural limitations, it was still a wonderful place, and Milton was still here. Townes found an open seat.

"There he is, the California Kid," Milton greeted.

"Good evening, sir."

"And how is our friend from the wacky coast this evening."

"Oh, I am not sure."

"Not sure? That mean I have to cheer you up?"

"Do you ever have to cheer me up?"

"No, and I didn't want to start today."

"Well, you don't have to start today. I just have some things I need to figure out."

"Well, I hope whatever you have to figure out can wait until I can make you a drink."

"Everything can always wait until then."

"Good."

"Something light. I'm meeting Ashley after a bit, and I don't want to be … you know."

"No, I don't know. Do I usually send you out of here heavy?"

"No, I guess not."

"You're damn right not."

"Sorry."

"Ashley, she is sweet, isn't she?"

"She certainly is. Thank you for the good reference."

"You could do worse, you know," Milton grinned.

"How's that?"

"Worse is nobody, and you are always with worse."

"You have a point."

"Yes, always … though sometimes it takes a while, and even I am not always sure what it is. What were we talking about?"

"Ashley."

"Right. I would rather talk about her than you. She's better looking," Milton said.

"No argument here. More interesting than I am, too."

"You meeting her after the show?"

"Yes, late dinner, at Marea."

"How about that."

"Can't figure it myself."

"What's to figure?"

"She's in a different league," Townes said, tapping his fingers together.

"So maybe it's time for you to get out of the minors and into the big leagues."

"Not sure about that."

"The big league calls you up, you gonna tell 'em to call back later?"

"Not sure they are calling me up."

"Sheesh! You west coasters aren't very bright. She's seeing you, isn't she?" Milton said, waving his hands.

"Yes."

"You think it's out of pity?"

"Could be."

She doesn't invite pity to walk her dogs, go to her show, and have dinner ... twice."

"You seem to know quite a bit."

"Of course I do. I made it through the eighth grade," Milton said, puffing his chest out.

"That's not what I meant."

"No, you're questioning my education? I learned a lot those eight years. It was Brooklyn, ya know."

"Book smart, way beyond your years."

"Hah! Street smart, baby. Sort of where you need some more schooling, my friend, but you're not from Brooklyn. You live in California, so I don't know if I have time to teach you all this stuff."

"I do appreciate your trying," Townes nodded.

"Who said I was?"

"Ashley asked you about me."

"She supposed to go out with a stranger ... not do some checkin' around?

How do you know I gave you a good recommendation?" Milton shrugged.

"Well, someone did."

"One of the door guys probably, they're always telling stories."

"They know me better than you?"

"Probably few people know you better than me. Even more reason not to suspect me ... sayin' somethin' nice."

Townes laughed. "Yes, now that I think about it, it must have been somebody else."

"There you go."

"I'm glad we got that settled."

"Me too. Now let's settle this 'something light' thing. Maybe I could get the kitchen to get some cotton candy ... since Coney Island is closed."

"I don't think ..."

"You eat yet?"

"Meeting Ashley for dinner...."

"Yes, but that's not 'til after the show. You might starve to death by then."

"I doubt it. I had lunch at the Four Seasons."

"I love that place. I had money, I'd eat there," Milton nodded.

"Pretty sure you have more money than me."

"How about a Negroni? One of my, if not my favorite, drink. It has a lot of depth of flavor. Or now that you are dating an actress, you are drinking some sort of ..."

"Wouldn't call it dating," Townes cut him off.

"I'm old, remember?"

"You're not old, and I'm not dating."

"What would you call it?"

"I wouldn't call it anything."

"Well, it's not nothing."

Townes started to respond, then paused. "It's not nothing."

"That's right," Milton said shaking his head.

"Maybe."

"Maybe what?"

"Maybe you're right."

"That's what I been tellin' you," Milton rubbed his forehead, looking at Townes like he was crazy.

Townes laughed, looking around bar, rubbing his eyes. He glanced back out to the lobby bar area. The piano player was on a break, or maybe not there.

He didn't remember whether he saw someone sitting there when he came in. He looked up at the high ceiling, wondering why he had written a book in the first place. All the work, all the money spent, and what did he have to show for it?

"Any goddamn chimp can write a book," he muttered. When he turned back, there was a Negroni in front of him.

Townes smiled. "Thank you."

"Maybe this will help your head."

"What's wrong with my head?"

"I don't know, but it's something, based on the conversation we just had. How was your day today?"

"Hard."

"I grew up in Brooklyn, before it was *trés chic* to live there, so hard is relative," Milton grinned.

"Let's see ... um, lunch with my editor."

"Yeah, Four Seasons. He fire you?"

"Yes, how did you know?"

"You said hard, so I didn't figure it was good news."

"Yeah, it kind of sucks. Maybe I need to find another line of work ... a couple, actually."

"All the way out in California, I can't look after you. Maybe you need to move here, so I can keep an eye on you."

"I, uh, hell, I don't know what I'm going to do but I'm going to do something."

"Be nice you come around here more often."

"You have been more than kind."

"Hey, you stand back here long enough, you start to figure out who's worth a damn and who's not worth a damn."

"Yeah, I'm not sure how I made the cut. I never seem to see shit coming."

"You're fine. We just need to get you past this."

"You have gone above and beyond, introduced me to Ashley."

"You are seeing, or whatever the hell you call it, a very sweet girl."

"Whatever you want to call it."

"Anybody back home going to object to you seeing her?" Milton asked.

"Not really."

"'Not really?' What the hell does that mean? Sheesh! I need a book to figure out what you hippies out there are talkin' about."

"Hippies?" Townes laughed.

"What do you mean 'not really'?"

"I'm not seeing someone," Townes paused. "I have seen someone a couple of times and she seems to be really a great person. I think she wants to leave the country, work overseas, and I think that is going to happen very soon, so that makes things a bit difficult. I just, by chance, saw this other woman, before I met this one. Turns out, it's her best friend. I had no idea. I feel bad about ... well, not bad, but I do feel weird about it."

"Hah! This is gettin' good."

"Yeah, forget I said anything."

"About the one you're seeing, or the one you want to see."

"Both. She is just so...."

"Just so what? And which one!? I need a program to follow this."

"Me too, and it's me we're talking about. You know I don't operate this way. I haven't been with anyone in ... forever."

"You go from nuthin' to somethin' in a helluva hurry," Milton laughed.

"Not really. One is leaving the country, and I don't even know the other one."

"Well?"

"Well what?"

"Well ... I got to tend to the other folks here, but I need to think about this a little."

CHAPTER 26

It was a short walk down Central Park South from the Ritz to Marea. It was later than he thought, probably due to his extra-long nap, induced by the stress of the day. The Negronis and a visit with Milton had helped his disposition, but he was still discouraged from the lunch conversation with his editor. All the time and effort now seemed wasted. He would probably not be good company tonight for Ashley, and he didn't think she needed to hear his problems. She was a very genuine person, which was not an invitation for him to dump his troubles on her. This friendship had evolved fairly quickly, thanks to the referral from Milton, but he wasn't going to pour his heart out to her about how disappointed he was that his editor had gone off the deep end of the martini pool and was now deserting him, how the book maybe have been a waste of time, and how he was rattled down to his very core about the possible mistake he had made by leaving corporate America, starting his own thing, and now not even wanting to do that anymore.

Yep, she is going to love talking to me, one of the characters said, as he walked along, glancing across the street to where the hansom cabs were lined earlier in the day and would again be tomorrow. Looking at the wall he had focused on earlier, Central Park on the other side of it, the messages of these things made his head feel like stirring concrete.

He found himself seated at the bar, the back wall some sort of caramel and white granite, backlit to give it a rather mesmerizing quality, like swirling illuminated ice cream. He ordered a club soda and bitters. Ashley was not here yet. He was starting to have trouble keeping track of time. He didn't know whether to think Ashley was late, or if he was early. He really only hoped he had the day right. It was starting to run together like the colors on the back wall of the bar. He had been on the book project a long time, and the recent setback made him consider the possibility of moving on, working on other things. He wasn't sure if he was even glad he wrote it, taking all that time, time he would never get back. He was disappointed that the project had reached a less-than-desirable conclusion and it gave him an empty feeling, not because someone had again turned him down, but more that people he had trusted had been less than upfront with him. Now here he was, drinking club soda and bitters.

Someone touched him on the shoulder, whispering in his ear.

"Sorry, I'm late."

It took Townes a second to respond.

"What? Oh, you are not late, I was probably early. My sense of time seems to be ..."

"I don't want to talk about time. I want to talk about your day," Ashley said, kissing him on the cheek.

"Could we talk about you ... how was the show?"

"It was good. Not as good as when you were there, but still good. I want to talk about your day," Ashley persisted.

"No, I think talking about the show would be more fun."

"Oh, that doesn't sound good."

"Well, I gave it a shot. Lots of shots, actually. More shots than I can count. Probably time to move on. Please sit, you have to be tired," Townes said, standing, pulling a seat out for Ashley.

Ashley smiled and settled in to her seat next to him. "You can't say that. Not yet."

"Well, I can say that. I've been at this a while. Maybe it just wasn't meant to be."

"Listen, I don't know you all that well ... yet ... but I am a pretty good judge of certain things, and I think you just need a break, and believe me, I know how it is to need a break. I appreciate you sharing this with me, so you just need to hear me out."

"I have to tell you, I have enjoyed spending the time with you, I really have. Milton always says I can only talk with him so long, and I need to get out more, though he sometimes doesn't let me leave."

"He truly is like being with family."

"Better. Family doesn't treat as well."

"Good evening. What can I get for you tonight?" The bartender asked.

"I'll have what he's having," Ashley said, pointing to Townes.

"Pretty exciting, club soda and bitters. You may want to reconsider," Townes said.

"No, I'm fine with that."

"Very good," the bartender said.

"So back to you."

"Hey, you have to be tired after doing a show. We could talk about that, or something, anything else."

"Like I said, I know what it means to need a break, and I think you deserve a break. Milton would not have said the things he told me about you if you weren't somebody special."

"He's getting older. He probably got confused and was telling you about somebody else."

"Stop it. I can feel something about you, so it isn't all just Milton. Everybody needs help. So start thinking about that. Then I want you to think about the concept that all things are connected. It is sort of difficult to grasp at first, but not all that difficult, if that makes sense. When you start understanding you are more connected to certain people you will see a difference between them and those that you maybe do not feel connected with. It's possible that then you will notice that someone that you are feeling closer to has an additional … I don't know, a certain light about them. When you begin to realize that all things are connected, it becomes easier to recognize someone that has the energy, has the light."

"The light?"

"Yes, the light."

"What light?" Townes said, looking up at the illumination around the bar.

"Stop it. All people have an aura, but most are hard to see because they are so negative in their lives. By that I mean the people are so negative that their aura is not seen. If you are so fortunate, and believe me, not everyone is, you can see the auras. To take it a step further, when you see someone with the light, it really stands out. Milton has the light. You have the light."

"I have the light?"

"Oh, most definitely. I saw it the first time we met, felt it before we met, actually."

"I think you are thinking about somebody …"

"Here you are, club soda and bitters," the bartender interrupted.

"Oh, thank you." Ashley said, smiling. She waited for him to move until she continued with Townes. "No, you have it."

"I don't know about that."

"Look, if you just start training yourself to notice what is different about the people you are attracted to, you will start to see what I am talking about, and I'm not talking about people that are pretty, or just good looking on the outside. I'm talking about the thing that leads you to them, connects you to them more than others."

"You said all things are connected."

"Yes, they are. Some things are more connected. You encounter someone with the light, well ... it just sort of changes you. It changes you for the good."

Townes squinted, pressing his lips together and shaking his head. "Well, there are certain people that you just know are different but ..."

"Well, now you know what it is, and why. You are going to be surprised at the changes this will bring to your life. Provided that you pay attention to it, which is not so easy at first," Ashley said, making a circle on the bar with her finger.

"Light. Not so easy?"

"Yes, light. Yes, not so easy. You already have it, you probably have just been fighting it."

"That and everything else," Townes said, moving his glass in small circles on the bar.

"What do you mean?"

"Nothing, just a little overwhelmed. But I would say you have this light."

"How do you know?" Ashley asked, leaning closer to him.

"Well ... if things are as you say ..."

"They are," Ashley nodded.

"Well, then I think you have it."

"And you know this because?"

"I don't know why I know, I just know," Townes said, staring at the designs of the back bar.

"Because I'm an actress, you can't be sure."

"No, that's not it. I am out of touch on a lot of things, like if not knowing who you were, was not example enough, but I knew there was something about you." Townes paused. "Pretty deep stuff, you know, for club soda."

Ashley laughed and put her hand on his arm. "Something?"

"Hey, I'm brand new to this. I just knew there was a thread somehow."

"You might get this faster than you think."

"I never get anything fast. I didn't know who you were, remember?" Townes said, raising his eyebrows.

"That was not important, who I was. What was important was that you knew there was a connection, just like I said," Ashley said, touching him with her finger.

"Maybe I'm not supposed to have this thing, this light."

"You don't have a choice, it just happens. The ones that recognize it, well, they have a more fulfilled life. I think you will have a great life, based on what I'm seeing."

"You can see all that? Are you sure that's only bitters in that club soda?" Townes asked, looking at her glass.

"Yes."

"In just this short time?"

"Yes."

"How long have you been able to see, er, to do this?" Townes asked.

"A long time."

"What's a long time?"

"A long time," Ashley smiled.

"A long time."

"See, now you're getting it."

"I told you, I never get anything."

"I think you do, you just process it so fast that you think you don't get it."

"I don't know about that."

"You will, you will," Ashley smiled. "You need to put your mind at ease about the events of today. This book thing is going to be very good for you. You just need, as I said, a break. I think this break will be easier than you think. It is always difficult to explain these things that I see. That's why I am very careful about who I mention this to. I only trust a few people with these things I see, these things I know."

"You know this because of this light thing?"

"This light thing. You are funny. How much longer are you going to be in New York?"

"If I hadn't met you and you weren't sitting here, I'd leave hours ago, leave now. Hmm, probably tomorrow. I have to finish a couple of things. Maybe an extra day," Townes said, moving his hand back and forth.

"I hope it's an extra day."

"Well, I've taken quite a bit of your time."

"You have not."

"How much longer are you in New York?"

"The show runs for another month. It is a limited run, and was supposed to be done by now, but we have been so fortunate with the attendance, so they extended it. It has been a fantastic experience," Ashley said smiling and nodding her head.

"I loved the show, and I thought you were great."

"You are biased."

"Yes, I am now, but I think that all right."

"Of course it is."

"Can I ask you a question? It's probably stupid."

"Certainly, and I'm sure it's not stupid."

"Have you ever been to the Beverly Hills Hotel?"

"Yes, many times, why do you ask?"

"I just always wanted to go there … stay there," Townes said, looking out the window at the passersby.

"What's stopping you? You go to nice places here in New York."

"I go to nice places … by myself. I'd like to double the guest list."

Ashley smiled and reached over and touched his hand. "So much is possible, if you are open to the possibility."

"Is that a play on words?"

"Being in my profession, I suppose I see how you might come to that, but no, it's not. If you are open to it, anything can happen. I would gladly go with you, and would very much like to go with you when you go."

They talked more, over Billecart Salmon Rose Champagne, poached oysters with prosciutto, and bowls of lobster risotto. The effervescence helped wash away the clumps of doubt from the day. The bites of the delicate but assertive flavor of the main course diverted the attention just enough to remind them this was supposed to happen. Their discussion was serene. With Ashley's reassuring voice, Townes was thinking less and less about how things with the book had gone sideways. He did not know how he was lucky enough to meet this woman, aside from Milton's introduction, of course, but the more she talked, the more she spoke of everything being connected, that things meant to get together would get together, the less he thought their encounter to be chance. She asked him for a copy of his manuscript and Townes agreed. They talked until they were the last people in the restaurant, the lights starting to come up.

They left Marea and walked back along Central Park, in no hurry to be anywhere, pausing to look at the light of the buildings, the darkness of the park, Ashley on his arm. It was very comfortable and unforced. Townes was baffled at how easy it was to talk to this woman, this famous person. Whenever he asked her about her life, she wanted only to know about him and his life. He was not used to talking about himself, but she made it easy to do so, remembering and talking about things he had not spoken of in a very long time.

Whenever he would stop, she would urge him on to tell her more, saying only that in her world she just had a difficult time relating to people because they all wanted something, wanted to get close to someone famous, so they could become famous themselves. Maybe it was because Townes didn't know who she was when they met. Maybe it was that he had not asked anything of her. He had not asked her out. She had asked him out. It could have to do with her talking about the light, though Townes was still trying to get his mind around it. Strangely enough, he thought he understood it, though he couldn't see how he could so quickly, since he didn't seem to understand anything quickly, except for business at first pass. Understanding this light concept gave him a really good feeling … that and being with Ashley, though it was not in the way one might think.

He was not smitten with her, like he was with Annie. He had such a calm come over him with Ashley. Just thinking about Annie made him nervous. He was trying not to read anything into either vibration. He just tried to maintain his balance. So here he was, walking along Central Park, late at night, with a very keen spirit holding his arm, telling him it was all right to be whatever he wanted and that given the opportunity, she would help him every possible way she could, and he hadn't even asked for any help. Walking along this serene stroll, he was not thinking of help. He *thought* he was not thinking anything at all, and yet somehow this woman was getting him to really *think* about things that before tonight were not familiar to him.

As they finally made their way back to the Ritz, they were both silent for the last block, speaking only to the doorman as they entered. They rode in the small elevator and walked to her room, the dogs not even barking as they entered her room and closed the door.

CHAPTER 27

La Jolla

Townes was happy to be waking up in his own bed back in La Jolla. He thought about Ashely and their conversation about being connected to people and about the light. He avoided thinking about the book, the editor. He got up and looked around for Angelina until he remembered she was still at Zeeder's. He showered, dressed in jeans and a sweater, and made the short trek on foot to Zeeder's apartment. Zeeder was outside again doing his thing, playing the guitar and painting at the same time, Angelina sleeping in the sun, her head popping up quickly when she heard Townes's familiar gait on the patio.

"Well, here he is, Mister Big Apples, his own self," Zeeder said, hitting a chord on the on the guitar.

"It think it's Big Apple, but I appreciate the vote of support. And you did say Big Apple, and not something else?"

"Nope, too early in the morning to discuss your actual real type traits. How's travels? Was it any count?"

"Oh ... was it any what?"

"Nothin'. Please continue."

"Hmm, well, travels is travels," Townes said, now laying down on the patio to get in a scrum with the dog.

"A bit of a piss-poor description from a writer type."

"Yeah, I don't know what to say. How you holding up?"

"Pressure somethin' fierce as you can see, but I am a tryin' to cope the best I know how," Zeeder said, looking out at the view of the Pacific seascape he was painting. "Dog's a pain, women calling for us to come play a private party, stuff like that. Doesn't sound like much, but it adds up," Zeeder said, putting paint to the canvas.

"This paint and play the … at the same … never mind."

"Let's hear about this trip you's just on. Try to be more descriptive this time. You see that bartender feller friend of yours?"

"Always. He's like the emissary of goodwill of New York, at least for me. You need to come meet him," Townes nodded.

"Nosir. Too big a city fer me. I'm a little cramped just being in La Jolla."

"La Jolla's not big."

"My point exactly. Tell me 'bout the travelin'," Zeeder strummed a chord on his guitar.

"You painting or playing or talking to me?"

"Haven't decided. I start paintin' on the guitar, you might want to recalibrate me. How did it go with the, what was it, secret agent, editor, whatever in the fuck it was you was talkin' about."

Townes stopped wrestling with the dog and started to laugh. "Secret agent?"

"I am not familiar with the vernacular of the book business and you said agent, so I was just trying to ascertain the nature of said agent and that was the phraseology that came to mind," Zeeder said, hitting another chord on his guitar.

"Where are you from again?"

"Kentucky, last time I checked."

"They got secret agents there, do they?" Townes said, cocking his head.

"I hears they's ever-where, but ain't never met one my own self … least not knowingly, course."

"Of course. Hate to disappoint you, but she is a literary agent, not a secret agent…that I know of. Whatever kind of agent she is, she isn't going to be my agent, other agents don't want to be my agent, and my editor doesn't want to be my editor anymore."

"So all sorts a good news then. Sounds more fucked up than a soup sandwich," Zeeder said, not taking his eyes off of the painting.

"Something like … like a what?"

"Well, maybe we ought bust open a bottle of Woodford and help you forget about it."

"A little early for Woodford, isn't it?"

"Ok, but I don't think we can find J.T.S. Brown in these parts."

Townes laughed, lying back on the patio, Angelina resting her head on his chest. "Then Woodford would be fine."

"I was a fixin' to get rid of that dog, thinkin' you wasn't comin' back. She's a lot of trouble."

"I noticed that when I walked up, and I think I remember you mentioning it before. Is she adding to your stress level?"

"I'm hidin' my true feelings. It's how us complicated artists are. Outside I'm calm, inside I'm thinkin' about hackin' off my ear. A veritable melange of inspiration and angst," Zeeder said, motioning to his ear.

"Right. That's pretty much how I see you."

"Yep. I'm just a tick away from goin' off."

"Should I be worried, you know, move a little further away?"

"I reckon not. Anything good happen while you was gettin' turned down?"

"Actually, yes."

"Well, unless you is just wantin' to add to my obvious angst, would you care to 'laborate?"

"You first. You said something about someone calling for us to play a gig?" Townes said, scratching Angelina.

"Gina called left a message a few days ago, said she runned into you sommers and you told her we would do that sort of thing for a ridiculously high price."

"I'm drawing a blank."

"Most of the time that I can tell," Zeeder continued on the painting.

"Did she say where?"

"Where what?"

"Where she ran into me," Townes said, looking at the sky.

"Here in La Jolla, sommers. Said she had dogs with her."

"The dogs. Gina. Yeah, that sounds familiar."

"I guess so, though I ain't sure what to picture there with that description. Tried to get her to come over here, but guess I forgot to call and invite her over. Called her about the gig though. That would explain why she didn't come over," Zeeder said, scratching his head.

"She had dogs, I had Angelina, leashes got tangled ... I remember now," Townes said, sitting up. "Traveling is not helping my memory."

"Maybe I want the rest of the details, maybe I don't," Zeeder said, looking back at Townes.

"A party: she wants us to play for a party she is having at her house."

"Sounded somethin' like that."

"What did you tell her?" Townes asked.

"Told her noooo disco."

"Ever."

"Ever."

"When's the party?"

"I fergit. Sometime," Zeeder shrugged

"Always the peak of efficiency."

"That's me. Good to know you can recognize true genius when you sees it. Might not have to cut my ear off after all, or at least—"

"Postpone it for a while?"

"Yeah. I'm inspired now so no need. Angst appears to be settlin' a might. Could have just been that burrito I had for breakfast," Zeeder said, looking at the painting, looking at the guitar.

"You can never rule that out as a possibility."

"What about the girl?"

"What girl?"

"Asked that kinda quick, didn't ya?"

"No, I just ... you mean Kat or who exactly?"

"What is the number up to now? I thought it was just Kat, or maybe the new girl you's in love with. You know, the one you seen and talked to for five minutes."

"Annie?"

"Who else you got bouncin' around that melon of yourn?" Zeeder said, pointing to his head.

"I met an actress in New York," Townes said, petting Angelina.

"Yeah, was that any count?"

"She was really nice. She asked me to send her my manuscript and she would see if she could help me. Can't hurt, since everybody else bailed."

"You are amazin', truly."

"It's not like that."

"Like what?"

"Like you are thinking."

"You know what I'm thinkin', does ya?" Zeeder asked, pointing at his head with the non- paint end of his brush.

"Well, no, but I could see how you could think ..."

"Watchit! I'm thinkin' about cuttin' my ear off again, so back the hell off of what you think I'm a thinkin', 'cause you don't know. I don't give a shit how many girlfriends you have."

"I don't have any girlfriends ... except this one," Townes said, scratching Angelina.

"Sounds to me like the paddock is full."

"Kentucky."

"The Bluegrass State and you wishes everyday of your life that you was from there so you could be more like me," Zeeder said, puffing his chest out.

"Every day."

"True genius."

"Yep."

"Then say it."

"True genius," Townes repeated.

"I wish I'd said that."

"You did say that."

"I can't remember everything I say. Us true genius types are like that," Zeeder said, putting more touches of the paint brush to the canvas.

"You are a musical genius, I do know that."

"Maybe I'm glad that yer back. Keep a talkin' ... about me, I mean."

"Never seen anybody as good with the guitar as you."

Zeeder held his brush in the air, raising his other hand. "Welcome home, let's celebrate! Don't forget, you still owe me an explanation on the actress."

"If you insist. We don't have to sing for our supper tonight, do we?" Townes yawned.

"Actually, we do, I forgot to tell ya. Jack's needs somebody to fill-in, and I said we would, dammit! I was lookin' forward to just straight up eatin' and drinkin'. Guess we'll have to do it tomorry night. But that don't mean you can still keep avoidin' tellin' me about the actress."

"I like the straight up eating and drinking part."

"We could sit down, I ain't decided. I'm tired of eatin' over the kitchen sink, so sittin' would be good," Zeeder nodded.

"Well, let me know," Townes said, rubbing his hands over his eyes, forehead and back through his hair. "'Cause I'm a bit tired. Or 'tard,' as you would say."

"Yer startin' to get the hang of things."

"I should probably call Kat and tell her I'm back."

"You gonna have her come with us to the dinner we was gonna have tonight, but now have to wait 'til tomorry night? She might get in the way of our eatin' and drinkin'."

"I've seen you eat. I don't think a truck could get in your way."

"I'm artistic, but also determined," Zeeder said moving his upper body, strumming some chords, trying not to get paint on his guitar.

"I'll tell her you and I are having dinner and she and I can get together afterwards."

"I's just messin' with ya. I don't care if she comes along. Maybe she can bring her friend. You can tell 'em you like 'em both. Tell them you was just talkin' to yer New York actress girlfriend. Tellin' her about how much you liked the two of them."

"It's not like that. Since you've know me, how many women have I had around?"

"I don't live with you, how would I know?"

"You see me more than anybody I know, so how many."

"Roughly, or do I have to be exact."

"How many?"

"Uh, none."

"None!" Townes said standing up. "You are absolutely right."

"Does Norah count?"

"Norah was right when you came to town, years ... I can't remember how many years. So no."

"Thought not. But you now have these three bouncin' around in your head ... hell, there may be more in there. It's like I don't even know you anymore," Zeeder said, laughing.

"What's funny?"

"Everything is funny."

"Everything is funny?"

"Pretty much."

"Well, I could see how you would think that."

"You got dumped by them book folks, but you're a thinkin' about three women, one's a actress, and ... yous a livin' in La Jolla. Seems like a feller could at least smile about them things."

"I think the guy from Kentucky living in La Jolla, that might be funny," Townes said, smiling.

"I'm seekin' political asylum."

"You maybe should be in an ..."

"Don't say it. Man, yer gettin' predictable. I needed to get away, and this was as far west as I could drive, so I stopped. I kinda like it here, it's nice here. I miss Kentucky, but I'm dealin with it."

Townes shook his head. "Is it too early to go to dinner?"

"It is still mornin'. I don't know how they do it in New York."

"Same as here."

"Well, go inside, get a cup of coffee, bring the Woodford, and come sit here with your dog and me, and tell us about all that stuff rumblin' 'round in your head. I don't really want to hear about it, but the dog probably does."

"You sure?"

"Pretty sure. She mentioned it earlier."

Townes went inside to get the coffee and the bourbon, Angelina following him every step. He called Kat's office and left a message that he was back in town. He returned to the patio to sit and watch the ocean.

CHAPTER 28

Townes and Zeeder saw the two women enter the bar. Townes smiled and nodded as the two waved. Zeeder looked at Townes, and laughed, turning away from the microphone. The women sat in a booth, again waving, Kat motioning for them to come over there, Townes again nodding. Townes glanced at Zeeder, who was now staring at Townes, rolling his eyes. They played two more songs before they took a break.

"We're not goin' to deal with that foolishness about bein' invited to the table again, are we?" Zeeder asked.

"No, I'm past that."

"That is a huge relief."

"I am nothing, if not accommodating."

"I was gonna say weird, but whatever."

The two headed over to where the women were seated.

"Hello again," Townes greeted.

"Welcome home," Kat answered.

"Thank you. How is everyone today?"

"We are good," Kat smiled.

"Yes, all good," Annie added.

"Ladies," Zeeder said, now getting to the table.

"Please, sit, if you have time."

"A few minutes, we have time," Townes said, sitting, Zeeder following suit.

"How was New York?" Kat asked.

"Long way away from here, but good, it was good."

"Did you do anything besides work while you were there?" Kat asked.

"Well, I, uh, I saw a Broadway ..."

"Well, look what we have here," a man's voice from behind them said loudly.

Kat did not look up, but crossed her eyes as she turned to Townes. "Shit," she said.

Annie knew the voice as well. Her posture tightened when she heard it. Townes also recognized the voice.

"You a groupie now, Annie?" the man asked.

Kat grabbed Annie's knee under the table, motioning with her other hand. "Well, Clement, what a ... oh, gee, I'm looking for the right word ... somehow pleasant doesn't cover it," Kat said, not turning to face the voice.

"Kat, it's OK," Annie said.

"It's OK when I say it's OK," Kat said out of the side of her mouth, now turning towards the man and giving him a less than friendly look.

"Easy there, slugger," the man said, taking a step back, bumping into another man that was with him.

"This the one that punched you?" the other man asked.

"She was lucky ... I'm not punching a drunk chick," Clement said.

"You are the one that was lucky, but I don't think we need to talk about that. If we were going to talk, and I am not advocating that we do, I would say we have talked enough already," Kat grinned, not showing her teeth in the smile, muttering something with her closed mouth.

Clement looked around the table and did not respond. His friend stepped forward and started to introduce himself. "Hi, my name is ... Townesie!? Holy shit, is that you!?"

"Alvin, how are you?"

"Oh, ho, ho, this is too much. I didn't know you were friends with Clement. Hi, hi everyone, I'm Alvin," he said to everyone at the table.

"I ... is that his name? I have not met him until ... hello, I'm Townes," Townes said, extending his hand across the table in Clement's direction. Kat grabbed his arm before he could get there.

"Tell you later," Kat whispered.

"Whose boyfriend is Elvis here?" Clement asked, looking at Townes.

"You really don't have to try to live up to all my expectations, Clement," Kat said, not looking back his way.

"If this one's your girlfriend, Elvis, you better watch out. She's got a helluva right hook."

"You want to see my left hook?" Kat said, narrowing her eyes.

"Kat!" Annie said.

"Annie, he's not worth punching twice. I shouldn't have done it the first time, but he was such an asshole ..." Kat growled, clenching her fist.

"Wow, Clemmie, this one's gonna kick your ass again," Alvin said, trying to be funny, but no one was laughing. "Forget it. Hey Townesie, you ready to come back to work with us? We got the big show coming up in Vegas, and we have a couple of monster big suites and we are going to stay over and party hearty. I could maybe get you on the list."

Townes looked at Annie, who was clearly uncomfortable, then at Kat, who was now way outside her normal Zen space, if a clenched fist were any indicator.

"Hello, name's Zeeder," Zeeder said to Alvin. "Your partner there 'pears to be upsettin' the ladies a might, so could be a good idea to have this discussion another time.'

"Who the fuck are you?" Clement asked.

"Clement!" Annie said quietly, but with enough force that it was apparent this was not heading in a good direction.

"I'm Elvis's band, so I'm not leavin' anytime soon," Zeeder said blankly.

"I really don't think you want to fuck with me, music man. I probably would be less inclined to hold back on you, like I would some drunk chick," Clement said, taking a step forward.

A phone started ringing and Alvin took it out of his pocket. "I gotta take this," he said, moving away from the group.

Townes watched him, Zeeder not moving his gaze from Clement. "I'm still here, music man."

"I am quite aware of your physical location at the moment. I am a might perplexed as to why you are attempting to congregate with a group that is clearly reluctant to add you to the guest list."

"What!?"

"Just an observation. I personally do not have a beef and mean no disrespect."

"This the kind of shit you are hanging with now, Annie?" Clement laughed.

"You just never seem to get it, do you, Clement? Nobody likes you.

Zeeder is just being polite, being from the South, which you could certainly learn from. It just seems like you might be incapable of good manners, which is sad. You could leave, as I think that would be an improvement for the entire room," Kat said, doing her best not to bite her lip in two.

"I really don't know why you don't like me, Kat," Clement said, shaking his head.

"I don't know either, Clement. I have a theory though," Kat smiled at Annie.

"And what's that?"

"Umm ... that you are a classless asshole."

Annie started to laugh.

"Don't be poisoned by her, Annie. You and I know what the real truth is," Clement said, moving closer to Annie.

"Clement," Annie said.

"Yes, sweetie?" Clement leaned in.

"There is no you and I," Annie said, looking relieved.

"We can talk about it another time, without them here," Clement's eyes shot around the table.

"We talked about it before, so there is really nothing more to talk about," Annie said, looking down at the table.

"Good, good," Kat whispered.

"OK, I'm back," Alvin said loudly.

Kat flashed an insincere smile.

"So, Townesie, you gonna come back to work for us? Be a lot of fun. Headin' to Chicago after Vegas. You get me your resume, I can probably put in the good word and get you back. We got a big team-building thing coming up and it would be good for you to be there," Alvin said, fidgeting.

"For the team," Townes said.

"What's a team building?" Annie asked.

Townes leaned close to her and whispered. "It's for people that don't know how to lead, to try to act like they do. They usually pay somebody to do some insane exercise so they don't actually have to do it, but they can put in their personnel file that they held a team-building event."

"Really?"

"Unfortunately, yes, really."

"That sounds kind of dumb," Annie said, shrugging her shoulders.

"It is beyond dumb," Townes smiled at Annie, Annie smiling back.

"So what do you say, Townesie boy, you in?" Alvin asked, still fidgeting.

"Uh, I ..."

"Ho ... hold on a second," Alvin said, his phone ringing again. "I gotta take this."

"Must be some purdy important feller," Zeeder said.

"He would have you think that," Townes said, looking around and turning to Clement.

"So what's your deal?" Clement said.

"My deal?"

"Yeah, what do you do, Elvis? Or is this it, waitin' to get discovered?"

Townes paused before answering, looking at Annie, then Kat.

"You can hit him if you want," Kat whispered.

Townes smiled back at Kat, glancing at Annie. "Yep, that's my deal, waiting to get discovered."

"Thought so. What do you get paid for something like this?" Clement asked, trying to sound important.

"Clement!" Annie said.

"I'm just curious, Annie. Just want to know about the guys you are hanging around," Clement huffed, looking around the room.

"Like it's any of your goddamn business," Kat said quietly.

"What?" Clement asked, turning to Kat.

Kat turned to Clement and smiled. "I said, and you might want to write this down ... like it is any of your goddamn business. Need me to spell any of those words for you?"

"Hah, funny."

"Oh, but it wasn't meant to be funny." Kat said, still smiling, then letting her smile fade to a more disgusted look.

"So how much, Elvis?"

"I pay them, they don't pay me. Valuable experience, you know," Townes said, looking at Clement, not blinking.

"Experience? That's messed up."

"I'm a slow learner, I guess," Townes said, drumming his fingers on the table.

Clement did not respond. He looked around the table as if to gauge whether Townes was putting him on or not. He looked like he did not want to appear stupid, but somehow could not help it.

"Clement."

"Yes, Annie?"

"OK, I'm back," Alvin said, popping back in to the group.

"Fabulous," Kat muttered.

"Yeah, yeah ... Annie wants to say something to me," Clement said, pushing on Alvin's shoulder.

"Oh, OK," Alvin said, looking at his phone.

"Well?" Clement said, turning back to Annie, the whole group now looking at her.

Annie took a breath, releasing it quickly. "Why don't you leave?"

The group stayed quiet, except for Kat, who seemed to shout something with her mouth completely closed. Clement said nothing, but glanced around the table and back to Annie, then quickly away. Kat looked at him with a smile that seemed to be growing by the second. Clement started slowly shaking his head up and down and looked like he might throw up.

"Alvin, we're outta here," Clement said finally.

"OK," Alvin said, shaking his head, not really understanding what had transpired. "Be in touch, Townesie."

Townes shook his head up and down as the two left. "No."

Kat and Annie began to laugh.

"Townesie? Do you like that name?" Kat asked.

"You like to be called Katty?"

"God, no."

"There you go," Townes said, raising an eyebrow.

"That was a might unusual," Zeeder said, looking after the two. "That one fellow was some sorta jittery, and that other feller wasn't what you'd call very polite."

"Not very polite is probably the nicest description anyone has ever given him," Kat said, drinking her wine.

"And how is it you know ... Clement, was that his name?" Townes asked.

"It's a long story," Annie said. "Well, it's not that long of a story"

"We can talk about it some other time," Kat said.

"Or not," Annie added.

"And Alvin, you used to work with him?"

"Something like that."

"And he wants you to go back to work with him? Is that something you want to do?" Kat asked.

"I want to do that. About as bad as you want Clement to come back here and sit with you," Townes said.

"Got it."

"Hate to bust up this conversation, but we need to get back to playin', else we get run off," Zeeder said, standing.

"Yes, we do," Townes added.

"Well, we'll see you later?" Kat asked.

"Sure," Zeeder said.

Townes paused, looking at the two women as if he were going to say something.

"Yes?" Kat asked.

"He's shy sometimes," Zeeder laughed. "Come on, shy guy. Ladies," Zeeder bowed, and the two started to head back to their instruments. Zeeder saw Clement re-enter, looking like he was coming back to say something to Annie and Kat.

"'Scuse me," Zeeder said, turning and going to intercept Clement before he got back to the women.

Townes could see Zeeder saying something to Clement, Clement not looking like he had a verbal response. The women were watching from their table. Townes moved toward the instruments, preparing to continue their set, feeling awkward standing there between everything. Zeeder ended his exchange, walking past the women again and waving, then returning next to Townes.

"Everything all right?"

"Is now," Zeeder said, tending to his guitar.

"You know that guy?"

"Nope. Know a bunch just like him, though. He's all talk, and not very interestin' talk at that."

"Well?"

"Well what?"

"What did you tell him?"

"Told him I wasn't generally a physical sort."

"OK, and?"

"And that he should just go 'bout his bidness without them two girls."

"Right, and he said 'you betcha'."

"He didn't say nothin'."

"No?"

"Started to, but I told him I would personally slit his sack and put his foot through it ... iffins he did."

CHAPTER 29

Clement leaned back in his leather office chair. Around him the walls were covered with photos of himself. Marlin fishing, holding up awards, driving a very large boat, leaning on a red Ferrari, standing next to a red Ferrari, sitting behind the wheel of a red Ferrari. The only photo that had anyone besides him in the picture was one where he had his arms around Annie. Clement was smiling, while Annie's expression looked more like she was being hugged by a dirty diaper. He had the same photograph with her on the wall and on his massive desk. He propped his feet up on the desk, expensive Italian loafers with no socks. He punched in a number on the nearby desk phone, the ringing probably audible outside the building.

"Yeah?"

"Topper baby. How the fuck are ya?"

"Who the hell is this?" the voice on the other end asked.

"Topper baby, it is Big Clement. Quit fuckin' with me, you know who this is," Clement said, opening a desk drawer, reaching in to extend a pop-up mirror. He looked at his reflection, side, side, then checking to see if he had anything caught in his teeth, then checking the shine on his shaved head.

"Oh yeah, Clement. Why the fuck am I on speaker phone?"

Clement scrambled to pick up the phone. "Sorry, I was in the middle of something. Thought I'd give you a toot on the old blower."

"A toot on the old blower? You been watchin' old gangster movies again? What do you want?"

"I need your services, and quickly."

"Quickly? You think I'm FedEx?"

"Funny. I got a couple of yokels I need you to dig up some dirt on."

"Yokels? What the hell kind of movies you been watchin', anyway? You're a lawyer with a computer. What do you need me for?"

"Your skills are what I need. The computer is only going to tell me where they live, maybe where they used to live. You're going to find out all kinds of things."

"You know I don't work cheap. Rates just went up, in fact."

"Went up? You just raised your rates the last time I used you."

"You can get somebody else."

"No, no, nobody else."

"OK, who you wantin' dirt on? You should do something with your life, you know."

"Thank you for the motivational non sequitur. A couple of guys ... live here in La Jolla, I think," Clement said, rubbing his shaved head, and fidgeting in his chair.

"You think?"

"I'm a lawyer, I don't know where the hell they live. I saw them in La Jolla, with people I know from La Jolla, so I figured ..."

"Brilliant work. You should become a PI. Don't tell me you don't know their names," the man on the phone said.

"I know one of them is Townes Mantle, other guy's name is Zeeder, I think."

"First, or last?"

"Zeeder, that's all I know."

"Sounds like a nickname. That's a big goddamn help."

"I'm going to pay you, so what does it matter?" Clement asked, drumming a pen on the desk.

"What's that knockin'?"

"Nothing, nothing. So you'll take the job?"

"Un, I'm kinda busy right now," Topper said.

"Yeah? Doin' what?"

"Who the fuck are you to ask me what the fuck I'm doin'? You're some pissant lawyer, wantin' dirt on some guys. Bet the bar association would love to hear that. What'd these guys do, splash mud on that fuckin' red car of yours?"

"You want the job, or not?"

"Can I think about it?"

"No, I want to know now."

Clement could hear whistling on the other end, then what sounded like a splash. "What in the hell are you doing?"

"Fishin'. What's it to you?"

"Fishing ... you in or out?"

"I'm in. I'll be in touch."

"Good luck with the fishing."

"Maybe you are the one that should go fishin'. Branch out, do something with your life."

"Whatever."

The five band members sat outside on a patio, a large blue and white cooler of beer next to the picnic table where they were seated. On the table was a spread of sandwiches, chips, dips, and a salad.

"Are we going to practice or have a luncheon and guest speaker?" Stretch asked.

"Dude, what do you think?" Fudgie asked.

"I don't know, that's why I asked," Stretch replied.

"I'm thinking ... luncheon," Saxman said.

"Dude, you put this together, it's your crib. I just don't want to suck at this country club gig, so we had better practice," Fudgie said.

"Do not suck," the group said, in unison, clinking their beer bottles together.

It was a warm day, a good day for a cold beer, and all were dressed in shorts, T-shirts, and sandals. If there were a luncheon and guest speaker, it was going to be casual.

"What kind of beer is this?" Stretch asked.

"The best kind of beer. Free beer. A buddy of mine works at for a local brewery. I get it from him. It's righteous," Fudgie nodded.

"I don't drink much beer. It's a bit problematic for me. Good day for it, though," Zeeder, the only one without a beer, said quietly.

"Dude, grab a brewhaha," Fudgie said, gesturing towards the cooler.

"Gives me gas. Don't drink it, like I told ya."

"Gotta have something, dude. Don't want you gettin' philosophical on us if we're drunk monks," Fudgie said, taking a long drink from his bottle of beer.

"I'm good … lessin' 'course you got some bourbon, I'd drink that," Zeeder said, smiling.

"On a hot day like today, no way! You and Fontleroy here been playin' the hoity-toity circuit too long," Stretch laughed, looking at Townes and Zeeder.

"Fontleroy, huh? Make sure you spell that right. Come to think of it, a Pimm's Cup does sound good," Townes said, grinning.

"You two have lost connection with your home boys, all these highfalutin concoctions," Stretch said, pushing Townes on the shoulder.

"I fails to see how bourbon is highfalutin. You's needs to get outta yer camp trailer more often," Zeeder said, scratching himself.

"OK, bourbon's not highfalutin, but I never heard of that Fim's, or Jim's, cup, whatever he said," Stretch said, again pushing Townes on the shoulder.

"If we started flailing on each other, it might be harmful to the group," Townes pushed Stretch back. "Let's get along, you know, for the sake of the kids," Townes said, tilting his head and looking sad.

"Oh, I can't stay mad at you, you big lug, give me a hug," Stretch said, moving towards Townes, his arms outstretched.

"No sex in front of the kids either," Townes said, putting his palms out in front of Stretch.

"Later," Stretch whispered and winked.

"OK," Townes agreed, shaking his head in a vehement *no way*.

Saxman reemerged from the house with a bottle of Old Crow bourbon. "OK, didn't think I had any, but here it is," he said, holding the bottle up triumphantly.

"Let's all take a snort," Fudgie said.

"Holy dithers! I didn't think they still made that," Zeeder said. "You cretins drink your beer. Could I get about three fingers of that in a tall glass of ice, and fill 'er up to the top with water? Iffin's you would be so kind."

"Yes sir," Saxman said, returning to the house.

"That sounds good," Stretch said.

"Called Kentucky Tea, good for what ails ya on a hot day," Zeeder said, pounding a fist on his chest.

"You feeling sick?" Stretch asked.

"Nope, and don't plan to, neither," Zeeder replied, pounding his other fist on his chest. "I drink that beer, I might get sick."

Stretch looked at Fudgie. "You believe those two? No wonder we're playing at a country club."

"It's good money, so why do you care where we're playing?" Townes asked. "Old Crow?" he said, quietly.

"Do we have to wear double-breasted blue blazers with brass buttons?

"No, and say that three times fast. The part about the blazers, I mean," Townes laughed. "Actually, they said *you* had to, but none of the rest of us."

"Dude, we should get some and wear them—that would be funny," Fudgie said, finishing his beer.

"Wear what you want. I'm not wearing a blazer," Townes said, "but I think you boys would look cute in them."

"I'm not wearin' one, I don't want to look cute. Well, maybe a little ... but I ain't a wearin' that." Zeeder said.

"Wear what?" Saxman asked, coming out of the house with Zeeder's drink. "Here you go. What's the wardrobe discussion?"

"Them two's a wearin' some sorta blue blazers. Thank you for the drink," Zeeder said.

"Hey, wait a minute. I didn't say I would wear that," Stretch said, shaking his head.

"Then how come you're asking so much about them?" Townes smiled.

"I thought we were going to practice," Saxman said, "not talk about clothes."

Fudgie let out a large burp. "I need another beer, and those sandwiches look like I'd better get into them. I suppose these two sissy boys don't want to practice. We have to practice and make sure Stretch lays off the cowbell."

Stretch looked down at the ground.

"We're here, aren't we?" Zeeder said, taking a drink. "Ah, that's good."

"Where's my Pimm's Cup?" Townes smiled.

"I don't know what that is. I was lucky to find the Old Crow. I might have a bottle of knotty head gin in there."

"You had Old Crow, would stand to reason you'd have knotty head. Any tonic?"

"Probably, can't guarantee it's not flat, I'll go check," Saxman said.

"No, sit. I'll go find it," Townes said, getting up. "You can find out if these two are planning on wearing pants to the gig with their blazers, 'cause with Fudgie, it's never a given."

"Free spirit, dude," Fudgie said, opening another beer. "Can't cramp my creativity."

"I wouldn't dream of it. The management might have a dress code, however." Townes said, going into the house.

"None of us should wear pants, dude! And by that I mean no pants, nothing!" Fudgie hollered at Townes, raising his beer bottle. "Who's with me?"

Zeeder, Stretch, and Saxman all looked at Fudgie, saying nothing.

"You fuckers deaf? I said who's with me?"

"We heard you," Zeeder said, looking back at his drink, taking a sip. "We always hear you."

Fudgie looked at Stretch.

"I like you, but I'm not playing a gig at La Jolla Country Club not wearing any pants. I'm not playing anywhere without pants."

Fudgie looked at Saxman.

"I was out for this part of the conversation, but, uh, I'm with the guys on this. Pants. Unless we're playing on a nude beach, in which case ... I'm... uh, you need to get another sax player, 'cause I'm not playin' that gig."

"Yer all a bunch of pussies."

"I don't think it's askin' too much to get paid for playin' a gig, and not showin' up nekkid from the waist down," Zeeder said, not looking up from his drink.

"Yep, gotta go with Zeeder on this one," Stretch nodded quickly, looking at Zeeder, Saxman, then Fudgie.

"Agree," Saxman said.

"Got a chance to be ground-breaking, and you mama's boys don't have the guts. Disappointing, disappointing," Fudgie said, draining his beer.

"Iffin you was to pick yer battles, this would not be the one to pick. Common sense has to enter into the equation ever now and again," Zeeder said, tapping his finger to the side of his head.

"I shoulda been alive in pirate times. You bitches would been walkin' the plank right now," Fudgie said, reaching for another beer.

"Can't kill your entire crew. Who would man the ship?" Townes asked, coming out of the house.

CHAPTER 30

Townes sat at Manhattan Bar, in the Empress Hotel in La Jolla. Manhattan was the name of the restaurant, so he figured, or hoped, he could not go wrong with a name like that. Zeeder had said he felt like "diving into some meat," and Manhattan was a good place in La Jolla to do that. A place more like the city it was named after than a place in southern California. It was an unpretentious, no bullshit kind of place, fairly loud, smelling of countless years of steak and Italian dishes. He was beat up with the book news, but getting together here would be a good thing. He sat quietly with the Sazerac he had ordered. He didn't spend that much time here, so he didn't know the bartender. He looked into the glass and looked around the room. He thought about taking Angelina and getting in the car and just driving until they ran out of road. Maybe a little time like that would do him some good.

"Welcome back," Kat said, touching him on the shoulder.

"Oh, hello. I didn't see you come in. I wasn't expecting you. How are you?"

"I could leave," Kat said, still standing.

"No, no. I just didn't think I would see you until later. Sit down, please."

"You're sure?" Kat asked, hesitating before she sat.

"No. Zeeder and I need some alone time, he's feeling neglected … of course, I'm sure! Sit down," Townes said, standing.

"I wouldn't want to break up the band."

"Hah. Sit."

"We didn't really get a chance to talk the other night. That asshole Clement has a way of messing things up, no matter the situation. How was the trip?" Kat asked, as she sat down.

"Hard to say, hard to say. Some business things went OK."

"What about your book business things?"

"Different ball park. Not sure I am allowed to dress in that locker room"

"Hmm. I don't know what that means."

"I don't know what that means either," Townes said, looking at his drink.

"Well, you're the one who said it, so the one of us that is familiar with that kind of business would maybe know."

"I know as much about the book business as you do, less than you do, probably. Can I get you a drink?"

"Ok."

Townes motioned to the bartender. "My friend here would like ..."

"Maybe a glass of Pinot Noir. California, please."

"Sure thing," the bartender said.

"So?"

"So ... I may not be cut out for the book business. Maybe I could join a monastery."

"Things went that well, did they?" Kat asked.

"Oh, swimmingly."

"I've not heard that word before, at least not that I can remember," Kat smiled.

"I may not have ever used it before."

"So it didn't go well?"

"Another agent passed, editor quit, said he wouldn't put it in front of any more agents, and he knows dozens, more probably. I think he ran off to join the circus, hell I don't know. This must be what being around me does to people, so watch yourself."

"Oh, I'm sorry."

"New guy, first book, no following. Sort of like having a contagious disease. Folks want to help you, but not really. You want to join us for dinner, or are you afraid you'll get sick too?" Townes said, covering his mouth.

"Very funny, but I'll take my chances. Though I'm not sure I want to witness you boys ... what did your message say, 'get your beef on,' was that it?"

"Yes."

"Maybe. I was going to call Annie and see if she wants to stop by. I heard you were playing for a party at my Gina's house."

"I guess we are. I don't know why I keep forgetting … everything these days."

"You are playing her party and you don't remember?"

"She was walking her dogs the other day, then I went to New York, got lost somehow. Zeeder took the booking, I didn't. I do feel bad that I don't remember. I now question her taste in music, but I can get past that. My memory has been for crap lately."

"Don't be so hard on yourself, you have a lot on your mind. I actually feel things are going to work out very well for you. Wait 'til you see her house, it is amazing. Too big for me, but it is phenomenal. I like things a bit more simple."

"I am simple, so I have no choice."

"Maybe that's why I noticed you, because of your simplicity. When you become a famous writer, you will probably wish things would go back to being simple," Kat said, moving closer to him.

"I appreciate your optimism about the fame, misplaced as it might be. I think I will always be simple."

"You might be, but when you become famous, it may be out of your control. Things changed when I became a doctor, having nothing to do with fame. You will be dealing with fame, which will be a completely different thing."

"This goes back to that 'we need to have a conversation about how you know things that are going to happen … before they happen.' You were going to enlighten me on that. Plus, I don't think my work is anywhere near the magnitude of yours."

"I don't mean that way. I mean I am still simple, but my profession is complex. Yours is about to become so," Kat said, tapping her index finger on Townes's hand. "I don't really want to get into that other right now."

"I don't see … I don't think …"

"Well, you probably can see it, but …"

"Somebody else just told me that same thing … in that vicinity anyhow."

"And they would be right. I want to meet this person."

Townes scratched his head.

"Look, it's not like there is a book out there on how your life is going to change, right?"

"Not if was written by a first time writer," Townes said.

"Funny, but stop it. A long time ago, I put in for a job in India. It looks like that is going to happen. It will undoubtedly change my life."

"Really, India? Wow. You said out of the country, or overseas … memory is … anyway, go on."

"Yes. I've always wanted to go there."

"You've not been there and you want to go work there? Seems like you might want to visit there first, see if you like it."

"Well … I sort of made up my mind, but that was before…."

The bartender was back with the glass of wine for Kat. "Here you are."

"Thank you," Kat said, happy for the interruption.

"You still good with your drink?"

"Yes, fine, thanks," Townes said, wondering what 'before' Kat was referring to.

"So back to New York, tell me more," Kat said, picking up her glass of wine. "Oh, here's to your successful book."

"Yes. Should change the name of it to 'Longshot: A Novel' by Contagious Disease, but thanks," Townes said, touching glasses. "Would have just about as much of a shot at getting it published."

"No! So tell me more," Kat said after she took a very healthy sip of wine. "You know, the fun stuff."

"Fun stuff. I saw my dear friend Milton, that is always fun. He is a great soul."

"I think you mentioned him before. He's a bartender, right?"

"Yes, but he is much more than that. I don't remember talking about him, but my gyroscope is a bit off."

"How is that?"

"It is hard to describe, so I won't go into it. He sort of knows everyone and everyone knows him."

"That's sort of the credo in that profession, isn't it? We'll get back to the gyroscope thing, I might add."

Townes looked at her, knowing she wasn't going to let the gyroscope thing go. "Yes, but it's more than that with him. He knows everyone, more like he knows everyone of substance, or if he introduces you to someone, they are pretty much going to be a solid person, not just someone famous, or someone at a bar. Does that make sense?"

"Yes it does. I don't see you just hanging with the barflies."

"I'm in a bar now."

"With me."

"True. I never considered you to be a barfly," Townes laughed.

"My theory proven," Kat said, then leaned over and kissed him.

"What was that for?"

"Proving theories ... and getting closer to book fame."

"Not even close to book fame."

"Closer than you think."

"If you say so."

"I do. Maybe we should skip dinner, have dinner later," Kat said, leaning in closer.

"Zeeder should be here ..."

Kat narrowed her eyes at Townes.

"Oh ... oh! I thought you were going to call Annie."

Kat narrowed her eyes even more.

"I guess we could eat later ..."

"I'll make sure you don't starve," Kat smiled, her eyes still narrowed.

"What about Zeeder?"

"He'll have to find his own girl, and there's food in the restaurant."

"I suppose so," Townes said, leaving money on the bar.

The two got up and headed out the door.

"I shouldn't have to explain things like this to you."

"I'm slow, sorry."

The two moved out the door and headed down the sidewalk. Townes stopped and turned, running back to the restaurant. He yelled back at Kat.

"Hang on a second."

He went back inside and Kat stood alone, looking around, not quite sure what to make of him going back in.

Townes quickly returned, smiling and breathing hard.

"Sorry, had to tell the bartender to be on the lookout for Zeeder to tell him I had to go."

"Oh, I thought you changed your mind."

"I'm just happy you believe I have a mind," Townes said as they walked down the street.

CHAPTER 31

Townes heard knocking on the door. He knew who it was. He got up off the couch, moving to the door and opened it slowly.

"You forget somethin' last night?" Zeeder asked, Angelina immediately jumping on him. "That's right, I know who my real friends are," he said, hugging the dog.

"Did the bartender find you?"

"What the hell kind of question is that, and find me where?"

"At Manhattan."

"Nope, was he supposed to?"

"Yes, he was supposed to find you. Sorry."

"What was he supposed to find me for, to tell me you's a shitbag for not showin' up? I surmised that my own self; didn't need assistance with that one."

"No, to tell you I was there and that a good-looking woman offered to make me a late dinner."

"Oh. Well ... that's different than just being a shitbag."

"I hope so. This kind of thing never happens to me."

"Sounds to me like it's happenin' a fair amount these days."

"It's not like that," Townes said, closing the door.

"Like what? Like a good-lookin' woman feelin' sorry for ya and takin' ya home, walkin' her dogs and shit?"

"You know this isn't normal for me."

"It is lately."

"How about before then?"

"Not many came a callin'."

"Quarantine would be more accurate."

"You gonna let me in, and is this vicious hound gonna shift into attack mode, forcin' me to flee for my life down the streets of La Jolla?"

"Sorry, come in," Townes said, opening the door wide.

Zeeder looked around, shaking his head and let out a sigh.

"Inhospitable, thoughtless sonofabitch."

"Sorry."

"There's more, I was just a bein' polite."

"I completely understand."

"See, at least someone appreciates me," Zeeder said, patting the dog on the head, the dog licking his leg.

"You want me to lick your leg?"

"Not on a bet. You could make me somethin' to eat, since I was deprived last night of a proper meal."

"You could have had dinner there."

"By myself? No sir. I get to do that all the time."

"You are going to make me lick your leg now, aren't you?"

"Again, not on a bet. I just wanted to make sure you are properly chastised for standin' up your best friend so's you could go have yer way with some poor gal."

"Not like that, I told you," Townes said, moving into to the kitchen to find Zeeder something to eat. "I've been out of town, so help yourself to whatever you can find."

"Good, I like to go through other folks' cabinets."

"Knock yourself out."

Zeeder started piling things up on the counter, intent upon not leaving hungry.

"I didn't realize you had so much food, else I'da been over here a eatin' whilst you was away."

"It's a standing offer."

"I didn't know that, but I will from now on, what with you bein' with all the women and all. Let's hear about it, don't make me beg ya."

"About what?"

"About last night, dumbass," Zeeder said, his mouth now partially full.

"You're something else."

"I'm just kiddin'. I don't need to hear the details about some gal ravagin' ya. You been pretty pathetic, so I guess you deserve a break."

"Really?"

"Yep," Zeeder said, feeding some of the crackers he had found in the cabinet to the dog.

"You really think so? And quit feeding crackers to her, she's going to want them all the time."

"They's good crackers, that's why she wants 'em."

"She wants them because you are giving them to her."

"That don't make no sense. My giving 'em to her don't make her want 'em. She wants 'em before I give 'em to her. Are all you writers this fucked up?"

"Are all musicians as fucked up as you?"

"Nope, just you."

Townes sat down on the kitchen floor, his back against the cabinet. He held up his hand, and Zeeder gave him a cracker. Townes held it there until he gave him several more.

"I just am not sure what to do."

"Do what now?" Zeeder slid down on the floor across from Townes, reaching back over his head and pulling the box of crackers down in front of him.

"This book shit. I probably need to just say fuck it and get on with doing something else."

"You got another vocation, last I checked."

"Yeah, and I'm tired of that."

"Well, you could do music full time. That pays, oh, let's see … that pays less than nothin'."

"You seem to be getting by."

"Not hardly."

"You must be doing something right, you're living here."

"Won the lottery once, that's runnin' out."

"I'm curious, but it's none of my business."

"Makin' a run at the music, ain't no different than makin' a run at the book. Timin', luck. They is everything." Zeeder pushed the box of crackers across the floor to Townes.

"I am thinking about going back to my old gig."

"Corporate shit? You hated that."

"Not all parts of it," Townes said, crunching a cracker. "OK, all parts of it, but it pays the bills."

"You got your own gig now—what about that?"

"Good when it comes, famine-like when it doesn't. Expensive to be out beating the bushes all the time. I don't know what the answer is. Why don't we talk about you?" Townes slid the crackers back to Zeeder.

"There's nothin' to talk about me. We play music together, remember?"

"I've been out of town, something could be new."

"Let's see. Oh, I remember now."

"What?"

"While you's gone, I got married, had a couple kids, they growed up, some went to college, some didn't … wife and I are plannin' on sailin' around the world next week … after we get back from Paris. Paris, Kentucky, that is," Zeeder said, sliding the box of crackers back to Townes.

"I was gone less than a week."

"We packed a whole lotta livin' into that week."

"I missed a lot."

"Boy howdy, I reckon."

"Next time, let me know when you get a wife and have kids in the same week."

"Do my best."

"Speaking of women …"

"In my observation, not that that means anything, but it appears that you is a hoggin' them all."

"Not really."

"Not … really?"

"Never. Seriously. I told you that lots of times."

"But you wouldn't mind iffin it was serious, 'ventually."

"You are confusing me a little, but no, I wouldn't mind. I really want to be with somebody… seriously. I really think we are supposed to be talking about you. You, we're supposed to be talking about you," Townes pushed the crackers back Zeeder's way.

"This some sort of ritual thing, where you have to have the crackers to talk? I heard about stuff like that, beatin' a drum and shit. I met a gal the other day, what was kinda nice, though she's tryin' to get me up to the glider port, get me to ride some sorta flyin' lawnmower-parachute-thingy-contraption."

"And?"

"Not gonna happen."

"Why not?

"If the Almighty had intended me to do that, he'd give me a lawnmower engine and parachute thingy, so no, not gonna happen."

"So you like her?"

"Aside from her fascination with flyin' contraptions, there is some promise there. I haven't knowed her very long. You know what a conversationalist I can be."

"I do know that, though I am not sure anyone else does."

"Not important that they know. I come up with something good to say, I'll say it. Maybe."

"Maybe."

"I been thinkin' about movin', maybe."

"Movin' where?"

"I don't know, someplace that ain't so expensive."

"Different part of town?"

"Different town altogether. Costs a lot to live here."

"Whereabouts, back to Kentucky?"

"Don't think I could do that. I got friends there that just want to get me into the same trouble we got into when I was growin' up there, so sorta don't think that is an option. I am supposed to be growed up a might more than that, so startin' that shit up again don't really have a bright future attached to it. May just go disappear up in LA sommers."

"I thought you said La Jolla was too big?"

"It is."

"Then LA would be …"

"I know what I said, just leave it be. I don't know what I want to do, just like you don't know what you want to do. Only difference is, I don't know that I can afford to hang around here 'til I figure it out."

"Me either. Maybe we shouldn't think about it today."

"You's pretty smart, fer a feller from up north."

"We live as far west as possible."

"Yeah, I knows, I drove here once. Maybe we just hang until we play that private party. That probably won't suck. Can't speak to that other country club gig Fudgie booked us at. We'll be in a better frame of mind, maybe. Course, private parties always have somebody who wants to sing."

"They pay us enough, they can do whatever they want."

"That don't make us hookers, does it?"

"Umm, I don't think so."

"Good, I gots to draw the line there."

CHAPTER 32

Townes's uneasiness after he returned from New York seemed to grow quickly. He was enjoying his time with Kat, but she was starting to focus more and more on her pending move to India. Townes knew how much it meant to her, and understood that would preclude more serious involvement with each other, but that did not mean they could not have fun while she was still here. He still thought about Annie, and saw her more often, as she came with Kat to listen to him and Zeeder play. Townes was not sure if her coming around more often was helping or not. She was always so pleasant, but with a certain sadness about her, and she never revealed much about herself, always responding with the same "busy," when simply questioned how she was doing. He had asked Kat about it, though not wanting to seem too obvious about wanting to know more about Annie.

His questioning her underlying sadness was a fair question, as it was definitely something that could be noticed if someone were paying attention to Annie, and Townes was certainly paying attention. Kat was distracted in her own right, but would tell him Annie had only really been close to one person, and that was someone named Grant. They had met in college and had been together for many years, not saying what had happened. She had only seen a couple of people since. Clement was the son of a close friend of her parents, and she only saw him to please them. Kat told him that was just a "colossal fucking mess," and that he was lucky he did not know Clement, and that he had only met him the one time, and that if he knew him better, he would understand why she described it that way, or something along those lines.

Kat had indicated there had been a resurfacing recently of Annie's other old boyfriend Grant, and that this resurfacing was not helping Annie's peace of mind. Kat really liked Grant, saying he was nothing at all like Clement. She said that things had just maybe run their course with Annie and Grant, that they had tried and were back together for a while, but it did not work out. Annie felt bad that it didn't. Kat would not usually elaborate about things like this, instead asking about Townes's past, to which he would change the subject, which was not easy to do with someone as intelligent as Kat.

Townes thought he only got away with changing the subject because her mind was elsewhere. He usually just told her he had been too mistakenly consumed with business, and that his work didn't leave enough time to get close to anyone. They had both had their jobs get in the way of settling down, which they agreed was sad. Now that they were starting to get close, it seemed almost certain that her leaving the country, and his continuing to travel around this one would not make a deeper relationship with them much of a reality.

Townes and Zeeder headed out to play the party at Gina's house. By then it had become a running joke with them previously forgetting her name. Her house was just above La Jolla Shores, so it was a short drive.

"What was her name again?" Zeeder asked, continuing the joke, though he knew full well what her name was.

"You took the booking."

"Yeah, you'd think I'da written that down sommers."

"You'd a thunk."

"I bet it's on the check."

"Strong possibility."

"Wonder what I call her ... miss, missus, miz, or Miss Dog Lady?"

"Maybe just lady. That always wows 'em."

"Preferred customer?"

"Who doesn't like to be called that? A charming icebreaker in any country, locale, or social setting," Townes smiled.

"Mizz Lady ..."

"You should be a dignitary or maybe an ambassador."

"That's what I was a thinkin'. I could use my natural charm to make folks feel comfortable."

"I thought that was what you did with your music?"

"Well, I suppose so ... or hope so."

"All this time and you don't know?"

"I guess not, er ... no I don't know. I mean, you play too."

"You are the musical genius. Hacker that I am, I'm just lucky you haven't been working with Angelina to take my place. I always hope you don't listen too close and fire me."

"I'm watchin' ya, just be aware of that," Zeeder said, "and the dog is gettin' purdy good, so just be aware."

"You gotta do what is best."

"Well, doin' what's best ain't always easy."

"I wouldn't know. I never did what was best."

"Me neither."

"Friends gotta stick together, even in repeated wrong decisions."

They drove the short distance up out of La Jolla to the cliffs above La Jolla Shores, finding the correct address. Kat had told Townes that the house was quite large. She had understated her assessment. They had been playing more private parties in the area which generally presented more of an element of civility than playing in bars, even nice bars. People were less likely to shout out some song they wanted played. There were other attributes that came with this sort of thing, all good conversation points for what Zeeder called "post-concert debriefing," saying that if he called it "coming off the gig buzz rap," then business geeks like Townes wouldn't know what the hell he was talking about. They approached the gate of the large home where a massive, tanned man in a Hawaiian shirt asked them if he could help them.

"We are the boys in the band."

"Yup, both of us," Zeeder added.

"There more of you?" the man asked.

"Nope, just us."

"All right. You need help?"

"No, just a couple of trips should get it," Townes said.

"You can drive in if that would be easier for you."

"We don't want to clog up the driveway."

The large tanned man pushed a button and the gates began to open. "Little chance of that. Have a good time."

Townes and Zeeder now viewed a driveway that looked like it could accommodate at least twenty five cars, and was on its way to doing so.

"You reckon we's at the right place," Zeeder asked.

"Pretty hard to say, since the place is this nice and we're the ones playing here, so I have my doubts."

"Me too."

"This big guy is letting us in."

"S'pose he's drunk?"

"Maybe Gina was when she asked us to play here."

"No accountin' fer taste, my Pappy used to say. You figure they's gonna make us play on this drive-a-way, or you think we get special shoes so's not to mark up concrete? Maybe no shoes and play in the house?"

"I am certain no one here wants to see your feet. Aside from that, I would not be able to say at this point," Townes said, pulling the car inside the gates, down the long drive.

"I think we done traded up," Zeeder said, his head out the window of the vehicle.

"Or they traded down."

"Do we need references, er letters … er somethin'?"

"She already invited us, paid a deposit, remember?"

"I really have no recollection of my life previous to this moment," Zeeder smiled, gazing at the large house.

"It seems that way every time I ask you something."

"Well then, I must be a tellin' the truth."

"The truth about what?" Townes asked, not looking up.

"The truth about no recollection."

"From one day to the next."

"Pretty much."

"How can you do that?"

"Makes things a might easier iffin you don't have to remember a mess a useless stuff," Zeeder said nodding.

"Useless stuff, what useless stuff?"

"I have no recollection."

"These days, I'm having trouble remembering anything."

"Yer thinkin' too goddamn much."

"Nobody ever accused me of that."

"First time for ever thing. Maybe you just need to back off a might."

"From…?"

"From ever'thing. It's all a gonna pan out, or it ain't, so no sense a worryin' 'bout it. Women, jobs, book, and such. Go play music for these nice folks, see what happens after that."

Townes stopped and stared at Zeeder.

"I know, I surprises myself sometimes too."

They got to the front door, where they were greeted by Gina and several dogs.

"Oh, hello! It is good to see you again," Gina said.

"Yes, good to see you as well," Townes

"Hello Zeeder," Gina said. Her light brown hair, tied back, wearing a Hawaiian shirt, a grass skirt, a flower in her hair. She smiled again at Zeeder.

Townes and Zeeder glanced at each other.

"I will show you where you can set up. The weather looks like it is going to cooperate, so I hope playing outside is all right."

"We play inside all the time, so being able to get outside once in a while is great," Townes said.

"If it gets too cold, which I don't think it will, you can move into the house, if that is not too much trouble. There are heaters on the patio, so I don't think there will be a problem," Gina said, as she walked them through the house.

"I'm sure we will be fine," Townes said, looking around the expansive house as they walked. "This is a beautiful home. Have you lived here a long time?"

"No, I just recently moved here."

"Where did you move from?"

"Too many places. I think that's why I moved here."

"Too many places?" Zeeder asked.

"Yes. We lived all over, which was great at first, but then you just sort of feel like you never get grounded. That, and it seemed like we were never with the dogs. I need to be with my dogs. You saw them that day," Gina said, looking at Townes.

"I understand that feeling completely. Where are they now?"

"Probably out back, waiting for the caterers to make a mistake."

"You said 'we.'"

"Oh, yes, things were different then, it's just me and dogs now."

"Oh, I'm sorry," Townes said.

"Don't be. This is better," Gina smiled.

"Oh, well, good."

"I was with somebody, but should not have been ... so this is better."

"It's none of our business…I mean—" Townes stammered.

"No, no, it's OK, I don't mind. I was with that person because I thought that was the thing to do, which it is if it's for the right reasons. I'm not against being with somebody. Some friends of mine got me to wake up and get some better goals in my life. They saw I had lost my passion, and you should never lose your passion," Gina said, waving a finger at Townes and Zeeder.

"Sounds like smart friends," Zeeder said. "Wish I had me some," he muttered over his shoulder to Townes so Gina could not hear.

"They are indeed smart and you know them," Gina said.

CHAPTER 33

"We do?" Townes asked.

"Well, of course your know Kat. I don't know if you know Annie, or not. She knows of you, I know that. She said she had heard you play, and agreed that you would be a good fit for the party; then running into you with the dogs, it just seemed right."

"Yes, we know Kat," Townes said.

"Townes here knows Annie too. Can't say as I really do," Zeeder said, winking, Townes shooting back a disapproving glance.

"I've met Annie a few times, but don't really know her," Townes said clumsily.

"Well I hadn't seen them in a long time and we got together, and they made me realize I had gotten off track and so ... so I decided to make a change and here I am," Gina motioned, her arms wide.

"Looks like a good change to me, but I don't know where you were, you know, before," Townes said.

"Too much useless stuff, no love to speak of, so much better, yes," Gina nodded.

"They ... Annie and Kat, got you to do all that?" Townes asked.

"It's a long story, but essentially, I was giving them a hard time about how they were living their lives, when I was the one that was in the wrong situation. Their drive, their level of commitment, their ... passion, showed me that I was lacking all of that. So I did something about it."

"Boy howdy, I'd say," Zeeder said.

"Boy howdy?" Gina laughed. "I just love the way you talk."

"It's all right if you tell him he talks funny, I do it all the time," Townes said, looking at Zeeder.

"No, it's refreshing."

"Hear that?" Zeeder said, looking at Townes.

"She's just being nice."

They made it out to the patio area, where they were greeted by several dogs and a whirlwind of party preparation activity.

"You can set up where you would like," Gina said as she moved away from Townes and Zeeder to tend to the flurry, the dogs following.

"Thanks, we …"

"She can't hear ya, she's outta earshot. Lord o' mercy would you look at this view," Zeeder said, facing the ocean, Townes turning to get the same vantage point.

The house sat on the last fringe of high land, the left side overlooking La Jolla, the right side up the coast, the expanse of the Pacific stretching endlessly, the sun still shining though it would be below the unseen edge of that ocean in a few hours.

"Holy schmoly."

"Wow is correct. What a shack, too. Gotsta be ten thousand square feet, just that I can see, and I bets ya there's a good more to see. I wonder iffin she wants to adopt me. Think she would. She said she liked me," Zeeder said, puffing up his chest.

"She's the same … she looks to be the same age as you. If she were going to adopt, she would get a little kid … instead of a big one, a big one that drinks bourbon like water."

"I could wet my pants … cry and make a fuss and such, iffin you think that would improve my odds."

"Remind me to ask her."

"I can wet 'em right now, if you think it would."

"Maybe wait until we get done playing. Man, what a view."

"If she adopted me, you could come up here lots and look at his view. Maybe she wants a big family and can adopt you too. Maybe she needs a live-in dog walker. You could get a recommendation from that actress lady what you walked dogs for."

"Maybe."

"Good to have a fallback plan."

"Fallback from what?"

"From what yer doin' now, like we was a talkin' 'bout earlier."

"I'll keep that in mind. Adoptee, and live-in dog walker."

"I would."

"I know you would."

"I could live here."

"You think so?"

"Yessir," Zeeder nodded.

"Creative juices flow OK here. No having to cut your ear off, or anything like that?"

"I reckon I wouldn't have to."

The two stood there for a few minutes, feeling both the tranquil energy of the now calm ocean and the nervous energy of the people doing the party prep around them. They set their equipment down, starting their own preparation, pausing every so often to look at the full-scale vantage point of such a large chunk of the Pacific. Gina made her way back over to them.

"Sorry to break away like that, but I had to get some details straight."

"No explanation necessary, we understand you have a lot to do," Townes said, still tending to his set up.

"I just wanted this to be my coming to La Jolla party, and now with Kat moving out of the country, incorporate that into the gathering as well."

"I didn't think that was final yet. I mean I knew it was going to happen; I just didn't know when," Townes said.

"You didn't know that she got the final word and is leaving really soon? Oh, I'm sorry, I thought you knew already when she was leaving."

"Where's she going?" Zeeder asked.

"She's going to India," Gina said to Zeeder, then turned back to Townes. "You knew she was wanting to work there, right?"

"Yes, yes, I knew. I just didn't know … know that it was final with dates and all that."

"Well, I'm sure she was going to tell you; she's just rushing to get things together to go. Maybe you should act surprised when she tells you. I'm sorry, I shouldn't have said anything. I have to tend to some things inside. Do you have everything you need?"

"I think we're OK. We make another couple trips to the car, we're fine," Zeeder said.

"Good. Tonight should be fun," Gina smiled. She was uncomfortable that she had been the one to tell Townes, and her discomfort showed.

"We always try for fun," Zeeder said. "And to not suck."

"And not to suck," Townes repeated.

Gina left to go back in the house, leaving the two to continue setting up. Townes was pausing, again looking at the ocean.

"Guessin' you won't have quite as many women to worry about now," Zeeder said.

"What?"

"Nothin'. You OK?"

"Yes, fine."

"Yer not upset, are ya?"

"No, I'm not upset. We haven't been seeing each other all that long, and this was important to her."

"You just think she might have mentioned it sommers in the conversation."

"She doesn't owe me anything. She's been wanting this for quite a long while. It does maybe explain the other night ..."

"I guess now you can focus on her friend and the actress lady."

"What!?"

"Nothin', nothin'. Ya know, once I throwed in with this group in Nashville. Good group, good fellers. They told me when I hired on that it was temporary, 'cause they had a guy out sick, or hurt, arrested, or somethin', I don't remember. Anyway ... wait, I think he rode some two wheeled electric contraption into a pole, that's what it was. Laid hisself up somethin' fierce."

"Is there a point to this country yarn?"

"The point was ... is, that it was a good gig while it lasted, and I knowed it wasn't gonna play out very long. I took it, I did it, and I wasn't pissed when it was done. I mighta liked to have had it goin' on a might longer, but no regrets. Git while the gittin's good, to simplify it a might."

Townes stared back at Zeeder. The silence that followed seemed longer than it was. A slight gust of wind brushed by, sending some paper goods on a nearby table across the yard, people hurrying to contain them. Townes looked again at the ocean, then smiled at the paper that was moving about.

"Why is it, in your very own twisted Southern way, that you seem to have such a knack for capturing the essence of things?"

"I calls it a gift."

"A gift that you have, or a gift that you gave to me?"

"I ain't a givin' you nary a thing. You still owe me fer takin' care of that beast of yourn, whilst yous away courtin' actress ladies in New York."

Townes started laughing and held up his hands to his mouth, as if to say he couldn't respond to that. He left to go back to the car to get the remaining equipment, smiling at Zeeder as he left.

The evening was as perfect as if it had been specifically ordered. It had been a while since Townes and Zeeder had played outside and then it was some small patio, some backyard that did not quite measure up to a backdrop like this one. The view of La Jolla, the view of the ocean, the setting sun. They had never played in such a spectacular setting.

The guests were all attired in Hawaiian garb and all seemed to be festive spirits. Townes thought about what Zeeder had said about doing something good that you knew was only going to be for a short while. He was still baffled that it was as he said it was, and that he should not be upset about Kat leaving when he knew that day would come. They were getting closer and they had fun together but there were other things for her to do now, things she had been wanting to do for a long time.

Townes was just not sure what he was going to do. There was nothing said about not keeping in touch with each other. There was nothing said about anything. He cleared his mind, they played their music, and enjoyed their surroundings, the time passing very quickly. Townes looked at his watch and could not believe they had been there as long as they had. With the occasional light Pacific breeze, and all the stars beginning to come out, it felt like they were suspended in time and it seemed like they had just gotten there. This night could make up for some of the times they played that seemed to last a week, with no one showing up, except for a couple of drunks that kept requesting songs they would never play. This was better. The crowd was amusing, very enthusiastic. *How could you be depressed in Hawaiian gear?* Townes thought. Many of the guests stopped by the area they were playing to show their approval. Townes recognized some of the people from when they played around town, though he did not know their names. They were all nice people. Being here had a great feel to it. He was taken away by the scenery but also hopeful to see Kat and Annie show up. There was no reason they wouldn't. Gina expected them, and Townes wanted them there. He wasn't sure what he would say to either one, so he did his best to not worry about it. Between songs, Zeeder would goad him about not paying attention and would laugh at what he perceived Townes's predicament to be. None of Townes's concerns could take away from how nice it was here. Maybe neither woman would show up and maybe that was all right, too. *Ashley said I should live more in the moment*, Townes thought, but as soon as he did, they showed up together which made him nervous and relieved at the same time.

"See what ya gone and did," Zeeder said.

"I didn't do anything," Townes responded.

"Uh huh, ya did so. Ya thinked about both of 'em, and now here they be."

"You are twisted."

"I know, but I've come to live with it."

CHAPTER 34

Townes and Zeeder watched as Annie and Kat entered the party. Townes kept a close eye on both of them. Zeeder would glance at them, look at Townes, and laugh. Townes would do his best to suppress a laugh in response. The party guests thought the two musicians to be some of the happiest they had ever seen, with all the laughing. Zeeder caught on to their watching and he laughed more. The laughter started to spread, with people moving more to the music, trying to get the rest to do the same.

"Now look what you've done," Townes said, away from the microphone.

"Yeah, hell. I hate it when everbody is a havin' a good time."

The all-inclusive wave caught Annie and Kat by surprise. They stood, watching all the others, wondering what joke they had missed. In no time people were forming a conga line, moving around the immense patio area. Annie and Kat looked at each other, then looked at Townes and Zeeder. Both men shrugged without stopping the music. Women in the line stopped momentarily to remove the flower leis they were wearing and quickly place one on each musician, then rejoin the conga line, continuing the merriment. It was difficult not to get caught up in the revelry. Gina was ecstatic, and Annie and Kat looked like they wished they had gotten there earlier.

When the music stopped, everyone in the line clapped and cheered until they started playing again. The line would start moving again. It was a tossup as to who was happier, the crowd or the band. Somehow they had hit the right button with the group, something that was never guaranteed. They never knew exactly what was going to get a crowd going. There was no set formula. They didn't play in venues with a great deal of room for crowd participation, certainly not of this magnitude. Most places were not large enough for any kind of crowd involvement. The lively people in their bright regalia, parading by them with the sun setting on the Pacific, was more than just all right.

After the conga line had again wound its way around the patio, everyone was clapping and singing. At the exact moment the song ended, they all yelled in unison, waving their hands in the air. The conga line slowly dispersed. The people returned to various locations around the party, still buzzing. Annie and Kat looking for the root cause of the merriment, made their way over to Townes and Zeeder, who thought it an opportune time to take a break, seeing a very happy, if slightly winded crowd.

"You boys seem to be in good form this evening," Kat said.

"I'll say," Annie added.

"Just a good crowd," Townes laughed.

"I think it was more than that," Annie responded.

"His multi-dynamic personality," Zeeder gestured. "Least that's what I keep tellin' him."

"That's for sure," Kat smiled.

"We all know that is not it, but thank you for the collective fabrication. It always sounds better when friends say nice things about you … that aren't true. Zeeder got the crowd laughing," Townes said, grinning.

"I don't know what yer a talkin' about," Zeeder said, turning to tend to his musical equipment.

"So how are you two?" Townes asked.

"Busy, very busy," Annie said, but looking happy to be there.

"And how about you?" Townes asked, looking at Kat. "I heard you are going on a trip."

"Something like that. I meant to tell you the other night that the time frame had been finalized … but I …" Kat turned to look at the ocean.

"That's all right. Congratulations. I know you have been wanting to work out of the country, make a difference and such, so now here it is. I think you make a difference here, but what do I know?" Townes said, hugging her. I'm happy for you. I'll miss you, but I'm happy for you.

"Yes, it really has been a long time getting to this point, so … I don't really know what to say. Be careful what you wish for, I don't … I'll be right back," Kat said, as she turned and walked quickly away.

The three watched her, with Annie the first to show that this was now uncomfortable, but not knowing what to do about it. She looked at Townes, who was already looking at her.

"She has ... um, been wanting to do this for a long time," Annie said, not knowing what to say.

"I know she has."

"So that's a good thing."

"I agree."

"Always hard to leave things behind."

"It is."

"So ..." Annie, now very uncertain of what to say.

"So it is not a problem," Townes said, trying to make Annie feel more comfortable.

"No, I suppose not."

"You've known her longer than I have, so I'm guessing I'm not the authority here. We only ... we ... it's not like ..."

"Not like ...?"

"Not like it's as uncomfortable as you and I are making it."

Annie laughed, realizing the tension Townes had tried to ease. It was indeed not as bad as they in fact were making it. "She is a wonderful person, and she will do well, wherever she is," Annie smiled.

"You are right. She is a wonderful person and we both hate to see her leave." Townes nodded. "Wow, I guess that last bit we played tired me out a little."

"When do you have to start playing again?"

"Oh, pretty soon. I need to get something to drink. Would you like something?"

"Oh ... I ... "

Townes noticed she was feeling uneasy. "If it is uncomfortable for you, don't—"

"No, I ... I don't think it's uncomfortable. I'm just not sure I ... I don't know," Annie said.

"Your choice. That's OK. I'm just thirsty after the conga thing. Almost feel like I was in the line." He paused. "This is the first time I have been alone with you. Well, sort of alone," Townes said, looking at all the people at the party.

"Alone with me?"

"Yes."

"What do—"

"I remember seeing you one time, the first time I saw you, at the restaurant."

"I'm confused."

"You're confused? I'm the emperor of confused," Townes said, scratching his head.

"What restaurant?"

"The first time I saw you."

"At the bar, where you guys were playing that time?"

"No, at the ... it was at the tables outside that day at the restaurant. You were with someone, he was a very vocal fellow ... kind of a prick," Townes said, the last part under his breath.

"What are you talking about?"

"The first time I saw you. You were with a guy. It was outside at the restaurant, the Coffee Cup. I was there with my dog. I wanted ask you out for coffee ... whatever, after I saw you," Townes said, looking down. "Funny, huh?"

"Really?"

"Yes. I'm sorry, I shouldn't have said."

"You said that already," Annie said, cutting him off, "So let's get past that. You wanted to ask me out since ... I'm sorry I don't remember that day."

"There is no reason you should remember that day. You were, or are with someone so."

"I'm not with anyone."

"It appeared that day that you were. At least he seemed to think so."

"I'm not ... wait."

"Wait?"

"Clement."

"Clement?"

"Clement. I was with Clement. Oh, gosh."

"Clement? The guy from the other night. I don't think he had a shaved head, and he had sunglasses on when I saw you with him that first time, that must have been it. He looks a lot different with a shaved head. Knew it was a stretch for two different guys to be ... such total fuckwads," Townes said, the last part under his breath.

"Yes, but he's not ... I'm not with him."

"Kat told me."

"No, I'm not with anyone, why? Why would you—"

"It came up in conversation."

"Because ...?"

"Because I asked if you are ... if you were with someone."

"I guess I'm really confused," Annie said, pulling at her ponytail.

"Well then, if you feel confused, then you know how I feel most of the time," Townes said.

"You don't look confused to me. You might be saying some confusing things, but that's different."

"Maybe we should just forget I said anything."

"I'm still confused. She just said she was leaving, and now you are asking me."

"I didn't mean anything by it. Not anything," Townes said, appearing uncomfortable.

"And?"

"And Kat told me that I really should be spending time with you."

"She didn't say that," Annie said, moving closer to Townes.

"She actually told me that a while ago," Townes said, appearing embarrassed.

"Why didn't she tell me that?"

"I am sure I don't know."

"So today she says she is leaving, and you ask me if I'm seeing anyone?"

"No, I asked Kat. It was just conversation. I have been traveling a lot. My social rhythm is a bit off."

"Traveling."

"Traveling. I couldn't very well just call you up to have a conversation. Also, traveling is code for I was ... I was afraid."

"I'm not sure you should be asking me at all."

"That thought has haunted me since I first saw you."

"Really?"

"Yes, really. There is never a good time, never an easy way," Townes said, looking into Annie's eyes.

"So, you spent time with Kat, so you could ask me out?"

"Hardly. I didn't know you and Kat were friends. Zeeder introduced me to Kat after I saw you that time. They have an art class together."

"Art class ... yeah, yeah, I know."

"Well, he introduced me to Kat, I had no idea you two knew each other. There was no—"

"No what!?"

"There was no plan. I'm not smart enough for that."

"Plan?"

"I wasn't ... oh, forget it. I saw you that day with that guy, and I just thought—"

"You just thought what?" Annie interrupted again.

"I've said too much already," Townes said, shaking his head, looking at the leis he had around his neck.

"No, I want to hear this," Annie said grabbing two chairs for both of them. "Let's hear it. Nice flowers, by the way."

CHAPTER 35

Clement walked up to the gate of Gina's house, intercepted by the large fellow in the Hawaiian shirt.

"Yes, can I help you?"

"Sure, sport. I'm here for the party," Clement said, straightening his bright, lime-green golf shirt.

"Great. You didn't happen to bring your invitation by chance?"

"Nah, I forgot it," Clement said, starting to fidget.

"No problem. I got a list," the man said, producing a clipboard, looking up at the shirt. "Name?"

"Shit," Clement muttered.

"What was that last name?"

"Uh … she said I could just swing by. She was supposed to put me on the list."

"Hmm, well, she didn't tell me that."

"Well, we've been friends a long time, she might have forgotten to tell you."

"Just doing my job, man," the large man said, putting down the clipboard.

"Listen, sport. How 'bout I give you this twenty and you just be a good dude and let me in?"

"Nah, couldn't do that … sport."

"Gonna be an asshole about this, huh? What's your name?"

"You got it right. My name is Gonna."

"What the fuck kind of name is Gonna? What's your last name?"

"This is too easy. Gonna. Gonna kick your ass, if you don't leave."

"I'm going to remember this, Gonna," Clement said, walking away.

"You do that, sport."

Townes looked around as if he was wanting someone to rescue him. Zeeder had wandered off and was over talking with some of the women at the party, too far to see Townes was cornered. Townes took a deep breath and quickly let it out.

"I thought, here you are with this guy—"

"Here I am with this guy, and?"

"If you would stop cutting me off, it might be easier to follow," Townes said. "So you looked incredibly sad. It just got to me."

"I looked sad?"

"Yes."

"You didn't even know me."

"Just because I don't know somebody, doesn't mean I can't see that they are in pain," Townes said, leaning closer.

"You notice that a lot, do you?"

Townes took another breath, holding it in. "Yes, actually."

"How ... why is that?"

"Somebody gave me a theory the other day," Townes said, looking away.

"What?"

"Nothing," Townes said, still looking away.

"So you notice ..."

"I travel, travel all the time. I'm by myself and I notice people. "

"You notice people?" Annie asked.

"Yes. I can tell when they are happy, sad, drifting."

"And you can do this because?"

"I don't know; it just happens."

"Just happens?"

"Yes, it just happens," Townes shrugged.

"Well, I suppose anyone can tell what someone is, or how someone is feeling by looking at their expression," Annie said, matter-of-factly.

"I suppose so, but it's not like that."

"So you saw me, looked at my facial expression and determined I was sad.

Maybe I was just having a bad day."

"That's probably it," Townes said, seeming to drift.

"And because of that, you wanted to ask me out?"

"It's not like ... never mind."

"Well, tell me what it is like. I mean, you see me, you want to ask me out; instead you go out with my friend. Now she's leaving, so you want to ask me out again. That pretty much sum it up?"

"No."

"Well, sum it up for me."

"I really don't ... I'm not ... I probably should start playing the music again."

"Your partner is not back yet, so go ahead and tell me."

Townes was uneasy. The conversation just seemed to be getting worse. He took another deep breath. "I felt a connection. I tried to repress it. I felt you were sad, and I wanted to help you; you seemed like you wanted help. I repressed that. You show up later with Kat and I realized I should not have repressed everything."

Annie looked at Townes, looking to sense whether this was a come on. She continued to look at him, to see if he was going to give her some pick up line, but he didn't. She could see that he was sincere, or if he wasn't, he was quite persuasive in his ruse. She softened a little.

"So why did you repress everything?"

Townes waited several seconds before putting his hand on her shoulder. "Because I didn't want to intrude into your life. I could see that others had done that before, and that some were doing it now ... er, doing it then, when I first saw you," he said, letting the last of the air out of his lungs.

"How did you see that?"

"I have no idea."

"Did Kat tell you about me?"

"No. Besides, I did not know either of you then. I hadn't even met her yet."

Annie did not know what to say. She continued to look at him. His touch on her shoulder felt good. She glanced quickly at his hand. Townes saw her look and started to take his hand away.

"Sorry," he said.

Annie grabbed his arm before he could take his hand away. "How did you do that? How could you know that?"

"I don't know, but I'm sorry I bothered you, sorry I saw you."

They sat looking at each other, Annie holding onto his arm, so he could not pull it away.

"What do you expect me to say?" Annie said, looking into his eyes.

"Expect? I don't expect anything. I don't understand any of this."

"You had to expect something."

"No. The whole thing sort of took me by surprise."

"Surprise how?"

"I wouldn't know where to start."

"Why not?"

"Because it's all new to me."

"Really?"

"Yes."

Annie was still holding onto his arm, looking at him, not looking away. "How am I supposed to interpret this? I mean, you have been going out with my best friend, and now you ask me if I … if … I don't remember what you said, or something. How … how am I supposed to process that?"

Townes paused, letting out another breath. "I really just wanted to go get something to drink during the break. I don't know how we got to this point. But, since we are, I don't know how to interpret this, so I can't tell you how. I am baffled by it and I really wish I hadn't said anything."

"Is this something you normally do?"

"I don't normally do anything … except get on airplanes."

"Then why are you doing this now?"

"This … this, I don't know what this is. Like I told you, I felt a connection, but I'm new at this."

"You are new at this?"

"You are not making this easy for me. New at this … yes, that's what I said."

Annie squinted her eyes at Townes. Her look told him she was not particularly comfortable, but her holding on to his arm told him she was not totally disgusted with him either. Townes was not sure what to do or say. It was awkward but he did not mind her holding on to him. She continued to look at him, her eyes still narrow.

"So?" she asked.

"So, have you ever looked at someone and felt that … I don't know, felt that there was something … something there?"

"You are going to have to be more specific."

"I saw you were with someone. You looked troubled. You looked at me and I thought we connected. I wanted to help you, but I couldn't ... more like I didn't ..."

"I was just having a bad day. Everybody has those."

"Yeah, well, this was more than that."

Annie continued to look at Townes, finally glancing away, then looking back at him. "This is sort of going in circles, so I should probably go," she said, still clinging to his arm.

"Based on Zeeder and the person that hired us don't appear to be in any hurry for us to start back up again, I'm going for a walk. Would you join me?"

"Funny."

"I'm serious."

"I don't know."

Townes took a deep breath, and let it out. "Come walk with me. You don't like it, you don't ever have to talk to me again ... or walk with me."

Annie looked around the gathering, which seemed like it had started to thin out. As large as the house was, it was possible that everyone was still there, just in one of the many rooms. She saw Zeeder and Gina sitting together, laughing.

Gina did not seem to care that there was no music, and since it was her party, she had final say. She looked happy.

"I should probably be a gettin' back to earnin' my pay," Zeeder said, scratching his head.

"No, stay here. You don't have to play anymore," Gina smiled. "I'm enjoying our conversation. I have to say good bye to some guests, then I'll be back. Don't leave."

"I won't. I'll pack up my stuff. Didn't seem like we played very long."

"You played a long time, and everybody loved it. I'll be right back. Do not leave!"

"All righty then, I won't leave. Do you need help cleaning up?"

"No, the caterers will do that, but it is sweet of you to offer."

"Well, without playin' fer very long, we want to be invited back."

"I wouldn't worry about a return invite ... I haven't asked you to leave yet. Your Southern drawl intrigues me."

"Do what now?"

"See, just like that. Nobody from here talks like that."

"I talks the way I talks."

"I'll be back in a minute, then you can tell me all about yourself," Gina said, looking around.

"Not sure there is much to tell."

"I think there is a great deal to tell. You're are just modest."

"Don't know 'bout that."

"We have lots to talk about, so stay put."

Gina gave Zeeder's hand a squeeze and rushed off to say good bye to her guests. Zeeder shook his head as she walked away. "Guess I'll be stickin' around."

"All right. Let's walk," Annie said.

"Good. You can keep holding on to my arm, if you want."

Annie looked at her grasp, taking it away slowly, one finger at a time. They walked along in the cool evening air, the now dark Pacific below their hillside vantage point. They walked slowly and silently, with no discomfort. Neither seemed to be in a hurry to speak, but each knew if someone was going to speak first, it was going to be Townes. Annie was not going to offer to break the silence, though was curious as to what Townes was going to say, should he decide to say anything. She knew people that were not real good about talking, so it was not going to surprise her if he said nothing. He invited her and was going to try to make the best of whatever time she was going to allot him. That was not going to make it any easier to not make a fool of himself. He already felt he was on shaky ground with her.

Zeeder got up and went back to where he and Townes had been playing, and began to tear down and pack the equipment, watching Gina while he did. He looked around for Townes, but did not see him anywhere. He laughed to himself. "Musta got a ride home. Feller sure got a lot a stuff goin' on." He looked back to where Gina was talking with her friends, and she looked over to where he was and smiled, seeing him there, looking at her. She continued to look at him, even with her friends talking to her, and it gave Zeeder a good feeling inside.

"Nice night," Townes said, thinking that was probably as stupid an opening as he could have chosen.

"Hmm."

"No, really. It has been a very nice night. It was a fun group to play for. Nobody called the police, which has happened before, and everyone seemed to enjoy themselves. And now ... I'm walking with you."

"So you are serious, not just making small talk." Annie smiled. "Yes, it was, is, a nice night."

"When we play private parties, it is different sometimes," Townes nodded, feeling a little more comfortable talking about something that was not going to create any controversy.

"How's that?"

"You'd be surprised. We get folks who want us to play stupid shit mus ... sorry, I mean stupid music that we don't know how to play, or things that we just won't play."

"No need to apologize. I've heard that word before ... once," Annie laughed.

"Good. Well, they want us to play stuff we don't do, which is one thing. The other is when they insist on letting them sing, or have one of their friends or relatives sing, or play an instrument and sing."

"Really!? People do that?" Annie asked.

"All the time."

"And?"

"And it never works out. It always comes after somebody is one cocktail too many past the mile marker of too far and then ..."

"Then what?" Annie asked.

"Then somebody, or a couple of somebodies, gets really embarrassed and it ... well, it isn't us. It's awkward, 'cause they are paying and all. It just always ends poorly ... for them."

"I would think so."

"Well, what are we going to do?"

Annie stopped walking. "What do you mean?"

CHAPTER 36

Townes kept walking a few more steps before he noticed Annie had stopped. He turned to face her. "As I said, what are we going to do? They paid us, so we have to let them sing, or whatever. Long as they don't bust up the gear."

Annie chuckled a relieved laugh. "Oh ... yeah, what else could you do?"

"Yes, what else. Wait, what did ... did you think I was talking about you and me?"

"No, no, I wasn't thinking that. I ..."

"I just said a walk, no deep dive into that darkness down there. I put you on the defensive earlier, I won't add to that."

Annie did not know what to say. She just looked at Townes, glancing down at the ocean, then back to where they had come from. Townes could sense further uneasiness from her as he again put his hand on her shoulder.

"What would you think if halfway through the party tonight, Gina brought you up to the microphone and announced you were going to sing?"

Annie's eyes widened, visible even in the darkness. "I would die."

"No, you wouldn't die, but you might feel a bit embarrassed."

"No, I'm pretty sure I would die," Annie said, laughing.

"Well, I'm sorry I brought you to the microphone tonight," Townes said, pausing for a moment. "I didn't know Kat then, then when I saw you, so it just was what it was. My telling you was not to do anything but tell you."

"But you can see how it would, I don't know, make me uncomfortable."

"Yes, and that was not the intention."

"Sometimes intention …"

"I know, I know. People don't intend to get in a car wreck, they intended to go to the grocery."

"That wasn't what I was thinking, but …"

"Yeah, I just keep making points here. You don't have to be nice and walk anymore, we can go back. I just wanted to let you know, that's all. I did that, and probably shouldn't have, but I did."

Annie looked at Townes, but made no effort to move back in the direction they had been. She stood there, looking at the dark ocean below them, as if she were gathering strength from the distant waves, before turning back to Townes.

"Look, I am not sure what to say here," she paused. "I am, or I was with this guy for a long time. It sort of, as Kat describes it, ran its course, or at least I thought it had run its course. We hadn't seen each other in a long time."

"The guy I saw you with at the restaurant, and the shaved head version the other night."

"I … what!? God no. That wasn't him, that was … I … no, not him."

"Sorry. You were with someone for a long time and?"

"Yes, I was with … I don't know why I'm telling you this. Did you drug me or something?"

"Yes, it was subliminal in the music. Sometimes it puts people to sleep."

"Ha, funny. So I just recently saw this guy after all these years and …"

"And you picked up where you left off."

"I wouldn't say that. It's a little more complicated, but …"

"But you are back together, that's probably good."

"We're not back together. We've seen each other, but it is not the same. Lots of things have happened, and I am not sure it feels right."

"I am sure you will do what is right," Townes said.

"I'm not so sure. I seem to have a block sometimes in that department."

"I would find that very difficult to believe."

"Why? Can you see that too?"

They were walking again, strangely enough, not heading back to the party, the walk much easier now than at the beginning. Townes was struggling that he had told Annie in the first place and surprised at the exchange they were now having. Annie was more surprised that she told him about details from her life. They continued their walk.

"I don't know you, that's true but you do not seem to be a person that would have a, what did you call it, 'a block,' about anything."

"How could you know that? Did you see that?"

"Maybe I'm just a pretty good judge of character."

"And that led you to notice me at the cafe?" Annie asked.

"Something like that."

"Hmm."

"Hmm, what?"

"Sounds fishy."

"It's not fishy. I have spent an entire lifetime ... so far, failing to maybe do what I was supposed to do. People describe listening to their inner voice. Hell, I've got so many inner voices ... anyway, A short while ago, I sort of started trying to tune out the multiple voices ... and act more on what I was feeling. That led me to notice you."

"Really?"

"Yes. That and the thought that you might be in the place where I was before I started paying attention," Townes shrugged. "Not that you're not paying attention, but I wasn't."

"You got all that ... from seeing me that one time?"

"Mostly from that one time. I've seen you since, so it wasn't all from that one time."

"That's still quite a bit to glean about me, in such a short time."

"It's hard to explain."

"I should think so. Do you use this approach with all the women you want to see?"

"I'm gone too much to see any women. My dog is even thinking about leaving me for another guy ... it is not an approach. I was just being honest, telling you what I felt, what I saw. I have never told or 'approached' anyone with this sort of thing."

Annie stopped walking, looking up at the stars. She blinked a couple of times and rubbed her eyes with the palms of her hands. "So what am I supposed to do?"

"What do you mean?"

"You are going out with my best friend, and you tell me this, so what response did you think you would get?"

"I didn't know. All I know is how I felt that day, how I feel right now. I just wanted to tell you. World ends tomorrow, list of regrets, this one's not on there," Townes said, seeming to relax.

Annie stepped back, as if to watch Townes's reaction. She could see, even in the dark, he was relieved about what he had said. Annie could see him very clearly and could tell he was not going to move towards her. She seemed to now find comfort in his company, in contrast to her feeling baffled only a short time ago at his disclosure. She now felt very warm, as if she had known him for a long time and was closer to him than she was letting on. There was a peaceful pause.

"I should get you back," Townes said.

"Wait," Annie responded quickly.

Townes didn't move. He held his breath, though not intentionally. "Yes?"

"I used to go out with the guy you saw me with," Annie said, tugging her ear.

"You don't have to explain to ..."

"No, I do, er, I want to. I used to go out with that guy, though not a lot, which is a good thing. It wasn't really a good ... it's a long story, not important," Annie said, tugging on her other ear, and looking around the now starlit evening. "So anyway, I went out to the desert, with Kat, a while ago and met up with some old friends, friends I hadn't seen in a long time. A real long time."

"That must have been good."

"I don't know. It was good on some fronts, not sure about the others. Anyway, one of the friends was somebody I used to be really close to."

"So it was good to see them."

"It was a guy, a guy I used to go with."

"And not the guy I saw you—"

"No! I mean, no, not him, but he did show up later."

"Wow. How did that go?"

"Badly."

"I should think."

"So anyway, this guy I used to go with, we had a real good ... I don't know what we had. We came back here, thought we might try again, but I ... I don't think I, we can. I've thought about it a lot and I just don't think it's going to work."

"So you're staying with the guy I saw you with."

"God no!"

"Oh, sorry."

"Which brings us to now."

"Which brings us ... to now," Townes repeated.

"I ... um, I don't ... I did ... I can't ... I ..."

"You don't have to tell me."

Annie took a breath, scuffing her foot on the ground. "I'm the one doing all the telling. Let's hear about you—what's your story?"

"I don't have a story."

"Everybody has a story."

"Mine is dull."

"Ok, so a guy that writes a book must have something to say. Lost loves, things like that. I told you about ...you know."

"I have to know you a while longer to talk about things like that, lost love and such."

"Why? I told you and I haven't known you any longer than you've known me. What was her name?"

"Are we really having this conversation?" Townes said, locking his hands behind his head.

"You started it, your idea. Give me a name, you don't have to go into details."

"You didn't give me a name."

"I asked first."

"A name?"

"Grant, his name is Grant," Annie said, looking at the ground. "Now you."

"Now me ..."

"What was her name?"

"Norah."

"Norah. All right. When was the last time you talked to her?"

"Years. It's been years. All I do is travel around for work, play music sometimes, and I have a manuscript, but it hasn't been published. A monkey can write a manuscript. In my case, pretty sure one did."

"OK, now we are getting somewhere, evening things up a little, but I want more."

"That's it, sorry."

"Doesn't sound like it from what Kat has told me. Travel all over, play in a band, wrote a book. Doesn't sound like dull to me. Let's hear it."

"Sounds like you summed it up," Townes said, now feeling uncomfortable

"I put it all in there, alter ego, and all that."

Annie laughed. "Don't give me the stage fright dodge, you get up there and play music, you can't be afraid of anything."

"To the contrary."

"Yeah, what are you afraid of?"

Townes scratched his head. "Lately, air travel … Ongoing …rotten produce … brought in by the audience."

Annie laughed more. "That's a good one. What else are you afraid of?"

"You."

She stopped walking and took a long pause, brushing the ground with her foot, looking around, then closing her eyes for a few seconds. "I felt something too, that day you saw me," Annie said, looking away.

"I thought you said you didn't remember me?"

"Well, I did remember you."

"Really?"

"Vividly."

"That never happens."

"I bet it does."

"No, I think I would know."

"I remembered, and I didn't even know who you were. So that night when Kat had me meet her at Jack's, and it turned out to be you, I just … I didn't know what to do, so I left," Annie said, turning back to Townes.

"I remember. Things happen sometimes, you had a patient to take care of."

"That's what I said, but—"

"But …?"

"I didn't have one."

"Wow! Scared you off?" Townes asked. "That sounds about right for me."

"You didn't scare me off. I just … I just didn't know what to do."

"Things happen sometimes, I don't know. We meet people we all of a sudden feel comfortable around, and we don't know why. Sometimes things happen … and sometimes, even though they are good things, they scare the hell out of us."

"Do they ever."

Annie and Townes walked back to the party, much closer together than before. They bumped into each other as they walked. When they did, neither one seemed in a hurry to break the bond of contact, their shoulders touching for the last part of the walk. The party had quieted down, the music equipment in cases. Zeeder was not to be found. The staff was cleaning up. Annie did not see Kat or Gina anywhere.

"Thank you for the walk," Townes said.

"Thank you for the walk," Annie said, more softly.

"I am going out of town for a while, and ..."

"And what?" Annie asked.

"I think there is, or ... there could be more"

"We'll see."

CHAPTER 37

Townes pulled into his driveway and started to unpack his equipment from the trunk. He turned to go into his house and saw Kat sitting on the front step. It was late and the sight of her startled him, causing him to stagger backwards, but managing not to drop the guitar case and amplifier.

"Need a hand?" Kat asked.

"Uh ... I ... no ... yes, if you want. There's a small bag in the trunk with some stands and mics and such, not heavy."

"Didn't mean to scare you," Kat said, as she reached in for the bag. "Close this?" she asked, her hand on the raised trunk lid.

"Sure, thanks."

Kat closed the trunk and moved behind him, on the front porch, Townes fumbling in his pockets for his keys. "You been here long?"

"No. I don't know. I don't think so. Is it OK?"

"Of course, come on in," Townes had found the keys, opening the front door, where they were immediately greeted by Angelina.

"Oh, look! Aren't you cute. I guess I've never seen her. You told me about her. Hello there!" Kat placed the bag on the floor and immediately kneeled down to embrace the dog. "You are so pretty. What is her name?"

"Angelina."

"Oh, you are so pretty, Angelina."

The dog thought this newcomer was worth the wait, clearly enjoying the attention.

"She probably needs to go out. I'll just let her out back," Townes said, the dog moving towards him the minute he said "out." "Be right back." He put his equipment on the floor and headed towards the rear of the house, the dog following quickly behind him.

Kat could hear them stop in the kitchen, with Townes asking a one word question "Biscuit?" then the sound of closing a ceramic container top, and moving to the door. Kat smiled when she could hear crunching for a brief second before the dog left the house. Kat got up off the floor, slowly looking around the sparsely decorated house. There were a great deal of books on the shelves, framed photos on the walls. There was a large wooden desk facing the window with writing journals and some coffee cups full of pens to the side, a desktop computer, a small laptop. Around the house, several dog toys and tennis balls. The photos were of landscapes, Townes with Zeeder, another with Townes and what appeared to be a bartender, the bartender older. Townes and another man, in what looked to be a winery, as there were large wooden barrels all around them. The man had long curly hair and was wearing a Hawaiian shirt. At closer look, Kat could see a grape cluster pattern in the shirt. There were lots of pictures of the dog. There were also several photos of a different dog. One of the photos of the different dog had a dog collar draped over it. Kat held both hands up to her chest and smiled. She heard Townes and the dog reenter the house.

"Sorry about that. She needed to go out. Can I get you anything?"

"Are you having anything? I should probably go," Kat said, still looking at the photo with the dog collar.

"Go? You just ... er, I just got here."

"Well, if you are having something. Otherwise don't go to any trouble."

"No trouble," Townes said, now back in the room with Kat, the dog coming to reacquaint herself with her, then veering away, quickly finding a tennis ball and bringing it to her, dropping it at her feet.

"What would you like?" Townes said. "Hey, you know better than that. No fetching in the house." Both Kat and the dog turned to look at Townes. "I'm talking to her," Townes said, pointing to the dog.

"I don't mind."

"Nope, she knows. Go get your bone. Where's your bone?"

The dog looked around quickly, then moved to a wooden barrel, not unlike those in the photo, only much smaller. She stuck her head in and began nosing for her desired item. After a brief perusal, she came up with a large bone, a triumphant look on her face.

"Good girl. Now go get in your place," Townes said, the dog moving over to a dog bed on the floor, putting herself in the best position to watch and chew.

"Impressive," Kat nodded.

"As soon as we go in the kitchen, she'll be up on the couch. What can I get you?"

"What are you having?"

"I'm having bourbon, but you can have anything else you want, except for scotch. I don't like scotch, or cheap white wine."

"Bourbon sounds fine."

"You can stay here with the monster or come in the kitchen."

"She's not a monster, she's darling."

"You wouldn't say that when she was standing on you, at four in the morning, wanting to go outside."

"I wouldn't mind."

"You say that now," Townes laughed, moving back into the kitchen. "How do you take your bourbon?"

"However you do."

"Good, best way."

Kat resurveyed the room, now noticing several Navajo rugs draped over some of the furniture. She could hear Townes filling a container with ice, a cupboard door opening and closing. Townes returned with the container cradled in his arm, glasses with ice in each hand, setting them on the desk. He opened a cabinet filled with bottles."

"A couple of flowers OK?" he asked.

"Flowers?"

"Four Roses. It's the brand of bourbon. Weak play on words."

"Sure," Kat said, raising her eyebrows.

Townes poured the bourbon into the glasses, about one-third of the way up, then brought them over to the table in front of the couch, moving a couple of coasters out of a stack there and placed the glasses on them. "Please, sit." The dog raised her eyes. "Not you," he said, then turned to Kat. "I meant you, please," motioning to the couch and chair beside it. "Wherever you are comfortable."

"Where are you going to sit?"

"Uh, does that ... sit where you want."

221

"You first."

"Ok," Townes said, moving to the couch. "How's this?"

"Good," Kat said, as she joined him on the couch.

"Better than the steps?"

"The steps were fine, it was nice out. You know, you were at the party. You guys really made it. Did you have fun?"

"Yes, but you didn't seem to hang around."

"Yeah, I, I don't want to talk about that."

"OK. Well, yeah, the party was great. Sometimes a mixed bag, parties, but not this one. Some house she has."

"Gina has always done well. She was kind of adrift for a while, but I think she found herself again," Kat laughed gently.

"Why the laugh?"

"We got together out in the desert several months ago, and we ... some of the ... she had an epiphany, of sorts. It was quite a weekend," Kat said, raising her eyebrows.

Townes paused at the familiarity of the description but said nothing. He reached for a glass, swirling the contents, then passing it to Kat, repeating the process for his own.

"To your new adventure."

Kat raised her glass, managing only a half smile, and clinked glasses. They both drank and both seemed to be thinking about something they thought funny.

"I hope I'm doing the right thing," she said, quietly.

"Well, now is the time to figure it out. A lot easier to get home if you are still at home."

Kat smiled. "I know. You know something? I never second guess. I always just do whatever," she said, taking another drink. "These flowers are really good," she nodded. "I mean, indecision is not something I struggle with, you know? I just need to do something different. But by different, I don't mean different from you. That part I am actually not wanting to change. I had this travel thing in my mind for a long time. It just seems like I have to do this. It's not a reflection on you."

Townes took a taste of his bourbon. "You're right, good flowers," he paused, looking at his glass, then at Kat. "I didn't think it was a reflection on me. I know how important this thing is to you."

"It is. Thing is, I don't know if I'm going to come back."

"You'll come back."

"How do you know?"

"I just do. The thing is, from previous experience with you, I think you know that too."

"It might be a long time."

"Maybe, maybe not. Which part are you afraid of, the going there ... or the coming back?"

Kat looked at him for a several seconds. "Like I said, I'll be there a long enough time that while I'm gone you should continue to drink bourbon ..." Kat said, taking a taste, "and continue to have fun."

The dog chewing on the bone was suddenly louder.

"Is that what you wanted to tell me?" Townes asked.

"I didn't know what I wanted to tell you. I'm not in a position to tell you anything. I haven't known you that long, so ..."

"So. You can tell me whatever you want."

"No, not really."

"Sure you can."

"I didn't come here to tell you anything. Well maybe ..."

"Maybe what?"

"Maybe ... I don't know."

"I think you do know, but what?"

"I think you and Annie should spend time together."

"Hmm. You said that before."

"She could really use somebody in her life, and I just think the two of you would be good for each other."

"I don't know how to ... what to say to ..."

"You don't need to say anything to that. You two were sort of meant to get together, and things sort of got shifted."

"Shifted? That part of your seeing things?"

"Yes, it is, and yes, shifted. It happens sometimes." Kat finished her drink. "So many things, so many places," she said, swirling the ice in her glass.

"Yeah, you told me some things about me when we first met, and I didn't ask you how you knew those things without meeting before. I probably should have had you elaborate. For the record, I have been trying to get you to elaborate."

"I know you have." She took a breath and let it out. "I haven't read your book. I'd like to, but I can see, I can feel ... that it is going to be successful, and I'm not saying that because I like you, which I do. I don't like to talk about how I know, or how it is that I come to know things that much, ya know?"

"Why is that?"

"Sort of a conflict of Eastern and Western philosophy that I am not always prepared to engage in."

"Boy, do I have someone for you to meet. You two would have a lot to talk about."

"Who is this person?"

"Care for some more fresh flowers?" Townes asked, scratching his head, trying to back pedal from a conversation that might be at least as difficult to explain as the conversation he was in.

"Please."

Townes finished his drink, getting up to repeat the process from before. When he turned, Kat turned quietly and turned off the light, moving through to the unseen section of the house. Townes returned with the fresh drinks, surprised that Kat was no longer in the room. He stood there, holding the two refilled glasses, one up to his head as he scratched. He hesitated before he put the glasses back on the table.

"Bring them back here," Kat said.

CHAPTER 38

The day was clear as could be. The blue sky projected its mirror image on the ocean, giving it a cyan hue. There was no missing the intensity of the reflection. The wind was light and a few sailboats in the distance looked like small, multicolored flags moving across the blue glass. The light rose-colored walls of the La Valencia Hotel were the proper selection from the palette to coordinate with the turquoise, with the added green accents of the palm tops dotting the canvas. Kat had her sunglasses on, taking them off momentarily, as if to verify that the colors were as vibrant as they appeared to be. She took it all in, and smiled, returning the glasses to her face.

"I am going to miss this," she said.

"How could you not?" Annie replied. "This place will miss you. I will miss you."

Kat smiled and touched Annie's hand. "I'll miss you too. Thanks for meeting me for lunch. I wanted to meet for breakfast, but I just couldn't get up. I think it was the flowers," Kat said, rubbing her head.

"Flowers?"

"What?"

"You said it was the flowers."

"I did? I meant bourbon. It was the bourbon," Kat said, still looking towards the ocean.

"You were drinking bourbon?"

"Yes. Apparently more than I thought."

Annie laughed. "I don't think I have seen you drink bourbon. Is this something new?"

"No, not new."

"Huh. What do you know? Kat likes bourbon."

Kat said something Annie could not make out, sounding just like humming. Annie looked out to the water, as if to find what Kat was focused on. They sat there quietly, each comfortable with the silence and enjoying how nice the outside felt. They may have sat there longer but a waiter interrupted their respite.

"Coffee for you, and green tea for you," he said, placing the tea in front of Kat. "Are you ready to order?"

"What? Oh, yes. Annie?"

"Um, how about the fruit, and some yogurt."

"All right, and for you?"

"Eggs Benedict please. I'm hungry," Kat smiled.

The two sipped their beverages and continued in the contentment of silence. Annie fidgeting slightly, turning her knife on the table with the tip of her finger, all the while scanning the ocean view.

"Gina seems to have really found her way. That weekend in Palm Springs must have struck a major chord with her. I'm glad," Annie nodded.

"She is happy and on a new path."

"Yes, that's good."

"Hey, we got through to her."

"I don't know if we did."

"Of course we did. She would still be doing stupid stuff with those other two if we hadn't gotten through to her," Kat said, rubbing her eyes under her sunglasses.

"Well, I don't know."

"Just once, you could give yourself credit for something."

"You did most of it."

"No, it was equal."

"I don't think so," Annie said, fidgeting more.

"It was, it worked, leave it at that."

"All right, we got through, that's what counts."

"Right. Listen, I have a suggestion for you ... changing subjects," Kat said, stretching her arms.

"Sure, what is it?"

"While I'm gone."

"OK," Annie said, sipping her coffee.

"While I'm gone, I want you to go out with Townes."

Annie choked on her coffee. "What!?"

"I want you to go out with him while I'm gone."

"I heard you," Annie said, wiping her chin with her napkin.

"Did I say something wrong?"

"I ... no ... I just, would not have expected you to say that," Annie coughed.

"I don't know if I am coming back, and ..."

"Shut up! You're coming back."

"Well, maybe, maybe not. Regardless, it is going to be a long time and you two should spend some time together."

"Because?"

"Because you both deserve to be happy," Kat said, moving the teapot that was in front of her.

"What about you and Townes deserving to be happy?"

"I can't ask him to just hang around, while I'm out in the universe."

"Maybe he wants to hang out."

"Maybe he's been hanging out his entire life life. Work has been his total existence. Sound familiar?"

"Hah, funny," Annie said, tilting her head.

"I know you had rekindled something with Grant, but that seems to have stalled, hasn't it?"

Annie put her napkin down and looked back out at the ocean. She looked like she was wanting to say something, but was having trouble putting the words together. The light breeze kept the flags moving on the horizon. "I don't know."

"Maybe the trip to Palm Springs and the time you spent was just closure."

"Closure?"

"Closure on where you were, versus where you are now. I was hoping, for your sake, and for Grant's, that things would work out. He is really a great guy, and I am glad I got to know him better. You both tried to start things up again, but it didn't work out, and that is not your fault ... at least I hope it isn't. That knucklehead friend of Grant's never seemed to help things, but I guess in the end, Rex wasn't so bad, he's just full of shit," Kat sighed. "But it was closure on something that happened when you were younger. You looked at it again through older eyes, and an older soul, but it just didn't happen. But now that you have that closure, that closure you needed, you need to move on. More than that, you need to have fun. I think Townes does too, and I think you would be good for each other."

"And he can't have fun with you?"

"I'm going to India. That's not his idea of fun, and I wouldn't ask for that to be his idea of fun," Kat said, pausing. "I'm not sure bourbon helps my conversational skills."

"Don't you like him?"

"Yes, of course I like him."

"If you like him, why are you trying to get me to see him?"

"Because I think you two belong together, or are supposed to be together. It's hard to explain."

"More than you two belong together?"

Kat took a drink of her tea, picking up a small leaf that had blown on the table. She held up the leaf, turning it around to view all sides, then blew on it, letting it go. "Yes, more than that."

"How can you say that?"

"I just can."

"I'm going to need more than 'I just can,'" Annie said, giving Kat a scowl.

"Trust me on this," Kat said, again sipping her tea.

"I trust you on everything."

"Well, then this shouldn't be a stretch then, should it? You deserve to be with someone."

"You haven't been with anyone in, I don't know, in … forever? So maybe you deserve to be with someone."

"But I'm leaving, starting over, I can't be with someone … at least not right now. Maybe I'll find someone in India. Maybe I'll find myself. Either way, I won't be here. I won't be with Townes."

"And you think I should be?"

Kat smiled, then rubbed the side of her head. "You might have to learn to drink bourbon."

"I don't want to learn to drink bourbon," Annie said, tapping her fingers on the table, in time with every word.

"Why not?"

"It doesn't appear to be doing much for you today."

"But it was great last night," Kat smiled, putting her hand over Annie's, also tapping in time with every word.

"Maybe you are still drunk," Annie laughed.

"No, I'm pretty sure I would feel better if I was. Maybe a drink would help."

"Listen to you! What's the matter with you?"

"I want you to spend time with Townes. The rest should fall into place from there."

"I'm not so sure."

"Well, I am, so do it!"

The waiter came with their food and they said nothing while he saw to his task. "Let me know if you need anything else," he said.

"How about a Bloody Mary?" Kat asked. "Absolut Peppar."

"Certainly. And anything for you?" The waiter asked, turning to Annie.

"I, uh, I don't think I—"

"Come on! We aren't going to be able to do this for a while," Kat said, pointing her butter knife at Annie.

"Well, OK. But only because you pulled a knife on me."

"Darn right," Kat said, continuing to motion with the knife. "It's got to make my head feel better."

"Very good, coming right up," the waiter said, leaving the table.

They waited until he was gone before they spoke again.

"Lighting it up a little early, aren't you?" Annie asked.

"Aren't we?" Kat corrected.

"I'm not lighting it up."

"You might as well. It's a beautiful day, we're outside, I'm hung over, and I'm going to miss you so much," Kat said, looking down.

"I'll try to keep a handle on things, so you can drink as much as you want."

"I don't want you to keep a fucking handle on things. I want you to have some fun and not worry about what anybody thinks. You want to keep a handle on something, keep a handle on Townes. And by that, I mean a good, fun handle. Don't let go," Kat said, her fist clenched.

"Are you feeling all right?"

"Hell no. I've got a hangover the size of this hotel and I'm trying to convince my best friend that she needs to loosen up, so ... no, I'm not."

"I have plenty of fun."

"No, you don't."

"Since when?"

"Since always."

"Always?" Annie asked.

"Look, you started to loosen up a little when we were out in Palm Springs..."

"And how did that turn out?"

"If that asshole Clement hadn't come along, it would have turned out fine. Certainly better for me. I don't generally punch guys in the nose," Kat said, pressing her fist up to her face, then pursing her lips. "Not very Zen-like."

"Well, I don't know."

"You and Grant had some fun, and now you're figuring out that maybe you can still be friends, but that you maybe don't belong together."

"I just—"

"Don't over-think it. Townes needs somebody. Townes needs you. You need Townes. Trust me. I have a feeling he's going to hit it with that book of his, and having you in his corner is only going to make it that much better for both of you."

"And just when did you—"

"Here are your Bloody Marys, Absolut Peppar. How is everything?" The waiter asked.

"Ah," Annie let out a breath through clenched teeth. "Everything is fine, thank you."

"Very good," the waiter said, not convinced by the sound Annie made.

"She's fine. She just got a new boyfriend," Kat said, smiling.

"Oh, I see. Well, congratulations," the waiter said, departing.

"I didn't—"

"He's gone," Kat said, watching the waiter walk away.

"Ahhh! You are making me crazy!"

"Not the intention," Kat said, turning back to Annie.

"When did you, you decide I was supposed to be with Townes?"

"Not that long ago ... a while. I don't know. Here's to my dear friend Annie, and her new, loosened-up ... is that a word? Her loosened-up lifestyle," Kat said, raising her glass.

Annie raised her glass slowly. "You are determined to make me crazy before you leave, aren't you?"

"Just fun crazy, not the other one. I've seen too much of the other one."

CHAPTER 39

Clement stood next to the red Ferrari, occasionally wiping off specks of dust with a large white cloth. The license plate read "FASTLWYR." He saw his reflection and rubbed his shaved head, and examined his teeth, attempting to sing some song that he didn't know all the words to. The phone in his pocket rang, the ringtone a loud, misplayed guitar riff, the same tune as whatever it was that he was trying to sing.

"Talk to me."

"You always answer the phone like that?" the person on the other end asked.

"I don't always do anything the same," Clement said, puffing his chest out.

"I bet you're shining that fucking car, aren't you?"

"No ... I'm in my office," Clement said, stepping back from the car.

"Bullshit, you're outside."

"What have you found out, Topper?" Clement said, twirling the white rag.

"There's not much to tell on your boy. He's just a guy."

"Just a guy? What do you mean he's just a guy?"

"Hey, he's nothin' special. Lived all over, has his own consulting business, plays music in clubs, never been married, no kids, no arrests, just a guy," Topper said.

"I'm paying you to find out what I already know."

"Hey, what can I tell you?"

"You can sure as shit tell me more than that for the money I'm paying you!" Clement said, starting to throw the rag at the car, then stopping mid-throw, letting the rag drop to the ground.

"Hey, easy, lawyer boy. Your homeboys might be afraid of you but I ain't beyond emptying your garage, sending you back a big red square paperweight."

Clement stood, stewing, picking up the rag, placing it in a nearby bucket, then getting a new one from a large stack he had.

"Sorry."

"You'd better be, 'cause I'll do it."

"Just see what else you can dig up, OK?"

"It's what I live for, to make you happy," Topper said.

"I'm sure it's not."

"There is one other thing."

"What other thing?"

"He's got a buddy."

"Who doesn't?"

"Besides you?"

"Ha, ha. A buddy."

"The guy he plays music with, in the clubs."

"Yeah, so?"

"I'm pretty sure I know who he is. I seen him before. I just need to verify it with some guys. I'm waitin' for them to call me back"

"Everybody looks familiar."

"To you maybe. To me they're all different dipshits walkin' around, sorta like you."

"You are really trying to be friendly today, aren't you?"

"Hey, just bustin' yer balls. Sometimes it's too easy," Topper said, crunching some food.

"What are you eating?"

"Potato chips, pastrami sandwich."

"You can't wait until ..."

"I seen this guy, or a picture of this guy, but I don't remember where it was. I got some guys, they been outta town. They can verify, when they get back," Topper said, his mouth full.

Clement pulled the phone away from his ear, shaking his head. "I don't give a shit about him."

"You might."

"Why?"

"Trust me. You just might."

"I'm interested in the blonde hair, not the brown hair."

"And why was that again?"

"Because I think he's making a move on my woman."

"He's makin' a move on that fuckin' car?"

"No!"

"That's the only thing you give a shit about. That and money."

"Ha ha … again. I think he's trying to put the moves on Annie and that ain't gonna happen."

"Last I heard, she ain't your woman."

"Well, contrary to what you believe, you don't know everything," Clement said, his face starting to match the color of the Ferrari.

"When was the last time she went out with you?"

"She's been busy."

"I thought so."

"That's none of your fucking business. Your business is what I tell you is your business."

"Two words."

"What?"

"Paper weight."

Clement took the phone away from his ear, placing it on mute and bent over facing the ground. "Aghhh!" he yelled until he was out of breath. He straightened up, closed his eyes and took a deep breath.

"You still there?"

"I'm here."

"Hello?"

Clement realized the phone was still on mute and pressed the button. "Yeah."

"Thought I'd lost you. Anyhow, I'm gonna see if I can verify who his buddy is, see where that takes us."

"But you are going to keep looking for anything on my guy."

"Yeah, yeah, whatever. You could save yourself a shitload of cash by getting another girlfriend that doesn't want to go out with you."

"Just do it and get back with me."

"Your money," Topper chomped and hung up.

Clement put his phone back in his pocket and rubbed his forehead back over the top of his shaved, shined head. He picked up a clean rag, twirling it in his other hand as he continued to rub his head. He pulled the phone back out of his pocket, and pushed the button of a number that had been saved in speed dial. The call went straight to voicemail.

"This is Annie. Please leave me a message."

Clement paused, letting out a breath before he spoke. "Hey, baby, how ya doin'? Just calling to say hey, and see if you want to get together … er something … so call me back. Love you." He again put the phone in his pocket. "Fucking musicians."

He put the Ferrari back in the garage. The garage had photos of him in various places with the car. The garage was spotless. Immediately after getting out of the car, he put a cover on it, tapping the hood, rubbing it slightly, once again trying to remember the words to the song he was singing earlier, but the results were the same. He walked back into his house, looking at himself in every one of the mirrors that hung in every hallway and every room. He still carried the white rag he had been using to remove dust specs from his Ferrari. He walked to the bar area of the house, drawing himself a beer from the tap installed there.

"Brewski always helps," he said, drinking the beer in loud fashion, finishing it quickly, holding the glass up to the light. "Yeah, baby!" he said, letting out a loud belch. "Man, that's good!" he shouted, waving the glass around, as if to show someone in the empty house.

He walked around the house taking his clothes off as he walked, revealing a body that had been completely shaven and skin that looked like there had to be a tanning bed somewhere in the house. He grabbed a remote off the kitchen counter, activating a sound system within the house with a decibel level that could make a person's ears bleed. He flipped through the music until he arrived on the song he was trying to sing.

"Yeah!" he said, trying to sing along with it, still not getting the words right.

By now he was down to his underwear, shouting words to the song, until it ended, holding his arms in the air at the conclusion. He was out of breath. He backtracked through the house until he found his pants, retrieving his phone.

"Alvin. Yeah, baby, it's big Clement. What the fuck you up to?"

"Hey, BC. What's up?"

"Just got done working out, polishing the car, feeling the burn. You want to go get in some trouble tonight?"

"I got some stuff I need to—"

"Pussy! You are a complete corporate toady, pussy."

"Listen to you, big time lawyer."

"That's right, big time Clement."

"What you got in mind?"

"Go get some tails in us, gobble a steak, stuff you're good at."

"Yer killin' me."

"Yeah, baby!"

"OK, but only 'cause I don't want to hear you bitch."

"Yer a bitch! Cool school. I knew you had it in ya."

"Where?"

"Jack's."

"All right."

"So solid."

"You are a weird dude, Clement."

"That's me. See you at six-thirty," Clement said, ending the call. He looked around the room, starting to pace and began talking to himself in a low tone, then raising his voice. He turned the music back on, shouting the same song he always seemed to be trying to sing. He looked at the only photograph that had more than just him, or more than just him and his car. The expression on the attractive blonde woman he had his arm around, looked like someone had put her hand in something slimy.

"That's my girl!"

CHAPTER 40

Northern California, Wine Country

Townes looked over the hood of the old Jeep, the top and doors long since gone. The view of the vineyards starting next to them stretched into the distance, and the mountains behind them made for a picture so calming that it actually frightened him for a second. The complete absence of noise except for the slight sound of the grape leaves fluttering with the breeze. The uniformity of the rows of vines, seeming to stretch on forever, following the contours of the hills. The air was much drier here than La Jolla, but the sky was the same deep blue. Townes set one foot outside of the Jeep, stepping where dirt clung to his boot. He took his other foot out of the Jeep, now standing, bending forward to place his elbows on the vehicle. He looked down, knocked his boots together to watch the dust come up. He looked back up to the grapevine view and smiled.

"This is what I have been needing," Townes said to the driver of the Jeep, a taller, stocky man, with shoulder length curly, dark hair and a grape cluster print Hawaiian shirt.

"Well, fuck, I been tellin' you that for months," Crosetti replied. "Get out there and talk to the grapes, you'll feel even better."

"Talk to the grapes?"

"Fuck, yeah, I do it all the time."

"Yeah, but you are fucking crazy."

"I know. You have to be to get into the wine business."

"No, you have to be crazy to get into the book business."

"Ah, fuck that. You're gonna be fine, gonna hit it big, I know it," Crosetti said, making a wild gesture with his arms in the air.

"I think I should say to hell with the book thing and move up here and work with you."

"You're here now. Call 'em up and tell them to send your stuff up here, you're stayin'."

"I can't right now. I'm working on a couple of other things I need to finish up, but I won't tell you that I wouldn't ever do it, because I might," Townes said, still looking at the vines.

"You're always fucking working on something, but it's a standing offer. Let's go taste some grapes."

"I don't want to be eating what you are going to turn into vino."

"Well, if you eat enough grapes to run us short, I'm sending you a bill for the goddamn difference."

"Understood."

"You need to be drinking wine, not eating all the fucking grapes."

"It was your idea."

"I just want you to know how they start out. Don't be filling your pockets, or any shit like that," Crosetti laughed.

"You can search me."

"Like hell. That's what the girls are for. I'm not doing it."

The two men left the Jeep and walked out into the vineyard, laughing as Crosetti's dog trotted behind them. The allure of this setting was quite powerful. Crosetti had grown up here, so he knew the country well and chose for it to remain his home. Townes was weary of the airplanes, weary of the travel, weary of all the components that made up the engine for his business. He was more comfortable here with his friend.

"Do you ever get lonely up here?" Townes asked.

"Fuck no, I talk to the grapes."

"Do they talk back?"

"When I make 'em into wine they do. When I don't talk to 'em enough before, they hold back their full flavor. When I talk to 'em enough, they let me know by turning into kick ass wine. When they're pissed, the wine is just too hot. They let me know."

"What about when you are waiting for them to talk to you?"

"I take a trip somewhere," Crosetti said, taking a small cluster of grapes off the vine, biting into the entire bunch, juice running down his chin. "They're pretty happy with me right now. Go ahead, try some."

Townes found a small suitable cluster, taking a couple of grapes in his mouth. "Good."

"No, no, fuck no! Not a couple of grapes. Take a monkey bite and eat the whole goddamn bunch," Crosetti said, repeating the ritual.

Townes followed suit, taking the whole bunch. "You're right, it's better," Townes mumbled, juice running down coming out the corners of his mouth.

"Don't swallow the seeds," Crosetti said, spitting the seeds out on the ground. "You'll grow Pinot Noir in your belly. Too damned hard to harvest there. Let's go get some wine, this work makes me thirsty."

"It's only nine-thirty," Townes said, spitting the seeds out.

"Really?! Fuck, we're a couple hours late!" Crosetti said, moving towards the Jeep, his dog following, getting in quickly and starting the engine. "Let's go! Quit eating all my fucking grapes!"

Townes shook his head, laughing, wiping the grape juice from his face. "OK, OK."

Townes was not even completely in the Jeep when Crosetti pressed on the gas, the vehicle coming to life and moving down the dusty road. "Time's a wastin. There's wine to be drunk!" he shouted. Townes fell backwards as the vehicle lurched forward, grabbing for anything he could to keep from flying out of the now quickly moving, noisy transport.

"Ha-ha! I threw some fuckers out of here one time, tryin' to tell me how to run my vineyard. They flew right the hell out the back of the Jeep and I never went back to get 'em! I had to wash the inside, 'cause I think they shit themselves on the way out the back," Crosetti yelled over the noise of the engine, laughing harder as he shifted gears.

"I can believe it!" Townes yelled, still trying his best to hold on.

Crosetti kept laughing, rocking his head forward, as if that would get the Jeep to go faster, the wind in his face more considerable due to the long departed windshield. They sped up and down the roads between the vineyards, dust flying, Crosetti laughing all the while. The speedometer was broken, so Townes had no idea if they were going a hundred miles an hour or thirty. He only knew it was hard to hold on with no top, no front windshield, or doors. Anything over a little fast seemed like a lot fast. The calming symmetry of the vine rows helped to maintain some balance, even as they flew by. There was something in their uniformity that spoke to a better grounding of the soul. Something was as it should be, and even though the total spirit of the grapes would not be revealed for some time yet, their organization said that they were going to be happy, no matter what. They finally came to a stop back at the winery, a huge cloud of dust engulfing them as they did.

"Let's get some wine," Crosetti said, hopping out of the Jeep, the swirling dust collecting in his long hair.

"I asked before if maybe is wasn't a little early for that. I wonder why I would think that?" Townes asked, waiving his hand in front of his face, to clear the air, spitting out the dust from his mouth.

"It's never too early or too late in the day. There is so much great wine. We've only got so much time to taste it. We pass up an opportunity, we might not get to taste the best wine in the world at that very moment. We miss it, we're fucked. Don't wait, ever!"

Townes rubbed the dust out of his eyes, took his baseball hat off, slapping the dust off it against his leg, brushing the dirt out of his hair. He wiped the corners of his mouth. "I guess I never thought of it that way."

"Well your priorities are way fucking out of whack."

"I'm starting to think so."

"Let's go get some wine and see if we can get you recalibrated."

"I would think that wine at this time of the morning would recalibrate anyone, at least until the following day."

"See, there's another place you're out of whack. You're not just recalibrating for the day, you're recalibrating for the long haul."

They started walking towards the winery, the dust now clearing.

"For the long haul?" Townes asked, putting his cap back on.

"Yeah, the long haul. You taste that wine and you picture a morning like today if it's good. If it's shitty, you picture, I don't know, you picture some shitty place that you've been."

"I'm not sure I understand."

"Just about any winery where you drink wine, the ambience of the place is going to take over and add extra points to what you think of the wine, because you are only seeing what's in front of you. You need to take it deeper than that. I'm a farmer, so I always remember what the weather was like that year, what the grapes were saying to me when I talked to them. You would probably, as most people do, think about what you were doing, or where you were that year. Hopefully, you will think about a beautiful woman you were with when that wine was made," Crosetti said, the dust glistening in his hair as he spoke.

"My palate is not … not sommelier quality."

"No, fuck that shit. I'm not talking about that crap. I told you before, I'm a wine drinker, not a wine taster. That twirly glass shit puts people off. I hate that. I'm talking about visualizing, visualizing the connection everything in that glass has with the world. For that, sometimes you need to drink it at ten in the morning or whatever the hell time it is. The universe is leaving all kinds of clues just laying around. You just need to pay attention. It ain't about getting drunk, though that's not always so bad either."

"If it starts at this time of the day, the outcome seems pretty certain."

"Then you had better pay extra close attention. Man, it's hot out here already."

"And dusty."

"Yeah, 'cause you were driving so fucking fast," Crosetti grinned.

"You were driving."

"Why'd you let me drive so fucking fast and stir up all this dust?"

"I'm just shitful, I guess," Townes said, shaking his head, dirt still fluffing off his hair like a halo.

"Knock it the fuck off, then," Crosetti said, as he started to take his clothes off. "And let's get this dust you stirred up off of us," he continued, leaving a trail of clothes on the ground behind him as he walked.

"Got any vineyard tours coming through today?" Townes called to him.

"Fuck, I hope so. They'll talk about this around their dinner tables for years. How they saw the naked guy running through the vineyard," Crosetti said, picking up his now naked pace to a run, jumping into the nearby pond.

"How they saw Sasquatch swimming in the vineyard pond," Townes laughed. He watched the event unfold in front of him, not surprised at what he just saw. He moved towards the pond where Crosetti's wet head now sprang up.

"Man this feels good. Get your ass in here. It really wakes you up."

"I think the Jeep ride did that already." Townes said, collecting the string of clothing as he moved closer to the pond.

"You wanna be awake when you drink this wine we're gonna drink."

"I'm awake."

"You're awake, but you're dusty as hell. I don't want your dirty ass riding in my clean Jeep. We're wasting valuable drinking time, so hurry the fuck up," the bobbing head laughed, before going under again.

"Shit, all right, all right," Townes said, piling Crosetti's clothes on a rock and adding his own, moving slowly towards the water.

The head reappeared. "Fuck that, take a run and jump, otherwise you'll take all fucking day to get in. It's like the grapes. Get into the fucker!"

Townes took a deep breath, backed up a few steps and took a run and jumped into the pond, letting out a loud yell as he did, Crosetti laughing the entire time.

Townes went under, coming back up quickly. "Son of a bitch, that's cold!"

"I know it is. It's from an underground spring. Feels good though, doesn't it?"

"I'll tell you when I can feel my toes."

"It probably ain't your toes yer bitchin' about," Crosetti laughed harder.

"You got that right," Townes said, still gasping.

"Bring some girls with you next time to do this, it's more fun," Crosetti said, walking out of the pond to get his clothes. "And quit fucking around and get out of there, we got wine to drink!"

CHAPTER 41

The smell of the wood smoke burning, and the food cooking on the large Tuscan grill by the winery cave reminded Townes of someplace he had been before, and smelled like the Fourth of July of his youth. Asparagus, tomatoes, chili peppers, and meat combined with the sweet fragrance of the smoke was near-intoxicating. The scent seemed to stick to Townes, even though he and Crosetti sat far enough away that it could not reach them. Townes thought the Pinot Noir they were drinking acted like an organic magnet for everything else.

"So what's on your mind?" Crosetti asked, running his fingers through his hair, still damp from the bath in the pond.

"Do I have to have something on my mind to come up here?" Townes said, looking at the color of the wine as he continued to fill his nostrils with the smell of the cooking.

"Fuck no, you don't, but you're always so goddamn busy that you don't ever get up here, so I figured you must have something bouncing around in there," Crosetti said, taking a large drink of wine. "Fuck, that's good. Who made this?"

Townes laughed, taking a drink. "Yes, it is good, and I think you did."

"That food smells pretty good too, doesn't it? Mariano knows how to do everything around here, especially cook."

The Mexican man tending to the grill looked over when he heard Crosetti mention his name. Crosetti smiled back at him and raised his glass.

"Si," Mariano replied, adjusting the height of the grill above the wood coals, turning a large hand crank on the side of the apparatus, also raising his glass. He brushed some sort of marinade on the meat, releasing even more powerful smells for Townes to try to make room for. Mariano took off his well-worn cowboy hat, removed a bandana from his pocket, and wiped the inside band of the hat, placing the hat back on his head.

"Caliente?" Crosetti shouted. "He's a hard working son of a gun, works all the time, sort of like you."

"Got to, got to get it done."

"Get what done?"

"Everything ... get everything done."

"How much wine we gonna drink, you work yourself to death? You need a good woman, that's what you need. She'll make you slow the fuck down."

"I see you don't have one."

"Hey, I was married once. That's ahead of you."

"So?"

"So shut up and drink your wine, and don't be talking when I'm telling you what to do," Crosetti laughed.

"That's how it works, is it?"

"I just want you to think about what it's gonna take to get you to live a long life. I can't drink all this wine by myself."

"No?"

"Oh, fuck no. I've tried, I can't do it."

"If I can get a couple of things to fall into place, then maybe."

"Things are gonna happen, or they aren't gonna happen. The key is to still be alive when they do. What's the latest on the book, and how many women are you seeing?"

"Not sure that those two subjects are related."

"They're not. I just lost my train of thought, then got it back again. I meant to ask you about the women when I was giving you shit about not having one."

"OK, got it."

"You still have to answer the questions though," Crosetti said, gesturing with his wine glass.

Townes shook his head and took a drink of the wine. "I'm not sure how to answer that. Book is just sitting there. Editor had a meltdown, agents hate new guys, which makes me hate them. Toss my manuscript in that fire over there, probably have about the same chance," Townes paused, looking up at the rising smoke. "I did have someone I met on this last trip to New York say she would try to help me."

"Help you what, marry you?" Crosetti laughed.

"Help me with the book."

"She in the book business?"

"No, she's an actress."

"An actress!? They're fucking crazy. I went with one once ... fucking nuts. Who is she? Do I know her?"

"I don't know. Her name is Ashley Meacham."

"Ashley Mee ... oh yeah, I've seen her in a movie. Where ... how did you meet her?"

"She was in a Broadway show, staying at my hotel."

"Probably wasn't the Stick It Inn, if she was staying there. And you were staying there too. You break in her room?" Crosetti chuckled.

"Yep, that's how I meet most women. No, my bartender friend ... well, he's actually the head barman at the hotel."

"Sounds serious. He's the barman, I like him already. How come you always stay in those nice hotels?"

Townes didn't say anything, just looking in the wine in his glass, then looking up in the sky.

"Well?"

"Well what?"

"Why do you always stay in those really nice hotels?" Crosetti asked, looking in his wine glass, mimicking Townes.

"I'm not going to tell you."

"Why not?"

"Because."

"Just because. That's a fucked up reason," Crosetti said, taking a drink of his wine.

"Yeah, well, that's me."

"Tell me, you fucker."

Townes paused, took a drink of wine, and looked at the rising smoke. "I stay in those places ... because ... I'm lonely. The people in those places always talk to you, always care about you," Townes said, looking off in the distance.

"Hey, you got a friend here that will talk to you, so drink up, and I'll talk to you 'til we fall over. So the bar guy ..."

Townes gathered his composure. "So he introduced us, or more like he gave her a referral on me. I walked her dogs for her."

"That code for something dirty? Tell me, tell me!"

"No. I had been in New York and was missing my dog. I ran into her and her dogs in the lobby and offered to walk them. Hell, I didn't even know who she was, I was just being nice. My friend told her I was OK, so she let me walk her dogs."

"And that's really not something dirty and you're just not telling me?"

"Nothing dirty."

"Shit. Then what?"

"So I took her dogs to Central Park. She gave me a ticket to the Broadway show she was starring in, but she hates that word, 'star.' Anyway, we had dinner and she said she would see if she could help me on the book."

"Because you walked her dogs," Crosetti said, a huge grin on her face.

"Yes, because I walked her dogs. I had no idea who she was."

"Sounds like you should get in that business … you'd have 'em lined up around the block. Women, I mean, not dogs. Are you sure?"

"Yes, walking dogs is walking dogs."

"So what's the book thing she's doing?"

"She says she knows people, and I can believe that. Hell, she's in the movies and on Broadway, so she probably knows a ton of folks."

"So she's going to talk to them?"

"That's what she said."

"And all you had to do was walk her—"

"Just fucking stop, all right?"

Crosetti laughed and sipped his wine. "That would be pretty neat if she could do something."

"That's what I was thinking."

"It pays to be … to be … well, it pays to not be an asshole, and I'm an expert, 'cause I know a lot of assholes. You got a bunch of wine, or a bunch of something to drink, it attracts assholes. It attracts good people too, but you get a lot of assholes. You treat people like people, it's going to work out better. Life's too short to be a prick. I got all these people trying to get close to me now that the wine is a big deal. Thing is, they treated me like shit when I was first getting started, told me I didn't know what the fuck I was doing, told me to stick with growing fucking lettuce. One motherfucker told me I should probably be pickin' fuckin' lettuce."

"You're kidding, someone told you that? To your face"

"Sure as fuck did."

"What did you tell him?"

"After I punched him in his pasty, arrogant, know-it-all face, I told him that the people that pick my lettuce are a hundred times better people than he is, and they are welcome in my house every day of the week. And, that he could stuff a head of lettuce up his fucking ass."

"Holy shit."

"Yeah, it was lucky for him I didn't get pissed."

"I should think so."

"I could have gotten really pissed," Crosetti nodded.

"Instead of just punching him in the face."

"Fucker was lucky I didn't throw him through the fucking window."

"You like that word 'fuck,' I noticed."

"No, I like wine. I hate getting pissed off. Just want to make my wine, make people happy, drink my wine with them. They like it, I'm happy."

"Well, you make the best wine I've ever had," Townes said, shaking his head.

"That's 'cause I talk to the grapes."

"I think you mentioned that."

"I did? I can't remember everything I say. I've got a lot on my mind."

"Like what?"

"Like what I'm gonna say to the grapes, like how I'm gonna get my friend to quit workin' so fuckin' much, and how I'm gonna to get my friend to find a girlfriend, stuff like that. That's a lot for me."

"And you didn't say 'fuck' but once."

Crosetti laughed, drained his wine and looked around the vineyard, drumming his fingers on the side of the glass, the purple lace of the wine still clinging there. "I've been a farmer all my life. Don't know how to do anything else."

"You are really great at it."

"I wanted to do all sorts of things to get out of being a farmer."

"Like what?"

"Like all sorts of things. I didn't mind being a farmer, I just wanted to be something bigger. You know, get away," Crosetti said, a distant look in his eyes, running his tongue over his teeth, then looking down at the ground. "You know what I wanted to be? I wanted to be a fucking professional baseball player, more than anything. My dad loved baseball. It was the only thing we could talk about without getting into an argument. He didn't want me growing grapes, said it was stupid. He wanted to grow stuff to eat, that's it. He said wine was OK to make for us at home to drink at Easter, that it was stupid to think I could make any money from it."

Crosetti kept looking at the ground, shaking his head, his drumming on the glass softening. Townes could see he had moved into a part of his past that was uncomfortable for him to talk about and did not know what to say. He reached for the wine bottle and leaned over, pouring first into Crosetti's glass, then his own. Crosetti nodded, but did not look up.

"I wasn't any fucking good."

"What?"

"I was a terrible baseball player. I wanted to be good, and I wasn't."

"It's really hard."

"Yeah, it is. I just wanted to be good at it, so my dad could—"

"It's OK," Townes said, putting his hand on Crosetti's shoulder.

"It would have been fun, I think."

"It's fun now."

"Yeah," Crosetti sniffed. "Don't forget to tell yourself that."

CHAPTER 42

The food from the grill that Mariano manned was beyond description. The asparagus, artichokes, and peppers were all from Crosetti's farm. Grass-fed beef and wild boar were the meats of choice, the beef from one of Crosetti's neighbors, the wild boar also a local, one that had made a wrong turn into the vineyard, a serious miscalculation for the feral creature. Animals eating grapes in Crosetti's vineyard had a limited lifespan, as there was a zero tolerance policy for that violation. The aroma of the meats grilling a few yards away was impossible to ignore. Now it was time to indulge.

Townes now saw fresh loaves of bread, whole heads of roasted garlic, and lots of warm olive oil. These things would smell grand on their own, but after Townes and Crosetti had polished off a bottle of Pinot Noir, the aromas were lassos pulling them to Mariano's grill. Townes thought the food was a great idea, the timing could not have been better. There would undoubtedly be a great deal more wine that would figure into today's program. Being able to continue in an upright position would be achieved only with the introduction of food.

Mariano motioned for them to come to the food, even though he knew he did not need to, as Crosetti had already become restless.

"I think Mariano wants us to move over there," Townes said, glad of the interruption.

Crosetti wiped his eyes and laughed. "Fuck, I hate it when I get leaky."

"Don't worry about it."

"I get to thinkin' about stuff and that happens sometimes. You know what else happens?"

"What?"

"Somebody sneaks up and drinks all my fuckin' wine. Look, my glass is empty!" Crosetti shouted, holding his glass upside down.

"Helluva deal."

"It is. Let's go get some wine."

"Food might not hurt, since Mariano went to all the trouble and all."

"Trouble? That ain't no trouble. He does this all the time. Gotta eat up those hogs that eat my grapes. They eat my grapes, I eat them."

"I might have thought twice about the monkey bites, had I known that."

Crosetti laughed loud and long. "It's OK if you eat them. You aren't going to invite all your relatives to come eat my grapes like that fucker was going to," Crosetti said, pointing to the grill and the meat. "He won't be telling his relatives now, will he?"

"I imagine not."

Crosetti kept laughing as they moved to the grill. "Nice out here, huh?"

"No, it's perfect out here," Townes said, taking a huge breath, taking in the vines, the soil, the air, the smoke, and the cooking food. "Just perfect. What would you charge me to come hang out here?"

"Nothing. You can live here free if you want. Got to shoot your own hogs though."

They sat out in the open, their plates full of the freshly grilled meats and vegetables, their glasses full of the rich, crimson Pinot Noir. Townes could not think of a better setting, nor any place he would rather be. Though he was already thinking about it, this made Townes want to quit the airplanes, quit the hotels, and leave the sidewalks even more. If he never put on a sport coat again, that would be fine with him. He could go to work in boots and jeans, and thought just maybe he could learn to talk to the grapes.

"I think I know the secret," Townes said, between bites of the glorious meal, "but I want to hear it from you."

"The secret? There isn't a secret. It's more of a mantra."

"And that is?"

"Do what you love."

"But you loved playing baseball."

"I did, but I was fucking terrible at it. So maybe its's a two-part mantra. Do what you love, but if you aren't cut out for it … and are real shitty, you need to love something else. You can use that for occupations or women. You need some more wine," Crosetti said, filling Townes's glass, which was not empty.

"What do you mean?"

"You can't make 'em love you, no matter what. You love them, but they don't love you, it ain't gonna work. All you can do, is be the best you. They don't like that, hell with 'em."

"This may be getting too deep for me, at least after I have had a case of wine."

"It's not deep, and you haven't had that much to drink—yet."

"Yet."

"You ever like a woman that didn't like you?" Crosetti asked.

"Yes."

"When?"

"Right now."

"That's funny."

"No, really. Strange circumstances."

"It's always strange circumstances. These days, people think you fill out a form, like a fucking shopping list, and that exact person appears. This questionnaire shit is just wrong."

"I didn't do that."

"I didn't mean you. I was just saying how fucking stupid it is."

"It works for some people."

"Good for them. Tell me about this woman," Crosetti said, picking up and devouring a stalk of asparagus.

"I saw her one day and that was it. Couldn't get her out of my head."

"What did she say to you?"

"Nothing then. I didn't meet her. She was with some asshole, and I mean, he was an asshole."

"Boyfriend, husband?" Crosetti said, between bites.

"Neither."

"So what's strange? And by the way, I'm pissed at you that you didn't say something to her, but go on. This is good food, huh? We ain't ate like this since we were in Dallas. What was the name of that place where we ate and you made me drink so much?"

"Fearing's. I made you—"

Crosetti laughed. "Go on about the woman."

"I went out a couple of times with this other woman that turned out to be her best friend."

"Hah! No shit?"

"No shit."

"Did you know she was—"

"Of course not," Townes frowned.

"How did you meet her?"

"My friend, Zeeder. The woman was in his art class."

"This is funny. You need more food, get some."

"I'm pausing."

"So did you meet the first woman?"

"Yes. Almost fell over when her friend introduced me."

"What are you going to do?" Crosetti said, flicking a bug off the outside table.

"Well, I'm not sure," Townes said, looking around the area, the day seeming to just slowly drift like the few clouds dotting the blue overhead.

"What do you mean you're not sure? You playing hard to get?"

"Not even, not ever. The girl from the art class, Kat, is sort of, I don't know, mystical, I guess you would call it. She sort of knows things before you tell her those things."

"That's powerful shit. I believe in it."

"I never really thought about it before, but after the actress, and Kat, I do believe in it now. Ashley is mystical too, probably more so than Kat. She's an actress and is very guarded, so you don't really notice it, but when you do, wow! Maybe it's because I've been around Kat more, but she definitely is. I've not been around people like that before. Or maybe I have but didn't know it then. She wants to help me, and I'm not used to that. I feel very relaxed around her and I really like her. She really makes me feel good about things."

"Like I said, that's some powerful shit, and I don't take it lightly, and you shouldn't either. I think you should go with her. So let's see. The actress, this Kat gal, and ... what's the other one's name?"

"Annie."

"You need to buy one of them houses with three separate entrances, so they don't run into each other," Crosetti laughed. "Mariano!"

"Si?"

"Mi amigo," Crosetti pointed to Townes. "Tres amantes!" Crosetti roared.

"Loco!" Mariano laughed, shaking his head.

"What is 'tres amantes'?"

"Three girlfriends."

Townes looked at Mariano, who was still shaking his head, tending to the grill. "No," Townes said.

"No?" Mariano asked.

"No," Townes confirmed.

"Si, si, si," Crosetti shouted.

"It's not like that. I met the actress and—"

"I know, you walked her dogs," Crosetti could not stop laughing.

"I … never mind. Kat is going, is gone to India, and I'm not sure she if she is coming back. That's a shame. I really like her. We just didn't get to spend that much time together, but we probably could have become very close, had she stayed."

"She'll be back. She can't eat and drink like this over there," Crosetti said, motioning at the spread of food, and accumulating wine bottles.

"Not everybody eats and drinks like this. Come to think of it, I actually don't know anybody that eats and drinks like this."

"Yeah, and that's a good thing, 'cause it leaves more for us," Crosetti said, raising his glass briefly, then taking a drink. "If people did more eating and drinking like this, there would be a lot less trouble in the world. People aren't going to fight if they are eating and drinking together. You need more wine."

Townes looked at Crosetti and shook his head. "Maybe I do need some more. You say they would … you need to meet my friend Zeeder. You would like him."

Crosetti nodded and continued. "So the actress is somewhere, the other one is in India, and the third one is somewhere. So that means no matter where you are, you're near somewhere," Crosetti laughed again, filling Townes's glass.

"Where I have always strived to be. Near somewhere," Townes said quietly, letting out a long breath, holding his glass towards the smoke rising from Mariano's cooking fire.

"Hey, don't worry about it. You're going to be fine. I'm looking after you, that dog is looking after you, and it sounds like wherever she is, that actress is looking after you. The book is going to go, and we're going to get drunk, and everything is going to work out. Go tell that other girl, what's her name, Annie? You tell her you are in love with her, and that you are going to be famous. How could she turn you down?"

"This, from the guy that says you can't make them love you?" Townes asked, continuing to watch the smoke through his wineglass.

"Oh, that's right, I forgot. Well, just tell her you like to have fun, and ask her if she wants to have fun with you. She doesn't want to have fun? Her loss. There's always the actress, Meacham, and she sounds like she really likes you. That sounds like the start of a pretty good blend of grapes to throw in the vat. You could come up with the vintage of the century! This wild boar is pretty good, isn't it?" Crosetti said, his mouth full.

"Not sure it is that easy."

"Everything is that easy."

"Annie's not real keen on me telling her I wanted to go out with her. Seems kinda pissed that I went out with her friend, who is moving to India. Maybe I should have—"

"Bullshit! You like her, you tell her! You like that actress, you tell her! Don't ever hold anything back, ever! You have a passion for something, do it. You have a passion for someone, tell 'em. Passion, passion, passion!" Crosetti said, pounding the table with his wine glass with each word.

Mariano did not look up from his tending the grill. He had worked here a long time. He, like Townes, knew the fire that burned within this man. He had heard this before. All those that worked for and around Crosetti shared that commitment and intensity. Townes thought it to be the richest and best type of contagion. His friend was not speaking out of an abundance of wine, though the amount of wine was certainly a finger on the volume knob. The message was the same, wine, or no. Townes received that message, and it would stay with him. He had heard it before and it had started to grow in his heart. This time, it related to everything he was doing in his life. He was going to do what he wanted to do. He had been chasing a lot of things long enough. It was time for a change.

CHAPTER 43

New York

Brandon greeted Townes at the front of the restaurant. The giant art sculpture ears, eyes, breast and signature nose on the walls of Trattoria Dell' Arte restaurant might as well have been sitting at the table with Townes. He had dined there more times than he could remember, but now those art pieces seemed to be speaking to him.

"So good to see you again," Brandon, the maître d' said, shaking Townes's hand.

"Good to be here," Townes replied.

"How have you been?"

"I have been … been all over."

"That is good for you?"

"It must be."

"Come, sit, and we will help you relax a little."

"I'd like that," Townes said.

He sat, looking at the art pieces, hearing what Crosetti had told him again in his head. Crosetti had that way about him. Others misjudged him as just a guy that made wine.

"Everything all right here?" the waiter asked, breaking Townes out of his trance.

"What … oh, yes, fine Joseph," Townes answered.

"You looked like, I don't know, you was lost, or something."

"Yeah, too many trips strung together. Starts to blur after a while."

"Well, what you need, is you need a glass of the Antinori, a little grilled asparagus, a couple of meatballs, some shrimp and scallop salad, from the antipasto bar. A little linguini and white clam sauce, then you'll be right," Joseph said, without hesitation.

Townes didn't know what to say. Joseph had seemingly given him the exact antidote to break his road-weary spell. Dive into the local fare and it will be a lifeline to normalcy. The couple of days with Crosetti had been a nice break for him. The trouble was, after a couple of days with Crosetti, Townes always needed a couple more days to recover from the days with Crosetti. Heading back to New York right after his trip to the winery left no time for recovery.

Recuperation would need to come from the local dining, from talking with the people that worked here. Like the Ritz, these people made him feel like he lived here. Seeing the same faces every time he came here made him feel comfortable, made him feel like there were still places in the world where people worked in the same place for a very long time, and took great pride in the work that they did. More of Crosetti's passion. Townes lived in a place where most thought they were headed to bigger and better things. The day they started the job, just a stepping stone to something else, left a void and prevented any sort of pride. It was not a total indictment of where he lived, but it was true more often than not.

"You've worked here a long time," Townes said.

"Yeah, something like that."

"Ever think of leaving?"

"Nah, not really. I mean, they treat me good here. I got customers been coming here forever and they treat me good, too. I go somewhere else, I don't know what I'm gonna get. My old customers, maybe they can't find me, don't know where I am. I like my customers, they like me, we're all happy. I go somewhere else, maybe that don't happen," Joseph smiled.

"That's a great assessment."

"Well, love what ya do, ya know."

"What?"

"You gotta love what ya do. Let me get this order in, you look hungry," Joseph said, moving away quickly.

Townes looked around, half expecting to see Crosetti laughing behind a corner, having just told the waiter to tell Townes that. Crosetti was probably related to, or at least knew the waiter. There was probably some cosmic connection. Ashley would be proud that he had noticed. Crosetti was quite a legend in the wine business and everybody either knew him, or knew of him. Crosetti would tell you that he didn't do a third of the stuff people said he did. He would just laugh and tell you that the crazy stories were not true, but they could be. Joseph returned with the antipasto and the wine.

"Take your time, no rush. You spend as long as you want and be comfortable."

Townes could think of no reason not to do just that. His appointments were not until tomorrow. He could spend some time here, relaxing from the flight, then see Milton later. Ashley's play was still in town and he really wanted to see her, and she told him she wanted to see him again. He had Milton to thank for this. He had told Milton before that he wanted to adopt him, rather than the other way around. He thought about those conversations.

"A son who is a bartender, knows everybody, and has his own health insurance, what's not to like? And don't forget, that is also older than you," Milton would add.

"Exactly, so I don't have to put you through college."

"And I don't drive."

"This just gets better and better."

Townes would leave a message for Ashley when he got back to the hotel. He wasn't sure she was still at the Ritz, but she would keep in touch with Milton. Milton would know where she was. Knowing Milton was a serendipity when coming to New York. You could have a connection to everything by knowing him, because he knew everybody. If he didn't know somebody in a particular arena, he knew somebody who did.

"Even more reason to adopt him." Ashley's words about everything being connected seemed more accurate every day.

Townes enjoyed the wine, the antipasto, and was in no hurry to leave. There was a peaceful rhythm to what would be considered frenetic in Southern California. Everything moved fast here, but the competence of the participants made it seem all the more fluid. The precision of it all took away the feeling of chaos that might otherwise be interpreted. Now that Townes had spent so much time here, it did not seem chaotic at all. He wondered if Annie would like this place, would like New York. He wasn't sure what she liked. She was very driven, very sure of herself, but there was still that sadness there. Kat said that Annie had not taken time to enjoy the things she should, that she had worked too hard, and didn't let her hair down. Townes could relate to that, *if sitting and talking to himself, at a great New York Italian restaurant, about adopting his bartender friend, were any indication*, one of the voices said.

Joseph brought the linguine with clams and another glass of the Antinori.

"How we doin' here?" Joseph asked, as another waiter cleared Townes's table and Joseph began replacing the plates with new ones overflowing with more delightful aromas.

"Very well, thank you."

"Attaboy. I brought you another glass of wine. Ya know, just in case."

"Good thinking."

"Gotta have a little more of the grape, right?"

"A friend of mine says the same thing."

"Very good. Ok, you lemme know if you need anything else."

"Yes, I will, though I can't imagine that I would."

"You never know. Enjoy your lunch," Joseph said, and left the table.

Townes took a deep breath, letting it out quickly. The linguine, clams, and garlic smelled exquisite, and the wine just made it all the better. He knew Crosetti would agree. This was a much larger midday meal than Townes normally ate, but today it just seemed right. He thought if he kept this up, he could go buy some new clothes in New York, because none of the ones he had would be big enough. He was bushed from all the travel. He was tired of talking with all his customers, telling them what was wrong with their business. If they would only use common sense, they could fix it without having to pay him to tell them how to fix it. The cycle had been going on too long, and Townes was ready for the cycle to stop. He thought two glasses of wine may not be enough. Crosetti was right.

He ate his lunch and ordered another glass of wine. The third glass of wine was enough to help him decide he was finished with doing what he had been and was going to do something different. All he had needed was three glasses of wine and some great New York Italian food to clear his mind. That and spending a couple of days with a guy who had vats and vats of wine. He reinforced his resolve with cannoli and Limoncello. He could not wait to tell Milton he was going to make a change. The smell of fresh-baked oatmeal raisin cookies being brought around the dining room on a tray did not help to pick up his pace.

"Maybe after one more Limoncello."

Townes walked the two block walk back to the Ritz, determining that a nap would be the right course of action. His steps back to the hotel, perhaps more animated, more unstructured than they normally might be. "Probably the cannoli," he laughed. He got in the hotel without anyone recognizing him which was rare, but in his state of marginal excess, he thought it best. Back in the room, now resting on the bed, his thoughts turned to starting a new, unknown job, to throwing his book manuscript out the window towards his view of Central Park. He laughed and closed his eyes.

He awoke laying crossways on the bed, his shoes somewhere in the room, he hoped. He felt very thick, his head especially. He searched in his mind for what had made him order so much food and drink. Apparently it was predetermined and the meal was to move him to another shore, and that, based on the quantity, that shore must be a long way away. He sat up and tried to clear his mind. He grabbed one of the bedside bottles of water that housekeeping had foreseen he was going to be needing and drank fully, emptying it quickly, letting out a breath only when he was done. He could tolerate the travel, provided he could jettison the new anxiety condition, but the line of work had to be revised ... or maybe he would lie back down and think about it a little more before he went downstairs and told his friend he was quitting the circus.

CHAPTER 44

"It doesn't hurt to change jobs once in a while," Milton said, filling a Boston Shaker glass with ice. "I'm going to make you a Martinez. I think you'll like it."

"I actually may not need anything to drink for a while."

"It's one drink."

"One, plus what I had earlier. I might have to reset the meter," he paused, looking around the familiar bar. Milton stared back at him in a way that told him he was holding up a great many things. "All right. I'll reset the meter. No scotch or cheap white wine. You know those are my only requirements."

"I remember, I remember," Milton said, shaking his head. "but gin you like, so I'm going to use this Hayman's Old Tom, some sweet vermouth, some maraschino liqueur, and a little bitters. Yeah, a job change might be good."

"Said the man who never changes jobs."

"That's because you're smarter than me."

"That's not even close to being true," Townes smiled.

"It's different for me. I'm not traveling all over the country, having to convince everybody I know what I'm doing. They see me back here, they figure I do. They don't think so, they can get the hell out and go to another bar. The ones that know me, they don't have questions about my abil-lil-a-tee." Milton laughed. "Plus, I don't want to stray too far from home."

Townes watched Milton prepare the drink, testing the temperature on the side of the mixing glass with his knuckles. There was always simplicity, always order here with Milton, but there was also that sense of passion for his work. He had been at this a long time and he still loved it. Townes could not help but make a parallel with Milton and Crosetti. They were really good at what they did. Some would say that it was time on the job. Others, including Townes, would say they were so good because they loved it.

Milton put the strainer on the mixing glass, and placed a napkin and a cocktail coupe in front of Townes. He placed a cherry in the bottom of the coupe, then began pouring the contents of the shaker. He started low, then gradually lifted his arm higher, filling the glass so the only thing keeping the liquid from falling over the top was surface tension. He had the exact amount to make the liquid bow at the top, yet not spilling a solitary drop.

"I like that, so will you," Milton said, moving away to see to the other customers, singing some sparse words to "Fly Me To The Moon," then assuring a woman a few seats down that she was first on his list of people to take care of. Townes looked at the cocktail, gently biting his tongue before taking a breath, then exhaling, knowing it had not been that long since his extended lunch. He leaned over to sip from the near overfull coupe. Any movement would require a bar towel. The taste was invigorating, making the drink tally since lunch rise to a place of unconcern. Townes closed his eyes and wondered if Angelina would like him working at a winery.

"That's an interesting looking drink. What's it called?" the man sitting next to Townes asked.

"What?" Townes opened his eyes.

"That drink. It looks interesting. What is it?"

"A Martinez. It's a very old, classic drink," Townes said, looking at the man drinking a white wine.

"Oh, I've never had one."

"Well, I'm sure Milton would make one for you if you asked him." Townes studied the man, who was in his dress shirt and slacks, tie loosened, no jacket. Townes had been drinking since lunch, but he still had the decorum to wear a jacket.

"Shithead," Townes muttered, his voices agreeing.

"I'm Arvin," the man said, extending his hand.

"Hello. Townes."

"Great to meet you, Townes. I hear this guy is a heckuva bartender."

Townes looked at the man's glass of white wine. "That what you heard?"

Townes asked, turning back to his own drink, now able to pick it up without spilling it.

"That's what I heard," Arvin said loudly.

"Hmm. That why you are drinking wine?" Townes asked, not turning back toward the man.

"Me? Oh, I don't really … I mean, I'm not really in the mood for … you know."

"So you came to the best barman in the city to have him open a bottle of what, Pinot Grigio?"

"How did you know I was drinking Pinot Grigio?"

"Wild guess," Townes said quietly. He had seen this act before.

"Just letting off a little steam. And, I heard this is a good place to do that. My boss told me this was a good place to go. What business are you in?"

Townes took another sip of his cocktail, then paused. "Chinchilla ranch and bait worm farm," he said, smiling forward, not turning to look.

"That's a real growth … wait, what?"

Townes turned slowly to the man. "Don't tell me, let me guess. You're with a hedge fund."

"Well, yes, how did you know?"

"I am goddamned clairvoyant … least that's what the actress said," Townes said, turning back to his drink.

"Seriously, what line of work are you in?"

Townes paused again, taking another taste of his drink. He looked to see that Milton was at the other end of the bar, so there would be no imminent rescue. "Investigator for the Securities and Exchange Commission."

"What?!" Arvin did not know which, if either to believe. "Uh, what … I…?"

"Writer, I'm a writer."

"Aren't we all," Arvin said, fiddling with his glass of white wine, breathing a sigh of relief.

"Apparently."

"We have a couple of opportunities coming up that might be of interest to you. We only have a few spots left, and, well, since you are a friend of—"

"A friend of whom?" Townes said, turning towards the man.

"You know, a friend of Milton's."

"Since I am a friend of Milton's, you are going to offer me an investment deal? That the baseline, is it? How long have you known Milton?"

Arvin paused, moving his wine glass to his other hand, then back to the bar. "Well, I don't actually know him."

"Obviously, or you wouldn't be drinking cheap white wine."

"What?"

"You fucking guys kill me. You come here because somebody, probably your boss, told you that you were gonna lose your job if you didn't get some numbers on the board, and you'd better get your ass over to the Ritz, or the Four Seasons, and scare up some business. I'm just relaxing, here with my friend, whom you don't even know, and after thirty seconds you give me a pitch. You don't even have the decency to have him make you a drink. You just order the cheapest wine on the list. I've seen hookers put down ten bucks for a goddamn club soda, out of respect. Hell, to think they have more integrity than you! Tell you what. Why don't I come over to your place Sunday morning when you are reading the paper in your sweatpants, and I pitch you on my book."

The man was speechless.

"I don't begrudge you trying to make a living, but that's the only reason you are in here, and it is not the reason I'm in here. I actually think I have been propositioned in New York bars more by you guys than I have by hookers and that is a little scary, 'cause I'm in New York a lot. You financial guys all have the same script, too, which is goddamn pathetic. 'Ooh, a Manhattan, I've never had one of those.' Even the hookers are smart enough to not all have the same fucking line," Townes said, downing the rest of his drink, holding it up until the cherry slid down into his mouth, catching it with his front teeth then turning towards the man, biting into the cherry. "Ya know."

Arvin's eyes widened and he reached into his pocket to place a ten dollar bill on the bar. He started to leave but Townes grabbed his arm.

"That's not enough."

Arvin, with a scared look on his face, dug back into his pocket, placing a five on top of the ten.

"Really?" Townes said, crunching the cherry.

Arvin reached into his pocket again and pulled out another ten.

Townes let go of his arm. "Good luck with the numbers."

Arvin left quickly. Townes held his glass up to the light, looking at the reflected light it cast onto the back of the bar, moving it around and watching it move around the bar. Milton came back, looked at the money, then held his hands in front of him, palms up.

"He had to go, work stuff," Townes said.

"I didn't even give him his bill."

"Folks are sure in a hurry these days."

Milton looked at the money then toward where the man had exited. "You go into a bar and don't have time to wait for the check, maybe you should go to a liquor store instead. Looks like he left enough."

"More than enough. He was drinking Pinot fucking Grigio," Townes smirked.

"I don't drink much wine," Milton said, scratching his head, "but people seem to like this stuff."

"Cause they think the name sounds good ... and it's cheap."

"Doesn't anyone drink gin anymore?" Milton said, loudly.

"I do," Townes said, gently nudging his empty glass.

"Good," Milton said, clapping his hands together. "That's my boy!"

CHAPTER 45

It was late and Townes wanted to go to bed. The aftermath of his lunch was now putting him on the groggy side. Milton would want him to stay just a bit longer, not to drink more, but because that's how Milton was. The bar was always incredibly peaceful after everybody left and it was just he and Milton. Townes often sat there, enjoying the quiet, noticing the rhythm of the take down, not unlike the rhythm of Milton mixing cocktails. It was a great place to write, provided there had not been a slight miscalculation, like today, on the number of cocktails. Whether the place was packed, or now at the end of the night, there was never chaos behind the bar. Even though it was late, Townes could stay a few more minutes.

"I'm sorry I'm so late," a woman's voice came from the other end of the bar.

"Hello, my dear Ashley, how are you, my darling?" Milton said, weary but happy.

"Oh, I'm running behind, running behind," Ashley said, walking over to Milton, the two kissing each other on the cheek.

"Would you like something? We're closing up, but whatever you would like, my dear," Milton said, bowing.

"I would like a writer, but also maybe a little Blanton's on the rocks," Ashley smiled.

"Lucky for you, I got both, the writer is down at the end of the bar," Milton said, moving his hand in a sweeping motion. "But he's pretty quiet, so you might have to nudge him to get him to talk."

"Is that what you do?"

"Please, I'm not supposed to touch the customers."

"Well, you just kissed me."

"You're better looking than him," Milton said, walking away to get Ashley her drink, pointing towards Townes as he walked.

"I think I see him, Milton. Thank you for pointing him out; I might have missed him," Ashley said, walking to Townes's end of the bar. She could hear Milton humming a tune behind the bar.

"She's looking for a bourbon … and a writer," Milton sung the words into the song he was humming.

"Hello there," Ashley said as she got closer.

"Hello there," Townes said, standing up. "I think I heard you were looking for a writer. Any particular kind of writer?" Townes asked, tilting his tired head.

"Uh huh," Ashley said, putting her arms around him, and giving him a kiss. Townes was somewhat surprised, but reciprocated. Ashley took hold of Townes's hands. "Mind if I join you? I'm sorry I'm late." The two could hear more humming behind the bar, and they both laughed. "He seems happy," Ashley smiled, still holding onto Townes's hands.

"He's an ambassador of life," Townes said, glancing at Milton, then back to Ashley. "Please, sit. Tell me about your night, tell me about this writer you are looking for. You must have hit your head during the show."

"Oh, I think I found him, and I did not hit my head," Ashley raised her eyebrows as she took the seat next to Townes.

"Fly me to the moon …" Milton sang from behind the bar.

"You were saying," Townes said, smiling.

"So I was saying, I was looking for a writer, but really I was looking for a specific writer."

"They are a shifty, unreliable bunch; you may want to look for someone of a different profession. Are you sure you didn't hit your head?"

"I knew where to find him. I didn't have to look hard, and I didn't hit my head."

"You haven't known me that long and already I'm that predictable?"

"Not predictable at all. It was actually that I knew who would know how to find you, versus me knowing you would be here."

"Hard not to let the big guy know. He gets upset if you don't keep him informed."

"He's not meddlesome, he just doesn't want to worry. He just wants to know you are OK."

"That is completely accurate, and you know it's comforting to know that somebody does care."

"I think you have more people that care than you know."

"I don't think about it that much, but you know I travel a lot, and when I come here, it's sort of like having a guardian angel."

"A guardian angel with a heavy Brooklyn accent."

"Something like that," Townes grinned, looking down at his drink, then back over to where Milton was standing behind the bar.

"I'll be right there," Milton said, his back turned to the two.

"He knows when I'm thinking about him," Townes said, still smiling.

"I think you and I had a discussion about that sort of thing, didn't we?" Ashley asked, turning her head.

"That we did, that we did."

"And yet you still question it."

"No, I don't question it. I'm just still getting used to it."

"Well, good! There are some other things you need to get used to also."

"Such as?"

"Such as giving interviews about your book, or about the movie. I'm not actually sure which one is going to come first," Ashley said, patting Townes on his hand.

"Here we are, my dear. A little bourbon nightcap, and I brought one for the writer here, too. I didn't want you to drink alone," Milton said, placing two napkins down, then placing the drinks on them.

"I'm never alone when you are here, Milton," Ashley said, taking his hand after he set the drinks on the bar.

"Oh, you are sweet to an old man, but with me finishing up here, I can't keep an eye on you, so I have enlisted my dear friend here to act as my emissary in that regard," Milton patted Townes on the arm, and kissed Ashley's hand. "Now I gotta finish cleaning up, or I'm gonna get in trouble," Milton said, moving away from the two.

Townes shook his head and started to say something to Milton, but stopped. "Wait, what did you say?"

Ashley grinned. "Have you been here with Milton all night?"

"It's sort of hard to tell, but I don't think so."

"That speaks to the question pretty well."

"What do you mean you are not sure which is going to come out first, the book or the movie? It's not published yet."

"No, but it will be."

"It will be?"

"Yes. I showed it to a friend of mine. He read it, he loved it, and said he would like to make it into a movie. I read it too, which I hope is all right, and I loved it too."

"Really!?"

"Really. Here's to that," Ashley said, raising her glass. "Don't you think that's delightful?"

"Wait, what does your friend do?"

"He gets things done. That's what he does."

"Well how, I mean, is he—"

"I told you, he gets things done," Ashley said, touching glasses with Townes. "He gets things done. It doesn't matter what he is. What matters is you are getting a book published, and a movie deal. I would say things are really looking up for you. We should buy drinks for everyone in the bar!" Ashley said, raising her glass and her free hand.

"There's only you and me and that man in the vest humming behind the bar," Townes grinned.

"We can buy everyone drinks another time," Ashley said quietly.

"Sooo ... how does this get done?"

"I don't know. He said he has some friends at a publishing house, but that they take forever to do this sort of thing, and that you can publish it yourself, and he would have someone fund that and get you distribution. After that, or before that, you can either write the screenplay, which I am sure you can do, or he can get somebody to write the screenplay. It's up to you," Ashley said, taking a drink of her bourbon. "I really like the taste of this ... but it tastes so much better when everything goes the way you want it to. Always celebrate the victories."

"Always celebrate the victories," Townes said quietly. He looked back and forth between Milton and Ashley. He set his gaze on his drink, moving it several times with his thumb and forefinger before picking it up and taking a large sip, placing it back gently on the bar, as if it might break. He repeated the glass movement routine, then removed his hands, making first a circle, then a pyramid with his hands.

"For real?" Townes asked quietly.

"For real," Ashley smiled. You might want to keep the movie part quiet, as that part needs to stay with just us, and Milton won't tell anyone."

"He knows?"

"Of course, he knows."

"How long has he known?"

"Not very long. I wanted to tell you, so—"

"So he kept me here so—"

"He didn't keep you here. You are here because you want to be here. He never keeps you here."

"But …"

"No buts. It's all going to be great for you, just like I said, and I am very excited."

"Well I … why did you do this for me?"

"I didn't do it, my friend did it."

"Well, why did you show it to your friend?"

"Because you just seemed like someone who would write something good. That's not a bad thing, is it?"

"No, it's not a bad thing at all, I just don't know what to say."

"Why don't you say … let's have fun with it."

Townes looked at this woman, sitting next to him, smiling at him, leaning towards him, her palms face up, her head bobbing slightly. "I'm stunned. Thank you. You can't believe how."

"That's not what you're supposed to say. What is he supposed to say, Milton?" Ashley asked.

The humming from behind the bar stopped. "He's supposed to say let's have fun," Milton said, over his shoulder.

"See? He agrees. Come on, let's go," Ashley said, taking Townes's hand.

CHAPTER 46

Townes rubbed his slow-to-open eyes. He recognized his surroundings, but there might have been some details about what had occurred before now that would take him a few minutes to piece together. Slowly he sat up in the bed, twisting his head from side to side, reaching towards the ceiling to stretch his arms. He went into the bathroom, hoping to get his bearings. He put on a bathrobe that was hanging there, the embroidery on the robe confirming he was still at the Ritz. He exited the bathroom and moved about the suite. He walked towards where he saw more daylight shining, soon greeted by two dogs.

"Good morning," Ashley said. "I didn't want to wake you." She was wearing the same robe as Townes. "The dogs wanted to wake you up, but I talked them out of it. Would you like some tea?"

"That would be great, thank you. What time is it? I have an appointment at one."

"Is it important?"

"Yes. I have to go see a client ... to tell them I'm not going to be seeing them again."

"Really? Due to your recent pending change of status?"

"No, I actually had decided that I didn't want to do this anymore before I got here, I think," Townes said, scratching his head.

"Oh."

"Yeah ... and ... that brings us to last night. Was that for real?"

"Which part are you talking about?" Ashley smiled.

"The … the book and such part. I know the other part was real. Well, I hope all of last night was."

"Come, sit, have some tea. Yes, it was all real."

Townes sat on one of the couches, the dogs getting up on the couch with him. He patted each of them on the head.

"Why are you doing this … this book part?"

Ashley chuckled and poured Townes some tea. "I'm doing this book part because I like the book, and I like you. Here's your tea. Anything in it for you?"

"What?"

"Anything in your tea?"

"Oh. No, that will be fine," Townes smiled.

"So you were saying that you were going to see a client to tell them you weren't going to see them anymore?"

"Yes," Townes said, sipping his tea. "I sort of hit the wall on this and want to do something else."

"Like get books published and get them made into movies?"

Townes let out a breath. "That was always in the back of my mind, but not really something I had connected the dots to, or certainly not something I was even close to banking on yet."

"Well," Ashley said, putting her tea down, "it would appear that the dots are getting connected."

"Thanks to you."

"You looked like a break wouldn't be such a bad thing."

"No, it wouldn't be such a bad thing."

"Especially since you were planning on going on hiatus anyway."

"Yeah, I hadn't really worked those details out yet."

"You could stay here in New York for a while with me."

Townes rubbed his hand on his beard-stubbled chin. "That is a wonderful offer," Townes said, pausing to think. "But my dog back in La Jolla would be very upset. She is probably upset now," Townes ran his other hand over Ashley's dogs. "You know how it is being away from your dog."

"Yes, I do, and I can't do it," Ashley nodded. "You could bring her here."

"She's never been to New York. It might be a pretty big adjustment for her."

"For her, or for you?"

"For her. I'm OK with New York. Maybe not permanent, but for a while, anyway. She … is in good hands, however, so maybe a little longer. This other crazy band that I play in has a big gig coming up, and I have to be back for that. How much longer are you here?"

"The play runs another month."

"And where to after that?"

"I planned to take a little time off after that," Ashley said, picking up her tea. "It's fun doing this and I really enjoy doing it, but it really takes it out of you. I am going to need to take a bit of a break after this. Maybe out to Southern California. After this, I could really use some sun."

Townes put his tea down and leaned forward, running his hands through his hair, letting out a breath.

"It's all right. It's all going to work out. This is all good, so let's have some fun with it. You heard Milton."

Townes laughed, not looking up or taking his hands away from his head. "I seem to recall hearing that from you and him. Starting to think you two are working together."

"Always," Ashley said smiling, getting up from her chair and moving to sit on the couch next to Townes. "We are always conspiring to make someone's life better."

"So what do I do next?"

"I will send you, or my friend will send you some contact names of some folks for you to get in touch with to get this rolling. You get it rolling and the rest will all start to fall into place."

"Just like that?" Townes turned to Ashley.

"Just like that," she said, putting her arms around him.

"You don't know that much about me."

"True, but you have exemplary references," Ashley said as she kissed Townes, "and I'm sure they are not wrong."

"Exaggerated, perhaps."

"Never," she said kissing him again.

"Right. I've never heard him exaggerate."

"He might to you, but he wouldn't do that with me."

"He exaggerates with everybody."

"You're too hard on yourself. Give yourself some credit. Plus, you are suggesting that I am not a good judge of character, which makes me feel bad."

"That was not the intention. This is just a lot to digest, so much happening this quickly."

"You're not prepared to succeed?"

"Sort of, but you know what I mean."

"Sort of."

Townes got up from the couch and moved over to the large window, the view of Central Park in front of him. It was raining. He was having trouble concentrating. He thought about what he was going to say to his customer, he thought about what Crosetti had said, thought about Kat leaving for India, about Milton always singing or humming a song. He moved his finger in a circle on the window. "It just sounds too good to be true," he said, locking his fingers together on top of his head.

Ashley got up and moved to the window and stood next to him. "I said the same thing when I got my first break. You think it can't be happening because it hasn't been happening for so long, and you think that it is never going to happen. You start to doubt yourself, doubt your choices, doubt your ... everything. You start to wonder about paths you think you should have taken, things you should have done. You think you should have gotten in line with all the others, and that by now you would have had kids, and be hanging out with all those that you stood in line with, and that you all would be vacationing together and watching your kids together at the pool. Driving minivans and pushing strollers the size of small cars, and memorizing the kids menu at the neighborhood restaurant." Ashley took a deep breath. "And then you say fuck all that, I'm going to pursue this dream and not settle. You crash and burn, you crash and burn, but you don't say 'I wish I would have tried,' because you did try, and you succeeded. That is what this is all about, and you are taking that step off the curb and into the good street, not the shitty one. The fact that I can help with that makes us both feel good. I'm not in the habit of getting very close to anyone, certainly not someone I just met at the hotel. In this business, profession, whatever you want to call it, everyone always wants something. Everyone wants to get close to you so they can get something. You ... you didn't want anything. You just missed your dog. I checked you out with the big guy downstairs and he said he trusted you implicitly. He said you never asked him for anything. You came, and all you wanted was friendship. He said it bothered him that two people he loved were both lonely ... and that it would not be such a bad thing if you and I spent time together. Milton has always looked after me, always protected me. When he tells me you are one of his favorites, and that I can trust you, for me that goes a long way. You put that together with the fact that you have the light, and this all seems pretty right to me."

Townes looked away from the Central Park view and into her eyes, not knowing what to say. Ashley smiled back at him.

"I thought so. Come on. Let's get you cleaned up to go tell those folks you got a better offer."

CHAPTER 47

La Jolla

Townes's phone rang. He had gotten back late from New York and forgotten to turn it off. The sound of the phone vibrating on the dresser top awakened him from a deep sleep that he had not wanted to leave. He had a dream where he was just sitting, looking out over the ocean, just watching the waves. Townes lumbered out of bed to get the phone, not getting to it in time. He let out a sigh as he looked back at the phone. "Good."

The phone vibrated again, the caller was back.

"Townes Mantle."

"Townesie boy!"

"Yep."

"It's Alvin. Get up, boy! Money never sleeps."

"Umm ... what's, uh, what's going on?"

"Just seeing if you got that resume in so we can get you back in here."

"Uh ... I have been on the road the past couple of weeks, so no, I have not done that. I might not ..."

"Listen, fucker, I think I can get you back in without you sending one. We still have your old one, so I just need to tell them you are working on your own and just killing it, and they would probably just go with that. That would be good for me. That good for you?"

"You know, this might not be the time for me to come back there. My plate is sort of full right now."

"Bullshit. You gonna pass up these good bennies, stock options to get beat up out there by yourself?"

"Last time I checked, your stock was for shit, but I appreciate you looking out for me. I'm not getting beat up. My clients like me 'cause I tell them the truth. The ones that don't like me, I get new ones. Nobody up my ass to get somebody else's ass out to dinner, get my ass on a plane. All the ass stuff is tiring," Townes said, his voice trailing off.

There was a pause. "That a dig at me?"

"No, just a generalization of the life driven by the dreaded organizational chart," Townes said, nodding his head up and down. "I don't have an org chart now, just me and the dog, and she doesn't ask for weekly reports, also a plus."

"Come on, you can't be happy out there by yourself."

"How do you know that? Actually, I'm quite happy. I had dinner in New York with an actress."

"Porn actress?" Alvin asked.

"Movie actress, currently playing the lead in a Broadway show."

"Whoa, Townesie! Listen to you, Mister Big Time. I thought you were hittin' that gal that's friends with Clement's ex-chick?"

"Hittin'? When did everyone become so uncivilized?"

"Come on, you know what I mean. You got 'em on both coasts. You da man!"

"I don't have them on both coasts. They are both really good friends, that's all." Townes did not see any benefit in telling him Kat went to India. Alvin would tell Clement, and Clement would start bugging Annie again, without Kat around to get in his face, or punch him in the face when he did.

"Whatever, big guy, you still the man! Listen, I'm going to get this paperwork rolling. You want to be a dumbass and turn it down, that's up to you. Don't say no 'til you hear the offer."

Townes paused and looked around his bedroom at the photos on the wall, but only of places, none with people. "I don't know."

"I'm gonna put this together, so don't fuck it up, dumbass. I'll be in touch. Way to go with the porn actress. Goodbye." Alvin laughed as he hung up.

Townes tossed the phone on the bed, lying back down. "Great. Now I have to listen to that fucker," he mumbled as he moved around the room to clear his head.

He walked outside to get the newspaper, noticing a note stuck to his door. He opened the note.

Don't fergit yer dog.
Band practice today.
Don't fergit that neither.
         Z

"Band practice?" Townes said, scratching his head. "Oh, yeah ... country club gig."

He went back inside and showered and readied for the day. He had a lot to do, but needed to make sure Zeeder and the dog were on the top of his list. "I piss them off, I'm done."

He looked at the stack of mail that Zeeder had piled up for him, quite a large stack after so much time away. He paused to wonder if the travel would ever stop. The new projects would probably require travel.

"Maybe I'll get a bus," Townes said, downing a glass of orange juice.

He continued to look through the mail until he came to an envelope, fancier than the standard correspondence. Opening it, he saw it to be an invitation to the party where the band was playing.

"Wine Fundraiser, La Jolla Country Club."

Wait 'til they get a load of us," he laughed. He looked at the invitation, turning it in his hands. It was ornately done, by a specialty printer, probably Crane, he thought. It was nice to see someone still gave a shit enough to send a fine invitation, as most were email, or some cheap do-it-yourself version. This was not a wedding, but the person had cared enough to make it nice.

"Hell, I'm in the band and she sent me an invite," Townes muttered. He knew she was friends with Annie, and the invite reminded him that he had been wanting to see Annie, wanted to call her, but he was not sure what to say. Though their last meeting ended fine, she still seemed distant, seemed to be carrying some burden ... he wasn't sure what. *It couldn't hurt to call her*, he thought. *She doesn't really like me anyway, so it's not like I would move any further down her list.*

He walked back outside and sat in one of the Adirondack rockers he had on his front porch. He had dressed, jeans and a linen shirt, all but his shoes and socks. He sat there, rocking, looking at the invite in one hand, the phone in the other. There were a few clouds in the blue sky that was the canvas for all the palm trees. It was quite the difference from the rain and concrete of yesterday. Even with a slight marine layer hanging off the coast, it was still near perfect. He looked at the phone again, looking up Annie's number.

"What day is it?" he asked, looking around, as if someone would answer. "Friday, it's Friday. Her office is closed on Friday ... shit."

He started to put the phone down, but changed his mind and placed the call. "I'll leave a message, less pressure."

The phone rang twice, and the recording came on, the usual instructions, with caveats for emergencies, then the beep.

"Yes, this is Townes Mantle, calling for Annie, er, Doctor Simms ... no medical malady ... just wanted to talk. Give me a call if you can. Thanks," he said, then left his number and hung up. "That will probably get deleted quick," he said, leaning back in the rocker, looking out at the palms.

He closed his eyes, rocking gently, the creaks of the wood the only sound. He could go back to sleep without any problem at all. Alvin had gotten him up much earlier than he wanted, and there was nothing keeping him from just sitting here and listening to the palms. It would be better if Angelina was here. She loved to lay on the porch, standing sentry to the world outside the rocker, outside the sun-warmed wood of the porch. If she had a bone, she could stay out there all day. Townes thought he could go get her and come back and slide into relax mode, stay on the porch, smoke a Fuente Don Carlos Number 2 he had been saving in his humidor. Band practice wasn't until later. His phone began to vibrate, but he did not recognize the number. He considered letting it go to voicemail in case it was Alvin calling back but thought it could be a client, so he answered.

"Townes Mantle."

"Hi Townes, it's Annie."

He paused, not believing she had called him back.

"Are you there?" Annie asked, after the pause.

"Yes, yes, hello ... sorry. Hey, how are you?"

"Busy, busy... but ... I'm fine thanks. How are you?"

"Good, good," he leaned forward in his chair, nodding his head, then leaning back, his posture gaining a couple of inches. "I'm good. Hey, it wasn't a medical emergency, so I appreciate you getting back with me. I just thought I would leave you a message ... I just got back in town last night, thought I would give you a call."

"Well, gosh, I'm glad you did. I haven't see you since ... where have you been?"

"All over. Northern California, New York. There was someplace else, but I forget, I think."

277

"Those sound like good places to me. I haven't been to New York in forever, and even then, it was just a stopover. Do you go there a lot?"

"Yes, actually, I do."

"Do you like it there?"

"Very much."

"I couldn't imagine living there, you know, after living here."

"I didn't like it at first, but after I got to know some people there, spent more time, I really like it."

"Maybe I'll get back there sometime."

"I'll give you a list of my favorite places. That way you won't have to be quite so overwhelmed. Go see my friend Milton at the Ritz on Central Park. That is where you have to start."

"That would be great. Thanks."

"Sure. Listen, I would like to have dinner with you ... er ... it might be nice to get together for lunch, dinner, whatever fits your schedule. I'm not—" Townes stammered, rubbing his forehead. "It might be nice."

After a slight pause, Annie broke the silence. "Sure, that would be good."

Townes took the phone away from his mouth, releasing the breath he had been holding, rocking faster in the chair. "I know you are extremely busy, so whatever your schedule will allow."

"I had something tomorrow, but that got cancelled, so would that work?"

"That would be great. Tomorrow would be great. Can I pick you up at, what, six-o'clock? I'm not sure where you live. I was going to walk to George's, but I can still come get you."

"Six would be fine. Walking would be good. I can meet you at the restaurant, or I can meet you somewhere else."

"Great. Thank you for making the time, I really appreciate it."

"Sure, thank you for the invite."

"I'm really looking forward to it. A lot has happened, and I ... well, I just wanted to talk to you about it."

"Gosh, well, I don't know what ... yes, it will be good to catch up."

The view from George's was always inspiring. The higher vantage point of waves and shoreline, above the palms, above the runaway bamboo, showing the enclave where they lived, and the sweeping arrow of where things could go from there. The massive hillside homes that just seemed too large for less than a dozen inhabitants. Annie looked radiant. The blue blouse she wore made her azure eyes seem all the more so. Her hair was down. Townes had never seen it that way before today.

"Have you heard from Kat?" Annie asked.

"She sent a note, a brief note, saying it was not like she expected."

"That all?"

"Uh, no, she asked ..." Townes paused.

"She asked what?"

"She asked if I had been to see you."

"She asked you that?"

"Yes, she asked me that. Have you heard from her?"

Annie moved uncomfortably in her seat and Townes leaned closer to her. "Yes."

"Yes?"

"Yes."

"And?"

"And she said the same thing."

"Which part?" Townes said, tilting his head.

"Both parts."

"Really?"

"Really."

"So, what do you make of that?"

Annie looked around, then back at Townes. "She wants us to see each other, that's what I make of it," Annie said, continuing her gaze at Townes.

"Me too, but you know that's not why I called you."

"I ... I know."

"Is that why you said you would come?" Townes asked. Annie again moved in her chair, then looked away from Townes. "I'm sorry, I shouldn't have said anything. Let's—"

"No."

"No?"

"No, it's not why I said I would come ... well, maybe ... I don't know."

"Why did...? No, I don't need ... whatever reason, or no reason. I'm just glad you did," Townes said, trying to be confident, but his voice softening.

"About that day at the restaurant."

"Yes?"

"Well ..."

"You said you didn't remember, then you said you did remember."

"I know I said that, I just—"

"You just …?" Townes pressed.

"No, I remembered the first time I saw you. I mean the second time I saw you, I remembered seeing you the first time."

"OK."

"Yes. Funny, huh?" Annie said, attempting to lighten the conversation.

"OK, if you say so."

"I didn't know what to say."

"I guess not," Townes said.

"Don't be upset. It's been kinda weird, I guess."

"How's that?"

"I … um, I don't usually talk about this stuff … stuff about me."

"We don't have to talk about it."

"I … I … I mentioned that I was, that I wasn't wanting to get involved in anything, or get involved with anyone."

"Ever?"

"Not, not ever, just not right now."

"Because?"

"Because I got back into something that I thought was right, but it wasn't right. Too much time had passed and things were different."

"I'm not sure I understand, which is usually the case, but—"

"It was someone from my … it was someone I knew before, and it looked like we could start over," Annie said, looking off in the distance. "And I wanted to, I really did, but too much had changed, you know, and it wasn't going to happen. We're still friends. We didn't have a falling out, or anything, we are just different now."

Townes did not know what to say. He lightly patted his hand on the table, scratching the back of his neck with the other.

"Sorry." Annie tightened her lips, nodding gently.

"Um, well, I don't want to intrude, I just … just thought we—"

"Thought what?" Annie asked, turning her gaze back to Townes.

"Thought we connected, like I said, and I never say that, by the way. I'm sort of surprised I said it now, again," Townes said, his voice trailing off. "I'm glad we got a chance tonight to spend a little time together." He looked around, looking at the view of the ocean. He thought it might be a good ideas to change the subject. "Have you ever been to the Beverly Hills Hotel?"

"What?"

"The Beverly Hills Hotel. Have you ever been there?"

"Um, no I haven't, why?"

"Just curious. I have just always wanted to go there. It sounds funny, I know, but I just always have. I remember seeing photographs of it in magazines when I was … well, a long time ago, and for a long time, maybe that is more accurate."

"Well, you should go." Annie saw he was uncomfortable, but that this question was something that meant something to him, and was not just an invitation. She wondered why it did, but did not want to push him about it.

"It's silly, but it is something I am going to do one of these days."

"I think you should go."

"Yep. Always celebrate the victories," Townes said quietly.

"What?"

"Nothing. So I'm going to write Kat back. What should I tell her … about you and me?"

Annie looked at him and sighed. "Sometimes things, life, just gets in the way of doing other things. Maybe it just wasn't meant to be, I don't know. You don't have to tell her that. I just meant … I don't know." She looked at him, narrowing her eyes, looking for some expression from Townes that might contrast what he had just said, what he had just asked. Townes returned the look, not wavering, putting his hand up to his chin, smiling a slight smile.

The break in the conversation seemed long, yet neither Annie nor Townes seemed uncomfortable with the pause, and each continued to look at each other. It was good just being here with Annie but Townes thought there was not going to be any deeper conversation tonight, and maybe not ever. Annie had deep-seated issues with mistrust in her life and no matter his candor, no matter his intention, those issues were probably not going to go away. She seemed, in spite of her composure that never wavered, to be damaged. She always had sincere things to say, always found the good in things, but there was a hurt deep down. He first thought her manner to be part of a doctor thing. Something that spoke to the intensity of the profession, to life, or possible loss of it. The more he was around her the more he saw this reluctance she had was not coming from her profession. It came from inside her and this hurt did not look like it was going away. She would be the greatest of friends to those closest to her, but it did not look like she was going to get any closer to someone than that. Somewhere, somehow, someone, maybe multiple someones, had really let her down.

It was a disappointment to Townes that things with he and Annie were going to stay at arm's length. He thought there could be so much more. Crosetti was right when he had said you can't make them love you.

CHAPTER 48

Zeeder watched as the two men took turns looking through a pair of binoculars. He had noticed them several times, several places earlier, and the thought of being a coincidence was no longer so. They had been at the coffee place, they had been in Jack's, they had been in the market. They were not police, Zeeder was sure of that. He got his phone out of his pocket and dialed a number.

"Holy shit, no way!" The voice on the other end said.

"Yep," Zeeder said.

"Man, we been a wonderin'. You OK?"

"Yessir, so far, but that could be a changin'. What you don't get out here and help me?."

"OK, but you have to tell us where here is."

"La Jolla, California," Zeeder said.

"Where the hell is that?"

"Just a hair above San Diego, on the coast."

"How long we got?"

"Not long, so's how long 'fore you can get here?"

"You needs us, we be there tomorrow," the man said.

"OK. I'll get you some money, some plane tickets, you know the drill. Sorry for the short notice."

"Hey man, we's just glad you's OK. Who is it, you know?"

"Not certain, but got an idee. This feller been givin' this friend a mine a hard time. Reckon he put some PI's on him, and they somehow figgered out who I was. Don't know who they is. I seen 'em a few places, watchin' and such."

"We'll be there. OK we call you on this number?"

"Fer now. Let you know what that changes," Zeeder said, looking around.

"I can't help but notice this is gettin' to be a regular thing with you. That being said, I have a recommendation for you," Topper said, coughing.

"Yeah, what't that?" Clement asked.

"Get a different girlfriend. One that actually likes you."

There was a pause, and Clement let out a long breath. "This some kind of a joke?"

"Nope, I'm serious. I know you got a lot of money and all, but I'm startin' to feel bad takin' it so's I can chase down guys that looked at this girl that doesn't really like you anyway. Don't want to keep takin' your money."

"I'll bet."

"Really, I don't."

"Uh huh."

"Look, I promised some people I would look after you, not for free, but still look after you."

"And did they tell you to tell me this? Seems like you got a conscience ... all of a sudden."

"They didn't tell me nothin'. Thing is, with pokin' around for stuff, sometimes people notice the pokin' around."

"I thought you were the best, so why would we, you, need to worry about somebody noticing ... if you were the best."

Topper was making a clicking sound on the other end, combined with what was either humming, or groaning. "Even the best get noticed sometimes. I like my batting average, but I don't like swinging a bat at bugs in the garden, it ain't worth it. I swing my bat, I connect, but bugs—"

"I'm not sure I understand what you are getting at. I pay you, you perform a service. Seems pretty straightforward to me."

"Suit yourself. Just thought I would save you some money."

"I appreciate your concern, but just do what I tell you to do, you got that?"

There was a pause on the other end, with more clicking.

Clement repeated himself. "You got that?"

"Here's what I got. You ask me things you would like me to look into or take care of. You tell me what to do, and I am going to go to the people I promised that I would look after you. I do that, you can pretty much go fuck yourself, because they are not going to want to hear that. You, left on your own, they just might have to do something to put a quick stop to that, and believe you me, fancy boy, they can do it so fast you won't know what red Ferrari drove over your ass. There won't be enough left of you to put in the glove box, so you might keep that in mind. You got that?"

Clement paused. "I got it."

"Good. We shouldn't have to talk about this again. Here is a recommendation for you."

"What's that?"

"Let it go on the one musician because there ain't no dirt on him, this Townes Mantle. But, I can maybe give you a finder's fee on the other musician, this Zeeder fellow."

"Why is that?"

"I told you I had some folks might know him. Turns out they do, and that means a finder's fee for you. It really doesn't, but I felt bad about takin' your money on the other. I ain't a bad guy. I just got my way of doing things. You ain't experienced in this stuff, so you just need to know when to step out. You gettin' a fee for this Zeeder guy, that ain't so bad, is it?" Topper said.

"What did he do, and why do you want him?"

"I'm not goin' into details but he's an heir to a family in the bourbon business in Kentucky, worth lots of barrels, I guess," Topper laughed.

"So?"

"So, seems he's been missin' for a long time. I got people pay me to get him back."

"What if I brought him back myself?"

"That ain't your line of work."

"Well, what if I did?"

"I would kill you dead."

Clement started laughing. "What's the punch line?"

"There ain't no punch line. I would kill you, and they would never find you. Or, they might find parts of somebody washed up in La Jolla Cove that the sharks had spit out, but it would take 'em a while to figure out who it was," Topper said, matter-of-factly.

"You're serious."

"As a fuckin' heart attack. This ain't your line of work, so just leave this stuff to me. You and your posse, you're good at corporate bullshit, gettin' money under the table for makin' introductions to places to sell some guy's shit, coverin' up little shady investment crap, inside tradin'. Some corporate toady gets an envelope full of cash to take somebody into someplace, tell 'em this is the guy they need. Settin' up guys with hookers so they'll sell your stuff. I don't give two shits about that kind of stuff. You make somethin' on it, more power to ya. This stuff is different, and believe me, you ain't got the stomach for what I do, and for the things that the people that we both know do. You best stay with your buddies, goin' around slappin' each other on the back, drivin' your fancy cars, lyin' about your golf handicaps. This other stuff, it ain't you. I told you I'd give you a finder's fee, which I don't have to do. I was only bein' nice. You walk away with some jack, everything is good. You try to take this guy in … you don't walk away from nothin' ever again. Pretty much sums it up."

Clement tapped his pen on the desk but said nothing.

"You still there?" Topper asked.

"I'm still here."

"We clear on this?"

"We're clear on this."

CHAPTER 49

Zeeder stood with Skinny and Landon. Skinny took a bottle of bourbon out of his backpack and opened it.

"Man, it's good to see ya," Skinny said.

"Sure is. You doin' OK?" Landon asked.

"Not sure how to answer that. I like the weather, not hot like back home," Zeeder said. "Folks is kinda into they ownselves a bit here. Their manners ain't so good. Could stand less of that. Got a good buddy here, you'd like him. He ain't like them."

"He's the one you plays music with."

"Yep."

"And he don't know about you … I mean know about you from before?" Skinny asked, passing the bottle to Zeeder. "I brought a bottle of Eagle Rare ten year, hope that's all right. Brought you an Ale-8 too."

"It sure is all right. No, he don't know about me. He's a good guy, reckon I shoulda told him, 'cause somethin' like this was bound to crop up," Zeeder said, taking the cork out of the bottle, offering it to Landon and Skinny.

"Hells no! You first, man. We ain't seen you in forever, so you take the first pull," Landon said.

"Well, thankee, I will. Here's to you fellers," Zeeder said, raising the bottle and taking a long drink out of it, then passing it to Skinny. "Man, that's good. So, you know what yous a gonna do?"

"I think so," Skinny said, repeating the process with the bottle. "They're gonna come up missin' for a while."

"Then they'll wander back from they don't know where … maybe with shaved heads, fancy designs painted on them, or tats," Landon said, taking the bottle from Skinny. "I ain't decided yet."

The night of the country club gig came and the band was ready, or so they hoped. They convinced Fudgie to wear pants, and he wore what he claimed was a pirate shirt. Stretch found a double-breasted blue blazer, white slacks, and white captain's hat. Saxman, Townes, and Zeeder said they had decided against costumes, wearing dark pants, dark shirts. The function was a benefit wine tasting, so Townes had mentioned this to Crosetti. Crosetti said it might be nice for the people at the event to "see what good wine tastes like," so he came to town and brought some of his wines.

They did their usual equipment setup, with Crosetti bringing a couple of bottles of wine and glasses for them to keep tucked away, "in case they got thirsty," Crosetti said. There was supposed to be a large crowd but they were going to be focused on the wine and not necessarily on the band.

"We are just background music, dudes," Fudgie said. "But even though we are, Stretch, lay off that fucking cowbell."

Stretch looked down at the ground.

"What do you care, we's gettin' paid purdy good for just bein' background music, so's I'ds just be grateful, I was you," Zeeder said.

"Sellouts! You land lubbers is all sellouts," Fudgie said.

"Well, Captain Rook, you could give us your share of the booty," Saxman said.

"I'm keeping my share, you wussies, and I'm buying some … some …"

"Some what?" Townes asked.

"I don't know, but I'm buying something. Booty? You think maybe I could get me some …"

"Attaboy!" Zeeder laughed.

A woman came to the microphone, thanked everyone for coming, introduced the band and encouraged everyone to donate more money for the cause, and proclaimed the event underway. She left the stage area and they got ready to play. It would be an easy gig for them, as the crowd was busy going to all the wineries represented at the gathering, and the band did not have to keep anyone focused on them. Townes and Zeeder recognized some of the people from the clubs, but as with Gina's party, did not know their names. Annie and Gina were involved in the event. They came and talked to Townes and Zeeder and said to let them know if they needed anything. Annie seemed very happy to see Townes, hugging him when she saw him, which she had never done. Gina gave Zeeder a note and smiled at him as they walked away.

"What was that, you two?" Stretch asked.

"Yes, what was that?" Fudgie followed.

"Just adoring fans," Zeeder said. "You get out more, you might get some."

"Some what?" Fudgie asked, sneaking a drink of Crosetti's wine.

"I didn't get a note," Townes said, his eyes still following Annie around the room.

Zeeder opened the piece of paper. "No after-party for me tonight boys ... I got a better offer." He scratched his head. "Wonder if she's a plannin' fer us to go boll weevilin' at her place like last time?" He said quietly. "Oh, and no offense."

"Offense taken," Fudgie belched. "Now let's play some music, you bitches."

They started to play. Fudgie wanted to play loud but the others managed to prevail upon him, and kept him in check. They seldom booked events like this, but Townes enjoyed it as a nice change from the usual gigs with just the two of them. The bigger band dynamic could become pretty raucous, especially with Fudgie left unattended, but for the most part it always came out fine. With a gathering like this, people were not paying strict attention to the band, so they could do some different things than they normally would with an audience more focused on them. It was a contrast to the music Townes and Zeeder played with the only caution being the band after-party, which had a tendency to be longer in duration than the event they played for. Even an event relatively early in the evening, like this one, might not end until the early morning hours with the addition of the band after-party. Townes was very careful about not scheduling anything for the day following an event. He thought it better to make at least some sense when he was meeting with a customer.

A slight pause in the festivities brought one of the organizers to the microphone again to give some information to the attendants. The band took the opportunity to enjoy a sampling of Crosetti's offerings. Townes tended to his guitar.

"Hey," a woman near the stage called out.

Townes looked up to see one of the country club wait staff. He thought it was the waitress he had met from the cafe the first time he saw Annie but wasn't sure. Her hair was red and this woman had jet black hair.

"Hey, it's me--Savannah, from the restaurant."

"Hello Savannah … how are you?" Townes said, unsure because of the hair.

"Working, as usual," she said, noticing Townes was looking at her hair. "Yes, it's me; I got tired of red. You ever find that blonde woman you were looking for?" Savannah said, looking at her own hair.

"Yes, I did, thanks to you."

"Are you with her?" Savannah looked around.

"No, I'm not with her. We're just friends, kind of," Townes said, looking at his guitar.

"Well, that's better than nothing. At least you got to meet her and got to be kind of friends, which is cool. I've seen her somewhere before, but I say that a lot about a lot of people. I got to get back to work. I wish I had known you were going to be playing here, I would have brought some of my songs for you to look at. Maybe I can get in touch with you and you can take a look at them."

"I'm not sure I am the best judge of music, as evidenced by this collection of misfits, but I will be happy to look at them. That guy in the pirate shirt back there drinking wine, he loves things like that, and he is the band leader. I'll take a look and make sure we all look at them. His follow-up is suspect, so I promise I will follow up. You were nice enough to help me," Townes smiled. He reached in his pocket and pulled out a business card and gave it to Savannah. "You don't even have to buy breakfast."

"Hah! That's funny. I would appreciate any help I can get. You probably don't need help, but I do. OK, back to work … call you," she said, quickly walking away. "How do you like my hair?" she called back.

Townes laughed, looking at Savannah moving quickly through the crowd, trying not to run into anyone as she did.

"Townes," Annie called. "How's it going up there?"
"Oh, hey. Fine, fine, everything is fine. An event like this is pretty easy, pretty fun. Toughest part is keeping the band mates under control. We'll see if we can be successful with that. It's never a given."

"It looks like everyone is having a good time. Who was that you were talking to?"

"That … that was somebody I met … Savannah, her name is Savannah. Listen, I have been meaning to call you to see if we could get together again. Things have just been so hectic, that I haven't had a chance to. I'm sorry I haven't," Townes said. He had never seen her dressed this nicely. A blue blouse and black pants, both somewhat iridescent.

"She looks really familiar," Annie said, tugging on her ear. "Yes, me too … I mean, I have been really busy also, helping Gina with this, and with work."

"I wanted to see if we could have dinner, or something, again. It has been … I don't know, it just seems like we should."

"I would like that very much, so yes."

"Well, let me know when is a good time, and we'll do something. You can choose, if you like."

"No, you choose. I will like whatever you decide, I'm sure," Annie said, smiling at him.

"Things are moving pretty quickly for me. I wanted to get some time with you before things, I don't know … before things got too crazy. There is a lot happening and a lot that is going to happen. I might not be around for a while."

"I'm not sure what you mean by that but all right. I think we were supposed to talk about that last time. That's my fault, that we didn't," Annie said, looking down.

"I just wanted to see you, that's all, before I—" Townes smiled.

"I'm here now."

"Yeah, I was thinking a few hundred less people," Townes said, looking around. He thought he recognized someone but Annie spoke and he turned back towards her.

"I understand."

"I'm going to have to get back up there. You probably don't want to get together afterwards but if you do …"

"Yes, I think that would be good," Annie grinned.

"Great. I just have to tear down but that won't take too long. Might need to go clean up real quick."

"Whatever works."

"Good," Townes said and leaned over and kissed her on the cheek and gave her a hug. Annie didn't pull away. They stayed in the embrace longer than Townes thought they would. Finally, each moved back slowly.

"I'll see you after we're done playing, if that's still OK."

"Yes, it is," she said softly.

"Good, see you then," Townes said, walking away.

Annie stood there watching him, a small, but meaningful smile on her face, a look of relief. She let out a small breath and adjusted her ponytail, turning to find Gina. She turned and there stood Clement in front of her. Her small smile disappeared.

"That how it's going to be, is it?" Clement said.

"This … is none of your business," Annie said. "Nothing I do, is any of your business. Why can't you get that through your head?"

"You don't want him. He's a fuckin' nobody."

"What I don't want, is you."

"You and I go way back. Have you forgotten that?"

"I have known you a long time, but that is all. There is no you and me, and I would really appreciate it if you would leave me alone. Forever."

"You don't mean that. What, that musician slip you some drugs? Musicians are always on drugs. You're not seeing things clearly."

"I see things more clearly now than maybe I ever have. If you do not leave me alone, I promise you, you will be sorry."

"What, you going to sucker punch me like your hard-ass friend Kat?"

"She didn't sucker punch you, and I'm not going to sucker punch you, but I am going to call the police and tell them all about you."

"You wouldn't do that. It's not in you," Clement said quickly.

Annie reached in the small clutch she was carrying, pulled out a phone and held it in front of her. "Watch me."

"You will regret this."

"You'll regret not leaving me alone when I asked you to years ago."

"You'll change your mind."

"I will not. Now go, before you wish you had. I am done with you and you are done with me."

Clement turned and walked away. Annie stood there, her jaw clenched tight, her face red, the phone still in her hand. Gina came up behind her and put her hand on her shoulder.

"Is everything all right? What's going on?"

"Everything is fine," Annie said firmly.

"Who was that?"

"Clement."

"Oh, no. Really? What did he want?"

"He wanted me … and that's not going to happen, ever."

"So that guy up there is the bourbon heir?" Clement asked.

"He's the one," the man said.

"What's your name?" Clement asked the man.

"Danny."

"How about you?" Clement asked the other man.

"Billy," the other man said.

"So you just going to go get that guy and take him somewhere?" Clement asked.

"You don't really want to know, do ya?" Danny said.

"Just curious, but I guess not," Clement answered. "Sure you can't do something with that other guy up there, too?"

"Topper says no. That girl you was just talkin' to, she looked like she didn't like you anyway. Topper says you should—"

"I know what Topper says," Clement responded. "May just have to take care of him myself."

"Whatever. We're here for that guy, so we'll be in touch," Billy said.

The band started reforming to play another set when a woman came up to the stage. Her cobalt blue blouse shimmered with the incoming light from the windows. "Could you gentlemen please play a slow song, I would like to dance with my friend."

"Well, generally we don't …" Fudgie started to say.

"Sure, Miss. We would be happy to," Zeeder interrupted.

"Great, thank you. And could you tell that man back there that I would like to dance with him?" The woman asked, pointing at Townes, whose back was turned.

"Townes, someone here to see you," Zeeder said.

Townes turned. "What, who … Scruff!"

"Hello, my friend. Could I have this next dance? I'm sure your bandmates can do without you for one song," Ashley smiled.

"Well—"

"Hey, dude, we can play one song without you," Fudgie said. "Go dance with the pretty lady. Hello, pretty lady."

"Hello," Ashley said.

"Are you sure this is the guy you want to dance with?" Fudgie asked.

"Oh, quite sure," Ashley smiled.

Townes put his guitar in a stand and looked at Fudgie as he got off the stage area. "Ashley, I didn't know you were coming."

"I just got in today. I am staying with a friend here in La Jolla that told me about the event. I was going to call you afterwards, but to my surprise, you are here playing for the event. I should have known. I guess I sort of did know you would be here. I wanted to see you," Ashley said, putting her arms around Townes and kissing him on the cheek. "Is that all right?"

"Of course, it's all right. I'm just surprised to see you."

"It was a last minute thing. She thought I was busy, but it doesn't matter. I'm here now. I like your band," she said, looking around Townes to see Fudgie and Stretch watching them, her arms still around Townes. She waved back to them.

"They are something, all right. Zeeder is my good friend, the one I play music with most. He is that one over there," Townes turned, pointing to Zeeder.

"They won't miss you for a minute so I can dance with you, I'm sure."

"No they'll be fine," Townes motioned for them to start playing.

A slow number started. Ashley and Townes danced, Ashley holding him close to her. "So is this OK … I mean, that I came to see you?"

"Of course it is! Why wouldn't it be?"

"No reason. Some people just don't like surprises. I generally don't."

"It's great to see you. You have helped me so much. I don't know how to thank you."

"You don't have to thank me. I told you, I know what it means to need a break and to have someone give me a break. I wanted to help you," Ashley said, pulling closer to him. "But it seems to have gotten to be a bit more than just helping you."

"Well, you have helped me, and yes, I think it has. I'm glad you are here."

Annie was still clearly upset from her confrontation with Clement. Gina tried to calm her but it wasn't working. Annie had wanted to say more to Townes, but there just wasn't time, and now here was Clement. She wished Kat were here.

"Just go sit down for a minute. If he comes back, I'll go get Zeeder and Townes and they will help Clement find his Ferrari keys," Gina said, looking up to the stage area. "I can see Zeeder, but I don't see Townes."

Annie looked that direction and saw that Townes was not with the band. She knew he hadn't left yet. She looked around, spotting him on the dance floor, with a very attractive woman, someone she didn't know, and she knew almost everyone in La Jolla.

"Who's that dancing with Townes?" Annie asked.

Gina looked to the dance floor. "I'm not sure," she paused, "but it looks like Ashley Meacham, the actress. She is friends with a friend of mine here in La Jolla."

"How does she know Townes?"

"I have no idea. Maybe she doesn't know Townes."

Annie continued staring at the two. "Dancing that close ... she knows him," Annie said.

"Oh, my," Gina whispered.

Clement and Alvin started to leave the gathering. They walked past the dance floor to find the door when Alvin spotted Townes.

"Hey, give me a minute," Alvin said. "Be right back, gotta talk to somebody." Alvin went over to Townes and Ashley, tapping him on the shoulder. "Hey, Townesie boy, I just wanted to—"

"Excuse me," Ashley said, turning towards Alvin.

"Well, hello there!" Alvin said, leaving his mouth open wide.

"You will just have to wait. Townes is quite busy at the moment. He might be free in a day or two, but more like a week, maybe two, so could you be a dear and run along now, please?"

Townes said nothing and just smiled.

"Uh, sure," Alvin said quietly. He turned and walked into one of the wait staff, knocking an empty tray out of her hands, making a crashing sound. "Whoa! Sorry about that," he said, then walked away.

Savannah rolled her eyes as she picked up the tray. She turned toward Townes and Ashley. "Asshole," she mouthed and then flashed a thumbs up gesture. "Way to go!" She looked at Ashley. "Love your movies. Gotta run," she said, quickly moving away.

Clement had seen Alvin talking to Townes and heard the tray crash and moved out to the dance floor to intercede. Zeeder had been keeping an eye on Townes and now saw Gina motioning him to go get involved. Zeeder leaned over to tell Fudgie to keep the music going and that he would be right back.

"Rock on, dude, and get me some more of that vino," Fudgie yelled, turning his amplifier volume up.

Zeeder moved down to the dance floor to where a group was now forming. Zeeder motioned to Gina to come help him. She moved quickly to where he was. Zeeder grabbed her and started to dance towards the group.

"Gotta help 'em," Zeeder said.

"I don't mind."

"Good. 'Fore things get outta hand, just want to tell you that I'm gonna be headin' out for a while."

"What? Where are you going?"

"Just headin' out for a while. Soon as I can, I promise I will get up with ya, OK?"

"Are you in some sort of trouble?"

"Not yet and don't plan to be. I ain't broke no laws. I just don't like folks meddlin' in my things," Zeeder said, keeping watch on Townes.

"It isn't something I—"

"Nope, nothin' you did. I would like to, you know, see if maybe we is any count, so long as that's all right with you. I'll be seein' you again, I just can't tell you when."

"Well, I…"

Zeeder leaned in and kissed her. "I'll see you soon as I can. Promise."

He moved over to where the others were, breaking his embrace with Gina. "Hey Rube, I needs some help with the gear out back. You wanna come give me a hand?" he called to Townes.

"You are sure popular," Ashley said.

"A little too popular," Townes replied, but looked around for problems, having heard Zeeder's code for trouble.

"Hey, Elvis, how about I have the next dance with your lady here?" Clement said.

"Nosir, I don't think that's gonna happen. You was rude the first time I met you and you ain't improved nary a lick. I suggest you leave these folks be and you and I can take care of this outside," Zeeder said, stepping between Clement and Townes.

"Who needs some wine?" Crosetti said, now approaching the group, holding magnum bottles in each hand.

Fudgie and the band saw the congregation forming and stepped the number up to something faster, turning the volume up, and the dance floor began to fill even more.

"I know who you are, bourbon boy!" Clement shouted, trying to be heard above the music.

"That so? Well, let's go out back and talk about it," Zeeder said.

"I'll bring the wine," Crosetti yelled.

"Who the fuck is this guy? Which one of these assholes are you friends with?" Clement asked.

"I gotta take this call," Alvin said, walking away.

Crosetti looked at Townes, then at Clement. "I got some special wine for you. Come on," Crosetti said, putting a headlock with his large arm around Clement.

"I have to go, but don't leave," Townes said to Ashley.

"I won't leave. Be safe."

Annie watched as the group continued to get larger and moved out to the dance floor as they started to exit, intercepting Townes. "What's going on?"

"Everything, everything is going on. You should probably stay in here."

"Clement is crazy, so watch out."

"He's about to see all kinds of crazy, so I hope you don't still have feelings for him, cause he is going to look a lot different in a few minutes."

"You can do whatever you want to him, I was about to call the police."

"Did he hurt you?"

"No."

"Good."

"Be careful!"

Townes smiled. "I just want you to know, I think maybe we could have—"

"Hey, Townes! Come with me to give this guy some wine," Crosetti interrupted.

Townes moved forward to the group that was now Townes, Zeeder, and Crosetti, with Clement still in a headlock. They moved through the crowd, Crosetti and Zeeder smiling and waving to the crowd to make it look like it was all in good fun. People laughed, waved back, and started crowding the dance floor. Annie watched as the group made its way through the crowd in the opposite direction of the festivities. Annie closed her eyes, putting her hand up to her forehead. She opened her eyes and saw the black-haired wait person that Townes had been talking to. She smiled, but said nothing.

Savannah smiled back at Annie. "He's a really nice guy. You should go out with him. Gotta go," she said as she darted off.

Annie then saw the woman Townes had been dancing with standing next to her. The woman was beautiful, impeccably dressed. The woman looked at Annie.

"I hope everything is all right," Ashley said.

Annie found it difficult to produce the smile that she could always seem to muster. She noticed they were both wearing the same color top. She looked at her own top, then back to the woman. "Are they friends of ... is Townes a friend of yours?" Annie asked, her hand still to her forehead.

Ashley paused, her eyes glassy, and exhaled a slight sigh. She smiled at Annie and walked away without saying another word. Annie watched the woman disappear into the crowd, Townes and the group now out of view. She suddenly felt very empty.

Townes and the group made it out back of the building, Crosetti releasing his hold on Clement.

"So what the fuck is the problem here?" Crosetti asked, setting down one of the magnums.

"Don't touch me again or you are going down!" Clement yelled, trying to straighten his obnoxious patterned bistro shirt. "This guy here a friend of yours, curly?" Clement asked, pointing at Townes.

Crosetti looked at Clement but said nothing.

"I asked you a question ... this asshole a friend of yours?"

Crosetti tipped up the bottle, took a large drink and wiped his mouth. "Yes, he is," and turned and punched Clement in the face. Clement dropped to the ground, out cold.

"You guys want some wine?" Crosetti asked, turning to Townes and Zeeder.

Townes and Zeeder stood looking at Clement in a heap, slowly nodding their approval. They passed the bottle, saying nothing.

"This is quite the shindig. Lots and lots of pretty women. Man, I kinda like it here. Your band sounded really good too. I'm hungry, let's go get some food. And some more wine. Somebody drank all my fucking wine!" he said, shaking the now empty magnum. "You know what we should do? After this, we should go back to Dallas, eat at that guy's place again. I like that. Lots of pretty women there too. What was the name of that place?" Crosetti asked, looking into the setting sun, wiping his forehead.

"What?" Townes replied.

"That place in Dallas where we ate that great food … and you made me drink so much. That guy can really cook. His food is so good, all the pretty women come there to eat!"

"Fearing's. It's called Fearing's."

"Yeah, that was it. I liked that place. Lots of pretty women like here. Let's go back there. Can we go there tomorrow?"

Townes rubbed his eyes and let out a deep breath. "Not tomorrow. I have some comp—I have another friend that just came to town that surprised me, so we can't go tomorrow."

"Did they bring a lot of wine, like me?"

"She didn't say."

Crosetti laughed loudly and turned to head back in the building. "See you back at your house later … maybe!" he said over his shoulder.

Townes looked at Clement lying there in a heap. He looked back towards the building, thinking about Annie, her reticence to get close. He thought about Ashley and how she had helped him, and how she had opened his eyes to a new dimension. He felt great when he was around her. Now here was this joker that seemed to be obsessed with Annie laid out in front of him, and that joker would probably never go away. He just shook his head. Townes started to follow Crosetti, getting almost to the door when he turned. Zeeder had not moved, still holding the bottle, taking another drink. "You coming?"

"Don't think so."

"Too much excitement for one day?"

"Somethin' like that," Zeeder said, taking another drink.

"I think I am booked for after, so may not see you 'til … after I'm … not booked," Townes smiled.

"I reckon you is booked, maybe double booked."

"We'll catch up sometime."

"Plan on it."

"Yep."

"All right then. Hey!" Zeeder called.

"Yeah?" Townes said, turning back.

"You's a good friend. I'll get with you soon as I can."

"I've got lots of company, so it might be a day, maybe more, I'm told."

"Think it's gonna be a bit more than that … for me, but I'll get up with ya, I promise."

"You know it." Townes turned back to look at Zeeder as he walked away.

CHAPTER 50

Beverly Hills
Present Day

Townes sat looking over the glistening blue water of the massive swimming pool, thinking it the largest he had ever seen, the landmark pink building of the Beverly Hills Hotel resting softly as a backdrop to the near blinding reflection of the Southern California sun off the immense swath of turquoise. It might not have appeared of such a shimmer to the other inhabitants, they more accustomed to the absolute shine of prosperity, but for Townes today, the luminous expanse was overpowering. Even the fragrance of the water was impossible to ignore. All the travel, all the nights alone, all the people he had connected with around the country had brought him here. He had always wanted to come to this place, never wanting to just come here by himself, like all the other nice places he had been. He wanted to come here with someone that he cared about, someone that cared about him. He wanted the ache to stop. He wanted the voices in his head to check into a different hotel. Maybe his friend Crosetti was right. Maybe now he was finally near somewhere.

So much had happened. It was going to take some time to determine his next move. The most troubling thing was his best friend being missing. Townes was still not sure what to make of that. He was going to try to put that out of his mind, hoping nothing terrible had happened and that his friend would make his whereabouts known when he thought the time was right. He reached for a newspaper. The paper felt odd, scratchy to his touch and decided he was in no mood to read. He brushed his now-long blond hair back with his hands, pausing momentarily over his eyes, wishing his headache had also checked into a different hotel. He looked at the woman in the chair next to him. Seeing her there, reading, brought back a great deal of memories, some he wanted to forget. She was so tan. Her hair tied back, the ponytail poking out the back of her blue baseball cap, the same blue as her bikini. Her slight scent of coconut oil blended nicely with the entire scene. He wanted to say something but it was difficult for him. Talking to her might not go well and he did not want to take that chance. Maybe they could talk later, that might be easier. If he waited, maybe he would not have to talk about how everything had happened, and why he felt stupid about some of what happened, or what didn't happen, in the first place. She could be understanding or she could be annoyed that he brought any of it up. Maybe she did not want to talk at all. She had been quiet the entire time she was there. She probably did not want to talk.

So much had happened. Seeing Annie that first day. Spending time with Kat. Meeting Ashley. Wondering why Zeeder was gone—missing. There had been so much and now all of this. The thoughts just made Townes's head hurt more. He didn't know if he had done the right things, made the right choices, or not. He thought the choices were the right ones, but he couldn't help but wonder. All the hotels, all the restaurants, all the bars all over the country that he had seen by himself had now brought him to this one place. People would ask him about it and that is what he would tell them. More importantly, that is what he told himself. He took a sip of his Old Tom Gin Collins, and closed his eyes.

He was exhausted. This spot by this magnificent swimming pool would go a long way towards catching up on his rest. He did not have to hop on a plane, head to some cold city for a useless meeting. He did not have to attend some idiotic sales meeting, make some ridiculous slide presentation. No more team-building events, no more motivational speakers, no more of that kind of mindless bullshit. The world would be different now and he was just fine with that. Being here at the Beverly Hills Hotel, he could think about how it was going to be now. He didn't need to have his phone with him, didn't need email. This was the first day of a legitimate vacation with no end date scheduled. A nap was not out of the question.

He could not take his eyes off her, sitting there reading, still wondering if he should bring it up. She was in her bikini. Maybe she would go in the pool soon and it would be left to speak of at another time. He suddenly felt himself drenched with ice cold water. He jumped up from his lounge chair.

"What the—"

The woman startled and looked up from her book. Townes turned to see Ashley standing there next to him, waving a large, empty cup, her other hand on her hip and an annoyed look on her face.

"Looked like you needed to cool off a little."

"Really?"

"At least get your eyes back in your head."

"I was …"

"You were what?"

"I was looking at the book," Townes said, toweling off.

"Right."

"Well, it's not like I've seen it in a setting like this," he said, leaving the towel over his head. "That was cold."

"Uh huh," Ashley said.

The woman next to Townes was perplexed at the exchange and looked first at Townes, then at Ashley.

"Sorry to bother you," Ashley said to the woman. "He wrote that book and isn't used to seeing it out in public … with someone in a small bikini reading it," her voice trailing off.

The woman looked back, skeptical, as she scrutinized Townes, who was sporting a grin under the towel over his head. Ashley motioned for the woman to turn to the back cover. The woman was either slow to understand or perturbed that her concentration had been broken by this unusual exchange. She looked down at the book, then back to Ashley and Townes. Ashley smiled and repeated the gesture to turn to the back of the book. The woman let out a sigh and turned to the back cover.

"Inside," Ashley nodded.

The woman turned to view the inside back cover, then looked at Townes, his head bobbing slightly under the towel.

"Dummy," Ashley said, backhanding him on the shoulder.

"Oh," Townes said, taking the towel off his head, brushing his hair back.

The woman moved her sunglasses down her nose looking at Townes, then at the photograph inside the book, repeating the process.

"Well, what do you know?" she said.

"We're sorry to bother you," Ashley said, sounding embarrassed, but proud of Townes at the same time.

"No problem," the woman said, looking at the photo, then again at

Townes. "You wrote this?"

"Yes."

"Hmm. Well, it's very good," she said, smiling. "Would you sign it for me?"

"What? Oh, sure," Townes said, patting his trunks. "I, uh ... don't ..."

"I have a pen I think," the woman said, reaching for a cloth drawstring bag she had on the small table beside her lounge chair, digging in it to feel if the contents included a pen.

Townes smiled at Ashley, shrugging his shoulders. Ashley gave him a cocked-head stare, accentuated when she moved her sunglasses down her nose, showing her squinted eyes, tapping her foot. Townes moved his closed lips from side to side, holding his palms up.

"Got it!" the woman said, producing a pen and handing it to Townes.

"Great. Who can I make this out to?" Townes asked, taking the book and pen she handed him.

"Kimla," the woman said, smiling at Townes.

"Yep," Townes paused, looking at Ashley, then back to the task at hand.

"This his first autograph?" Kimla asked, looking at Ashley.

"Second," Ashley smiled.

"Do I know you from somewhere?" Kimla asked.

"I can't imagine where it would be," Ashley said, pressing her sunglasses firmly on her face.

"There you go, Kimla," Townes said, handing the book back to her.

She turned to where Townes had placed the inscription. "Thank you, that's really sweet of you. You want some advice?"

"Sure he does," Ashley said, still tapping her foot.

"You'd better start carrying a pen. You're going to be signing a lot of these," Kimla said, as she packed her things and got up to leave.

"I'm sorry I interrupted you. You don't have to leave," Townes said.

"Oh, you're not interrupting me. I am running late anyway ... had to get one more chapter in," she said, hoisting her bag on one shoulder and extending her other hand to Townes.

"Townes, I am Townes," he said, reaching for her hand.

"I know. You're funny. Thanks again," she said as she walked away. "And don't forget."

"Forget what?"

"To start carrying a pen," she said, still walking.

"I will … er, I mean, I won't forget," Townes said, tapping his head, watching her walk away. He smiled and let out a breath. "How about that?"

Ashley looked at him, still tapping her foot. "How about that?" she said, feigning disgust.

"What!?"

"What!?" she mocked.

"I'm not used to that."

"Used to signing the book, or used to the blonde in the bikini?"

"Come on," Townes tilted his head.

Ashley started to smile, laughing to herself, throwing the last few drops of water out of the cup in Townes's direction. Townes jumped back, thinking there was more water than there was. She laughed out loud, putting the cup on the chair next to his. "This seat taken?'

"Uh, no."

"Good." She took off her T-shirt, adjusted her blue bikini, tossing the shirt on the lounge chair. "Now, will you sign my book?" she asked, scrunching up her nose.

Townes paused, took off his sunglasses, tossing them on his chair. He moved towards Ashley, reaching up and taking off her sunglasses. He put his arms around her and kissed her, in no hurry to curtail the gesture, Ashley appearing in no hurry either. Slowly, they broke apart, with Ashley slowly opening her eyes.

"Well?" she asked.

"Well what?"

"Well, are you going to sign my book?"

Townes picked her up in his arms, carrying her towards the pool. "Already gave you the first signed copy, remember? And I thought you didn't want me signing books for women in bikinis."

"Other women in bikinis," she said with a laugh.

"Come on, Scruff, let's go for a swim," he said as he jumped in, holding her in his arms, and very, very happy that the voices usually in his head had not checked in to this hotel.

ACKNOWLEDGEMENTS

I'm not sure if this second book was harder than the first book or not. Some parts were easier, some parts were more difficult. What I do know, is that I am very fortunate to have some wonderful people that help a great deal in this process.

My editor, Kristina Blank Makansi and her staff. After being tortured with working with me editing my first book, Nowhere Yet, she came back for more with this book. This certainly makes me question her overall judgement, but when it comes to books, she is who I want.

My cover artist, Patricia Bacall. You have a great eye for details, a fine gift of tying them all together, and the important team prerequisite of being fun.

Chef Dean Fearing. If only I could cook like that. Great times at your fine restaurant and am looking forward to getting back down there. So kind of you to do the foreword for this book. Always loved your grub, but it wasn't until we became friends that I came to know the reason that it is so good, is because you are such a fine person. I suspected that all along.

Remy Haynes, who photographed the cover, and we had a lot of fun doing it (Well I know I did, and she is still speaking to me).Along with her worldly photography skills she always brings a nice joy and calm with her wherever she goes.

My dear friend Norman Bukofzer. I have said before that from our very first meeting, it felt like we had been friends for a very long time. Nothing puts years back on my life more than spending time with you.

Edward Mady, Stephanie Wagner, Leslie Lefkowitz and all the other truly gracious people at the Beverly Hills Hotel for their tremendous support and hospitality.

Starla Fortunato for her truly difficult task of making me look good in pictures (As good as I can possibly look). A really fun person, and wonderful photographer. She has taken so many incredible photos of really great looking, and famous people. She must have lost a bet to then have to photograph me. I'll make it up to you, I promise.

My guidance counselor, Benjo. Thank you for continuing to be such a positive influence in my life, and the lives of so many others.

The wonderful folks at Warwick's Bookstore in La Jolla, CA. They have been such a help to me over the years. From all the stupid questions I asked(and continue to ask them) about the book business, to all the encouragement they have given me. To make their Top 50 Bestseller List with my first book, Nowhere Yet, truly was an honor. The best way to pay them back for all their kindness, is to sell a lot of books in their store.

Gary Pisoni and family for their great friendship and support, and for continuing to be the best example of the fabulous things that can happen when passion is what drives you.

Crawford Brock, Keith Carlisle, Chris Wright, Salvador Martinez and all the great folks at Stanley Korshak in Dallas. I hope we can get together again for this book, the last one was great fun.

Phil Terry for his work as my de facto agent. Lousy pay, bound to get better.

Vick Chen for her work as my de facto advisor (same pay structure as Phil).

DeBusk for always being the reality check (same pay structure as Phil and Vick).

Tara for helping me find my center. I'm not quite there yet, but am working on it.

Lester Hayashi for teaching me a great deal about golf, but for teaching me more about life. I still miss him more than anyone can imagine.

The great staffs of:

The Ritz Carlton Central Park South, New York
The Ritz Carlton Dallas
Fearing's Restaurant, Dallas

The Four Seasons Restaurant, New York
Felidia Restaurant, New York
Marea Restaurant, New York
Trattoria Dell' Arte Restaurant, New York
Nederlander Theater, New York
The French Laundry Restaurant, Yountville
The Craftsman, Encinitas
La Valencia, La Jolla
Manhattan Restaurant, La Jolla
The Coffee Cup, La Jolla

ABOUT THE AUTHOR

Edward Cozza is a Colorado native now living in Southern California. His debut novel, *Nowhere Yet* won an IPPY Gold Medal, and 3 Beverly Hills Book Awards. He has traveled on five continents, with his favorite travel being in the United States, and at this writing is eight states shy of tramping in all fifty. This travel allowed for experiencing the different flavors and cultures of the country and experiencing and enjoying the diversity of regional language. He has, unfortunately, noticed the near extinction of the art of conversation.

Always willing to take time and help to keep verbal dialog from becoming an entirely electronic application, he takes great pride in spending time with loved ones and friends, old and new, preferably over food and drink wherever he goes.

Near Somewhere is the sequel to *Nowhere Yet*. Edward is working on the third in his trilogy.

CPSIA information can be obtained
at www.ICGtesting.com
Printed in the USA
LVOW12*1651130416
483455LV00006B/34/P